Sevens Wild

Hounds of Dawn Book 2

H.S. Torben

SIMPLY ABSURD
PUBLISHING

ISBN: 979-8-9863141-3-6 (ebook)
ISBN: 979-8-9863141-4-3 (print)

CONTENTS

For Rusty.

Without you, my friend, this book and so many other things would not be possible.

You are a lifesaver.

Sunday 7:00 AM

***

The Hounds of Dawn in Blues of Bell
Wild Children War Upon the Dell
Roar of Brothers. Seven and seven.
Vortex Cross a Violet heaven
Splintered Time. Forged Love. Staunch Friend.
Together Stand or All Will End.

***

1

BLUE

B lue camouflage. It was everywhere. Every single person in this building wore some piece of clothing made from blue camo, making her wonder what they were trying to blend in with. Some people also wore oversized glasses with blue lenses. Others wore brightly colored blue wigs, fake blue beards, and an occasional boa. Some even sported blue glittery tutus and sparkly tiaras. She would never understand the obsession some grown-ass people had with tutus and tiaras.

Blue stared at her shoes, trying her best to pretend that the small coffee shop she stood in was not filled with people preparing to run in the Race for Rhodes 5K to support missing country music star Cade Rhodes. But the Caffeinated Cougar was filled to the brim with them. He supposedly went missing in a violent home invasion and the world lost its ever-loving mind. As evidenced by the impending 5K. How was a 5K helpful? It wasn't. It was an excuse to wear tiaras and post on social media. She shook her head. People were strange.

This "race" started in less than an hour at a giant arch made of blue balloons erected in a park across the street. Half the racers stood here trying to get their pre-run coffee. She and Ava had been here for the past twenty-five minutes. Every employee was in training. Which begged the question of who was training whom. The line wrapped past the door and around half of the seating area, which was standing room only. The place had to be exceeding fire codes right now.

The soft thump of a DJ in the park spinning dance mixes of Cade Rhodes' most popular songs washed over them as they waited in line. It was unfortunately not loud enough to drown out the prattling of a woman in the corner who had no qualms about letting the whole café know how much she loved Cade Rhodes' new look. The beard was so hot. And she didn't flinch from sharing information about Grandma's bowel movements or the dating eligibility of her daughter's soccer coach, either.

Blue pinched her nose and rubbed her eyes, wondering what this bunch would do if they discovered their beloved missing country crooner was sleeping soundly in a stolen RV in a neighboring parking lot.

"I'm still trying to wrap my head around all of this." The statement came whispered through barely moving lips from the teenager, Ava, standing next to her in the line.

"You and me both, sweetheart."

The girl hunched conspiratorially next to Blue, eyeing the sea of blue camouflage with derision. "So you think my mom left a note with Mister, uh, Westridge? And he gave it to you. But you didn't come to the café where Dad and I were just because of the note, but because you were helping a detective friend. That really serious Finn fellow, right? He was trying to find some missing people. The café was nearby, and you thought you would check it out and then save my life?"

"That's the gist of it." Blue nodded, grateful Ava used Rhodes' given name and not his stage name so that the surrounding people wouldn't know he was involved in what she was discussing.

"And Mom knew he would give you the note because you and Mr. Westridge were engaged. So she thought, you know? I don't know what she thought. But it worked. I think it was because you both used to be a part of this super bad ass magic soldier club with Mr. Ivan and did a covert hand off like in the movies." Ava leaned in closer and lowered her voice. "I can't believe you worked for the Cahlad. You are so... irreverent." She looked around to make sure no one around them heard her mention the most powerful and impossibly stuffy magic guild in the world. Currently, the Cahlad was a political hot-button issue and a bit of a disaster.

"Believe it." Blue nodded, still staring at her feet as the café grew more crowded and they got closer to the counter. She really liked Ava. She reminded Blue a lot of her mom, Amber, who was Blue's childhood best friend. But it was too early in the morning for this many words. Her stomach growled. Blue frowned, trying to remember the last time she ate. Didn't matter. Coffee would tide her over.

"But you got captured by the same guy who is trying to capture me. He started some magic terrorist group called the Sovereign and killed a bunch of people." The line crept forward again as Ava alluded to the concerning number of times in the past few days groups of heavily armed men tried to abduct her because she could supercharge magic. "Thanks for not letting him get me. Even though I don't think you or Mr. Rhodes like my mom very much?" Ava raised an eyebrow.

"You are welcome, sweetheart." Blue ignored Ava's last statement and focused on the thank-you. She would not share the gruesome and sad details of how her friendship with Amber ended with the woman's daughter. Probably ever, but certainly not in a coffee shop surrounded by what she was slowly coming to realize was the Cade Rhodes Army. That was the ridiculous moniker his fan club gave itself and explained the camo.

Ava wrinkled her nose when her not-so-subtle information fishing expedition failed. "So you met Ms. Devon because the crazy man captured her, too. She and some guy named after a color helped you escape, and now you live with them because Mr. Westridge broke your heart, dumped you, and used his magic to make you look like the definition of average in the dictionary."

Blue cut her eyes at the teenager and bit her tongue. It was an accurate assessment of how she came to be best friends and roommates with Greenlee and Devon and an honorary aunt to Devon's daughter, Lexi. It was also an accurate yet brutal assessment of her current appearance. She stifled a sarcastic retort and just grunted an affirmative as she shuffled forward once again.

"Oh, look." Ava pointed at a chalk sandwich board containing the shop's daily drink specials. "They have a Country Rhodes drink in honor of the 5K. It has blueberry syrup. That's clever." Ava snorted out a laugh when she reached the counter. As Ava placed their order, Blue fished cash from her pocket and handed it to the cashier, who stared at her like she had a second head and a third eye. As the teenager turned to another employee to figure out how to count the cash and make change, Ava stepped back to Blue's side, still whispering. "What I don't get is how Mr. Sam and Mr. Ivan ended up at that café with you."

Behind them, someone wailed about spilling coffee on their tutu. This was a nightmare. She should have gone with Devon and Ivan to buy clean clothes and supplies at the superstore next door.

"I don't get it, either." Blue watched in fascination as both teenagers behind the counter struggled with the money. Now a third person was involved. In the hours they spent running for their lives from a raving bunch of armed zealots, she hadn't found the time to ask the Cahlad Regent, Sam Sotach, and her ex-Zenith teammate Ivan Lacroix how they came to be at the same café that she and Ava were at when a bomb went off. She added that to her to-do list.

"I can't believe Lexi conned Lurch into agreeing to protect all of us, either." Ava snorted again. "It's a legal contract, right?"

The fact her ten-year-old niece, Lexi conned a magically binding protection contract out of the second-in-command of the world's most powerful magic guild last night with nothing more than sad puppy-dog eyes both amused and amazed her. She was so proud of that girl. "Even better. It's a magic contract. You might die if you break one on purpose."

"Really?"

"Yep."

Ava made a face. "That's a little scary."

"Oh. My. God!" the woman trying to date her daughter's soccer coach screamed in an octave so high Blue was certain dogs across Colorado were having seizures right now. She bunched up her shoulders to protect her ears from the annoying noise.

"And how did Dad end up in Colorado in a car with that nice Cahlad lady and your friends?" Ava glared at the cashiers who were not making coffee but still trying to figure out how to make change. "For real?"

"Something about an umbrella?" Blue shrugged. Finn and Greenlee provided details of how they teamed up with a Cahlad Stalker, Nisha Ravi, and Ava's dad, Ben, and ended up in Colorado when they talked to Sam on the phone last night. She was unconscious from some impressive blood loss at the time, and he hadn't done a great job of relaying the information when she woke up. She was still a little confused. Either way, Finn now protected the Cahlad's fugitive Paragon Mitch Collins and his wife, Zella, because the FBI raided the organization's headquarters and organized a manhunt for its senior leadership, including Sam and Ivan.

Blue rubbed her eyes again. If she didn't get coffee soon, she was just going to rob the place. Take the whole machine. It had been a hell of a week. No. Hearing Ava put it all into words put it in perspective. It had been complete insanity. If she didn't know any better, she would swear someone somewhere was pulling strings and making them all dance like puppets. Nonsense like this didn't happen by coincidence. It bugged her. "This is so fucked up."

"Yeah." Ava nodded in sympathy. Then she released a dramatic sigh when the cashier just shoved their money in the till and didn't offer to provide change. "So now you work for Mr. Sam? Was that the deal?"

"Noooo." She agreed to help him make sure the government and the psycho Sovereign didn't take control of the Cahlad. She was working with him, not for him. That meant keeping Mitch Collins, a man she truly despised, in charge as Paragon because he was the least evil option. And she was already regretting it.

"It's you!" The same woman's high-pitched exclamation rang from the back of the line. Blue groaned.

"Ms. Blue?" Ava intoned.

"Yeah, sweetheart?"

"Can Lurch make her be quiet?" Ava tapped on the marble counter impatiently, using her nickname for Sam.

"He's in the bathroom." Blue pulled her hat farther down over her ears to drown out the noise.

Ava smiled at the young man behind the counter. "It's just six coffees with some extra whipped cream. How hard is it?" He stared back at her like a deer caught in the headlights.

The voice screeched, "Oh, you poor thing! What have they done to you?"

Spinning around to give the most annoying voice in the word a piece of her mind about acting the fool before the world could caffeinate, Blue's morning went straight to shit. The ambient buzz of conversation in the room fell silent. She hissed, unable to find words.

Ava stopped berating the barista and looked for the source of Blue's concern. "Oh, Gods." Her eyes beheld the same disaster Blue's had. Then she turned her face away from their impending doom. Rhodes, the same Rhodes most of these people were here to exercise for, stood in the middle of the coffee shop. His eyes were bleary. He looked rough, dark circles under his eyes, hair asunder, covered in blood because of a minor incident the night before. They left him in the camper to sleep it off. She never dreamed he would wake up and wander around, especially through the crowd surrounding this café. "Nope. Don't worry about the lid. Just give them to me." Ava wiggled her hands at the barista. "Come on. I need that coffee."

Rhodes met Blue's gaze, eyebrows drawn down in a bewildered frown as he looked around the blue-clad crowd, some wearing shirts with his face on them. "Baby?" Half-asleep, he did not know where he was. She was going to kill him after she got them all out of here in one piece. A buzz rippled through the room at his words.

"Damn it, Rhodes." Blue tried to move toward him, but the crowd in the shop converged around him into a packed wall of bodies. Only Rhodes could make a week this crazy even worse. Why did he pick today of all the days to sleepwalk? He half-heartedly pushed at the crowd, still overwhelmed and drowsy. She needed to get to him before he did something stupid. Or more stupid than this.

Rhodes pushed at the someone with more intention. "Get your hands off my junk, lady!" Eyes now lucid, he looked straight at her. "Blue?" Reading her expression, realization crossed his features. Followed by alarm. "Uh-oh." Angry glares turned in her direction at his words.

"Oh Lordy, he's so delirious he's singing," the world's most annoying woman fawned. She wore blue camouflage yoga pants and, for some inexplicable reason, a gigantic pair of dark sunglasses, even though they were inside.

Blue pushed at the mass of people around him. But they were all determined to keep their front-row seats to the unfolding drama and refused to budge.

"Don't worry, Cade! We won't let them take you again!" The Audrey Hepburn-wannabe's statement energized the others, and the restaurant erupted in shouts and screams.

"That is Cade Rhodes!"

"Is he hurt?"

"He looks drugged! "

"Somebody call the cops."

"What happened to his beard?"

At that statement, Rhodes reached up and touched his freshly shaven face. His eyes grew wide when his inspection revealed no facial hair. Then he tilted his head in indignant disbelief and glared at her. She tried not to laugh and succeeded. But she couldn't hide her smile. Yeah. She and Devon had shaved America's beard this morning while he lay passed out cold in the passenger seat. Ava helped.

"I'm streaming this to the Cade Rhodes Army! Everyone knows where you are now!" another woman chimed in. Blue hung her head in defeat, knowing they were back on the Sovereign's radar.

Sam charged from the bathroom, shirt untucked and fly still partially open, throwing exasperated hands in the air. "What in the hell is going on? I was gone for two minutes."

"Stop him." A man in a business suit stepped in front of Sam, blocking his path. "Isn't that the Regent? The police are looking for him!" That statement stopped Sam in his tracks, not accustomed to needing to hide his appearance or being on the run from authorities. He took a moment to really look at the situation unfolding in front of him. His face, covered partially by the hood of a sweatshirt and two days' worth of facial hair, turned grim and he sent an irritated look in her direction. Like this was her fault.

Blue searched for exit options. They needed to get out of here. Now. A sea of glitter, tulle, and blue camouflage obstructed her path. A thin piece of tape holding a handwritten Private sign blocked a narrow staircase to the right of the bathroom. She peered behind the counter, unsurprised to find the staff far more focused on the celebrity sighting in their dining area than on making coffee for paying customers.

"Get out of my way." Sam scowled at the men blocking his path. They parted like the Red Sea, and another hush fell over the crowd as the residual effects of his magic took hold. He stepped forward, yanking Rhodes through the gap and away from the mob.

"Real smooth, Lurch." Ava lifted the tray of coffee. "I've got the coffee."

"Good job. Way to handle those priorities, sweetheart." Blue turned to exit through the kitchen, only to find two of the previously lethargic baristas wielding carafes full of scalding-hot coffee as their chosen weapon in the brewing fight to save Cade Rhodes. Resourceful. Yet inconvenient. They couldn't go out the back, and a mob of angry Cade Rhodes Army blocked the front door. They had to go up.

"Sotach!" She pointed to the stairway. Grabbing Ava's arm, she steered the girl toward the stairs, trying to stay between her and the mob.

"You are spilling the coffee." Ava struggled to juggle the full tray.

"So help me God, Ava!" Blue pushed with more urgency.

A full head taller than anyone else in the crowd, Sam spotted the stairs easily and shoved Rhodes toward them. "Run, asshole."

Rhodes broke into a sprint like someone was chasing him at Sam's poorly timed choice of words.

That is when the riot started. The crowd surged toward them as one. Every patron who waited long enough to buy and receive a cup of coffee launched it in their direction. Rhodes reached the stairs first and disappeared around the bend. Sam waited, arm flung up to protect his face from the scalding liquid. He reached for Ava as they approached, and a cup of caramel macchiato splattered next to their faces. A blueberry biscuit bounced off her temple. "Ow!" Ava wailed. "That was hot. Freaks!"

"Go." Sam swung Ava onto the stairway and motioned for Blue. "Come on."

Another scalding-hot splash of liquid soaked Blue's back as she rushed past Sam and hightailed it up the stairs, rounding the ninety-degree bend only to slam into Ava, who stood-stock-still halfway up the staircase. In front of her, Rhodes' shoulders touched both sides of the stairway, though it was an average width. "Is he stuck?" she asked, bewildered. A few stairs up, Rhodes stood with a furry neck. Large gouges marred the walls from the wicked claws jutting from his hands because of Ava's magic flare. He shifted into something without proper fingers and couldn't turn the doorknob.

She heard Sam say something to someone behind her, followed by heavy footsteps. Glancing over her shoulder, he bounded toward them, looking backward, yet somehow taking the steps two at a time. "That should buy us a few seconds."

The infuriated taunts and jeers of the frenzied mob grew louder in the confined space. The first few people stood frozen in the entrance to the stairway, unable to follow them and effectively blocking the path of the mob behind them. She really hoped the mob didn't trample them. But the tactic worked.

A cup of coffee somehow sailed over Sam's head and plastered her shoulder. He slammed into her, almost knocking her over and falling down himself. "Why?" He finally looked up and took in Rhodes' poorly timed transformation. "Shi..." He clamped his lips shut and flinched as another cup of coffee bounced off his back. Where was the coffee coming from? The reload should have taken at least twenty-five minutes with that crew of untrained employees.

Blue moved around Ava, shimmied through the area between Rhodes' hips and the wall, and ran up the last few stairs. Her movement jolted him out of his shock and he climbed behind her, shoulders dragging the walls, claws upright like a surgeon prepping for the operating theater.

She threw open the door and waved Rhodes through. He wiggled his shoulders, falling into the room and landing on the floor. His claws gouged the wood planks, and he spun and sat on them like a kid trying to hide something. Blue yanked Ava up the last three steps and Sam ran in behind her, slamming the door. He threw the lock, and they looked around at a disorganized storage room. Tables, chairs, and boxes obscured all the walls and most of the floor space. There were no exits, just a large plate-glass window on the front wall.

In the corner, a giant industrial ice machine loomed, inappropriate stickers covering its dented lid.

"That looks like a great doorstop." She pointed at the machine. If they could move it in front of the door, they might hold off the rioting Cade Rhodes Army.

2

BLUE

Blue slumped against the ice machine, gasping for breath, covered from head to toe in coffee and all the sticky accoutrements that came with it. And now she was sweaty.

Bam! The mob got past Sam's directive and now attacked the door. It shuddered. The distant sound of sirens pierced the air. She pinched her nose and squeezed her eyes shut. All she wanted was to drink a hot cup of coffee. Not wear one. Rhodes' fans called themselves the Cade Rhodes Army. But she did not know that they took the moniker literally or would turn their overpriced coffee into molten caffeine-laden projectiles. Shaking her shirt out to relieve the burns from the white chocolate mocha dripping into her bra, she picked a coffee stirrer out of her hair.

Sam, also covered in coffee, hunched in exhaustion next to her, with his arm and face resting on the machine, a dollop of whipped cream clinging to a tuft of hair on the back of his head. The Cahlad's second-in-command looked a little worse for wear. She suspected he already regretted their arrangement to protect the Cahlad from government and nefarious magic users. Neither of them imagined in a million years they would first need to protect a teenage girl and Blue's pain-in-the-ass ex from an enthusiastic and alarmingly organized fan club.

"Are they insane? They used espresso and breakfast pastries as weapons. Who does that?" A touch of hysteria laced Ava's voice. She knelt next to Rhodes, who now looked like the unfortunate love child of a Klingon and grizzly bear. The seams of his clothes ripped loose as his body grew larger. Ava still held a paper coffee cup in her trembling hands, raising it to her lips and taking a nervous sip. Blue did not know how the beverage survived their chaotic retreat.

"The crazy people who listen to this guy's money printing music. That's who does that." Blue stared down at Rhodes, who still sat on his hands, watching Ava with golden, glowing eyes.

"It is delightful music. You are biased."

In response to Ava's musing, he growled. This form couldn't speak. Rhodes' bulky frame grew even larger, and his shirt gave up the fight, falling away in pieces, trailing broken tendrils of thread to the ground. He huffed in frustration, squirming to more firmly encase his claws under his body.

"I know." Ava nodded like she could understand what the bear-man said. "I'm trying to calm down. Ms. Blue can't jump us out of here if I don't calm down. You don't want to be a hideous dog-man. I know all of this. You aren't helping."

Sam tilted his head, which was still resting on the ice machine, in her direction. He went silent in the stairwell when he realized why Rhodes shifted, not saying a word since. Sam's magic compelled others to follow his instructions. She appreciated his discretion but wondered if he was being too cautious. But the exhausted and irritated look he wore now telegraphed he thought the kid was losing it.

The sirens outside came to a sudden halt. The authorities had her trapped in a coffee shop with a were-bear, an emotionally compromised teenager, and a mute. Worse, she couldn't use her magic without a high probability of killing herself and everybody with her.

"Maybe we knock her out?" she whispered to Sam. She wasn't in love with the idea. But they were running out of options. "Her magic stops. Then I get us out of here."

Curling his lip, he shook his head. His soft spot for Ava was the whole reason they were in this coffee shop in the first place, instead of using the drive-thru of a national chain with "overpriced, overrated swill water" down the street. He did not yet understand children were master manipulators, and both girls had him wrapped around their little fingers.

Someone shouted, and the door rattled. He appeared to reconsider her suggestion, glancing at Ava with trepidation.

"Do you have a better idea?"

An exasperated and disturbed look crossed his face before the cell phone in his pocket rang. Fishing it out, he hit the button to answer before moving it halfway to his ear and opening his mouth to speak.

He stopped, closed his mouth, and handed the phone to Blue, with a frustrated gesture. She took the device and held it to her ear, catching her friend Devon mid-sentence. "Heck is going on?"

"Tell me about it." Blue moved to the window to look out over the parking lot. It was filling up fast. Five cop cars sat haphazardly parked, lights still flashing. A news van was on the scene to cover the 5K and now broadcasting the pseudo-riot outside. So far, she didn't see any cliché black SUVs filled with bad guys.

"Blue?" Devon sounded confused, probably expecting Sam to answer. "What happened?"

Blue could see their RV from here, parked in front of the regional mega-store across the street. It remained unobstructed so far, but that would change soon. She searched the rest of the parking lot for a viable means of escape. Ava joined her. Rhodes sat on his hands, looking down. Blue poked his dejected shoulder with her foot and watched as he cut yellow glowing eyes that were more animal than human, in her direction. She had never seen him this far gone before. "Rhodes happened."

Devon just sighed in frustration and understanding.

Unusual movement in the parking lot drew her attention, and she leaned forward for a better look. "Does that lady have a bullhorn?"

"I don't know, but I see a guy with a Cade Rhodes flag. Those are a thing?"

A woman standing on the hood of a car took a deep breath, raised the bullhorn to her lips, and screamed, "You Sovereign bastards. You can't have him. We are coming for you, Cade!"

The bullhorn fed back through the phone. "Are you hearing this?"

"Unfortunately," Devon said in a dry voice.

"You have got to be kidding me." Ava took another sip of her coffee. "Does that woman have beards painted on her boobs?"

Blue scanned the assembling crowd below. "Yep. Boob beards."

"Baby!" The bullhorn blasted the word, drowning out the noise of the frenzied army below and behind them.

An answering cry of "Blue" infiltrated the room in surround sound. The parking lot and stairwell echoed with the volume of the response.

Devon sputtered, trying to suppress a laugh. "Oh my God."

Ava slapped her hand over her mouth and looked Blue's way with wide eyes. Rhodes wrote his breakout song, "Baby Blue," about her using a pet name. Blue loathed the song and the reason he wrote it. Letting out a garbled sound of embarrassment, fury, and disgust, she stared at the woman with the bullhorn. That woman was evil and sent here to drive her mad. And she was wearing a tutu.

"Breathe, honey." Devon stifled a laugh. "Just breathe."

Rhodes yowled something mournful and unintelligible. Sam snorted in response. When Blue looked over her shoulder, the two men were glaring daggers at each other, and she would swear Sam understood Rhodes' yowling language.

"Baby!"

"Get Lexi out of here." Blue swallowed her mortification and glared down at Rhodes, who wouldn't meet her eyes. "Coward."

The answering cry of "Blue" made her clench her fist. "I'll figure something out."

"Okay?" Doubt filled Devon's voice. "Be careful."

"Baby!"

Rhodes let out another plaintive yowl.

"I know, dude. I know." Ava knelt next to Rhodes and scratched his ears like she would a pet dog four times her size, with razor-sharp fangs jutting underneath his top lip. "It's okay, buddy." Rhodes shook his head in indignation and tried to pull away.

Unable to form a response, Blue hung up and took a deep, not-so-calming breath. She closed her eyes and tried again. Still no luck. This was too much. She needed a break.

Someone bumped her arm, and she opened her eyes to find Sam pointing toward the corner of the room where the gigantic ice machine lived before they moved it. He held his shirt in his hands and wiped at the streaks of coffee trailing down his chest. Some patches of skin were still red and irritated from the scalding liquid.

"You've got something." Blue pointed to the tuft of whipped cream clinging to his hair. Wiping it off, he didn't even try to hide the smile that spread across his face when the crowd chanted her name back to the bullhorn woman, and Rhodes yowled again. The asshole thought this was funny. She shoved the phone back into his hands. Just for that, she would not tell him about his unzipped fly.

Ava planted a half-finished coffee in her hand. "You need this more than I do." Rounding on Sam, she put her hands on her hips.

"For real, Lurch. What do you have against keeping your shirt on?" She didn't mention his fly, either. Blue liked this kid.

Sam just raised his eyebrow and offered Blue his shirt-turned-towel, walking in the direction he pointed when she took it.

Blue sipped the coffee. Though already cold, something about the flavor calmed her brain, bolstering her focus and control. Tossing the rest of the cup back in a single gulp, she handed it back to Ava. "Thank you, sweetheart." She tried to smile at the girl, but ended up grimacing as another round of chanting grated on her already frazzled nerves.

Following Sam across the room, she used his shirt to wipe away the coffee still streaming down her chest and back and seeping into her pants. He pointed at a spot above a stack of boxes labeled cups and sugar packets, where the top two inches of another door peeked out. "That could work. Where does it go?" Sam shrugged. The fact that the only other functioning adult in the room refused to speak irritated her.

Another thud shuddered through the stairwell door, punctuated by a high-pitched crack as the frame gave way. The tall machine kept anyone from seeing into or entering the room, but it was only a matter of time before the lunatics outside got in and found a gigantic bear-man where their precious singer used to be. "Shall we?" They tossed boxes aside quickly. Sam moved the last box and pushed the door open. Peering outside, he jerked his head back into the room and closed the door, dragging her away from it. "What? What is it?" The chants were even louder now that the army scented victory.

Sam made a finger gun and then pointed it at the unlocked door, holding up four fingers.

"Four? Cops?"

He nodded.

The police were coming, and they were standing here playing charades. Mitch had himself one hell of an army. The world was in expert hands. "Perfect."

"Ms. Blue?" Ava sent the door a nervous look.

"It's okay. We have a plan." Blue sent Sam a pleading look, hoping he had a plan.

He glanced in Ava's direction to make sure she wasn't looking, made a fist and hit his open palm with it, jerking his head toward Ava. Then he pointed at Blue. Stunned, Blue stared at him for a moment as his plan sank in. He actually wanted her to knock Ava out so the girl couldn't overload their magic, and Blue could teleport them out of here. "Seriously?" Again she only mouthed the word, but she stomped her foot for emphasis.

Sam's eyebrows flew up, and he threw out his hands in a *it was your idea* gesture. It was her plan. But it was a terrible plan. The freaking Regent could do better than that. He glanced at the exposed door and then back at her impatiently.

"What's the plan, Ms. Blue?" Ava scratched Rhodes' ears, fear crawling back into her voice. Rhodes' furry frame grew again as another surge of Ava's magic hit him. His pants fell away this time. He whined.

Blue moved her lips but didn't make any sound. "I don't like it." She did not know why she was no longer speaking out loud.

Sam made an agitated waving motion, signaling she should get on with it. She glared at him. He hit his open palm two more times, but at least had the decency to look guilty.

Blue pointed at Sam and then at Ava, signaling that he should do it.

Horrified, he shook his head emphatically.

Rhodes sat on the floor, his head pivoting back and forth between them, the ridges of his furry brow drawing farther down with each round of their strange game of charades. A deep, growling rumble escaped his chest.

"I know. But you still can't eat people." Ava's gaze never left the cracked door. "Even if they are stupid, tasty, blueberry-infused sheeple." The three adults met each other's eyes, then sent concerned looks her way.

Shaking his head, Sam pointed to the other door. He mimicked a man firing a machine gun. He clutched his heart, stumbled back, and stuck his tongue out.

She still glared at him and, for lack of anything else to do, stomped her foot again to signal her displeasure.

He threw his arms out once more in a *do you have a better idea?* gesture.

She didn't have a better idea. Dammit. Her stomach sank. She was going to do this. She was such an asshole. She bit out a silent, "Fine." Sam tossed his head in a way that telegraphed a sarcasm-laden *finally*.

She moved behind Ava, acting like she was walking toward the window. Stepping in front of Ava, Sam motioned for her to give him her attention. Because the kid didn't dislike him as much as she let on, she turned his way, completely trusting. Blue struck her on the back of the head when she did. Ava crumbled, and Sam caught her before she hit the ground.

"We are such assholes." Blue shook out her aching hand. "I'm going to hell. And you are going with me."

Sam dragged Ava's body toward Rhodes without a shred of remorse. Without Ava's magic overloading his control, Rhodes morphed back into his less-hairy and much smaller human form. He sighed in relief. "Christ, Blue. What did you do?" He wobbled, pale and sick from the overload of magic. Rhodes pulled his hands loose and shook them out, grabbing his shredded pants and doing what he could to cover himself.

Sam dumped Ava unceremoniously in Rhodes' lap. "Rhodes, shut up and hold on to her."

Rhodes wrapped his arms around Ava's limp body and glared daggers at Sam.

"How long do we have?" Blue asked, then let out a "Whoop" as Sam's long arm reached out and snatched her by the wrist, dragging her toward him. She lost her footing and stumbled.

25

"Seconds. Not cops. Sovereign." He dropped to his knee next to Rhodes, grabbing him by the wrist as well. He kept pulling on her arm, fingers digging into her skin.

She landed hard on her knees, catching the knee of Sam's bent leg in her gut. She tipped forward with an "Oof", threw her arm out to catch herself on Rhodes' shoulder, and came to rest with her face pressed against the top of Ava's head. This was the most awkward game of Twister she had ever played.

"Get us back to Devon and Ivan. Hurry." Sam wedged Ava firmly in the middle of the adults.

She blew Ava's blonde hair out of her face and focused on Devon because she had jumped with her more often than with Ivan. The pull was stronger and easier to grab hold of. She started on her calculations, but she wasn't sure how accurate they were because Sam's order made her rush. Devon was moving fast, likely in the RV. A small moving target above ground level. How tall was the RV again? Four people. How much did they all weigh? How much space did they take up? Not much room for error.

"She's moving." Blue worked through all the variables in her head. The frigid rainbow of her magic clouded her vision. She had no choice but to trust Sam and Rhodes to keep them all together. She had to focus on the math. "This will be rough."

Rhodes flexed his arms, wedging everyone together even more. He shifted again to shield his body and, hopefully, Ava's from injuries during the jump. His animal and semi-human forms were much harder to hurt. He knew what was coming. "You've got this. I've got them. Just concentrate."

The back door flew open, shouts rang out, and bullets started flying. "Go now!" Sam shifted to put himself between their uncomfortable huddle and the door, curling his body over all of them. She screamed in frustration and let go of her magic with an incomplete calculation that sent them all careening across the electric rainbow trampoline from hell.

3

DEVON

"We have to go back for them. Please, Mom." Lexi kicked her legs frantically, squirming in the blood-stained passenger seat of their RV. The child still clutched a bag from this morning's interrupted shopping trip in her arms. The others lay scattered across the floor of the RV where they threw them in a rush to get inside unseen. Lexi's brown eyes were wide and brimming with tears. "You don't leave the people you love."

Lexi's words tore through Devon's heart. In a rush to get away from the chaos, she turned onto the first major highway they passed, unsure which direction they were going or where they were. Four members of their group, including her best friend, were still likely trapped there. She wanted to go back. And if she didn't have Lexi with her, she would. "I can't, baby. Tia Blue said she would figure something out."

Lexi blew out a raspberry. "That means she is flying by the seat of her pants!" Her voice went up with every word. "And they are probably on fire because she was lying!"

Devon cut her eyes at her daughter and took a deep breath, hating that she was right. That is exactly what Blue's statement probably meant.

Lexi zeroed in on Ivan, who stood against the counter in the small kitchenette, hands wrapped around the back of his neck, staring at his shoes. Because of his size, he filled the muscle role on Stalker Prime, the Cahlad's most elite investigative and enforcement unit, but looked like he was barely holding it together. Devon didn't miss the long look he gave the coffee shop before deciding to climb on board with them, as conflicted about leaving people behind as she and Lexi were. "Mr. Ivan, tell her!"

Ivan walked forward, kneeling next to the passenger seat so his eyes were almost level with Lexi's. "Sam made you a promise."

Lexi chewed her lip and frowned. "But he didn't promise to help Tia Blue."

"It will be okay." Ivan spoke quietly and firmly. She caught his eyes in the rearview mirror. He was probably trying to convince himself as well.

"I don't like this." Lexi crossed her arms in a huff when it became obvious he would not take her side. Her lip jutted out in a pout, and she squeezed the bag in her lap even tighter.

"We don't, either." Devon watched for signs so she could figure out where they were. Sam drove them here while she was still half-asleep. They were somewhere in Colorado. That was the best she could do.

"What's in the bag?" Ivan said in his same calm tone.

Lexi sniffled and glared at him. "I know what you are doing."

"What's that?" Ivan poked the bag.

Devon's phone rang as Lexi rolled her eyes and announced, "You are trying to distract me!"

Ivan didn't respond, and soon Lexi was engaged in a spiteful staring contest, arms crossed over her chest and a mulish expression on her face. Devon juggled her new phone out of her pocket and answered, "Yeah."

"Are you okay?" Greenlee's voice was strained and exasperated. She put him through the wringer during the past two days. First, she drove into a gunfight while he listened on the phone. Then she flew halfway across the country without telling him she survived the first thing. As usual, his voice helped calm her anxiety.

"How?" Emergency vehicles still whizzed by in the opposite direction, no doubt responding to whatever incident Rhodes had caused.

"It's all over social media, Dev. Some woman claiming to be the future Ms. Cade Rhodes is live streaming from the parking lot of a coffee shop. I saw Blue's face in the video. It's you guys this time, isn't it? Are you okay?"

"We left Blue behind." He would understand what she meant. "Ava, too."

He was silent for a moment. "Lexi is with you?"

30

"Yes. Ivan and Lexi. We left everyone else."

"Lacroix is still with you?"

"Yeah."

"Good." Greenlee sounded relieved. "Stand behind him if anything goes south."

"I will. What about Blue and Ava?"

Lexi blinked and then looked at Ivan with respect and awe. Nobody had ever beaten her kid in a staring contest before. And they had all tried.

Lexi pulled a crushed box of limited-edition cereal with rainbow unicorn marshmallows out of the bag she held in her lap, launching into a spiel about Tia Blue's love of weird cereal. Ivan gave her all his attention, nodded earnestly, and asked questions that drew Lexi's attention even further away from the horrifying reality of their current situation. For someone his size and with his reputation, the guy was a natural with kids.

"Blue will figure something out." Greenlee pulled her back into their conversation with worry in his voice. Blue was Greenlee's best friend, too. He was worried out of his mind. "She always does."

"That's what she said." Devon realized her mistake immediately.

He snorted. She rolled her eyes. Even Greenlee's juvenile antics couldn't move the ball of guilt lodged in the pit of her stomach. "She never would have left me behind, Green. Never."

"You had to take care of Lexi. You did the right thing. Sometimes it sucks."

Anxiety and guilt still overwhelmed her. But it was more manageable now. "I needed that."

"Where are you, Dev?"

"Um." She looked around for anything useful. Her eye caught on Lexi as she pulled another box of cereal from the bag, this one a lemon- and peanut-flavored abomination guaranteed to send Blue into fits of gleeful delight. Ivan couldn't suppress his grimace, and Lexi howled with laughter. "I see a sign for Durango."

"Which direction?"

"Forward?" she groused when she didn't see any other signs. She navigated by landmarks. Not that compass nonsense.

"That's not the type of direction I..." She didn't hear the rest of his sentence because an arctic blast of air exploded behind her. Something smacked the back of her head, and she dropped the phone to stay in the seat, hang on to the steering wheel, and keep them on the road.

Lexi screamed in terror.

A resounding crash echoed behind her, punctuated by the shattering of glass and the hiss of water, and the whole rolling structure jerked to the side and squatted low on its chassis under the weight of whatever had just hit them. Ivan flew forward, landing across Lexi's lap, his head slamming into the dashboard and his foot knocking Devon's arm away from the wheel. She shook off the pain and fought to keep them in the lane as the camper bounced upright and swayed, close to being out of control. "What in the blazes!" she screamed, wrestling with the wheel and pumping the brakes. Every drag of the brakes made it harder to steer.

"Dev!" Greenlee screamed from the speaker of the phone that she dropped when whatever nightmare they were dealing with hit them. Lexi still screamed, her hands in front of her face. "Dev! What's happening?" the phone barked again.

Ivan launched upright and whipped around to confront the threat in the vehicle's interior. His face was murderous as he crouched to spring. Staring behind them, Lexi let loose with another high-pitched scream.

"Lexi!" Devon wouldn't have any eardrums left at this rate. "Stop! For God's sake!" The RV hit a bump mid-sway and lurched to the side again. "Screw! This! Stupid! Thing!" She jerked the wheel, willing the metal behemoth to do her bidding.

"Dammit, Devon! Answer me!" Greenlee's angry voice echoed from somewhere on the floorboard. He never spoke to her like that.

"I don't fucking know what's fucking happening, Greenlee. Fuck!" A horn bellowed next to them. "Fuck you, too, you mother fucking asshole!"

Ivan tilted his head beside her and stood up straight. His gaze was laser-focused on the interior of the camper, but he no longer looked ready to murder someone. He looked confused and concerned. A plastic cup rolled by his feet and landed between the front seats.

"Ivan?" Devon looked up at him while still trying to stay on the road.

Lexi stopped screaming and stared at Devon in wonder. "Mom! You said fu..."

"Don't you even." Devon risked taking a hand off the wheel to point at her.

Lexi rolled her eyes. Then they grew wide. "Mr. Sam?"

"What?" Devon looked for the rearview mirror but this thing didn't have one. "Sam? Ivan! Somebody!"

An anguished cry followed by a low, keening moan of pain that sent shivers down her spine, rolled through the cabin.

The big man surged forward in response to the sound.

"Oh man." Lexi retched. "I think that's broken. It's not right."

"God. Bless. Sugar. Mother. Hockey Pucks!" Devon cursed and searched for a place to pull over and find out what was happening since nobody would give her any useful information. A hush fell over the cabin.

"Take her." Rhodes started handing out orders behind her, and her shoulders sagged in relief. Blue figured it out, and they were here.

"I've got her." Ivan's bulk rocked the camper as he walked to the back.

"Karma." Blue groaned, then whimpered.

"I rushed you. My fault." Sam's voice sounded strained, too. "Don't try to move."

"Hang tight, baby." Rhodes said the words just loud enough for Devon to hear.

"Oh." Lexi threw her hands over her face and peeked through her fingers. "My gosh." She shut her fingers and turned away. "Their clothes are gone."

Devon frowned. She couldn't stop herself from craning her neck to look behind her. Sam, cradling his shattered left arm to his chest, lay shirtless and entangled with another body that was motionless except for the rapid rise and fall of the chest that matched the panting she heard. His face contorted in pain, his other arm wedged under the body. The body's leg jutted at the wrong angle, and the shoulder twisted over the head and backward unnaturally. Devon's stomach flipped.

Sam held himself up awkwardly and tried not to move. His body blocked most of Lexi's view of the carnage, for which Devon was grateful. Judging by the calm, methodical way everyone reacted, it must be Blue, who could heal from virtually any injury, and not Ava, laying in a mangled heap on the floor. Sam looked up, speaking to Rhodes. "These are bad. She landed under all of us."

Rhodes leaned over Sam and Blue, assessing their injuries. His body shifted from furry and muscled, back to plain old baby-faced Cade Rhodes. Horrendous bruises covered his body, but he appeared otherwise unscathed. He had not a single stitch of clothing on. Turning, he made his way to the bathroom. "She did it on purpose." He sounded irritated beyond measure.

The shattered remnants of the kitchen's upper cabinets lay scattered all over the floor. They mixed with the now crushed groceries and clothing that Ivan and Devon tossed into the vehicle earlier. It was a disaster.

"Ava is out cold. Big knot on her head." Ivan reappeared, carrying blankets and sheets. "I put her on the bed." He knelt by Blue's grotesquely bent leg before Devon had to look back at the road.

"Wonder how that happened?" Rhodes' voice held sarcasm as he opened and closed the cabinet doors in the bathroom.

"She figured it out?" Greenlee inquired in a far more controlled volume than he had used earlier from somewhere in the floorboard.

Devon had forgotten all about him. She leaned down, fishing with her aching right arm until her fingers found the phone. She snatched it up. "We have them."

Lexi leaned closer to the phone. "They are naked, Tio G."

"They aren't naked." Devon pulled the phone away. "Well, Rhodes is. I need to park this thing. It's not good."

Greenlee grunted in sympathy, understanding her meaning. "Okay. Go take care of them. Call me back when you can. I love you."

"I will. Love you, too."

Devon hung up, spotted an off-ramp ahead and aimed the rolling beast that way. Rhodes wrapped himself in a threadbare towel and knelt by Blue's head, using two rolled-up towels to fashion a makeshift neck brace. Ivan rested on his knees beside Sam, helping to support his weight, inspecting the man's mangled arm and the bloody shard of bone that jutted from it. Devon swept the debris away so she could get close enough to help.

"We need to set these." Rhodes appraised Blue's broken bones with a clinical detachment Devon found disturbing. Blue's eyes were closed, lips thin, face pale, and she breathed in small shallow breaths with deep exhales, accompanied by the smallest whimpers of pain.

He put a hand on Blue's forehead. "If I don't do it now, they will heal this way."

Blue responded with the slightest nod of her head. "I know. Do it."

Ivan scowled. An almost growl emerged.

"You can't be serious." Sam stared at him in disbelief.

Rhodes lifted a hand to stop any further commentary. "Better than re-breaking them later. Trust us."

"He's right. Let him work." Blue and Rhodes exchanged a look Devon couldn't interpret. His face softened into pained dread for only a second before the detached mask slammed back into place. There was a story here. Ivan made another disgruntled noise.

"I'll keep her out while you set them," Devon volunteered. "If you think it's safe to put her under?" She sent the last statement to Rhodes because he took charge.

Blue's eyes snapped open, and a tiny smile crossed her face. "Hey, Dev." She exhaled a pained pant. "Told you I would find you."

"It's safe." Rhodes nodded. "Help her."

"Honey, this is getting ridiculous, even for you. And you still owe me hot coffee." Devon touched Blue's cheek and watched her friend's lips turn up as her face relaxed and eyes fell closed. Her breathing remained fast and shallow, but at least she wouldn't be conscious for the next part. Devon witnessed bones being set before and knew what it sounded and looked like. Hell, she knew what it felt like. And Lexi didn't need that knowledge.

She asked Ivan if he could take Lexi outside. He nodded and moved toward the passenger seat. In short order, he and Lexi were stepping outside to discuss cereal, and Devon took his place behind Sam to help support him until they could get Blue stable enough for him to move.

"This may take a few minutes." Rhodes grimaced at the extent of the damage. Devon sent an extra surge of magic into Blue's arm to make sure she didn't wake up while Rhodes worked.

Sickening noises rang out as bones snapped back to their original homes. Devon winced with each snap and twist. Sam kept his eyes closed, but he flinched with each sound, curling his broken arm closer to his chest. "One more." Rhodes' tone held no emotion as he moved to the leg that stuck out at a ninety-degree angle from where it should be. Another stomach-churning thunk and crunch had him standing up and placing his hands on his hips. "That's it." Rhodes made a splint out of a towel and a broken shard of cabinet. "Your turn." He finished with the splint and looked at Sam, who paled at the prospect of having his arm bones snapped back into place. "I can put you under." Sam looked suspicious. "Just long enough to set the bone."

"I'd take her up on it, man." Rhodes eyed the shattered bone. "That's a bad one. You will pass out, either way."

Sam looked at Devon with a hint of distrust. He just met her yesterday, learned who her father was, and discovered they worked in opposition to each other for years. This whole alliance was still very fragile.

While Sam stewed about whether he wanted to pass out from pain or magic, Rhodes knelt next to her, looking at something on his patient's exposed back with morbid interest. "Wow. Talk about good timing." He reached down and plucked at something, causing Sam to wince. Rhodes held up a still, almost perfectly formed bullet. "This was bad news for one of us. Good catch."

Any color that remained drained from Sam's face as he studied the bullet that had almost killed him. "What stopped it?"

"A rainbow of magic." Rhodes chucked the bullet to the side. "What's it going to be?"

"Fine." Sam hung his head. "I'm a sitting duck, either way."

"That's the spirit." Devon reached out and bopped his nose. Rhodes caught his collapsing body before he could fall on his face and rolled it backward, leaving one of Sam's arms still stuck under Blue's shoulders and his legs still flopped across her unbroken leg. It looked uncomfortable. Rhodes set the arm quickly. "I need to clean this wound." Rhodes glanced around with a frown. "Where is the first-aid kit?"

"We bought a new one." Devon searched through the pile of rubble. "It's here somewhere."

"Good thinking." He rummaged through the visible bags. He found the red box, ripped it open, and pulled out what he wanted. He went back to work cleaning and bandaging the ragged wound.

"Where did you learn to do this?" Devon watched Rhodes strip the sheet Ivan had brought over with a single wicked claw he materialized from his hand. "This is not basic first aid."

He fished out two pieces of shattered cabinet and fastened them to the arm with a compression bandage from the kit. Then he made a tight sling with the strip of cloth and tied it, looking at Devon, devoid of emotion. "Advanced medical training. Zenith program."

"You hate it." Devon couldn't stop herself from stating the obvious.

"I scored high on the aptitude test and did well in combat-casualty care. Rest is history." He tossed three blankets over Blue's body. "She did great in languages. She wanted to learn music. They didn't care. Eight languages. Only one instrument." He looked out the window to where Ivan helped Lexi pick flowering weeds. "Ivan loves literature. But he scored high on mechanics and computers. They forbade him to read fiction books because they were a waste of his time."

Rhodes studied Sam for a moment and tossed a blanket over him as well as he stood, a sad, contemplative look on his face. "He wasn't in the Zenith program. But he had no options, either. He wanted to be a carpenter like his dad."

"Hey." Devon snapped her fingers to turn his attention her way. He seemed so lost. She stood.

He finally looked over. She wrapped her arms around his waist and squeezed tight. "Thank you." He froze. "I'm sorry the bad stuff happened to you. All of you."

He stood stock-still and silent. He had made an awful choice and had an ego the size of Texas. But he wasn't the villain she thought he was. She squeezed harder. "Hug me back, butthole."

He brought his arm down and patted her back awkwardly.

"Aww," Sam slurred from where he still lay on the floor, contorted like a pretzel. "Hug her back, asshole."

Both of Rhodes' arms wrapped around her shoulders and squeezed, unsure if it was because of Sam's semi-coherent statement, or because he might genuinely want to hug her back.

"I see why she loves you." Rhodes hugged her.

"I see why she loves you, too."

"Still hate me?"

"Nah."

"So sweet. Tylenol?" Slurring his words, Sam tried to put his left arm over his face. The sling tied it down, so he tried with the arm still wedged under Blue. Flopping like a turtle trapped on its back, he gave up. "Please?"

"Oh, buddy." Devon dug a travel packet of painkillers out of the new but decimated first-aid kit. "Headache?"

"Yeah." He kept his eyes closed.

"That's my magic. Sorry." She arched an eyebrow at Rhodes while trying to help Sam sit up. "Could you put on some pants and help me?"

"In that order?"

"Yes, please."

"I don't care if he's naked." Sam covered his eyes. "I just want Tylenol."

4

SAM

Sam still sat in the dinette booth where he fell asleep earlier after Devon showed him mercy, helped him out of the floor, and gave him painkillers. And he was cranky. Not because his head hurt, or his broken arm bothered him. It was because neither of those things bothered him. He wasn't even wearing the sling or splint he had gone to sleep in. Someone healed everything and even pulled a clean shirt over his head and wiped away most of the dried, sticky coffee. The only evidence remaining of the morning's events was his exhaustion and a thin red scar on his left arm.

Not only had Blue healed him while he slept, but she also risked teleporting to a different coffee shop with Devon to bring back the fancy drinks the Cade Rhodes Army denied them. She currently sat on the debris-free floor in front of the remaining cabinets, leaning comfortably against Rhodes' shoulder. The man sat next to her looking relaxed and nothing like Cade Rhodes, the country music star, and exactly like an older version of Rhodes Westridge Sam remembered from twelve years ago, with dark hair and eyes an eerily transparent shade of glowing blue. Face clean-shaven and features sharp, he had an unsettling countenance. The man missed his calling as a vampire. Not the pretty ones that sparkled in the sun with a thing for underage girls, but the ones they made high-body-count horror movies about. There was nothing remotely charming about this version of Rhodes.

They both wore clean clothes that fit. Blue balanced a bowl of cereal on her knees. Her hair was down and covered with a knit beanie. She wore a pair of large silver glasses. The hair, hat, and glasses made her look like a completely different person. But they didn't hide the dark bags under her eyes or her pallid complexion. She was exhausted and didn't feel well. Healing him contributed to that. And she wasted additional energy going for coffee.

He took a hate sip of the coffee. Adding insult to injury, someone remembered his original drink order, and it was perfect. It only made him crankier. He glared across the dinette at Devon, whose hair was a wild mass of shoulder-length black curls. She wore no makeup and had removed her thick-rimmed glasses. The minor changes made her hard to recognize as well. She looked much younger. These ladies were no strangers to disguising themselves. She drank her coffee and smiled at him in a way that let him know she found his crankiness amusing.

"This is terrible." Rhodes made a face and held a bowl of cereal away from his body. They were engaged in some kind of time-honored cereal-tasting ritual.

"Here." Blue swapped her bowl with his. "It was pretty good. I'll eat it."

Rhodes did not reject the offer to swap cereal. He ate a spoonful from the fresh bowl and said around a mouthful of colorful marshmallows, "You lie."

"I've had worse." Blue shrugged and ate from the fresh bowl of cereal without complaint.

"You still lie." A wistful smile crossed his features. "I've missed this."

"I can smell that stuff from here." Ivan wrinkled his nose. He sat in the driver's seat, steering them leisurely in a northerly direction toward Nisha and Torrin. Ava sat on the couch behind him, also in clean clothes, reading a book Ivan picked out for her before everything went to hell in a hand basket. Ivan wrinkled his nose and shook his head. "It's just wrong. Why?"

"I'd rather try it and not like it than not try it at all." Blue shrugged.

"But why finish it?" Ava didn't look up from her book. "Just eat the other stuff."

"She will finish the whole box. Doesn't matter how awful it tastes." Rhodes finished his bowl of unicorn cereal.

"I'm sitting right here, guys," Blue said around a mouthful of disgusting cereal.

"It's weird." Devon wrinkled her nose, too.

"Oh, for God's sake." They were all getting on his last nerve and acting like everyone, except Ivan, hadn't almost died this morning, and the government and a bunch of psychopaths weren't looking for them. They were incapable of taking anything seriously.

He jerked himself out of the booth and yanked the bowl of hideous lemon- and peanut-flavored goo out of Blue's hands. Pouring the cereal into the trash can with an angry flourish, he refilled the bowl with unicorn cereal and milk. "Life's short. Eat the cereal you like." He thrust the bowl in her direction.

The RV fell silent. Rhodes shoved a huge spoonful of cereal into his mouth. Devon snatched the cereal box from his hand and fended off Lexi's attempts to get to the box. Ava popped a dry piece of cereal into her mouth like a kernel of popcorn.

"I don't like cereal." Ivan sounded smug.

Blue slowly took the bowl he offered, looking slightly heartbroken. As if she wanted to eat the nasty cereal. "Okay."

He tilted his head back in defeat. "I'm sorry. Stop. All of you. Blue, please eat the good cereal?" These were the times he wished he could curse like everyone else. Things got weird every time he said shit or fuck. Damn, just didn't have the same grit to it. "Do you want another bowl of the other stuff?" he offered. "I'll get you another bowl."

"I told you the coffee would piss him off." Ava looked over the top of her book at him with a smug expression.

"This is fine." Blue looked down quickly and tucked into the fresh bowl. She wasn't calling him on it. Nobody was. Sam sat back down, feeling like a complete asshole. It was a familiar feeling.

"Who gets mad about coffee?" Lexi demanded. "I get an apple and water. I'm the one that should be mad."

"No sugar." Ivan obviously remembered the night before when he gave her cookies and Twinkies. She chattered nonstop and bounced off the walls for three hours, testing even Ivan's infinite patience. Lexi stuck her tongue out at him.

"Oh, yeah." Lexi shifted to fish in her pocket for something. "I found this when Mom made me sweep." Her small hand extended toward Sam. Instinctively, he took what she offered. Knowing this child, it was a fake spider or one of those button buzzers that shocked you. Instead of a gag or prank, a small piece of metal fell into his hand, still warm from her pocket. "Tio Finn has four in his desk. I found them one day. He was upset about it. But he says each of them has a story and he will tell them to me when I'm older. Mr. Rhodes said this one was from your back." She gulped and looked up.

Sam stared at the tiny projectile in his hand, unsure of what to say. Chest tight, he looked to Devon for help and found none. Rhodes looked away. Blue sat with a spoonful of cereal halfway to her mouth, at a loss for words as well. Kids were hard. How should he respond to a ten-year-old who handed him a bullet as a keepsake? "That was very thoughtful of you?"

"It's the story of keeping your promise." Lexi nodded.

Devon blew out a deep breath and put a fist to her chest, over her heart. "Oh, my goodness, child."

"Tia Blue and Mr. Rhodes say it's just a piece of metal and has nothing to do with a promise, because you have to think about promises to keep them and you didn't think about it. I think that's a good thing?" The little girl shrugged uncertainly and glanced toward Blue, who gave the girl an encouraging smile, and Rhodes, who nodded in affirmation. "I still thought you might want it." Lexi looked at him hopefully, without an ounce of manipulation on her face. "Like Tio Finn." He just nodded and patted her hand, not trusting his voice to stay steady if he responded. She graced him with a glowing smile. "I'm glad you're okay."

Overwhelmed, his eyes fell onto two of the most dangerous magic users on the planet, sharing gimmick cereal on the floor. It was strangely domestic. They watched him but no longer with reservations or distrust. He saw respect. He had to look away.

"Zenith and I have each other's backs." Blue went back to eating her cereal. Rhodes tilted his chin in Sam's direction.

Devon gave him a gentle smile when everything clicked into place in his head. He wasn't sitting here healed and holding the perfect cup of coffee they knew would piss him off because of a magical contract, nor because he was useful to them. Sam was now on the inside of their tiny and remarkably dysfunctional circle of trust.

Needing a minute, he shot from his seat, stopped himself long enough to put the tiny projectile into his pocket, and hurried to the front of the RV, falling into the seat next to Ivan.

His abrupt departure didn't bother anyone behind him. Ivan allowed him to sit in silence for a few moments before glancing his way. "You need to call Mitch."

"That will be fun. Ready to be Regent?" If Mitch didn't kill him for the terms of his agreement with the Hounds of Dawn, he would fire him. Sam never wanted this job. However, he did not expect to lose it this way. No doubt Nisha was on Mitch's bad side as well. That left Ivan to fill the spot.

A long moment later, face fierce, Ivan turned to him, taking his eyes off the road. "Zenith and I have each other's backs."

5

FINN

The hush blanketing the car dragged on for so long, making even Finn, usually comfortable with silence, uneasy. His phone sat propped upright on the dashboard to allow him and Nisha to take part in a video call between Sam Sotach and Blue West, who were traveling in a camper full of powerful, magical fugitives and the currently displaced Paragon of the Cahlad, Mitch Collins, who was sitting in Finn's warehouse just outside of Nashville. He was there because Nisha, a member of his cabinet, negotiated a contract, giving Finn's company, Herne Tactical, the oversight of two of the Cahlad's most controversial regulatory responsibilities in exchange for protection.

Nisha's mouth gaped open, and she stared, speechless, at the four silent faces on the screen. The Paragon scowled at all of them with a thunderous expression.

Hale, Finn's right hand and point person on Mitch's security, sat next to the Paragon, tossing popcorn in the air and catching it in his mouth. Mitch's jaw twitched each time Hale crunched a kernel.

Sam Sotach, Mitch's second-in-command, just dropped the bomb that he, too, negotiated a contract as an authorized agent of the Cahlad with a shadow organization named the Hounds of Dawn, granting an unknown number of fugitive Sovaj immunity and forcing the Cahlad to rewrite the Sovereign Registration Act of 1978.

His friend, and sometimes employee, Blue, sat next to the Regent with an amused look on her face, gleefully watching the Cahlad's senior leadership implode. Even the other two passengers in Finn's car, Greenlee Anders and Ben Hughes, made no noise. The fury on Mitch's face burned so potent, they both hugged the doors to stay out of the camera's range.

The Paragon handled Nisha's stunt with surprising grace. Sam made an excellent case for agreeing to his deal with Blue and, by extension, the Hounds of Dawn and Rhodes Westridge, a former Zenith. Sam had a stronger case for his deal than Nisha had for hers. The Paragon clearly didn't see it that way.

Finally, Nisha's face turned furious. Finn prepared himself for the explosion, but she deflated and sighed. "Damn it, Sam." Nisha threw her hands in the air. "You always have to show me up."

The Paragon's face grew darker. Blue's smile grew even wider, and she bounced with delight. Sotach remained impassive, waiting for Mitch's response.

Composing himself, Mitch focused on the screen in front of him, studying something before tipping his head. "Indigo." He addressed Blue by her real name. Earlier, Nisha filled Finn in on Blue's life before she met them. Her real name was Indigo Vale. Raised as a ward of the Cahlad, she had worked for them in a lethal capacity for many years before an incident that led them to believe she died. Greenlee did not seem surprised, and it still stung. Finn struggled with the fact that Blue, Greenlee, and his sister-in-law, Devon, were all members of the Hounds of Dawn. The three actively hid fugitive Sovaj from the Cahlad for years right under his nose. Next Thanksgiving was going to be interesting.

"My friends call me Blue." She stopped bouncing and lounged back in a relaxed slouch.

Mitch responded with a bland look. "What should I call you?"

"Ms. West will be fine." The Paragon and his former Zenith operative had a history, and they didn't like each other. Finn ran a hand over his face. This signaled a poor start for their new alliance.

Hale's eyebrows went through the roof, and he tossed another kernel of popcorn into his mouth. Mitch's face turned red, and he twisted to glare at Hale. "Would you please stop that?"

"May I call you Blue, Ms. West?" Nisha inquired sincerely.

Blue graced Nisha with a million-watt smile. "Please do. It is nice to meet you, Nisha."

"Wonderful. You, as well." Nisha nodded. "I am grateful for your willingness to help us, Blue." She placed her hands in her lap and waited for someone else to speak, but the uncomfortable silence returned. Finn wasn't wading any deeper into this swamp of bad blood. Somebody else needed to go first.

Nisha looked between the phone and the people in the car, trying to make eye contact with everyone. "As freshly minted allies, we have much to discuss. Where would we like to start?"

Hale put his bag of popcorn down. "I'll start. The Coffee Chaos video has more hits than the Paragon's video Harper had me working on for four hours. Not cool, Angel. Not cool."

Blue frowned in confusion. "What on earth are you talking about, Hale?"

"The future Ms. Cade Rhodes live-streamed the entire show down in the coffee shop." Hale waggled his eyebrows. "You are famous. You, too, Sotach. Your fly was open. Excellent job staying off the radar."

Blue groaned and dropped her head.

Sam cleared his throat. "Moving on. Mitch needs to reestablish a public base of operations to quell any potential challenges from other Cahlad leaders, putting him in the FBI's and the Sovereign's line of fire. We also need to keep Ava secure. They could do irreparable damage if they got their hands on her. Those two objectives are of equal importance. How do we make it happen?"

Finn had been working this exact problem in his head for several hours. "If we rally, we are a bigger target, but have more firepower. If we split up into teams, we are a smaller target, but it leaves us more vulnerable."

Mitch waved a dismissive hand. "I can handle myself against the Sovereign. There is a reason they sent the government in to do their dirty work."

Nisha nodded as if the matter was settled. "Ava is safest with Mitch."

"I agree." Blue's statement shocked Finn. He watched the footage of Collins' first official duel. Anyone touching the magic community watched that fight. He also watched some of the subsequent challenges. Mitch was a dangerous man, but for both Nisha and Blue to imply that a high-value target like Ava would be safest with a single person as opposed to an entire team against a veritable army of truly evil bastards was ludicrous.

"Then we stick together and move Ava to Mitch as quickly as we can." Nisha twisted to look at Ben in the back seat. "Does that work for you, Ben?"

Ben didn't try to hide his skepticism. "The Paragon is going to protect Ava personally?"

"I am, Mr. Hughes." Mitch sounded sincere.

Sam looked almost as skeptical as Ben. "I've dealt with these guys twice. With two Zenith. One person isn't enough. How many can you offer as backup, Torrin?"

"If I pull everyone in, I have twenty."

Mitch's eyebrows rose. "Your men are all ex-military?"

"All of them. Some of the best I've ever worked with." Blue's tone dared Mitch to make a negative comment. As if she would somehow figure out how to kill him through the phone.

Hale ignored the drama and shook his head. "Lilac is not big enough to base a twenty-four-seven operation of that size. We need to move him."

Finn went over options in his mind. "We do. How long to coordinate a secondary site?"

Hale crunched a popcorn kernel. "At least a day."

"Get Trix on it," Finn said before Mitch could focus on the noise. "Call everyone in."

"Great. How will you handle the FBI and any other alphabet soup that comes your way, Paragon? Sir." Blue's tone dripped sarcasm.

Hale crunched more popcorn. "She's right. If you run them through the Mitch Collins bird blender, you will never recover from that press. Even Harper won't be able to save you. Game over."

"I don't care about the press," Ben said from the back seat. "Blend them."

"Amen." Greenlee twirled his finger in a blending motion.

Mouth thinning with impatience, Mitch cleared his throat. "Senator Miller is driving the government's efforts. It's a deeply personal vendetta. Ivan looked into it for me. Magic users burned Miller's childhood home to the ground with his mother and sister inside. It's a sad story, and he blames the Cahlad. No one else in the administration shares his zeal. But they are afraid to alienate his large vocal base."

The man's story genuinely saddened Nisha. "That's just awful."

"Great. It's a holy war." Finn tapped the steering wheel. "How do we force Miller to stand down?"

"I think Ms. West's unique skill set is best suited for this effort." Mitch said the words as if he was paying her a compliment.

Blue's face twisted into a knowing, humorless smile before she crossed her arms and looked up at the ceiling, huffing out a silent laugh.

No one said anything as his words and their implication sank in. Nisha's face twisted in horror. Sotach hid his reaction well but was clearly torn between the morality and effectiveness of assassinating a senator. Hale shot daggers from his eyes through the phone when he didn't object.

"Sir?" Nisha's voice lowered in disapproval. Yet she did not seem surprised.

"Who is on deck?" Finn interjected. "If Mitch loses control of the Cahlad, who takes over?"

"Larson." Nisha didn't hesitate. "Maybe the Brazilian Arcon."

"What about you or Sotach?" Greenlee asked from the back seat.

"Hell no," Sam and Nisha said in unison, both shaking their heads vehemently.

"Lacroix?" Greenlee leaned forward sot his face was in the frame, and everyone on the phone could see him. "You can't kill him. He is perfect."

Devon's face appeared between Sam and Blue, leaning into the frame. She looked mildly amused, gaze focused somewhere over the camera, and shook her head. "Pretty sure that grunt translates into a firm no." She stepped out of the frame.

"We know Larson is bad news." Finn raised an eyebrow in question. "The other guy?"

"Not much better." Nisha narrowed her eyes at Finn. "Four internal investigations into human rights violations. I've heard it in his head, but I don't have solid evidence yet. We are working on it."

Finn didn't censor his thoughts. He did not oppose dealing with Miller in any way necessary. Hell, he would handle it himself if it came down to it. Anyone in bed with the people who killed his brother and nephew didn't deserve mercy. Especially after his associates came after Lexi.

"Let me meet with him." Of course Nisha wanted to negotiate.

"They will arrest you the minute you surface, dear." Mitch shook his head. "Talking is no longer an option."

"Bottom line, the willing alternatives are worse than what we have now." Finn put it out there and didn't miss the Paragon's scowl. "If we don't help Mitch, none of us gets what we want. Miller is a significant threat to our goal."

"You are right." Voice flat, Blue looked back at the camera, her expression blank and her eyes cold. Finn had never witnessed this level of detachment from his friend. A stranger looked back at him. "I'll handle Miller."

Nisha squirmed in her seat. "Let's table this. We have time to solve this problem after we get everyone secure."

Frowning, Sotach sat back and crossed his arms, then turned his head toward the woman sitting next to him. "You told me you were done following orders you did not agree with. You don't have to do this."

"He didn't order me to do anything, Sotach."

Sam opened his mouth, but the sound of metal hitting metal echoed through their connection before he could speak. The phone in the RV tipped, its screen showing only the corner of something wooden. Shouts rang out from the background.

"Sam?" Nisha sounded panicked.

"Ava!" Ben leaned forward.

"Hold it together, Ben." Finn knew there was gray mist behind him. A quick glance at the floorboard confirmed it. "I can't drive if I'm dead."

"What in the hell is happening now?" Greenlee bit out. "How far out are we?"

"Fifteen, twenty minutes, I think." Finn pushed his foot to the floor of their rental car. He had a general location, but nothing specific. They were planning to coordinate where to meet when they got closer, to minimize any opportunity for the enemy to swarm their location.

"Make it ten." Greenlee sat back and started pulling items out of his backpack.

"Trix, I need a location on Devon and Blue." The lights went out at Hale's location. "Trix, was that you?"

The call remained connected, but Finn could not see Hale or the Paragon. "Hale?"

Distant echoes of gunfire preceded the distinctive sound of a *flash-bang* that strobed their square green on the phone's screen. "We need to move." Hale's voice carried over the speaker, though Finn still couldn't see him. "Stay on me." The line went dead.

Finn slammed his fist on the steering wheel, listening to shouts and crashes from the connection with Sam and Blue, still unable to see anything. This wasn't a coincidence.

Nisha leaned forward and twisted, looking in all directions. Either she came to the same conclusion or just used her magic to read his mind. "Eyes open." Greenlee continued shoving items from his bag into his pockets and hanging multiple pieces of jewelry around his neck. Ben joined Nisha in scanning their surroundings for potential threats.

"There they are." Ben pointed behind them to the left. Finn's eyes snapped to the rearview mirror. A red sedan careened around the bend on the road behind them.

"How many, Nisha?" Finn already had his foot on the floor, and they were gaining on him. "Get ready, Ben."

"Ssh. That's a long way." Nisha closed her eyes and frowned. "Three in that car. There are more cars behind that one." Her eyes opened wide. "Lots of cars, Finn."

"Hold up, Dr. Chuthulu." Greenlee pulled a toy car out of his backpack. Rolling down the window, he calmly unbuckled his seat belt. "I'm going to kill these assholes."

Greenlee twisted the toy car until it resembled a robot. When he snapped the head into place, a high-pitched whine filled the car.

"What is that?" Finn cursed the underpowered engine of the rental.

Greenlee started counting and boosted his upper body out of the window, sitting on the door, his legs extended across the back seat. "Get back in the car!" Nisha implored. "They have guns."

Greenlee's long hair fell out of the band containing it and whipped behind him. When his countdown reached twenty, he muttered the word apricot and hurled the transforming toy with everything he had. It bounced down the stripes in the middle of the road and lay there. Climbing back inside, he belted his seat belt, rolled the window up, and stared straight ahead.

"That's it?" Ben looked puzzled.

"That's it." Greenlee went back to inventorying the contents of his bag.

Finn kept checking the rearview mirror as nothing happened. The sedan got closer. "Ben, you are up."

A boom sent the red car rotating violently to the left, so fast it lifted off the ground, flying thirty feet into the air, still spinning in a colorful blur. Hovering for a moment, it plummeted back to earth. The vehicle disintegrated as it drilled itself into the ground. No one could survive that. "Jesus."

"What was that?" Ben looked at Greenlee with something akin to glee. "You have more of those?"

The dark smile that crossed his friend's features made the hair on Finn's arms stand up. He was seeing a different side of the man raising his niece.

Nisha's phone rang, and she answered on speaker.

"Finn." Trix spoke so softly, Finn struggled to understand him. "I don't have long. We've lost Lilac. Thirty-seven degrees, seventeen minutes, forty-seven seconds north. One hundred and six degrees, fifty-eight minutes, twenty seconds west. Nine miles. I released Gabrielle's Hounds."

"What does that mean?" Nisha asked him. "What about Mitch?"

Releasing Gabrielle's hounds meant Trix sent the scatter-and-go-to-ground order to every Herne team member. This protocol safeguarded his people in case the questionable nature of their artifact-hunting activities ended up on the Cahlad's radar and within their jurisdiction.

The line went dead again. Everyone needed help, and he couldn't do a damned thing about it. At least Trix got him Devon's coordinates. "Dev? Blue? Can you hear me? We are nine miles out. Hang on."

A deafening screech of metal rending apart erupted from the phone, lighting up the portion of the screen where Sam and Blue once sat, punctuated by screams, and the line went dead. His heart skipped a beat, and Greenlee and Ben cursed in the back seat. Nine miles never seemed so far away.

6

ZELLA

Zella's hand clutched Kendra's belt as the woman led them through the pitch-black facility. Not even the emergency lights illuminated their retreat. Zella couldn't see it, but Kendra led with her gun, moving forward as fast as they dared. Harper clutched Zella's other hand in an excruciating death grip.

After the initial loss of power and the quick barrage of gunfire and small detonations, the facility fell eerily silent. Each breath they took echoed in the inky stillness.

Zella hoped Hale got Mitch out of the building and did not wait for them. They were taking part in a call, with Sam and Finn in another room when the electricity failed.

Zella did not know where the two men on guard patrol who introduced themselves earlier as Caesar and Paco were, but suspected the gunfire had something to do with them. If Mitch engaged with the artifact he carried, the whole place would be in danger of falling on their heads. Kendra sniffed in front of her, then she came to a sudden halt. Zella stopped herself without bumping into Kendra. But Harper bumped into her hard enough that she barely stayed on her feet. "Not this way." Kendra sniffled.

"Is she smelling them?" Harper's drawl sounded incredulous. Zella didn't know and couldn't respond if she wanted to. Kendra changed directions and set off at a fast pace. Zella counted out fifty paces, a right-hand turn, and another eighteen paces before Kendra stopped again. Another sniff sounded in the darkness, followed by a low whistle that sounded like a finch or canary. An answering whistle sounded moments later. "Stay here." Kendra removed Zella's hand from her belt, leaving Zella alone with Harper clutching her hand in the silent darkness. Harper breathed audibly behind her. Zella patted her hand reassuringly, though her insides were churning. She had no foresight of these events and did not know what happened next.

Kendra's whispered, "It's Mitch and Hale" made her jump. Even in the stark silence, she did not hear the woman approach. Kendra brushed by quickly. "Harper, with me. Ms. Z., you are with Mitch. Hale has the rear." A moment later, a warm hand she would recognize anywhere clasped hers, bringing a wave of disappointment that he was still in the building. She needed to get him out of there. And she needed a damned gun. Mitch passed by her and tugged on her hand to follow.

Their group crept silently through the mazelike bowels of Herne's underground headquarters. Two almost inaudible clicking noises came from behind them. Mitch tensed, and the entire line of people come to a halt. She waited, her hand sweating in her partner's. A flash of white light filled her vision, then a rainbow-colored strobe. It took her precious seconds to realize it was a vision and not reality. She pitched backward against the wall, unable to adjust her equilibrium between the two vivid realities. Dim light illuminated a shadowy figure whose size shifted from large to average. A hiss sounded. It felt real, but this part was a vision. Something struck the shadow's neck. A dart? He fell hard to the earth. Another shadow that also grew and shrank stumbled, then fell to the ground in slow motion. A female form fell seconds later into a pile next to him. Black-gloved hands grasped the arms of the fallen and hauled them away. Another flash of white and rainbow strobe tore through her vision. "Zella, love? Listen to me. I'm right here." Mitch moved his hand up and down her arm in a calming gesture.

Real hisses sounded, followed by Hale's slurred, "Go!" Throwing her body in front of Mitch's, she hardly registered the sting of two objects piercing her shoulder. A tiny sliver of metal jutted from Mitch's right bicep, and she ripped it out, throwing it to the ground. Her muscles turned to jelly and Mitch stumbled sideways. Next to her, Hale's large body hit the ground. Lights erupted around them, and she collapsed. Men surrounded them, pointing weapons, breaking the terrifying silence with shouted commands and responses. Head falling to the side, she found the hallway next to her empty, holding no trace of Harper, Mitch, Kendra, or Lady Lucille. Where had they gone? How long had she been laying here? Seconds? It must have been longer. The shouting grew angry, unable to find what they were looking for. Her brain struggled to put it all together.

Someone lifted her roughly. Head lolling backward, she glimpsed Hale's prone form being dragged away, hands bound behind his back and chin falling to his chest. A flash of her daughter's face, screaming in agony, ripped through her mind. Another flash of the mountains interposed itself over her vision, this time with a purple, sparkling ring in the foreground. The figures surrounding it remained nebulous. Rainbow and pure white flashes of light strobed, surrounded by a black swirling galaxy of stars. And she didn't know if she was conscious or trapped in a vision. A soft snort snapped her reality into focus. She was still in the same hallway where they had fallen, with only Hale and the men who attacked them. Though she couldn't see her, a muffled snort sounded just like an irritated Lady Lucile should be right next to them.

7

DEVON

Devon pulled herself off the floor where she landed next to a stunned Ava when something hit the camper, rubbing her elbow with a wince. Lexi clutched the back of the sofa.

Sam surged off the floor and landed on his knees behind Ivan's seat while Blue crawled toward them, falling over when the camper took another hit.

"Mommy?" She barely heard Lexi over the crunch of metal and tires squealing as Ivan fought to keep control.

Blue tightened Lexi's seat belt. "It's okay, sweetie. You are going to be fine."

Devon helped Ava onto the couch and fastened the seat belt around the girl's waist. "I have them."

Blue rushed to the front of the camper and kneeled behind the passenger seat where Rhodes grasped the dashboard, glaring at the side mirrors, trying to gain a view of their pursuers. The goon squad found them. Again.

"Somebody tell me what is happening." She held each of the girl's hands in her own.

"Honey Badger?" Ivan glowed and struggled to grip the steering wheel because of the force field encasing his hands.

Devon looked into Ava's wide, frightened eyes. "I need you to calm down, honey." Letting go of Lexi, she placed both hands on Ava's face, holding her by her cheeks. "Calm. Down."

"I'm trying!" Ava's eyes filled with tears, and Rhodes made a noise that sounded like a rabid pack of wolves joined the party. The man now sported tawny-brown hair and fangs.

"Blue." Devon jerked her head, calling Blue back. They had to deal with this. Blue crawled over with a question on her face. "Check me."

Blue nodded in understanding and placed her hand on Ava's arm as Devon carefully sent a jolt of magic into the teenager, hoping that Blue's enhanced magic healing could counterbalance her own. Ava's chin hit her chest, and she snored deeply.

"Boom Kitty." Blue bumped Devon's fist. Ava was asleep and not comatose. "That would have been handy this morning. Go team."

"Better." Ivan no longer glowed.

"Thank you," Rhodes said.

"She's not going to hell with you?" Sam's words dripped sarcasm.

"You invited him? That was a girl's trip." Devon attempted to make Ava more comfortable.

Ivan jerked the wheel to the side, and she fought to stay upright. Fortunately, the road remained empty except for them and a white SUV trying to run them off the road.

"I can get to them." Blue crawled forward again, craning to look at the side-view mirror.

Devon joined in the loud chorus of exasperated and angry nos that rang through the vehicle. She couldn't believe Blue would consider a jump of that complexity after what happened this morning.

"This morning was a rush job." Blue winced and glared at Sam.

Kneeling on the couch between Lexi and Ava, Sam ignored Blue and peered out the window behind them. "They are going to wreck us." He looked down at Devon. "Can you knock them out?"

The camper lurched again from another violent hit. Ivan fought the wheel, and announced calmly, "They are backing off. Up to something."

"I'll try." Squeezing Lexi's arm, she stood and drew as much magic as she could from the world around her. "I'll be right back. Tia Blue has you."

Holding so much magic that it hurt, her stomach knotted, and her hair floated languidly around her head. She crawled across the bed and looked out the window. A cold chill ran down her spine. Two vehicles sat stopped behind a man standing, legs braced firmly, holding something large on his shoulder. They were definitely up to something. But her accuracy was terrible at this range.

"Rhodes?" Blue's question reached her ears.

"I've got it." Rhodes stood, and seconds later, the bed dipped, and he crouched next to her to look out the window as well. "Whatever you are going to do, do it now, Devon." Rhodes' eyes never left the scene behind them. "Now!"

His panic spurred her to action, and she released every ounce of stored magic with a shout and a visible ripple of energy. Collapsing forward, her face planted itself in the mattress, and she tried not to vomit, feeling the rear of the camper jolt and hop from the force of her magic surge.

Rhodes still looked out the window. "I think you got them."

"What on earth is that?" Lexi sounded awestruck as a bright purple light illuminated everything.

"Hold on!" Ivan locked the brakes, causing them to squeal as the light grew brighter. His arm flew up to protect his eyes. Devon tumbled away from the window.

"Brace! Brace!" Coarse hair scrubbed against her skin from an abnormally large arm that wrapped around her and threw her to the floor.

"What's happening?" Cocooned entirely in a wall of fur, she could hardly breathe.

The camper tipped from a thundering explosion. Everything slowed down, and gravity stopped working. The sounds of wood splintering, metal rending, and people screaming filled her ears even through the ringing caused by the explosion. Somehow Rhodes held her tighter as they tumbled, unable to tell which direction was up, though the deafening noise told her the camper no longer moved on its wheels. Gravel and rocks ground against the smooth exterior walls as it slid off the road. Infused with panic, she only focused on whether Blue got Lexi away in time.

The camper lurched to a stop with a sickening crunch, sending them tumbling forward. Pushing frantically on the pile of fur crushing her to the floor, she staggered to her feet. Miraculously, the section of the vehicle she and Rhodes occupied survived relatively unscathed. But the wreck obliterated the hallway leading to the rest of the camper, and she couldn't see anyone else. "Lexi!" She tore at the rubble in front of her.

Rhodes clambered to his feet behind her, still furry and larger than normal, but not so large that he shredded his clothing yet. Stumbling, he leaned against the vertical ceiling for support and shook his furry head to clear it.

"I've got her!" Blue's voice pierced the wall of rubble, and Devon's body sagged with relief. "She's good."

The vehicle shuddered, knocking Devon sideways into Rhodes, who kept them both on their feet with a grunt. Blue yelled something in a language Devon did not understand, but it sounded like curse words. Lexi squealed.

"Blue?" Rhodes said so loud, she flinched. His head was down and his fists clenched, eyes glowing bright gold. He huffed like an animal, fighting a shift into something not human.

Devon took a quick step back, remembering his claws. "Hold it together, Rhodes." He huffed like an enraged bull in response.

"We are stuck." Blue sounded frustrated.

"Ava is awake," Lexi said helpfully. "Mr. Ivan is glowing."

Devon looked around in despair, realizing they were stuck, too.

"Stay put, Lexi Lou." Rhodes pushed Devon to the side with his hip, mindful of his claws. "I'm coming to get you." Slamming a gigantic hairy fist all the way through the back window, he slung shattered pieces of glass everywhere. Devon covered her face as he hit it again, knocking the entire thing out of its frame.

Stepping through the broken window, they emerged in a field of blue wildflowers. A mountain range rose tall to their left. The front of the camper lay in a deeply shaded, dense grove of cedar trees on the other side of a gigantic portal, rimmed in sparkling purple flares. "What in the world?"

"Dev?" Rhodes' voice rumbled inhumanly deep.

Distracted, Devon shielded her eyes from the bright purple light, staring in wonder. "Yeah?"

"Hold my pants."

8

BLUE

Standing in the center of a once functional Class A motorhome, Blue's feet rested on the passenger side wall, and she leaned on the vehicle's roof. Lexi stood next to her, arms wrapped around Blue's upper leg, sniffling to keep herself from breaking down. Looking up into Ava's frightened eyes, Blue tried to hide her frustration. Ava dangled by the couch's built-in seat belt. The moment Ava's dazed eyes opened, an already unpleasant situation got worse. Blue abandoned the jump with the girls when Ava's magic surged. Ivan's shield flared golden-bronze, and the already mangled driver's compartment disintegrated, further pinching Blue and the girls between two piles of wreckage. Only Ivan's right hand stuck out of the driver's compartment. She could not see Sam at all. Her only viable exit appeared to be an eight-foot jump and chin-up out the broken window above Ava's head.

"I'll catch you." Blue held up her arms.

"What happened?" Ava's shaking hands tried to unbuckle the belt. She frowned and rubbed her head, disoriented and in pain. "Where is everyone?"

"Focus on your belt." Blue pointed to direct Ava's attention. Ava fumbled with the mechanism holding her in the air. A pained groan from behind her accompanied the shifting of rubble in the kitchen. "Sotach?"

Something between a yeah and an ow answered her. Ava won the battle against the seat belt and fell flailing toward the ground. Blue snatched her out of the air and helped soften her landing.

Ava's bottom lip trembled, and she let loose a wail that deafened Blue's still recovering ears. "Oh Christ." Blue wrapped the girl in her arms, bringing Lexi into the huddle, since her niece was obviously struggling just as much as Ava. "I've got you."

She looked toward the heap of building materials that had once been the RV's kitchen. The refrigerator lay among the debris, leaving only a portion of Sam's leg visible, the rest of his body completely buried. Ivan's situation wasn't much better, so pinned in by twisted metal, she had no way of helping him. "Ivan?"

"Working on it."

Blue searched for a way out. Before their vehicle turned into a stunt plane, she glimpsed a large, shining purple circle. It was magic, undoubtedly bad, and the Sovereign goons were still around somewhere. This situation was not ideal.

Rhodes said he would get them. And she trusted him. But a contingency plan never hurt. Maybe Sam could reach the window, or Ivan could lift the girls up to her if she could dig one of them out. Twisted metal and an entire tree encased Ivan. Sam only dealt with debris and a kitchen appliance. Untangling herself from Lexi and Ava, she turned her attention to the rubble that pinned Sam down.

He was making progress in shifting the items trapping him. Even with her help, it was taking too long. The camper quaked, and the rubble covering Sam shifted even more, and she threw herself back to keep from being buried with him. Something big had hit them. Ava and Lexi screamed. The camper quaked again, and the wall under her feet shifted and tipped upward.

Lexi's eyes grew wide. "Tia Blue?"

The roar of an animal vibrated through the space as the camper tilted. The structure groaned as destroyed joints and supports shifted. "Oh boy." Blue snatched both girls into her arms, doing her best to wrap her body around them. The camper continued to tilt, flinging them off their feet. All three of them slid down the wall. The rubble in the back of the vehicle thundered as it landed in a new configuration. Blue landed underneath both girls in a tangle of limbs on the actual floor and hissed as a sharp pain radiated from her back. The camper slammed onto its wheels and rocked back and forth as the momentum of whatever threw them back over subsided.

Ava, still screaming, stood up, looking around with wide eyes. Lexi leaned back on her knees, taking her weight off Blue, tears streaking down her face. Blue looked around, trying to figure out what was happening, and reached to the spot on her back where the pain radiated. An object stuck out just below her ribs. With Ava's magic flaring, her body was healing around whatever it was. She gripped it firmly and yanked, enduring a blinding flash of pain that made her scream.

"Ms. Blue." Ava stared in horror but didn't move to help. "Oh my God. Oh my God."

Blue looked at the object in her hand and stood slowly, aware a small river of blood now trailed down her back and pooled at her feet. She took a deep breath to handle the pain. This was getting old. The nova-fueled rapid healing hurt almost worse than the initial injury. The thing that stabbed her was an L-shaped piece of shiny metal, now covered in blood. She threw it to the side and looked the girls over. "Are you two okay?"

"I don't know, Tia Blue." Lexi shook her head, still sitting on her knees, dazed. Blue ran her hands over her niece and didn't find any physical injuries. But Lexi was reaching the end of her mental and emotional limits.

"Look at me, honey. You are okay. Ava?"

"No. I'm not okay! I want my dad!"

A horrific screech of metal rending ripped through the space, and Ava screamed in terror again, diving toward Blue. Blue slung the girl behind her and pulled Lexi across the floor away from the noise and put herself in front of them.

The rubble of the kitchen shifted, and Sam's hand poked out. "What in the hell is happening?"

"I'll tell you when I figure it out!"

The bent entry door of the camper ripped away with a screech, letting in a fresh wave of cool mountain air and revealing a nine-foot-tall bear-man with the face of a Klingon. The screen door dangled from claws as long as her feet, attached to arms that bulged with muscles and almost dragged the ground.

"What is that?" Lexi screamed as the creature leaned over and turned its head to look inside.

Ava exhaled a long, relieved breath and clutched her chest. "Mr. Rhodes?"

Rhodes' golden eyes landed on Blue, then moved to the puddle of blood on the floor beneath her. If a Klingon could look remorseful, this one did. She had never seen him attempt a shift into anything this large before. He had to be overdosing on Ava's magic. He yowled, unable to answer with words.

"Oh. Thank God. Rhodes." Blue sagged in relief and pushed a hand against the almost healed wound in her side.

"Get them out of here, Westridge!" Ivan thrashed to free himself from the twisted metal, slinging the steering wheel onto the floor.

Devon, clutching a pair of sweatpants and looking worriedly at the road, sidestepped the shrinking but still giant bear-Klingon, like it was an everyday annoyance and leaned into the gaping hole where the door used to be. "Come on, girls!" She reached inside, and Blue shoved Ava in her direction.

"Sam and Ivan are stuck. Get the girls clear!" Blue shoved Lexi into Devon's arms.

"Blue! Come on." Rhodes' voice rumbled deeper than normal and held a touch of howl. But at least he could speak now. He helped Ava down and pushed her toward a grove of trees.

"They have it loaded. I can't hit them from here!" Devon tried to climb back into the camper after helping Lexi down.

"Get them out of here, Rhodes! Please!" Blue turned her focus to the two men trapped in the mangled mess.

"Dammit, baby." Rhodes' words emerged slightly more human this time. At the edge of her vision, Devon's face morphed into a mask of surprise, and she disappeared from the door with a yelp.

"Don't make me carry your stubborn ass." Rhodes' warning preceded Devon's indignant oof. Arguing voices faded with distance. Blue sagged in relief. Rhodes might be an asshole, but he came through when it mattered.

Sam sat up, forcing away a landslide of debris and pushing on the refrigerator, still crushing his left leg. He bled from everywhere, and the refrigerator wasn't budging. Racing back to help dislodge the large appliance, she pushed as hard as she could in the same direction he was.

"You need to get out of here." Sam grunted with the effort to free himself. Blue didn't even acknowledge his statement, just ducked her head and kept working. The fridge lay wedged at an awkward angle and was stuck. Sam couldn't get out. "Damn it!" he screamed and pounded on the metal top.

A sharp crack sounded behind her, and part of the wall in the driver's compartment shifted. "I'm coming!" Ivan's glowing, shielded hand shimmied through the tiny space he cracked in the rubble. Next, his face, contorted in effort, appeared as he levered off the tree trunk, now embedded in the vehicle's driver compartment.

Devon yelled another warning. They needed to go now, even if Ava overloaded her magic. She grabbed the portion of Sam's leg that she could reach and stretched desperately across the space toward Ivan.

Ivan, still stuck in the collapsed driver's compartment, strained to reach toward her. His shield pushed in front of him, stopping Blue's hand each time her own got close to him. Everything slowed down.

"Vanya, I can't get to skin!" Choking out the words, she batted at the shield, trying to get through to his hand, and almost lost her grip on Sam's ankle. She could see the men Devon mentioned through the shattered side window. They had some kind of launcher, and it was ready to fire.

"It's okay." Ivan quickly pulled his hand back and out of her reach as he looked at the men over her shoulder.

Blue stared at him for a sub-second. An eternity. "I can't leave you again."

"Get him out of here." Ivan ripped at the mangled chassis that had become his prison.

She cursed and continued to reach out. She wanted to close her eyes, but she couldn't. If the assholes had that green gas, Ivan really could die if she left him. But they would all die if she didn't. Ivan had a better shot at surviving than Sam. It was math. Leave one to save two. She would deal with what that did to her soul later.

Realizing what she intended to do, Sam attempted to pull his leg away. She clawed into his skin so that she didn't lose contact. "Ivan! No!" He went still. "Damn you both. Throttle your magic!"

A roaring hiss echoed through the valley, and Ava screamed from outside the camper. Blue glimpsed flame and something flying toward them. This was it.

She mentally slammed the door on the massive amounts of magic that battered at her like an angry sea, trying its best to take her under. The golden outline around Ivan's hands receded. "Give me your hand!" she screamed, stretching her muscles until they burned with agony. He reached out, still pinned by the mangled metal and trees.

Numbers whizzed through her brain, and she let her vision fade from Ivan's grim face to the arctic rainbow she was growing to hate. A high-pitched whine filled the camper. Ivan's fingers brushed hers as he screamed at them to go, his calm dissipating. Something hammered the walls behind them and she released her magic, and flames erupted around them.

9

RHODES

They stood in a densely wooded cedar glade, the sun overhead blocked by the tall trees around them instead of the lush mountain-flanked field of wildflowers they had just been in. Rhodes placed a hand on Ava's shoulder, stopping the merciless push to get them away from the camper and out of weapons range. He had to pick Devon up and carry her away. After handing him Lexi, she tried to climb into the camper to help the people still trapped.

Ava stopped, chest heaving and face red from running at full speed. She clutched Lexi's hand in her own. He put Devon back on her feet.

She punched him in the stomach and yelped, shaking out her hand. Ignoring it, he stared instead at the gigantic purple outline ripping the world in front of him in half. On the other side, their attackers parked on the road they drove down only minutes ago. "What is going on?"

"I wish people would quit asking me that." Devon let loose a strangled laugh that bordered on hysterical. "Blue needs help."

"She has it under control." Rhodes ignored her murderous scowl. If anyone could get them out of that camper, it was Blue. She asked him to protect the people in front of him, and that was what he was going to do. It was the first time she said please to him since she begged him to change her appearance back, and it almost broke him.

"Bull!" Devon spat. "There is no controlling any of this!" She waved to the wrecked camper, the sparkling purple portal, and to his partially human form.

Rhodes herded them farther into the grove of trees, and Devon shook her arm loose angrily. "She will be right behind us." He looked back at the wreck. Blue reached for Ivan through the ruined door. The camper disappeared in an explosion of flame.

A wave of heat blistered his back as he fell forward, shoving Devon and the girls down as small pieces of debris pelted them, unable to comprehend the devastation. Devon lifted her head even as she clutched the girls to her and looked behind him. "Oh my God." The tone of her voice compelled him to look. The camper was nothing more than a flaming husk of metal. Black smoke billowed from the gnarled body, and a cloud of green gas seeped out, hugging the surrounding ground. "Where are they?"

Frantically searching in every direction, fear and fury warred for control. He couldn't believe what he just witnessed. Looking around again, he prayed three bodies would fall out of thin air. He would even take just one. But there was only dancing flames and the shapes of the men who survived Devon's attack advancing on them. A painful hollow ache took root in the center of his chest, and breathing became difficult. Devon clutched Lexi's face to her chest so the girl could not look toward the wreckage.

"This is bad," Ava said with enough trepidation in her voice that he pried his eyes away from the heart-wrenching disaster behind him and followed her gaze.

Five people stood among the trees. Not traditional soldiers, but he could tell they were here to fight. They ran right into a trap. He recognized a few high-level magic practitioners from his days at the Cahlad. He could handle them. Especially with Devon at his back. The person who worried him most, however, was the man who strolled out of the trees, hands casually tucked into his pockets, observing them with predatory calm. Larson Battle wore a smug smile that made Rhodes want to rip his evil face off.

"Rhodes." He nodded, as if they were old friends exchanging pleasantries. More figures emerged from the trees surrounding them. Too many to count.

Taking a deep breath, he drew all the extra magic he could get from Ava. His stomach lurched, and his body stretched by at least four feet and several hundred pounds. He let his claws extend, and fangs poked past his lips. He had channeled small amounts of magic every second of every day for the past ten years. But this much magic at once might kill him. He hoped to buy Devon enough time to get the girls away. He stepped between the biggest threat and the people he needed to protect. Larson's level of power would take him out quickly if he could only play defense. But he had to try.

"I want as many of you alive as possible. But, really, all I need is pieces." Larson's voiced dripped with menace and boredom. "Even you can't beat these odds. Do the smart thing for once in your life, and give up."

"Burn in hell!" Devon howled as she stepped from behind Rhodes. "Never!" Her hair danced above her head, and her eyes glowed a deep blue. She looked completely unhinged and danger-ous, and he suspected she was. This man murdered her oldest child and had his sights set on her youngest. Throwing her arms forward, she let loose a visible surge of magic that left her hands with a pop. Larson didn't even flinch, lip curling up as the energy wave ripped the ground apart on its way toward him.

"Yep. Bad. Let's go, Lexi." Two sets of light footsteps pounded back toward the flaming camper. Standing his ground, he roared to draw attention to himself and away from the girls. In this form, he could take a substantial amount of damage.

Devon's energy wave bounced off an invisible barrier mere feet from Larson's smiling face. "Hmmm." Devon's own face held a feral smile, as if the fact her magic hadn't touched a hair on his head didn't bother her at all. Her hair lifted in a crown of waving static once again, clothing billowing. She hovered over the ground, a terrifying visage. "Which one of you is protecting this turd hole?"

Another, smaller, wave of magic washed from her left hand, rolling toward the people on their left. Only one person remained standing. She shot another jet of magic at Larson, and it deflected again.

"Rhodes, did you see that?" Stepping back, she angled herself so she could blast the people still protected, from a different direction. He needed to find the person holding the shield and take them out fast. The girls were running, and Devon fought without magical healing or shielding. One hit would take her down.

Letting loose a roar that held every ounce of rage stored over the past decade, he lunged to the right. No mercy, no changing people to babies or kittens. He descended on those lurking at the edges of the ranks with claws and fangs, absorbing a volley of random magical attacks. Howling as the skin and fur on his chest sizzled away, he kept going. One of these bastards held that shield for Larson. Rhodes was going to find him and kill him.

Devon threw another visible bolt of her magic Larson's way, and it once again bounced off the invisible barrier. Changing tactics, she threw her hand upward. Twenty feet in the air, the wave of her magic continued on into the sky. She'd found another edge. Could he jump that high in this form? He swiped through another opponent and prepared for the leap.

"Do it!" Ava's scream came from far away. Lexi's scream followed, and Devon lost her focus on her attackers. A miniature bolt of lightning sizzled across her right side. Devon screamed and fell to her knees on the other side of the clearing, clutching her ribs. Swaying, she snarled and pushed another wave of energy at the three people standing in front of her.

Larson smiled as she fell, but his face twisted in horror and surprise when he looked up. A shadow blocked out the meager sun, drawing Rhodes' eyes to the smoldering husk of the camper hurtling toward them, thirty feet in the air and raining molten debris onto everything in its path. Lexi stood in the middle of the field, hands extended, hair standing on end, just like her mother's. Ava stood behind her, golden glowing hands wrapped around the girl's upper arms. Both of them were screaming. "Stop!" He doubted the girls could hear him or would listen if they did. That was too much magic for someone so young and inexperienced. There was a big difference between a fork and a bus.

As the camper cleared the barrier protecting him, Larson turned and ran like the coward he was. A few of the ever-increasing number of magical soldiers emerging from the trees, despite his and Devon's attacks, turned their efforts toward the girls. "Rhodes! Can you get to them?" Devon threw wave after wave of magic. She was exhausted, losing the battle, and still on her knees from the lightning bolt.

Rhodes needed to go after the bastard that ruined the lives of everyone he ever cared about. That Blue had not reappeared, devastated him. Larson's lackeys just took out two Zenith and two members of Stalker Prime with one shot. But Lexi just threw a ten-thousand-pound, flaming metal carcass on at least a few of them, and the girls were now sitting ducks.

The ground in front of the girls rolled like waves cresting against the shore, sending them both flying backward, and Lexi's arms dropped. The RV lost its momentum and fell. But it didn't fall straight down. It continued forward and over the place where Devon's magic crested the shield. Rhodes didn't wait to see if it hit Larson, tearing across the field, trying to get to Lexi and Ava. Ava pulled Lexi beneath her and huddled in place as fire, lightning, and ice rained down around them.

Behind them, on the road in Colorado, more SUVs than he could count sped toward them. Fire erupted behind the lead car, a gray SUV, as it barreled through the portal and drove straight at the girls. He roared and urged his legs faster. The SUV slammed on its brakes and threw dirt and a shower of blue flower petals in all directions, skidding to a stop sideways, blocking his path.

The rear passenger door flew open, and a tall man, with shoulder-length blond hair whipping around his head, leapt out, hitting the ground running. He pulled something from his pocket and threw it as he ran. It landed several feet behind Devon, and a surge of electricity ripped through two people lurking in the trees behind her.

A man with licking flames for eyes emerged from the car, a cloud of gray mist hovering around his feet churning the blue flower petals higher into the air. He took two gigantic steps toward the girls as a swirling dome of black mist enveloped them and blocked Rhodes' view of all three. He howled in fury. But the incoming magical attacks bounced off the dome without making a dent. The girls might be safe in there.

He spun on his clawed feet to help Devon, now on her hands and knees, head hanging so low, her hair dragged the dirt. Piles of people lay unconscious or dead around her, but others emerged from the trees. She held her arm out and continued to push magic, but she was pale and trembling.

The tall, blond man charged in her direction, arm in the air, a small glowing shield protecting him from most of the magical attacks aimed in his direction. This must be Lexi's beloved Tio G. The man threw a toy car onto the ground in the middle of the group closest to Devon and shouted something that sounded like *apricot*. Air swirled, and they flew into a vortex of arms and legs straight up into the air, hovering for a moment. Then they plummeted to the ground, landing with a symphony of disturbing squishes, crunches, and agonized cries. He threw something else too small for Rhodes to see, and an explosion tore another cluster of Larson's lackeys apart. A shimmer rippled through the air, and Larson's shield fizzed out of existence. Greenlee slid to his knees and scooped Devon into his arms, looking up at Rhodes without a shred of hesitation. "Help me, Rhodes." Rhodes made a noise he hoped the man understood was an affirmative and turned toward the never-ending wall of assholes trying to kill them with magic. Rhodes recognized many of them as convicts sentenced during Larson's time as Regent. Some of them were his arrests. He didn't see Larson anywhere. The bastard got away.

Greenlee stood and ran toward the car and the gray dome of mist behind it. Rhodes ran behind him, absorbing attacks.

Two people abandoned the car as a giant ball of ice shattered the front windshield. Rhodes recognized them both. Finn Torrin used the door for cover. Nisha Ravi held a similar position at the other door. They both fired into the wall of Larson's foot soldiers, slowing the magical bombardment but not stopping it.

"I've got her, Ben!" Greenlee sprinted across the field at a fast pace, completely unaffected by the extra weight in his arms. As he approached, a breach appeared in the dome, revealing a man he recognized from video calls as Ben Hughes, Ava's dad. His eyes were still aflame. Lexi clung to his leg while Ava buried her face in his chest. Ben stood in the center, looking up with one arm protectively around each girl, the gray that formed the dome swirling from his feet.

Greenlee rushed through, and the dome slammed shut behind him, leaving Rhodes staring at Nisha and Finn.

The cavalry had arrived. And it wasn't enough.

10

NISHA

Greenlee dashed past, carrying a dark-haired woman who barely kept her arms around his neck, but she left an impressive number of bodies in her wake. Nisha staggered under the mental weight of too many voices, many thinking in languages she didn't understand, and fired into the trees that hid dozens of Larson's minions. Even more hid behind the smoldering husk of a large vehicle. They were radical magic supremacists who genuinely believed in Larson's cause. And ex-convicts who owed him a solid for having the government call the Cahlad's methods into question and release them. Mentally, she could hear them all. Every single one of them had dangerous magic, and a giant shimmering portal that Finn drove their car through without a second thought did not surprise them.

A portal this size took massive amounts of magic, and very few people could hold it open for more than a few seconds, if they weren't feeding off Ava and well-protected. Devon and Rhodes littered the field with bodies before they arrived, somehow forcing

Larson to flee. But the portal still held strong. Did Larson intend to keep the portal open, or had he intended to open it just long enough to separate his quarry from any help, only to be stymied by the Ava effect? The answer hid in the scattered mental fragments bombarding her mind. Regardless, Larson was here and Mitch wasn't. She didn't know anyone else who could face Larson head-on and survive.

Her magic now fed off Ava's surge, and acid sandpaper scraped across her brain. She did a double take as a gigantic creature that looked half man, half bear, with ridges running down its forehead stopped next to Finn when Greenlee disappeared inside Ben's shield and looked at them. Magic attacks bounced off him with minimal impact. Her guess was that Rhodes Westridge stood in front of them. Where were Sam and Ivan? She couldn't isolate a singular mental voice in the chaos.

Fire, lightning, ice, and seismic magical attacks flew across the field, buffeting them. It felt like walking on the deck of a burning boat tossing violently in an arctic storm. Luckily, the attacks were uncoordinated and remained free from Larson's signature meteorites.

"We need to run!" Dozens of people surrounded them, harboring an intent to kill, and Larson lurked nearby. It was all so loud.

"Run where?" Finn ejected an empty magazine, tilting his wrist and reloading in one fluid motion. "They are swarming behind us. Greenlee is almost out of toys. Where's Blue?"

At Finn's words, Rhodes whined and shook his shaggy head.

"What does that mean?" Finn ducked a gout of fire that bounced off the car's hood. Nisha focused on Rhodes with a painful amount of effort and picked up pieces of his memory. A vision of Blue and Ivan in the exploding camper, surrounded by a gigantic cloud of green fog. His sorrow made her breath catch. She opened her mind back up again, the onslaught so intense her head jerked to the side. She searched through any mind she could hear, unable to isolate Sam, Ivan, or anyone who sounded like a teleporting Zenith operative.

"We are on our own, Finn." She swallowed around a lump in her throat and shot at the enemies that she could see in front of her. No doubt her aim was terrible. She would be lucky to not shoot Finn or Rhodes, she was so distracted.

Finn stopped shooting and turned his gaze her way. She nodded toward the wrecked vehicle in front of them. His face grew dark and dangerous as he processed what she was telling him. His mind raced methodically through scenario after scenario, prioritizing Lexi and Ava in everyone. "Can you shift into something that can fly, Rhodes?"

She didn't like this one bit. She wanted to chase after Larson. Rhodes longed to do so as well. But keeping Ava away from Larson and getting the other little girl to safety took priority.

The beast stood motionless, its glowing golden gaze boring into Finn. Finally, it huffed and nodded.

A barrage of a single word pummeled her mind: fire. She looked up as a meteorite hurtled toward them. Larson Battle had joined the fight. "Run!"

Finn's mind compartmentalized all of his options and focused on the immediate problem, without emotion. "Rhodes is our ride. Get him in the shield!"

Together they shoved Rhodes' lumbering form toward the gray dome behind them as they ran. "Ben!" A gap in the gray bubble formed. Rhodes' massive frame trundled through as a flash of light and heat washed over them.

"Close it!" Nisha shoved Rhodes through, barely pulling her arm back before the dome snapped shut behind him. Finn's acceptance of certain death flitted through her mind, and he tackled her from the side, slamming her into the ground as the giant gout of flame battered Ben's forcefield. Flaming bits of rock and magma bounced off, engulfed in roaring flames. Her skin tightened painfully as the scorching heat rolled over them. Finn yelped, his pain searing her mind and her nose filled with the smell of singed hair and burnt clothing. Pushing with all of her might, she rolled them away from the misty target of Larson's fury. Another ball of flame exploded against Ben's forcefield.

Untangling herself from Finn's body, she patted out a stubborn patch of flame on his back and assessed the damage. A small patch of minor burns marred his back and left arm, and something had hit him in the head. He was loopy as hell in there.

A steady stream of fireballs still fell from the sky, making it impossible to return to Ben's forcefield without being roasted. It stuttered and shrank with each blast of Larson's magic. Throwing Finn's good arm over her shoulder, she pulled him to his feet, thankful he could walk. Stumbling farther into the cedar glade, struggling to control the onslaught of frantic thoughts, she kept her weapon raised in case they encountered any of Larson's convict army. Waves of burning sensations scraped over her brain, and she fought not to vomit. No longer able to feel the blistering heat of Larson's fireballs, she let Finn flop to the ground. He leaned against a tree and panted, still clutching his weapon.

Turning, she contemplated trying to sneak behind Larson to distract him or catch him by surprise and buy the others some time. In the field, a flaming ball of fire so large that it took up her entire field of vision screamed toward Ben's shield. The gray bubble stopped the projectile, but wavered and dropped completely away on impact.

A blast of wind ripped outward as it fell, howling with the force of a hurricane, followed by a barrage of glowing golden magical discs that exploded in a wave from the center of where the dome used to stand. A ripple of force pulsed toward them, and the soft whoosh of thousands of discs cut through the air. It looked like Mitch's signature attack, except this was five times the size of anything Mitch ever released, and it had no focus. It simply radiated outward.

Screaming in terror, she dragged Finn behind a fallen log and threw herself down beside him, praying it would be enough cover as golden discs whizzed over their heads, obliterating everything in their path. Above them, the tops of trees sheered off and plummeted to the earth. Dirt flew skyward, then pelted them. Wood and twigs rained down around them, battering her back and legs. The sound of falling trees thundered in her ears. Terrified voices pierced her brain and slowly, one by one, winked out.

11

BLUE

Still reaching for Ivan, Blue landed hard on top of Sam, shaking and staring at her empty hand, where she still felt Ivan's fingertips, unable to move or process the fact he wasn't with them. An explosion cascaded across the meadow, casting a flare of orange and red across everything in her field of vision. Sam hurled her sideways, her armpit crowding her face, a reminder that none of them had a proper shower in days. "Get off." She pushed on Sam's arm and chest but remained trapped within range of his body odor until the rain of debris and noise subsided.

The following silence punched her in the gut, and she let her head fall back, clenching her fingers to stop the phantom tingling of her fingertips. She left Ivan behind again. Trying to locate him with her magic, she groaned as a wave of pain and nausea almost overwhelmed her, evidence Ava was still close. She craned her neck toward the sounds of crackling flames. Nothing but a smoking husk remained of the camper laying across the apogee of a gigantic portal, edges shimmering like purple sparklers. A cloud of green gas billowed around the camper, wafting off in tendrils on the wind. There was no way Ivan survived that without his shield, and that damned green gas would nullify his magic. She couldn't form words.

Sam stood with a pained grunt he tried to muffle and pulled her up with him, motioning for her to move. "Charades? Again?" She forced her knees not to wobble because she still pulled dangerous amounts of magic, despite actively trying to throttle it.

"Yes." The venom in his words drew her attention, and she tried to take a step back. He seethed and vibrated with so much anger that she shook, too, because he still held her arm. Her gut told her he struggled for control, and that was a bad thing. Especially if he was mad at her. An anguished whisper emerged: "I told him to throttle his magic. It's my fault."

She blinked. He didn't blame her. He blamed himself for giving the order to drop the shield so she could move them. "Hey. You said throttle the magic. Not kill it. That gas is the problem. Not you."

His hand squeezed her arm so hard, it felt like it would snap in two. Flashes of magical effects from the portal strobed at the edge of her vision. Helping Rhodes and Devon as fast as possible was a priority. "Rhodes is good, but they are in trouble, and I have to deal with the shooter and help them. I could use your help. Are you with me?" He nodded and met her eyes again. She wasn't sure if it was her imagination or not, but his eyes were much darker than she remembered, and it made her uneasy. She pulled her arm loose.

"Now." She twisted toward the two vehicles that pursued them. "Which of those bastards shot it?"

Rolling up his sleeves, Sam turned his attention to the cars. Men scurried around the vehicles, unaware that a furious Zenith and a raging Regent had them in their sights. They would all be dead soon.

Before either of them could do anything, two things happened at once. The husk of the smoldering camper quaked and groaned, levitating skyward, stopping to hover thirty feet in the air. Gravity sheered off the back third of the structure and it plummeted to the earth. The remaining mass catapulted forward all the way through the portal, raining debris as it went.

As the RV flew away, the screaming engine of a vehicle being driven far beyond its capabilities drew their attention away from the flying hunk of metal. A gray SUV sped down the straight stretch of road, heading toward the portal, followed by a fleet of cars, one closer than the others. A black sedan harried the gray vehicle's driver's side, trying to knock it off the road. A tall figure with familiar blond hair climbed out onto the edge of the rear passenger window. Greenlee threw something that resulted in two gigantic fireballs erupting in the middle of the road, melting it and forming a gaping crater several hundred feet long, and just deep enough to make it impossible for the trailing vehicles to continue through the narrow valley without four-wheel drive or magic.

As soon as he disappeared back into the vehicle, it slammed on its brakes. The black sedan next to it kept going. The gray SUV surged forward and clipped the vehicle's rear wheel, causing it to spin out of control. A wave of jealousy and relief hit her, knowing Finn was the madman behind the wheel. His SUV steered in the portal's direction and gained speed, hitting a bump that sent it airborne through the tear in reality.

"What just happened?" Blue looked over at Sam to see if she had imagined it all. He looked as flabbergasted as she was. Finn's stunt driving, while amazing, still left—she counted quickly—seven carloads of bad guys for Blue and Sam to keep from going through the portal. At least Rhodes and Devon had help now.

"You got this?" She motioned to the scattering of cars whose occupants abandoned their crippled or trapped vehicles to approach on foot.

He nodded without hesitation, like taking on that many enemies single-handedly didn't bother him in the slightest.

Leaving him to deal with the small army of murder hobos that just rolled onto the scene, she eyed the men who killed their friend, standing by the car a few hundred feet away. One busied himself reloading a shoulder cannon. Skipping to the space right above him, she plummeted as dead weight onto his head and shoulders and swung two quick brutal jabs at his kidneys on the way to the ground. Rolling forward when they landed, she sprung to her feet and spun, kicking him in the face before he could recover. Pouncing again, she landed on his back, grasping the sides of his head and twisting. His death gave her no satisfaction. He died too easily.

Counting her opponents, she snatched his holstered weapon loose. Four left. All looking at her. Death falling from the sky left them stunned, and she shot twice before they could react, each target collapsing with a satisfying thump to the ground. Skipping skyward to avoid the bullets the other two sent her way, she dropped out of the sky, once again forcing her victim's body to crumple. Still falling, she shot the last man standing, then swung the gun down to shoot the man below her in the head. The strain of both using and throttling the magic surge ejected the contents of her stomach onto the last body. Feeling better, she collected their guns. She preferred knives, but guns were better than nothing.

Standing to assess Sam's situation, she stared in confusion. Three men stumbled in circles next to him, motions frantic, clawing at their necks. One turned a horror-filled face her way, hands digging into the soft flesh of his own throat. "Help." His lips formed the words, but the distance between them swallowed the sound. Swiping at his own flesh again, a jet of blood spurted from his neck with the rhythm of his heart. His body fell and jerked. The man ripped his own throat out with his bare hands. She slapped her hands over her mouth in horror as the other two men followed suit and collapsed to the ground in jets of blood. "Sweet baby Jesus."

A horde of people descended on Sam, all shambling slowly forward, dragging their feet trying to stop themselves. Darkness settled around him, projecting an aura of doom.

She should cover her ears now. She didn't want to hear whatever he was about to say. Dropping the guns, she lifted her hands to do just that, but a sound, more of a loud exhale than a whisper, got there first. Her breath caught in her chest, muscles paralyzed and refusing to follow her instructions to breathe. Terror coursed through her. The horde surrounding Sam panicked and flailed, lips gaping like fish out of water. Everyone assumed Mitch chose Sam because he didn't have enough magic prowess to pose a viable challenge for Paragon. But he just sent a compulsion so strong it overrode the autonomic nervous systems of thirty people with only a breath, an unheard-of feat, even amped up on Ava's nova magic.

Blue lost control of her fear and clawed at her own chest, willing it to work. It only burned from lack of oxygen in response. Her hands clutched at her throat. Stumbling as blackness pressed in around her vision, she willed her muscles to respond and expand. Nothing happened. She had never felt this helpless.

Bright flashes filtered through the portal. But she couldn't focus on them. Her coordination faltered, and she crashed to her hands and knees, rocks digging into her palm. Footsteps thundered toward her. Looking up in relief, she shrank away from the grim sight before her.

A demon barreled in her direction. Its hair and lips were an unnatural coal black, dark purple veins lining the neck and face, gait jerking and unnatural, but the eyes caused dread to wash through her chest. They were inky-black cosmic orbs with silver flecks swirling throughout, extending into an endless abyss. Though she didn't have enough air reserve to spend the energy, she twisted and clawed at the ground to drag herself in the other direction.

Hands grabbed her under the armpits, spinning her around and swooping her off the ground like she weighed nothing. Flailing and kicking to free herself, a familiar face filled her vision, twisted in a mixture of rage and panic, eyes the epitome of cosmic evil. Sam leaned down, releasing a puff of air next to her ear. No words. Just the slightest of sounds.

Immediately, her muscles responded, and she sucked in the largest, freshest gulp of air she ever breathed. She breathed in until her whole body quaked, and her lungs protested. Sensation returned to extremities she didn't realize had gone numb, and her vision returned to normal. More explosions flashed behind them from the portal.

Sam's eyes still swirled black and silver, his face tense and lined with purple veins. She focused and regained control of her breathing. He exhaled a sigh of relief that made her cringe and try to pull away, but her feet still dangled in the air. She did not fully understand his magic, but he had not used words to either halt her breathing or allow it again. That was new. Bodies thudded to the ground behind them, the desperate swishing of their limbs against the grass as they died horribly, whispering across the field.

Staring at the visage before her, a primal warning coursed through her gut that she was in the presence of something fundamentally dangerous. "Put me down, right now."

He dropped his head and set her back on her feet, raising his hands and stepping away. Placing a hand over her thundering heart, she raised the other as a barrier between herself and the man she had mistaken for a demon moments ago and backed away. "Give me a minute."

12

DEVON

Devon sat on the ground next to a cloud of swirling gray mist erupting from Ben Hughes' feet where Greenlee had placed her just moments ago, exhausted and nauseous. She used entirely too much magic, and she would be dead right now if Greenlee hadn't charged his fool ass into the middle of a war and carried her out of it, then hugged her and Lexi so hard she feared their ribs would crack. Neither of them complained, hugging him back, feeling like everything might be okay, which was ridiculous.

Her insides tried to shake loose, but she clutched Lexi, face pale and eyes rimmed with dark circles, to her chest. She wanted to scold her daughter for throwing an entire freaking recreational vehicle at a sadistic madman. But it saved them.

Greenlee stood next to Ben, digging through his backpack, expression fierce, intending to run back into the fray. She did not like that one bit. "What's the plan, Greenlee?"

He cut his eyes over to Ben, who somehow cut his flaming eyes back in Greenlee's direction. They didn't have a plan. That exchange was two guys completely winging it and getting caught. "Um. The plan was to get to you before the Sovereign killed you." He looked around at the gray dome Ben generated. "Now we need another one."

"I love you, Dad." Ava wrapped her arms around Ben's torso so tight it might take the jaws of life to extricate him. Ava was a good kid, which spoke volumes about Ben's parenting, and the moment she laid eyes on the scene in the center of this strange swirling shield, she knew he was one of her people. Lexi, a child he had never met before in his life, clung to his leg, hiding her face. The terrifying man with flames shooting out of his eyes and swirling around his head held her gently, despite being mauled by Ava and generating a massive life-saving forcefield, telling her everything was going to be okay as he patted her back. Dad goals. He only let Lexi go when Greenlee picked her up.

"I love you, too, sweetheart." Ben's voice rumbled so low that it reverberated in her chest, sweet and unsettling all at the same time.

"How many are we dealing with, Dev?" Greenlee glanced back up at the dome. "Finn and Nisha are still out there."

"I don't know," she said honestly. "They just kept coming. I killed so many."

He plucked a few items from his backpack and stuffed them into his pockets. "You did good."

"Ben!" The urgency in Finn's voice from the other side of the swirling gray dome worried her. Immediately, a gap formed in the dome, and Rhodes' hairy face appeared, contorting his gigantic body to fit through the narrow opening.

"Close it!" a woman's voice screamed. Rhodes' body lurched forward, and he stumbled in. The gap closed, Rhodes fell to his knees, and something detonated against the barrier with the force of a bomb, shaking the ground beneath them.

Ben grunted and stumbled as the barrier he generated wavered but held. They all stared up with wide eyes as another blast hit the barrier and sent Ben to his knees.

"Daddy?" Ava's hands glowed as she clutched her father's shirt, true terror blanketing her face.

"It's okay, sweetheart." Ben stood back up. "Stay calm."

Rhodes shifted back to one of his human forms, the horror Gothic one he used in the camper earlier, looking at the place where he came through the barrier. Nobody else made it in after him. "Finn wants me to fly the girls out of here."

Greenlee stopped digging in his backpack and looked at Rhodes. "Why are you flying? Where is Blue?" When Rhodes didn't answer and looked away, Greenlee turned to her. She held Lexi's face close, knowing the girl wouldn't miss anything even if she didn't say it. She gave her head a small shake and mouthed, "Camper" so that he could read her lips and Lexi couldn't hear. Greenlee's face crumpled, and Lexi sniffled and shook in her arms. His arms fell to his sides, face hardening with anger as he looked up, scanning a sky he could no longer see. "No." The word wasn't a plea; it was a statement. An order.

"Ava's dad? How much longer can you hold that?" Rhodes scrutinized their shelter.

"Not long, man." Ben's voice belied the strain he was under. "What's hitting us?"

Devon looked up at the orange glow above them. "Larson Battle."

"No wonder." Ben grimaced. Everyone here knew the firepower Battle could throw around. The Cahlad never kept it a secret when he was Regent.

"How high can you make this wall?" Rhodes rolled his arms. "I need fifteen, maybe twenty seconds of not getting hit with a meteorite."

"How many can you take with you?" Greenlee turned his attention to her, clearly working through exit strategies.

"Two," Rhodes said almost apologetically. "I might have enough magic to shift someone else. They can fly with me."

Ben flinched as another fireball pummeled his shield. "You need this shield and cover from the ground. You won't have that if we are all in the air."

Greenlee studied Ben's hunched and sweating form, then took a deep breath. "Shift Devon and carry the girls. Ben's tapped out. I'll cover you from the ground."

Devon shook her head. "I don't think I can fly. I can't even stand. Does it give you extra energy? More magic?"

Rhodes took a closer look. "No. Assuming you survived the magic of the shift."

Lexi looked between all of them in desperation. "Shift me and carry Mom."

Rhodes shook his head. "Flying isn't an instinct. Steep learning curve. I can't risk you and Ava. Not here. I need to carry you."

That was it, then. Devon took a deep breath and closed her eyes. "Save your magic, Rhodes." Even though he used to be one of the Cahlad's super-magic soldiers, he had to be pushing his limits. "Use everything you have for the girls. We are out of time."

Greenlee looked right at her, an argument already forming on his lips. But she clearly had a severe case of magic poisoning. Using any more or adding the wrong type of magic would likely just kill her and waste Rhodes' resources. His eyes fell closed and his shoulders sagged.

Lexi stared at them in disbelief. "Mom? What about you and Tio G?"

"Baby." Devon ran her hands up and down Lexi's arms. "We have to keep you safe. We will be right behind you."

"You are lying." Lexi's lips quivered.

Devon's eyes filled with tears. They had to do whatever it took to get her precious little girl out of here. Even if no one else survived. "Tia Blue knew what she was doing. Mr. Rhodes is the best person to keep you safe right now." Her voice cracked. "I love you. Trust us. Please."

Greenlee dropped to his knees in front of them, cradling both of Lexi's cheeks in his hands as another fireball bounced off their shelter. "I love you more than anything." He said the words to Lexi, but his eyes met Devon's. "You are my heart."

"I know." Lexi clutched his wrist and sniffled, visibly fighting back tears.

"Good. So you have to go with Mr. Rhodes and stay safe. I can't live without my heart." He took a leather necklace off his own neck and fished a small silver bead from his pocket, weaving it on to the necklace before dropping it over Lexi's head. "Say coconut."

"I love you, too, Tio G." Lexi sniffled and clutched the necklace, looking away from them both, tears finally spilling over. "I love you, Mom."

Devon clung to her baby girl, her heart splitting in half. "I love you more than anything, Lexi."

Greenlee pulled them both into a tight hug, thunder booming above their shelter. Then he lifted Lexi from her arms, hugging her close. He took her to Rhodes and reluctantly sat her down next to the man.

"Ava." Greenlee pulled a golf ball from his pocket. "Give me all the magic you can spare. We are about to do something amazing."

Ben grunted as another fireball battered his barrier. "Can you handle that kind of overload? The umbrella had nothing on Ava."

Greenlee didn't respond to Ben's question but turned his attention to Rhodes. "You need twenty seconds?" The air surrounding him swirled, kicking up dust in their confined space.

Ben placed his face next to Ava's. She still clung to him after helping him back to his feet. He whispered something, and she nodded her head.

"Rhodes?" The warning tone in Greenlee's question was unmistakable as he leveled a hard look at the man they were trusting with everything precious to them. Ben turned flaming eyes to him as well but remained silent as his body flinched with each booming concussion of rock and flame above them.

"Please." Devon fought the urge to crawl to where he stood and hold on to Lexi.

Rhodes solemnly motioned for Ava to join him. "With my life."

"Okay." Ben nodded and pushed his daughter away reluctantly.

Rhodes rolled his shoulders again and transformed into a hellish, mutant bald eagle, easily the size of a minivan standing on its end even with his wings at his sides, and let out a terrifying caw that made them all flinch.

Lexi eyeballed the giant bird with uncertainty. "I don't want to."

"I know, morra. But you have to." Devon hoped Lexi wouldn't make her fight about it. "Please, baby."

The air continued to swirl as Greenlee's magic built into a frenzied vortex of potential. They all covered their faces to keep from getting dirt and pine needles in their eyes. The force of another fireball rippling across the surface of the shield in fingers of orange and gold drove Ben to his knees again.

Dragging herself across the ground, unable to muster enough energy to crawl, she collapsed behind Greenlee, who now vibrated with magic energy. His face had gone pale, and he was pulling so much magic that he was in pain. "Stay behind me, baby. Whatever happens."

Ben collapsed again on his hands and knees without Ava's help. Sweat dripped off his face onto the ground. "I can't take another one."

Ava whimpered and grasped Lexi's hand. "Oh my God. This is it. You are all going to die because of me."

As if Ava's words triggered the event, another ball of fire hit Ben's swirling wall. He strained and collapsed face-first into the dirt with a cry. The shield sizzled out of existence but stopped the incoming fireball.

"Now, Rhodes." Greenlee released the stored magic in a burst as bright as the sun. It rolled away from them, splintering into small white-and-gold discs rotating away in every direction except immediately behind him, where they all stood. The force of the magic pulsed and ripped the surrounding forest asunder.

The first flap of Rhodes' enormous wings generated a gust strong enough to flatten her to the ground and lift him five feet in the air, holding Lexi in one gigantic claw and Ava in another. Both girls screamed in terror as the second flap took him even higher.

The gold-and-white disc still radiated outward. People screamed among the carnage, and trees toppled with resounding crashes that echoed around them. An orange ball of rock and flame, smaller but still enough to kill anything it hit, clipped the edge of the disc attack.

Part of it broke off, but the rest sailed directly toward the giant bird and her girl.

"Coconut!" A small shield, the same one Greenlee used earlier, flared to life in front of Lexi. But that wouldn't be enough.

Greenlee couldn't redirect his attack without hitting the people he was trying to protect. "Ben!" she begged, crawling toward the man. He lifted a weary head and groaned. The flames in his eyes flared so weakly she could still see the brown of his real ones. A knot of black tentacles burst from his feet and spiraled at least fifty feet into the air, disorganized and flailing. She held her breath as two of the appendages batted the meteor off its path, sending it screaming into the woods where it decimated the ground and trees before Ben collapsed completely still, onto the ground.

With the barrier gone, a few stragglers lurking behind them focused on Rhodes, arms and hands moving possibly to point out the escaping bird or to hurl a magical assault at it. She didn't know their immediate intent and didn't care. They all died today. Pulling every ounce of magic she could out of the supercharged atmosphere Ava left behind, she hurled a wave of magic at them just as one lifted a hand aggressively. It rammed them just in time, and they fell where they stood, releasing a random jet of ice across the ground, never knowing what hit them.

Rhodes sailed into the sky, framed by the sparkling purple portal. Greenlee's wave of golden disks continued to tear through the forest, obliterating anything taller than two and a half feet and likely crushing anything smaller than that under a sea of splintered lumber.

The portal winked out of existence, taking her view of Rhodes with it, leaving behind a chorus of fresh screams and the echoes of a thundering detonation that vibrated the ground.

"They made it." She collapsed onto her side, eyes heavy as she retched. Greenlee gave her a sad smile and staggered. He let out one ragged breath and sank to his hands and knees, lips blue and eyes glassy, then fell sideways, lying as still as death.

She tried to crawl to him but couldn't even lift her head. "Finn?" They needed help. Could Finn have lived through the destruction outside their dome? Nothing remained of the car he stood behind. But maybe he made it. Where was he? There were so many bodies.

A deathly silence settled over the clearing. "Green?" Staring up into a beautiful blue sky now unobstructed by trees, only the wail of approaching sirens answered.

13

SAM

S am's heart thundered as he stared at the terrified woman in front of him and listened as the field of wild blue flowers behind him fell silent. He completely lost control and barely noticed she was in trouble before it was too late. He thought she was far enough away for the compulsion to miss her. The first one, drawing everyone to him, had. He turned his back to give Blue the minute she requested and force himself to look at what he had done.

A tall, slender woman with a halo of blonde waves stepped over a body behind him, her stance aggressive as she surveyed the field with a detached expression. He recognized this woman. Amber Collins, Mitch and Zella's presumed dead daughter, stood before him very much alive and rubbed absently at a gaudy bracelet made up of marble-sized beads.

Hackles up, he took a step back, bumping into Blue's out-stretched hand. His magic surged, desperate to be set loose on the new threat. Cold blue eyes appraised him, and she placed her hands on her hips. He didn't know how Amber Collins arrived in the same field where Larson Battle's sadistic army ambushed them or how she avoided the fate of the bodies surrounding her, but he seriously doubted she was one of the good guys.

"Amber?" Blue darted around him, and he grabbed her arm, stopping her short, and she jerked on her arm in frustration. Getting a good look, her jaw fell open.

"Blue?" A mixture of terror and elation warred for control on Amber's face.

He stuck his hand out in a clear sign for Amber to stop. He had already killed or almost killed two allies and a few dozen enemies today. He needed to keep his mouth shut and his magic under control, which was no simple task knowing that Ivan's body might lie somewhere behind him.

"I can't believe you are still alive." Amber approached cautiously. "Did you get to Ava? At the Canary? Oh God! You didn't get to Ava in time?"

"She's fine. She's, um, with friends." Blue stared at the portal.

"Thank God." Ava looked back over her shoulder. "There?"

Sam shook Blue's arm in warning. When she looked up, he shook his head. He didn't trust Amber.

Amber smiled. "I beat him this time. You both lived." Her laugh morphed into a sob. "I can't believe it. That's never happened before."

"What's never happened before?" Blue demanded as a blinding flash of light erupted from the portal, causing them both to cover their eyes.

"No matter what I try, one of you always dies." Amber sobered quickly. "This is a miracle. I need to get to Ava."

"You thought I was going to die at the Cat and the Canary?" Blue braced her free hand on her hip in irritation, still squinting from the surge of light. "Figures."

Movement behind Amber drew his gaze, and he blinked in disbelief. A demonic eagle, the size of a semitruck, flew over their heads, and the strange purple portal snapped shut with an audible fizz.

Completely focused on Blue and unaware of the events behind her, Amber's eyes filled with hurt and pain. "I'm sorry. For everything." She extended her arms and stepped even closer. "Please take me to Ava."

"I can't carry people right now." Blue tensed and tried to step back but bumped into him, her attention on the space where their friends had once been. He tried to back up as well, and several dead bodies effectively blocked his path, causing him to stumble.

Amber grabbed Blue's other hand. "Please, Blue. I need to see her."

The bracelet on Amber's wrist flared to life, beads spinning so fast around their chain that they blurred together, and a high-pitched hum cut through the air. Blue's body convulsed, and she screamed in pain. "What is that thing?" A mild jolt of electricity surged through his hand where he held Blue's arm.

He assumed Amber was attacking until her own body convulsed, and she screamed in agony as well. "What?" She stared at her bracelet in confusion.

He pulled on Blue's arm but couldn't dislodge Amber's grip, so he placed a hand on Amber's shoulder to push her away. A pulse of power exploded outward from her bracelet, morphing into a deafening and continuous roar. Their bodies surged together as if drawn by a high-powered magnet, crushing them. Pain seared through his skin. He fell backward. A tremor buckled the ground beneath them. They were falling, but they weren't landing. Strobes of blinding light alternating between rainbow waves and white took over his vision and more magic coursed through him than he than ever before. The world tilted sideways. Sam's veins burned with liquid fire and his muscles spasmed, locking his hands tighter around Blue's arm and Amber's shoulder. Jolts of excruciating electricity surged through his body. Amber's body glowed white, and blood seeped from her nose. Blue radiated prismatic light. Blood dripped from his own nose, but he dared not say a word. He did not know what would happen. What was this thing doing to them?

It was killing them. Crushed together by a force none of them controlled, they tumbled head over heels. Blue's colorful lights led the way, chased by Amber's white aura.

Blue grasped at Amber's hand to pull it away. Blood streamed down her face from her nose and eyes and ears. A burst of rainbow light washed away from her body, forming a swirling circle of multicolored magic around them, then she fell silent and limp, her chest no longer moving. "Keep breathing, damn it!"

Spurred by his words, more magic surged through his body and exploded outward in a sparkle of black light. His own grasp on consciousness faltered, and he didn't even know if he had a body anymore. The expelled magic twirled around them, slowly mixing with the rainbow magic forming stripes of sparkling color and blackness.

Amber's back arched unnaturally, white light beaming from her now bleeding eyeballs in columns straight up, generating a force that hurled their bodies in the opposite direction.

"This isn't right! Something is wrong." Amber gave up on words and just screamed.

No kidding, this wasn't right. A writhing electric ball of light and pain surrounded him. His muscles still jerked, and they still tumbled out of control. "Fix it!"

Sunday 11:00 AM

***

A most unusual buffet
Delights of soul amid silver and gray
Valhalla rides upon the trolleys
Unaware of phallic follies.

***

14

RHODES

Even with a living magic battery supercharging his magic, he had reached his limits. His body was shutting down, and he wouldn't be able to hold this form much longer. He needed to find a safe place to land before they all fell out of the sky and someone reported a monster bird to the news outlets or local wildlife officials, bringing the Sovereign and probably the government down on top of them.

The two girls who dangled from his claws had long ago fallen silent and grim. He didn't see what happened after he took to the air, but he had heard it, and it did not bode well for the people on the ground.

Ava and Lexi witnessed what happened. He heard their screams as he flew away. He did not know what emotions he would deal with when he landed. Their calm worried him.

They flew over pine-covered peaks on the southern edge of the Rocky Mountains. The area directly below them was mostly desolate, with some areas still covered in snow. He scanned the ground below him, searching for a safe place to land that offered shelter nearby but was still remote enough that he could recover before the Sovereign inevitably found them again.

He spotted a small cabin on the edge of a clearing near the top of one mountain below him. A long, treacherous gravel path led to it, littered with fallen trees and ruts, making it unlikely to be used by anyone without a chainsaw. Perfect. He banked and made his approach. Ava perked up and wiggled as their altitude changed. He cawed, trying for reassurance, but she flinched, so he remained silent until he could shift back to something with vocal cords. She had been through enough without fearing the person who was supposed to help her.

Swooping into the edge of the clearing, he set the girls down as gently as possible. They stood silently, looking around with blank faces, both in shock. Lexi's eyes were red-rimmed from crying, and her face was blotchy. Ava's face was devoid of emotion and held no color.

And he had no clothes. Landing next to them, he shifted into a small dog he hoped resembled a beagle. Neither girl reacted, just standing woodenly and shivering. He needed them to stay put while he inspected the cabin, so he walked in a slow circle around them, whined, and pushed Ava toward Lexi. She sat down hard, seeming to understand, and pulled Lexi over to sit next to her. Neither girl spoke.

Trotting toward the cabin, he made a slow circle around its perimeter. A shed out back housed a generator. The back porch sheltered a stack of firewood next to two rocking chairs and a small handmade table. His inspection revealed no alarms or signs of recent occupants. It was the first thing that had gone right for him in several days. Trotting up onto the back porch, claws clicking on the old wood, he shifted into his original human form, the one that didn't take any magic to maintain. His skull pounded, and his stomach threatened to empty itself, every step harder than the one before. Jiggling the door handle and finding it locked, he checked the usual places. Finding a key under the leg of a table, he opened the squeaky door and let himself into the dark cabin.

Stale air met him as he moved around without bothering to try the lights or open the blinds. His inspection revealed a relatively clean multipurpose room with a bathroom and a closet in the back corner. A small galley kitchen ran along the rest of the back wall. A double bed, a couch, a bookshelf, and a folding card table rounded out the furnishings. This would work.

Rifling through the closet, he found a pair of camouflage pants and a flannel shirt that belonged to a giant and put them on, rolling the waistband, pant cuffs, and sleeves to fit. Sufficiently covered, he gave the kitchen cabinets a quick perusal, finding them stocked with basic dried and canned goods and a few MREs. Not gourmet, but they wouldn't starve in the next twenty-four hours.

Letting out a steadying breath, he put on his game face and headed outside to get the girls. The girls still sat where he had left them.

Lexi's head now rested in Ava's lap as Ava trailed her fingers through the younger girl's hair soothingly. Lexi was sound asleep.

"Hey." He squatted to bring himself to their level. "Let's get inside."

"Sure." Ava stared straight through him. He did not know what to do. Screaming and crying, he could understand and deal with. This quiet brokenness made him feel helpless.

"I'm sorry, Ava." She handled herself impressively through everything that had happened. But she was still a kid who likely just watched her father die. And she was stuck in the middle of nowhere with a stranger. That was a lot to handle.

"She's asleep."

"I'll get her." Rhodes found enough strength to lift Lexi from the ground without waking her. Barely. But Ava made no move to stand. "Ava?"

"I'll be right behind you." Giving him a weak smile, she still didn't move. "I'm trying to keep it together."

"You don't have to."

Her eyes brimmed with tears, and she swallowed hard, finally standing, and they plodded to the cabin. Stepping in, she peered into the dark room cautiously and wrinkled her nose.

"We are going to leave it dark for now. Abundance of caution. But it's safe and clean."

"That's smart." She just shuffled to the bed and pulled back the covers. "Put her here."

Rhodes didn't argue. He put Lexi down, and Ava tucked the surrounding covers around tiny shoulders. She stood and stared at the sleeping child.

"I think." Ava shuddered. "I don't..." She turned his way. "My dad?"

Rhodes didn't want to lie to her. Ben might be dead. But in his world, you didn't count someone as down until you personally put the body in the ground. "I will look for him as soon as I can."

"What if he is dead?" Ava's voice was thick with emotion. "What do I do?"

Rhodes took a deep breath. He couldn't make this better, but he could empathize. "My dad died. Almost twelve years ago now. Sometimes I still don't know what to do. I just take it one second, one breath at a time."

"My mom died." Her voice shook and her hands trembled. "It never stops hurting."

"No," he said softly. "It doesn't."

She sniffled hard and wrapped her arms around her waist, curling in on herself. He expected this reaction when emotions boiled over and the mind and body could no longer contain it all. A sob ripped from her chest, and she slammed her fist over her mouth to muffle it, looking back at Lexi to make sure she had not woken her. Ava sat heavily on the end of the bed, another sob shuddering through her body noiselessly. "I'm sorry."

Rhodes sat on the bed next to her. "You have nothing to be sorry for. Do you need a hug?" She sniffled and leaned over, and he wrapped his arms around her. Immediately, his shirt soaked through with tears. "I've got you."

They sat for a long time in the semidarkness, rocking back and forth while Ava sobbed silently. When his father died, Blue sat on the couch with him, rocking back and forth for hours just like this. His own sobs hadn't been as silent as Ava's. Having some-one there, even sitting in silence, kept the grief from crushing him. Hopefully, it helped Ava.

Ava eventually ran out of tears just like he had all those years ago. Tired as he was, he would sit with her all night if that was what she needed. Finally, her shoulders relaxed, either from acceptance or exhaustion. She sat up and wiped at her face. "You don't look so good."

"I don't feel so good, kid." That was the understatement of the year. He felt like death. "Let's get some rest."

Crawling silently into bed next to Lexi, Ava pulled the blan-kets up to her ears and stared at the sliver of light peeking in through the drawn curtains. He did not think she would get any sleep, but he hoped she would.

He walked a quick circuit around their small shelter, making sure everything was as secure as possible. Sitting on the couch, he dropped his head into his hands, physically and emotionally exhausted and starving, but too sick to eat. He couldn't even think about Blue. Not now, while he had to keep it together for these kids. He was also worried sick about Harper, Kendra, and even his dog.

He was suddenly responsible for two traumatized young ladies and woefully underqualified for the job. People still wanted to kill them, and he had no way to call for help. He wouldn't know who to call if he did. Did Torrin make it out of that ambush?

He couldn't shift into anything useful for at least a day, likely longer, to allow his body to recharge. Sighing, he stretched out on the couch. That meant they were stuck on this mountain for the foreseeable future without answers, and he hated to admit it—with very little hope.

15

FINN

F inn peered over the fallen log that Nisha dumped him behind
seconds before whatever had torn this forest apart hit them.
She had saved his life.

Entire trees leaned over their heads, by some miracle, forming an
improvised and likely unstable teepee of shattered tree trunks. The
smell of cedar permeated his nostrils. Nisha huddled next to him in
the cramped space, rubbing a lump on the back of her head. She was
pale and her hands shook and she looked exhausted. Bodies littered
the clearing and the remains of the cedar glade. The melted remains
of their rental SUV acted as a centerpiece of the scene.

Emergency responders swarmed the area like ants minutes after
the last rumble of cataclysmic destruction echoed into the distance.
The seclusion and dense foliage of the clearing made it hard to reach
by vehicle. If not for the magic portal, their own car wouldn't be
here. A mix of state, county, and two different city police forces
scanned the clearing on foot to determine what could have caused

this kind of damage. A small army of firefighters and medics triaged the needs of a staggering number of dead and wounded.

Rhodes, Lexi, and Ava were nowhere to be seen. He did not see them escape but assumed they had since he couldn't see them or any identifiable parts of them. He prayed they made it.

Devon, Greenlee, and Ben lay in the middle of the chaos. Devon was still prone but communicating with a medic. Neither Greenlee nor Ben looked conscious. For a moment, he worried they weren't breathing, but the medics were stabilizing them and readying them for transport. That meant they were in serious condition, but alive.

He couldn't get to them now without raising suspicion, but he needed to know where they were being taken.

"What am I dealing with, Ravi?" Finn needed to know if the FBI or any agencies aligned with Larson's Sovereign group were on the scene.

Nisha joined him in peering over the log. "No ulterior motives out there yet." She took in the carnage and held her forehead with a shaking hand. "God. They are finding parts of their bodies. I only hear six conscious. All injured. Our people are stable enough to route to a local ER." Her words came with staccato breaks between the information. "The police are forming a search grid. Federal is a few miles out. It will be their scene. They will be on us soon."

"We should move. Did you catch where we are?"

"Lebanon, Tennessee, on the edge of the state park property."

They weren't in Colorado anymore. The portal had taken them to a suburb east of Nashville. He turned his gaze to their impromptu shelter, wondering how hard Nisha hit her head and if she held on to her weapon.

Nisha poked at the lump on the back of her head. "Still attached. But my brain feels scorched. And yes, I still have my gun."

He would never get used to that. "Take it easy, and keep an eye out." He began the slow, perilous process of moving logs and branches to form a gap large enough for him to crawl out of. The logs above them were large enough to do serious damage if they collapsed. Eventually, his efforts paid off. He crouched and observed the surrounding area. He didn't see any signs of movement. The search parties had plenty to occupy their attention within the first thirty feet of the ruined forest before they reached them. He trusted his eyes, but it didn't hurt to make sure. "Clear?"

"Yep. Let's move."

Finn climbed out and crouched low, waiting for Nisha to follow, hoping the structure remained stable. He watched in fascination and horror as her ankle caught a limb and got stuck, causing the whole precarious structure to lean. She wriggled to get loose, causing her shoulder to bump one of the larger logs, and he scrambled to catch it before it fell on her. He only slowed its descent. The whole tower crumbled in slow motion, missing her by inches. He didn't know whether to laugh or panic. He had never seen anything so ungraceful in his entire life. She sat on her bottom, glaring at the collapsed pile of wood before standing up without a word. She sent him a warning glance as he chose not to say anything and struggled to clear his mind.

Setting a brisk pace, he led them in the direction opposite of the search parties. Securing transportation and retrieving his people before the Sovereign did and contacting Hale or Trix were his priorities. A hand slammed onto his arm, pulling him to a stop. "Not that way."

Nisha took the lead, weaving through trees and shallow ravines. They traveled several miles in silence before she slowed. The hum of female voices reached his ears at the same time a twisted barbed-wire fence appeared, delineating the edge of a property line. Wooden bangs and creaks of large objects moving overtook the voices as he climbed over the fence and continued to follow Nisha, unable to decode the method to her madness. Where were they and where they were going? She could hear his questions and wasn't answering. She shushed him. "I didn't say anything." She shushed him again.

They stopped several feet from the edge of a tree line. An army of people moved around a clearing, setting up chairs and arranging flowers. A massive white barn loomed behind them. Strands of Edison-style light bulbs zigzagged overhead. A woman in a white dress stood with her hands on her hips, holding a bouquet. She did not look happy. Eight women wearing mismatched light-blue dresses and cowboy boots surrounded her. Who got married in a barn, wearing cowboy boots? No wonder she wasn't happy.

"It's the big trend in weddings now. I call it barnyard chic." Nisha leaned against a tree and scanned the area. The bride frowned at a petite, exasperated woman with salt-and-pepper hair, holding a camera. "She is going to be distracted for a while. Her car is over there." Nisha pointed to a large parking lot filled with delivery vans and trucks and hurried in that direction, still staying out of sight in the trees.

"How do you know which one is hers?"

"It has 'Photography by Sal' written on the door." Turning an appraising gaze his way, she smoothed her dark hair and brushed off her clothing. He couldn't stop his mind from calling her a smart-ass. "I'm quite intelligent. Yes. Meet me by the car. I'll be right back."

Nisha stepped out of the trees and strolled toward the rear entrance of the barn, where harried workers hustled to roll in trays of food and even more flower arrangements. He was not used to being blind to the plan, and he didn't like it. And he knew she knew that. Leaning against the tree in front of the photographer's vehicle, he stayed in the shade to keep from standing out. "Sure, I'll just wait here." He crossed his arms and kept a close eye on the activity in case she needed help with whatever it was she was doing in there.

Moments later, she strolled out the same door she entered, carrying a large purse and a brown paper bag. Her expression was all business, and she blended in with the workers like she belonged there. Tripping once, she caught herself, then walked to the car and hit the button on a key fob in her hand. The locks on the photographer's car clicked open, and Finn couldn't contain his impressed smile as he stepped away from the tree and approached their new ride. Nisha climbed into the driver's side, forcing him into the passenger seat. When he sat down, she dropped the purse and the brown bag in his lap. There was no hesitation but also no rush as she started the car, backed up, and drove down the bumpy gravel drive. "My God. She won't let them eat breakfast or lunch because she doesn't want them to look fat in the pictures. And the whole place smells like food. That woman just might be Satan." The scene behind him grew smaller in the side-view mirror. Nobody noticed their departure. "Do you have any idea what the inner dialogue of eight hangry women being suffocated by Spanx sounds like?"

"I shudder to think."

"You should. It's the stuff of nightmares." She pulled onto a two-lane road that looked the same in both directions. "There are cell phones in there. All the cash I could find. A laptop, too." Her hand disappeared into the brown paper bag and pulled out a handful of small appetizers on toothpicks. "They dropped some cash on the catering. These bacon-wrapped chicken things are amazing. I think they have brown sugar. The fried mac-and-cheese balls are so gouda. Get it?"

Finn rolled his eyes, grabbed a handful of mac-and-cheese balls, and fished through the purse. Three cell phones lay on top of a pile of random junk. Wondering how he was supposed to unlock them, he smiled again. All three were disgustingly sticky, and crusty patterns smudged the glass. Ravi was disturbingly good at criminal pursuits.

These belonged to women with small children who knew how to get into Mom's phone. Lexi broke into Devon's phone by the time she was five. He sobered, wondering if Rhodes got the girls to safety. Working his way through the list of memorized numbers in his head, he texted coded messages to systems that he hoped his men were monitoring. He posted ads for items his team knew to look for on two online marketplaces and looked up at Nisha. "Do you have anyone you need to contact?"

"Nobody left to call." Her words were tight and filled with emotion as she stared straight ahead and turned the car onto a side street. Faded brown signs directed them to a boat ramp sheltering one truck with an empty trailer. She parked and extended her hand. "We need to get rid of those."

"I'm sorry, Nisha." He lost friends and teammates before and understood what she was feeling. Taking the phones, she climbed out without a word, stomped on all three, and hurled the pieces into the water.

Jerking the door open, she sat down. "He killed two Zenith and two Primes in less than ten minutes. You don't know where Mitch is." She looked at him, daring him to contradict her. He couldn't. He had confidence in his team. But he could not confirm Mitch's safety until they received his messages and coordinated a place to regroup. "They scattered your men. Sam's new army is in shambles. We need to find Devon and Greenlee and hope they know how to contact the fugitives they hid."

"More people aren't the solution." Untrained people, regardless of their magical prowess, would fare no better against Larson than they had. "The right people in the right place are. Take out the key players. Give ourselves time and room to maneuver."

"You sound like Mitch."

"He wasn't wrong about this."

Nisha bit her lip and refused to look at him. She started the car, looking crushed and resigned. "There really are no good guys."

Finn turned away, looking out the window at the calm waters of the lake. He didn't know how she lived in this world, doing what she did for a living, and just now figured that out.

16

DEVON

Devon tugged at the armpits of the stolen too-small scrub shirt that stretched across her breasts and bunched under her armpits as she scowled at the tiny computer screen in front of her. Her glasses disappeared somewhere between the field and the hospital, making her task difficult. The person she borrowed the scrubs and badge from snoozed comfortably in Devon's hospital bed. The owner of the credentials she used lay neatly tucked by her feet under the desk at the nurses' station. Only one other nurse worked this floor, and she was busy giving a bath.

The hospital's patient management software was outdated and slow. Her search returned a result. It listed Greenlee as a John Doe because his wallet burned up when his car got hit by a meteorite. It listed Ben under his real name, which was a giant problem. She envisioned a giant blinking arrow in the sky, pointing at them right now.

Both Ben and Greenlee rested in a step-down unit and needed medical care. However, it was only a matter of time before the authorities and possibly Larson Battle's remaining minions showed up, looking for the survivors of the portal showdown. She fell asleep in the ambulance and remembered little between the field and waking up with a nurse changing her IV. They had been here for three hours. Too long.

She itched to get to Lexi, but she did not know where Rhodes had taken them. She couldn't do anything for Lexi without that knowledge, but she knew where Greenlee was.

Jotting the room numbers on her hand with the nurse's pen, she hit the print button on Greenlee's medical record, clipped her badge onto the scrub's front pocket, and pushed the nurse below her farther under the desk with her feet.

Devon took the papers, walking with purpose to the elevators, nodding and smiling at people as she went, pausing long enough to grab a wheelchair. In the elevator, she made faces at a little girl and exited onto her target floor with a cheerful wave. This is where it got tricky. Step-down units had more staffing than regular floor wards. Two men on one bed would draw attention, and she couldn't carry either of them by herself. Is this what it was like for Blue, always flying by the seat of her pants? How the hell would you plan for something like this?

Approaching the nurses' station, Devon plastered on another smile. Parking the wheelchair in front of the chest-high counter, she walked into the space where two women sat next to each other, entering information into neighboring computer stations and gossiping about a television show, where a bunch of women tried to convince one man to marry them. After watching one episode, she and Blue had to take a shower to wash away the icky. She did not know how anyone found it entertaining. But these ladies did.

Before she could consider that her next action could compromise the health care of seriously ill innocents, she placed one of her hands on each of their shoulders and sent a wave of magic into each of them before they even noticed she was in their space. She swayed on her feet and bent forward, grabbing for a trash can.

Gathering herself, she rolled both chairs back and shoved the women to the floor, folding them under the desk. Pushing the chairs back in and making sure no appendages jutted out to draw attention, she grabbed the wheelchair and rushed down the hall. She had little magic left, and she was sick. If she knocked anyone else out, she might die.

When Greenlee and Blue trained for the marathon, she heard them mention a concept of gutting it out, in which a person willed themselves to keep going past their body's reasonable limits. Now she understood what they were talking about.

Leaning heavily on the wheelchair, she staggered down the hallway. Ben shuffled from a room, and she stifled a potentially embarrassing shriek. His skin was ashen, and blood crusted at the side of his mouth. He wore a hospital gown, and his arm trailed a plastic tube once hooked to an IV bag. He leaned against the doorframe, face murderous, eyes glowing with black-and-purple flames. A small silver object dangled from a leather strap in his shaking hand. She recognized it immediately as Greenlee's craftsmanship. "Ben?" She rushed forward to help him without thinking. The flames in his eyes flared, and gray mist swirled around his feet, stopping her in her tracks.

"Stay away." His voice was rumbling with otherworldly menace and a trace of confusion. Raising the leather strap over his head, he dropped the necklace into place and tucked the silver into the neck of his gown, breathing easier immediately.

"Ben?" She raised her hands in a nonthreatening gesture. "It's Devon. Greenlee's friend. We have to get out of here. Let me help you."

His brows furrowed as he studied her face, eyes glassy from medication, fatigue, or trauma. There was something else, too, something scary. "Devon?"

"Yeah." She shoved the wheelchair forward. "Do you need this?"

He glanced over his shoulder, expression unreadable. "I can walk."

"Good. Greenlee is in 407, two doors down." She moved to pass him with a flutter of nerves. This version of Ben made her uneasy. There were no dad-goal vibes happening right now. She wouldn't let her kid anywhere near this version of Ben. She glanced quickly into his room and stopped. Two sets of feet, one in Crocs, the other in velcroed sneakers, stuck out behind the hospital bed. "What happened?" His entire stance and movements were different. Aggressive.

"Needed energy." Ben prowled down the hall, unconcerned that his gown hung open in the back.

Devon was pretty sure he meant he had drained their energy. Everything clicked into place. Ben was a soul eater, and his energy was coming from people's souls. A wave of apprehension washed over her. "Will they be okay?"

"Eventually." He reached 407, shoved the door, and lurched inside without so much as a pause. He was hunting. She shivered.

From inside the room, someone said, "You shouldn't be up." A croak and the loud thump of a body hitting the floor followed. She rushed forward but skidded to a stop with a gasp. Misty gray tentacles writhed from Ben's feet and wrapped around a middle-aged man in black scrubs. He lay on his side on the floor, pale and unmoving. Her gaze moved from the fallen nurse to Ben's feet, then up to his face. His eyes still flamed, but his color was returning, and he held himself straighter. He didn't seem to be interested in snacking on Greenlee.

Taking a deep breath, she reminded herself that this man had sheltered and comforted Lexi without a second thought. There was a decent man in there somewhere. Or there had been. And he had not tried to hurt her. Yet.

Shutting the door behind him, she skirted around the edge of the room until she stood looking down at Greenlee. He lay attached to oxygen, IVs, and so many wires, she couldn't count them all. Strands of hair plastered to his forehead, dark black circles rimmed his closed eyes, and his skin was cold and clammy. Her chest squeezed, and her eyes tingled with tears. She could not lose her family again. She wouldn't survive it, so she had to save them. Staring at the monitors and screens over his head, she wished she had any idea what the numbers meant.

Ben scrutinized the monitors as well, eyes returning to their natural brown once more, then leaned down and removed the nurse's stethoscope. He placed them in his ears and listened to Greenlee's breathing. Ava mentioned her dad was a doctor. "Can we move him?" She unfolded the paper she printed out upstairs containing the first three pages of Greenlee's chart and a bunch of numbers she had no clue how to interpret and offered them to Ben.

Ben read the pages and glanced back at his new patient, seeming uncertain for a moment, and sighed. "We shouldn't." But he began pressing buttons on the monitors and removing IV bags from the stand and laying them on the bed above Greenlee's head. He swapped the oxygen tube for a mask attached to a small tank secured to the bed and continued to unplug various wires and cables. "But I assume we have to?" He looked up and held Devon's gaze.

"I think we do. I can't let them get to him again."

His head disappeared below the bed. A rustling noise reached her ears, and a moment later, he stood, hopping from foot to foot. He ripped the hospital gown off and leaned back down, reappearing with a shirt that he pulled over his head. A badge still dangled from the front pocket, and it hung loosely around his shoulders. "Help me move this guy."

Together, they dragged the semi-naked man to the bathroom and closed the door. Devon fished the clear plastic bag containing Greenlee's clothes out of the small cabinet next to the bed, hoping that most of his little magic trinkets were still in his pockets and not lost like her glasses. They might need them if she could figure out what they did.

Ben's foot hit the brake release on the bed. "Get the door for me."

They maneuvered the bed into the hallway and back toward the elevators, passing the nurses' station. Devon bit her lip and glanced around. "Um, Ben?"

"What's wrong?" He stopped by the bed and looked around for threats, eyes flaring.

Unable to believe what she was about to suggest, she let out a shaky breath. "If you need more energy. There are two more behind the desk."

He tilted his head in surprise and stepped behind the desk, raising an eyebrow. "Thanks." It took less than a minute before Ben rejoined her, looking hale and fit. He was almost back to 100 percent. "Most people are afraid of me."

"Oh, buddy. I am freaking terrified." If she had to be trapped in a cage with a lion, she intended to keep it well-fed.

"I'm not going to hurt you." When she didn't respond because she didn't entirely believe him, but wasn't about to tell him that, he shoved the bed into motion again. "Where are we going?"

They hustled down the hallway, meeting a few visitors and a few support personnel moving patients or performing specialized care.

No one stopped them, all too busy and harried to notice strange faces. She shouldn't be grateful for a nationwide nurse shortage and woefully inept management practices, but she was today. She hit the down arrow button for the elevator. "I'm still working on that. If I found you, so can the Sovereign. I'm amazed they have not swarmed us yet. We need to get out of here."

No sooner had she answered than a loud, high-pitched bell rang over the building's emergency speakers. "Attention, all personnel. Code Gray. I repeat, Code Gray."

"Come on." Ben hit the button again several times.

Devon's heart skipped a beat. She didn't know what a code gray was, but judging by Ben's reaction and the timing, it wasn't good. "What does that mean?"

"Security situation. Criminal activity. Possible missing person."

"Well, foo." Someone found the nurses she left on the other floor. She shifted from side to side and watched the number tick upward on the elevator. Ben's only response was a noncommittal grunt. She casually strolled down the hallway and stood with her head down slightly to the side. If they discovered a patient was missing, they would look for a Hispanic woman in her thirties, about five feet two and a hundred and twenty-five pounds. She looked around, inspecting what they were dealing with. There were no visible cameras in this hallway. The hospital was older and a regional facility with a small budget. The elevator finally dinged, causing Devon to hold her breath in anticipation.

The doors opened, revealing two security guards dressed in dark blue uniforms, faces alert. "What's going on?" Ben projected just the right amount of innocent curiosity and expected trepidation. Color her impressed. "Gotta get this guy down to radiology. Is it safe?"

One guard peered past him, down the hallway. The other frowned and stepped out, placing his hand on his radio. "Take the patient back to the room."

Devon watched Ben closely. He nodded thoughtfully. What were they going to do now? The men would soon discover five unconscious staff. Her stomach flipped, and it had nothing to do with the magic poisoning. If she used any more magic to knock these guys out, Ben would have to move two unconscious bodies or save himself.

"Sure, man. No problem." Ben backed the bed up so that the men could step onto the floor. When both men moved to exit the elevator, gray mist appendages immediately engulfed them, and they fell limp across the gap between the elevator and the tile floor of the hallway.

"Oh, sugar!" She flinched, watching the men fall. This differed from seeing already downed bodies. The mist remained coiled around the men's torsos and dragged them from the elevator. She rushed forward to help.

"Hold that door." Devon felt his voice more than she heard it. She didn't look at him, knowing it would just creep her out. This was not convincing her he would not hurt her. She blocked the door with her leg as Ben pulled the men completely into the hallway. He pushed the bed into the elevator and slapped the button for the basement.

The doors closed behind them as Devon leaned heavily on the wall, staring straight ahead. Soothing music drifted through the speakers. This was all so surreal. What on earth had she gotten herself into? "You have a plan, I take it?"

"Morgue. Stick him in a body bag and get him into a vehicle somehow." Eyes brown once more, Ben appeared refreshed and almost glowing in direct contrast to how she felt. The security guards must have hit the spot. "Unless you have a better idea."

"Nope." She popped the P and looked down at Greenlee, hating the idea of putting him in a body bag. But it wasn't a terrible plan, given the circumstances.

"Thanks for taking care of Ava." The terrifying man next to her made polite conversation. "She told me how nice you were. And coming to get me. It's been a long time since it wasn't just the two of us."

"I'm glad I could help you. Both of you." She paused, taking a minute to form her next words carefully. "I'm drained, but I'm going to do everything I can. Whatever happens in the next few minutes, get Greenlee out of here."

"No."

"Excuse me!" Stunned, she turned to Ben in disbelief and indignation.

"This man put himself into a coma to save my daughter. He wants you safe. I'll keep you safe."

"That's some bro code bull hockey." Devon crossed her arms over her chest with a huff. "I just put people to sleep. He stands a better chance of finding Ava and Lexi than I do."

Ben studied her for a moment. "I'm not so sure." Ben shook his head as the display above them clicked over to the letter B and the elevator slowed. "You are all very resourceful people. "

The public announcement system wailed again with a startling siren. "Attention personnel. Code Silver. Code Silver."

"Ben?"

"Means active shooter at my hospital."

"Fudge."

17

NISHA

Nisha shuffled slowly down the corridor, her hand dragging the wall as hundreds of voices battered at her exhausted brain. Finn's mood was foul. EMS diverted their people during transport to the hospital while they walked through the woods, trying to avoid capture. It took them several hours to figure out which hospital they ended up in. Finn harbored the belief the Sovereign took them, and he wouldn't see his sister-in-law again. He loved that lady and his niece. No one from his team had contacted him yet, so he didn't know if they were safe. Everyone he cared about was missing or dead. It had been painful and exhausting to listen to. She was thankful for a few minutes away from the turmoil of his mind, even though the current situation wasn't much better.

The events of this morning, Finn's anxiety, and the time she spent sifting through the minds of hospital visitors and staff to find the name and room number of a patient they could use to gain access without drawing attention to themselves left her mentally and physically drained. There were two general types of magic. The first and most common kind you turned off and on at will, building magic muscles until you could channel the amount of magic you needed safely. The second kind was always on, and you learned to contain it. She had the second kind. So did Ivan and Sam.

Nisha was used to managing her magic at a low level all day, every day, with occasional spikes. However, today was pushing her limits. Her reflexes were sluggish, and her fine motor control was almost nonexistent.

She wore a ball cap low over her face and her hair shoved up inside of it to disguise herself since she was a fugitive from both the government and the Sovereign now. The longer this day wore on, the harder it became to shut out the noise or focus on an individual voice or even concentrate on basic tasks like walking without tripping. Soon she would slip up, and something bad would happen. Where was he? She wanted to find their people and get out of here. He should be right behind her.

A strong hand wrapped around her upper arm and jerked, causing her to stumble. She hadn't even heard anyone approach. If someone recognized her, she was a sitting duck.

Finn stood next to her, a concerned frown on his face as he glanced around to make sure no one was close enough to hear him. "You seem out of it."

She just shook her head. Sick people were as mentally loud as scared people, and this place was full of them. Except fear came in waves she could catch her breath between. This was a constant onslaught, and she didn't have the reserves to deal with it.

"Hang on for a few more minutes." Finn led her back to the lobby, and she tried not to trip as a dull ache settled behind her eyes. He recognized someone in the lobby. "We have a problem. I need you to listen to someone." He stopped them just at the edge of the hallway leading to the reception area. A group of official-looking people in suits crowded the receptionist's desk. "The short, round one in the middle. What can you tell me?"

Nisha leaned against the wall and focused. The man wore a cheap suit and a paunch short tie. He glowered at the receptionist and tapped his finger on the counter, separating them, projecting a slimy respect-my-authority vibe.

"Dick man?"

"What?" Finn scowled.

"He is referring to someone as a dick man." She scrunched up her nose. "Himself? He is referring to himself in the third person as dick man. In his head, at least."

"Wow."

"Yeah. Shh." She stopped following their movements visually and locked on to the group's thoughts, almost losing her balance.

Finn didn't make a noise, and his mind immediately went mostly blank, picturing plain white walls in a silent room. It was brilliant and very helpful for her focus. Her breath caught when she finally discerned the conversation happening in front of them. "FBI Magic

Taskforce. They are here to take custody of everyone brought in from Larson's attack."

Finn scowled. "I was afraid of that. Does he have warrants, or is he just throwing his weight around?"

"I don't know. But he has an anti-magic field equipped if he needs it. He isn't leaving here empty-handed. Finn, two of those guys aren't agents." Anti-magic fields were incredibly rare and very expensive. How had he gotten his hands on one?

"Our people? Do you hear them?" Even though her answer had been no for the past hour, he asked again. He swept the entire area with his eyes, mind active once again. He had no intention of letting FBI Agent Mann or his team inside this hospital. At least not without a fight.

"I'm sorry. Sick people are so loud, it hurts. I can't hear them."

"You got us in. I'll get us out." He dropped an arm around her shoulders and turned them away from the lobby. He wanted to stash her somewhere semi-safe and figure out how to deal with Team Dick Mann and get her out of the building.

"Oh, no you don't." She might be clumsy, but she could still help even if Finn thought she would fall over and that she looked terrible. Before the inner workings of his mind could offend her any more than they already had, the overhead announcement system chirped, and a tinny voice announced, "Attention all personnel. Code Gray. I repeat, Code Gray."

Jerking to a stop, they looked up at the speaker in the ceiling. "What in the hell is a code gray?" Finn pulled them to the side as a security guard burst through a door and jogged past them, brain screaming.

"Security incident. Two nurses injured. Third floor. Missing female patient." She placed her hands over her eyes and hunched her shoulders as the anxiety in the building skyrocketed and ripped through her brain like shrapnel.

"Gotta be Dev," Finn reasoned as loud, angry voices erupted from the lobby. Nisha didn't have to be a mind reader to know that the security alert had, at least momentarily, locked down anyone entering the building, including Agent Dick Mann, and he wasn't having it.

A wave of disembodied terror hit her mind, followed by a roar of familiar angry voices tipping her over the edge and causing a wave of vertigo that turned her stomach. She jolted sideways, her vision tunneled, and she threw her arms out to catch herself. She exhaled sharply. "Ben."

"Where?"

"Up?"

"Good Ben or bad Ben?"

"Dr. Chuthulu."

"That's not ideal." Footsteps echoed through the tall lobby as his brain ran through a few dozen scenarios. The possibility that Ben had lost control and was on a soul-eating rampage crossed his mind, but he settled on the probability that Ben was helping Devon, the missing female patient, escape. He wanted to buy them time to get out of this hospital. "Do you trust me?"

"Yes." Glimpsing his plan, she immediately regretted her answer. "No."

"Hey, Dick Mann." Finn projected his voice down the corridor. She watched in horror as FBI Agent Mann and five of his buddies rounded the corner from the lobby and looked directly at them. Finn reached up and knocked the hat covering her hair off her head, revealing her face. She was a more valuable target than any of the people the agent had come looking for. "Look who I have."

"Torrin!" The agent's plain face twisted in fury. "It's Ravi! Stop right there!" Already running, Finn pushed her down the corridor in front of him. They hit a set of double doors and entered a hall crowded with spare hospital beds and rolling racks of supplies.

"What the hell, Torrin?" She willed her feet to move faster and tried not to fall. She heard the minute Dick Mann realized this was a distraction and reacted. "He is sending two the other way."

They barreled through a set of doors and skidded around a corner into an area bustling with activity, but no urgency. A sign on the wall read Emergency Room. This hospital had the vibe of a place that mostly handled the occasional heart attack, Legos stuck up the nose, and periodic *hey, ya'll watch this* injuries. The patients and staff were bored and paying no attention to the two weirdos skidding around the corner *Breakfast Club* style.

Finn waved his arms wildly. "Gun! He has a gun! Get down!" Screams erupted, and people fell to the ground. Panic and terror overloaded her brain with spikes of pain, and she stumbled again. More shouted orders to stop echoed behind them.

A powerful wave of intent slammed into her, and she pushed Finn to the side with her shoulder, crushing him against the wall just in time. Loud barks of gunfire roared behind them, echoing in the cavernous space filled with hard surfaces. She threw her arms over her head as bullets pinged around them. Mann's men did not care about innocent bystanders, some only sheltering behind rolling carts and beds. "Thanks." Finn righted himself, grabbed a large laundry cart full of soiled sheets and gowns, and shoved with all of his might. The thing careened down the hallway, catching Agent Dick Mann in the gut and sending him flying.

"Go. Go. Go." Finn once again took over their mad charge through the hospital. They raced by terrified faces and barreled through another set of double doors into the waiting room. "He has a gun!"

Another spike of pain ripped through her head from terrified thoughts of terrified people she could no longer muffle. "Would you stop that?"

Finn shoved her toward the exit as panicked patients and their families scattered around them. A security guard emerged from the triage room. "Stop right there!"

"Keep going." Finn yanked on her arm hard enough she worried for her shoulder socket. The door behind them burst open and shouting FBI agents erupted into the chaos of the waiting room, causing even more terror and confusion. The overhead speakers wailed, and the voice from earlier announced a Code Silver, whatever that was, but it must be bad, judging by the wash of emotions she received.

She stumbled behind Finn, head now spinning, as he led them through the automatic doors into the sunlight and fresh air outside. Struggling to process anything more than shutting the voices and pain out of her head, she dodged a uniformed body flying as Finn wrestled it from the driver's seat of an ambulance onto the concrete of the portico. She yelped in surprise as he threw her into the vehicle and shoved her roughly across the seats.

"Get ready to run."

"What? Why?" They had just gotten to a vehicle. She struggled to right herself.

The engine roared, but instead of surging forward as she expected, they flew backward. Shouts pierced the interior of the cab as the ambulance struck the building behind it. Metal crunched, but the glass and doors remained intact. The impact bounced her body off hard objects in the cabin's interior. Finn threw the gigantic vehicle into drive and swung it sideways, dragging the driver's side across the bay doors, mangling them and wedging them stuck.

A look crossed his face that she did not like at all as he observed the parking lot that surrounded them. "Buckle up." She caught a flash of his plan.

His respectable façade hid a hopeless adrenaline junkie. She fumbled desperately for the seat belt and clicked it in place as his foot slammed on the gas. They lurched forward and careened around the building, tires screeching across the pavement. He put the gigantic, lumbering vehicle into a dead spin, almost tipping it over. He straightened them out. The two airborne wheels slammed back to the earth, and he shifted gears. His foot was on the gas immediately, and they sped backward at full speed, the engine screaming. She looked in the side-view mirrors, wondering what on earth he was thinking. A telephone pole towered behind them, topped with two oversize transformers. "What are you doing!?"

The rear of the vehicle hammered the telephone pole, throwing glass everywhere and slinging all the compartments in the back open.

Her head hit the back of the seat, causing stars to dance across her vision. Overhead, the pole cracked audibly. A flash of light blinded her, followed by a boom like thunder that shook the cab of the ambulance and made her cover her head instinctively. At least one transformer had exploded.

"Go." Finn unclicked her seat belt, then reached across to open the passenger door. A deep gash marred his forehead because he had not been wearing a seat belt. Idiot. The window behind his head offered a clear view of a live wire dancing feet from his door. While she questioned his mental stability, he climbed across the seats and shoved her bodily out of the ambulance. She fell ungracefully headfirst with an indignant oomph. Nisha rolled, shaking the sting out of her wrist and the rocks out of her palms, thankful that the felled power lines were nowhere near her.

The transformers dangled eight feet off the ground, still attached to the upper half of the broken pole, sparking, and swinging slowly. The windows on the hospital's upper floors were dark. What if people needed that electricity to stay alive? A low rumble started behind the building, the emergency generators priming and turning on.

Finn jerked her up, and they were running again before both of her feet hit the ground. Well, he was. She still stumbled like a drunk person, overwhelmed by the side effects of her magic. She didn't even know which direction they were running in or if anyone followed. "Hang in there."

They ran through a never-ending series of lawns and parking lots. The wail of sirens surrounded them. Her heart beat wildly from running and the threat of being captured by people aligned with the Sovereign. She remembered every image from Greenlee's memories of his time in the Sovereign-run facility, and the threat of falling into their hands terrified her.

"Slow down." She fell into step beside the man next to her, hand pressed hard into her chest as the distance from the hospital and the chaos surrounding it quieted in her mind. Her equilibrium returned to somewhat normal levels, and her mind cleared.

"You are completely insane." She fully digested her surroundings for the first time in a few minutes. They were in an industrial area, walking across a parking lot toward a warehouse with a tall loading dock running down the length of it. Two trailers sat backed up to the pier. The whine of a forklift whirred somewhere inside the building.

"I'm just good at improv." Finn's face remained grim as his thoughts wandered to some of the other dire or chaotic situations he had faced during his career. Many of them featured Hale and a man named Tanner. More than a few featured guest appearances by the former Zenith they all called Blue. It amazed her the man was still alive. They approached the end of one trailer and Finn peeked inside. "This one is almost full. Do you know where it is going? Long haul or local?"

She huffed and focused on the minds in the building, feeling the energy leaving her body. For a guy who didn't let magic users join his team, he had no qualms about using her magic. The forklift driver was thinking about a NASCAR race. The truck driver stood in the bathroom, thinking about working on a restoration project tonight. He wasn't driving far if he planned to be home. "Local."

"Up we go."

They climbed into the dirty trailer filled with plastic-wrapped pallets of boxes, wriggling their way through the tightly packed space. They found a pallet only partially full toward the front of the trailer and stretched out on top of it, keeping their heads low enough to remain out of sight.

"I did not want it to go down that way. I hope it bought them enough time."

"Me, too."

"We still don't know where they are." Finn paused. "How are you feeling? You looked like you were in pain."

"Yeah. I'm good." She stared at the trailer's roof, not yet relaxed but enjoying having fewer voices in her head. "I want to see if there is anything useful in Zella's journals. One page might mention Ben and maybe that café. She wanted me to see it. Maybe it will be helpful if we can figure out her gibberish."

"Let me see." He extended his hand, palm up, and she pulled the journal out of her waistband where she had carried it since they traveled by magic umbrella to Colorado, handing it over. He thumbed through the pages as the forklift rolled onto the truck and dropped a pallet, causing the whole thing to shudder.

"Last pallet." She closed her eyes and fought hard to stay awake. People were exhausting.

"This is like poetry."

"It is. Zella sees chunks of the future. But she hasn't been able to communicate anything useful in years. Maybe we can translate it."

Finn let out an amused snort and turned his head in her direction. "Here is something about fleeing phallic follies."

"That sounds far nobler than running from a dick man." Nisha yawned as the trailer door rolled closed, and the truck fell into darkness.

"That it does. Let's take a minute. Rest. Get somewhere safe, and we can put our heads together with fresh brains." His retreated to the mental white room from earlier, and she relaxed a little more.

"Thanks." She yawned and fell asleep before the trailer pulled away from the dock.

18

DEVON

The doors opened to a rather dreary vestibule with directions to the various departments painted directly onto the cinder blocks with cheap stencils. No one else occupied the hall. Ben steered the bed in the direction the words on the wall instructed.

Devon helped him push. She knew who was shooting, and they couldn't fight right now. Hopefully, putting six floors between themselves and where the computer said they should be would buy them some time. The lights blinked out, throwing the hallway into pitch darkness momentarily before dim emergency lights clicked on. An eerie silence descended on them as the typical buzz of modern air conditioners and appliances stopped. Neither of them said anything. They careened toward the double doors at the end of the hallway. She rushed forward to open the doors but could only get one open, the other locked firmly in place. Why was only one door locked? "I can't get it open."

"The bed won't fit through just one door."

"That's great information that does not open the door. Thing is stuck."

Ben stepped up and yanked on the door as well. It didn't budge. "What in the hell?" Ben disconnected Greenlee's IV and ripped off the oxygen mask covering his nose. He moved the bed up against the wall, leaned down, and pulled Greenlee's dead weight upright, hauling his much larger body over his shoulder. "Go." When she just stared, Ben rolled his eyes. "I work on football players for a living. You ever tried to lift an offensive lineman's leg?"

"Sorry. I'm going." Snatching the bag of belongings off the bed, Devon ran through the door first, determined to meet any threat and buy him enough time to react. He followed her more slowly, but at a brisk pace.

She glanced around the office as they entered. A small desk sat to the side, and several institutional gray doors led to other rooms. A whimper reached her ears, and she motioned for Ben to slow as she circled wide around the desk, and her eyes landed on two older gentlemen. One wearing scrubs and a lab coat hunkered, frightened out of his mind, covering his head. The other wore a golf shirt, khakis, and a pissed-off frown, glaring at them. A badge pinned neatly to his shirt pocket said he was Robert from Seven Points Memorial Chapel. Neither man had a gun. Not the shooters. "Where is the exit?"

"Don't kill me." The frightened older man squeezed his arms closer over his shoulders, refusing to look at them. His body quaked.

"I'm not helping you. Shoot me," the angry man hissed.

Devon put her hands on her hips and glanced back at Ben, fresh out of grace and patience. "Hungry?"

"I could eat." Tendrils flew out of his feet, encompassing both men before they could move or scream. They slumped into lumps on the floor, and Devon waited for the mist to retract before kneeling next to them and digging through their pockets.

She pulled cash out of both of their wallets and keys from the funeral director's pockets. She showed Ben the keys and stood. "Bet he has a van. Transportation secured. Let me find the exit."

Ben nodded and surveyed the room. "No time to find a body bag. We need to get out of here."

She didn't disagree with him and found herself mildly relieved Greenlee wouldn't be in one of those things. Devon pointed at the angry funeral director. "Will that one live without medical help?"

"Sure." Ben shrugged casually, causing Greenlee's body to shift.

"How long will it take him to wake up?" Devon leaned back down and took Mr. Robert's phone, using his thumb to unlock it.

"Usually takes two or three days."

Devon chewed her lip and cut her eyes up to Ben. "Think you could tack on an extra day or two?"

Ben studied her for a moment, clearly unhappy with the request. "You don't have to feed me. Your soul is not in danger."

Devon busied herself changing the password on Mr. Robert's phone. "It's not like that. He saw us together. The other guy didn't. We need to keep him quiet for as long as we can." She shrugged. "Or we can kill him."

Ben stared again, his tone dry and sarcastic, when he finally spoke. "Or we can kill him?"

"Not my favorite option. Can you buy us a day or two or not?"

"You are the first person who has ever asked me to suck someone's soul out."

"In my defense, how many people know you are a soul eater?" Devon raised an eyebrow and turned away, not eager to see the familiar judgment that she received when people got to know this side of her. She tried to open the three other doors leading out of the room. There were no exit signs. How did this place pass codes? One door was locked. Probably a closet. The other led to cold storage. The last door led to a long hallway. Door number three, it would be. She walked back to the room where she left Ben with a Robert-sized soul snack. "I think the exit is this way."

Mist snapped into his feet as she entered the room, and he turned flaming eyes to face her, Greenlee still thrown over his shoulder. "Lead the way." He followed her through the doors she held open for him. They reached another door, this one with small, white stenciled letters that read Exit.

"Do you think it's safe?" A window would be great right now.

"You have the keys?" Ben squatted and sat Greenlee down on the floor where he flopped like a rag doll, then stepped forward and motioned for her to watch over Greenlee. "I'll go first."

"Okay?" Devon showed him the keys clutched in her hand. What was this about?

Ben opened the door slowly, letting light into their small space. He glanced out. "I'm no good at this stuff. What am I looking for? I'm a doctor, for fuck's sake. Not a soldier."

"Did you just quote *Star Trek*?" Devon snickered.

"No? I see the van. It's not far."

"You quoted *Star Trek*."

"I don't think they say fuck in *Star Trek*."

"They do in the new ones."

Ben sent her an exasperated look. "Are we really talking about *Star Trek* right now?"

She huffed. This guy's personality was dry as a cracker. "I'll go get the van and back it up. Less suspicious than walking out with a body."

After another quick look outside to reassure himself, the coast was clear; he nodded and pushed the door open for her. Cute. Thankfully, it was a short walk to the van, clearly marked with the name of the funeral home down the side. This is what Blue would call a beater. The ripped seat stuck to her clothes when she sat down, and she worried for a moment that it wouldn't start. She climbed in and, much to her relief, it started on the third try. Devon backed it up, left it running, and helped Ben scoot Greenlee into the back while they both inhaled exhaust fumes. Sirens wailed in the distance, getting closer by the minute.

Without a word, Ben shut the door to the hospital's interior and helped her climb into the passenger side, then moved around the van to the driver's seat, closing the door and extending his hand for the keys. She handed them over and laid her head back on the headrest. She was exhausted and a little light-headed, either from magic poisoning or breathing exhaust. Maybe both.

"You are the criminal mastermind here." Ben put the van in gear but didn't hit the gas. "Where are we going?"

Devon opened her eyes and sighed. She didn't get to rest yet. She held Robert's phone up to her face. "Navigate home."

"Navigating home," the phone's robotic voice said.

They both looked at the results on the screen. They were going to Seven Points Memorial Chapel. Evidently, Mr. Robert lived with the dead people.

"Probably lives in an apartment on the property." Placing the phone in the cupholder so Ben could see the map, she buckled herself in.

"What if his wife is there?" Ben glanced back at the map on the phone and navigated out of the parking lot.

"Let's cross that bridge when we get away from the active shooters?" She laid her head back again and put her hand on her unhappy stomach. She might jump off the bridge when she got there. How on earth did she end up in a stolen van, carting an unconscious man in the back, being driven by a man who ate souls for snacks? And her baby girl was flying around somewhere with a giant mutant eagle. "I'm going to vomit."

Ben looked at her with concern. Two police cars screamed by them in the oncoming lane of traffic. "Do I need to pull over?"

"God, no. Keep driving."

19

SAM

Sam's eyes snapped open with a start, a rush of cold air filling his lungs. He squinted, the sun above him hurting his eyes, and a sharp rock digging into his shoulder. He wasn't falling anymore, but every square inch of his body still tingled painfully with residual magic. A head entered his vision, framed by a wild halo of hair, its dark outline blocking out the sun. He blinked and focused, only to find Amber Collins scrutinizing him with a sharp look that put him on edge. She no longer bled from her nose and eyes like the last time he saw her. She bit her lip and glanced around.

"Listen carefully, Regent. I only have a few minutes." She rubbed distractedly at her now stationary and silent bracelet. He hefted himself upright, something in her tone letting him know that the urgency was real and not manufactured. He sat on the ground at the bottom of a steep pebble- and brush-covered hill. A moving van lay on its side, crushed against two trees, walls mangled, and contents strewn across the hillside, its tumbling path clear from the gouges in the dirt and ruts through the pebbles. "I don't know why we're here, but you told me to fix it, and this is where we ended up." Blue rested on her side a few feet away, blood staining her face. Her chest rose in a slow and steady rhythm. Somehow they had all survived whatever happened. But now Blue looked like the girl he remembered from the Zenith program, with fair skin and freckles, her hair a strange mix of the dark brown Rhodes had given her and her natural red.

"Sevens. Remember. The pockets are sevens. Seconds. Minutes. Hours. Days. Weeks. Months. Years. Decades. Let's hope it doesn't come down to decades."

He scowled. None of this was making sense.

"Always sevens. I can't channel enough magic to get everyone back without Blue, even with this." Amber lifted her arm and flashed the bracelet. "She is the only reason we aren't all dead."

Confused, he opened his mouth to tell her to say something he could understand when she sliced her hand through the air.

"Shut up and listen. This is the hours. A couple moving here for a new job as a research director at Everdale University were the owners of that van. These two are shady as hell. I don't have many more details. They came from nowhere and then disappeared. Their bodies were never found, so it will work for now. His name is Samuel Keys. Hers is Ivy. Go with it."

"How do you know this? What are you talking about?" She spoke so fast he struggled to process her message. He jammed his palms into his eyes in frustration.

"They lived at 149 Kay Street. I can't change location, so stay close to this area. I will find you."

"Amber. Damn it. Where are we? What is that thing and what did it do to us?" He pointed at her wrist, still adorned by the mysterious bracelet of spinning death. He narrowed his eyes, noticing that she avoided touching him, and each time she leaned close, it glowed and emitted a low whistle.

"The Son Sovaj." The words emerged like she hadn't just dropped a bomb on him as she brushed her fingers over the beads distractedly. That was the name of the artifact from the red Project Zenith file that created a stable of powerful magic users and killed countless women.

"Are you insane?"

"Something has changed." Her brows drew together, and her eyes glazed over. "Everything feels off. Seven days." She scrunched her eyes shut as her hair stood on end, and a white glow enshrouded her body. "If you want to get back home, keep her alive, or find another powerful conduit." Sam didn't miss the emphasis she placed on the word powerful.

"Tell me..."

Amber winked out of existence before he could demand she explain herself better. He shook his head to make sure this was real. Footprints indented the dust and pebbles where she squatted seconds ago. What did getting back home mean? Where were they? If she couldn't change location, what could she change? His surroundings did not look familiar.

He stood on aching legs, dusted himself off, and eyed the treacherous hillside. Amber was gone for seven days, and Blue was out cold. He was positive she had stopped breathing during their nightmare trip through the world of light and pain. If he was going to keep her alive, he needed help.

Getting himself up the hill would be a struggle, much less hauling anyone else. His priority had to be figuring out where they were, considering zealots and government officials still hunted them. Worrying about getting cancer from Son Sovaj exposure would have to wait.

He scrambled to the top of the hill, only slipping back to the bottom twice before he reached the roadway above him. A narrow two-lane road greeted him, desolate in both directions with no clues to give him an idea of where he was, except for a yellow sign showing a sharp turn and a hill. He threw his arms out in exasperation and glanced back down the slope at the wreckage and the body lying next to it. She was still giving him shit about the last time he tried to leave her after an uncontrolled tumble through the electric nightmare light show that had almost killed her. This was becoming an obnoxious pattern.

An older model work truck rolled toward them from the east. It was brown with a cream stripe, sporting square headlights rimmed by chrome, designating it as an eighties' model truck. Lifting his arms, he waved, hoping that the person behind the wheel wasn't out to get them or a member of the Cade Rhodes Army, who would claw his eyes out on sight. He could use a break at this point.

The truck stopped next to him, and the driver leaned over and twisted the hand crank on the passenger window. An older man wearing a co-op hat and canvas coveralls took in his general state as an old country song reached his ears. "Everything okay?"

"No. Someone ran us off the road. There are injuries. I need help."

The man threw the truck into park and hit the button for his emergency flashers. He clucked as he waved at the yellow sharp-turn sign a few feet away and shook his head. "They need a guardrail here. Highway is getting too busy these days." Hopping out, he walked over, looking down the hill at the scene below. "Holy hell." He whistled and turned back to his truck. "You hang tight while I get some help."

Sam gritted his teeth, wondering if he was in the twilight zone or just surrounded by idiots. "Call someone."

Huffing, the man got back in his truck. "Did you hit your head, son? That's what I'm doing. I have to find a pay phone."

Sunday 6:00 PM

***

Dark the harbor to Soar round noon
Alight the Zenith by feral tune
Defy the dark. Be hope my child
Everlasting hearts and sevens wild.

***

20

FINN

Finn rested his elbows on his knees, holding yet another burner phone in his hands. They sat in the small office of a family-owned car repair business down the street from the delivery truck's last stop. An enormous banner decorated the building entrance, reading "Gone Fishing. See you Next Week." The building stood empty, and the old-fashioned desk calendar told him not to expect anyone until next weekend, and he hoped that meant they had a few days before anyone discovered they were here. He tried to stretch his stiff neck and shoulders, whiplash setting in with a vengeance.

Trix was alive and monitoring their preestablished communication channels but remained cagey about his own location. During the hours Nisha slept and Finn alternated between fitful rest and reading Zella's journal, Trix amassed a wealth of information. Gabrielle's hounds, scattering his people, kept the ones not at Lilac from being apprehended. Only Hale, Kendra, and the three people in their care remained unaccounted for.

Both Caesar and Paco suffered injuries during the attack on his offices. Paco got shot, and Caesar, the team's medic, took a drugged dart to the leg. It left him unconscious for a few minutes but allowed him to observe Hale and Zella being bound and shoved into a van as he came to. There was no sign of Kendra, Mitch, Harper, or the dog, even though Caesar performed a thorough sweep of the facility after he stabilized Paco. The Paragon's status and location remained a mystery.

The injury count from the hospital, mostly nurses and security guards, held at eight, all in comas but stable. Agent Mann suffered a severely sprained ankle when he tripped over a laundry cart, requiring a physical therapy appointment in a week. Devon, Ben, and Greenlee's locations also remained a mystery, but Mann left the hospital empty-handed. Finn's distraction worked to buy them time to get out; however, he still didn't know where they were.

Rhodes also remained off the grid, leaving no trace of him or the girls anywhere. Officials reported thirty-two bodies in the Tennessee glade where Larson attacked and twenty-six in the Colorado field where the RV crashed. Half of the RV was in one state and half of it was in another, both halves burned to a crisp, along with anyone still inside. Sam, Ivan, and Blue were missing and presumed dead. Finn struggled to wrap his head around it. Out of everyone involved, Ivan and Blue should have outlived them all. The official numbers did not count the two carloads of people Greenlee leveled with his strange bag of toys on the way there. Officials were struggling to identify the victims, particularly in Tennessee, where most of them were in pieces. The body count was staggering and a testament to Larson's desire to achieve his goal. So far, the press said the incidents were more magic surges. Either the non-magic authorities were unaware those events signaled the opening battles in an all-out war for control of the world's magic, or they just didn't want the public to know the truth yet.

Now, Trix awaited instructions. Did Finn want to rally the team or continue to lie low?

He glanced up at Nisha, who sat quietly on the floor of the small office with Zella's journal open on her lap, eating from a box of Cheez-its. "Anything we can use in there?"

Sighing, she closed the journal. "It doesn't make sense until whatever it is has already happened. There is a whole passage about discovering the secret popcorn castle in here."

"That's going to be the one that saves us." The journal was a waste of time. Laughing humorously, he held up the phone. "Did you catch all of that?"

She rolled her eyes at him. Of course, she had. "Kendra knows your protocols? Will she check in?"

He nodded, although he strongly suspected they loaded her and Mitch into vans before Caesar shook off the effects of the drug they hit him with. "If she can do so safely."

"We can't operate on guesses. We know they have Zella and Hale. Larson will use Zella to draw Mitch out, and that is checkmate."

"We don't know where they took her."

"Trix is certain Nolan Miller is working with Larson, right?"

Finn nodded again and leaned back gingerly on the ancient but comfortable couch. Trix intercepted messages between the two.

"That mendacious little prick has been strutting like a peacock across the front steps of the Cahlad Prime campus since this whole thing started." Nisha gritted her teeth as she spoke of Miller and tossed her head to calm herself. "He is in our house. That is his flex. I would bet my life that Larson is there, too."

"That would be ballsy. Larson blew up a city block and announced a terrorist manifesto. Even if Miller is in bed with him, he can't risk acknowledging that publicly."

"We know Larson is in the area. We saw him with our own eyes."

"He has magic portals. He could be anywhere."

Nisha crossed her arms and glowered at him. "Get me close to the campus. I'll tell you for certain."

He looked back down at his hands, wondering where on the Cahlad's vast campus Larson would hold Zella.

"The holding cells on the third floor of the Werner Building. Anti-magic designed to hold level-five inmates indefinitely." She stood, placing the journal on the cluttered desk, and paced. "That's where I would put them."

"Why are we still talking?" He stood as well, walking to the wall, suddenly frustrated with the whole situation. "You know everything before I say it."

"Verbal communication is the most effective way to work through problems collaboratively." She shrugged and stopped pacing. "Saying things out loud and hearing the words helps the brain process things."

"Fine." Pacing, he wished he had a few of those Cheez-its right now. "How do we get to them? Where is the building?"

She handed him the box of snacks with a sheepish look. "Dead center of the campus. Not visible from the perimeter."

"Great." He looked heavenward and tried to think. They needed to move fast. "It is just me and you, maybe Trix on comms. We don't have enough time to assemble my team." He had to raid a location harboring a well-armed and trained magical paramilitary force that was swarming with agents from several government agencies by himself.

"Stalker Prime handles high-risk extractions all the time. I'm not completely useless or untrained."

"We might have a contract. But you aren't my team."

They stared each other down. She didn't like his last comment, but it was the truth. He wanted Tanner and Hale at his back. Ideally, Paco as well. Two of those options were out, for obvious reasons, and he had to hold Tanner in reserve in case he needed an extraction, or Rhodes or Devon surfaced.

"Looks like I'm what you have, Torrin." She finally looked away, disgruntled because she knew he wasn't happy about it. "We don't know whether we need an extraction plan yet. They might not be there. Get me close. Let me listen and we will go from there."

Conceding unhappily that her plan was the best for now, he shuffled through the papers on the desk. Two cars waited to be picked up. "Toyota Sienna minivan or a Nissan Pathfinder?"

"Pathfinder."

Finn walked to the key valet next to the office door and plucked the Pathfinder's keys off the hook. "Let's go."

21

RHODES

"Mr. Rhodes?"

Blinking away sleep, he peered into the dark room, taking a moment to remember where he was and how they got there.

"Mr. Rhodes?" Lexi stood next to the couch, her voice an urgent whisper. She clutched a pillow to her chest, hair sticking in all directions, and looked around the small cabin with wide eyes. "I heard a noise."

He bolted upright. It was still dark outside, but the soft glow of the beginnings of sunrise filtered in through the blinds and threadbare curtains. He slept too long, but surely the Sovereign hadn't found them already. "What kind of sound, Lexi Lou?" He strained his ears for any evidence that someone had found their safe house. The night was silent except for Ava's soft breathing.

"Growling. I think it's a wild animal."

Rhodes relaxed slightly. Wolves and wildlife he could handle. A squadron of well-funded magic soldiers posed a larger problem.

"Crawl back in bed with Ava, and I'll look." He leaned over and shoved his feet into his shoes, looking up to find Lexi had not moved an inch. "Lexi?"

"I don't want to wake her up. Can I stay on the couch?"

"Sure, kid." Rhodes stood, ruffled her hair, and moved to the front window, peering out onto the dewy Colorado morning for several minutes. There were no footprints. No movement out front. He repeated his observation from the back window with the same results.

"Are you going out there? What if something happens to you? Tia Blue always looked for the noises, but Tio G stayed to keep me and Mom safe while she was gone. If something happens to you, who is going to keep us safe? You can't go out there." Lexi's worries tumbled from her lips in a torrent. "Stay inside with us."

"I'm not going anywhere." Turning back to Lexi, he hoped to head off an emotional breakdown. A low, rumbling growl reached his ears from the direction of the bed.

Lexi jumped up, clutching her pillow tighter and looking around with scared eyes. "Did you hear that? What if they are like you and are hunting us as animals now?"

"Lexi, it's all right." Rhodes knew what woke the child. In other circumstances, it would be funny.

"No, it isn't. I don't want to be eaten." She stomped her foot, and her voice took on a touch of hysteria.

"Lexi?" Ava jackknifed upright in the bed, threw back the covers, and jumped to her feet, arms wide and ready for a fight. "What's wrong?"

Fur erupted from his arms, and his nose elongated into a snout-like shape. His shoulders slumped in exasperation, and he closed his hands and stepped away from both girls in case he lost control of the shift. "It's okay, Ava." He hurried to reassure her while he could still speak. "Please calm down. You just need breakfast."

"Mr. Rhodes?" She dropped her arms and looked around in confusion. "Why are you a dog-man again?" Another growl rumbled through the cabin, and Ava grabbed her stomach. "Oh my God, I am so hungry, it hurts."

Rhodes exhaled with relief as his body returned to normal, grateful that his borrowed clothes were two sizes too large and had not ripped.

"When was the last time you ate?" Lexi stared at Ava in disbelief before turning embarrassed, watering eyes toward Rhodes. She blew out a breath and looked down at her feet, realizing that Ava's growling stomach had scared her senseless.

Given the heightened emotions they were all dealing with, he intended to forget she had said anything about wolves and never mentioned it again. He waved them both toward the kitchen. "Let's raid the cabinets, then. I'm hungry, too. I should have fed you sooner, but you needed the sleep."

Lexi didn't let go of her pillow, but she followed him into the tiny kitchen area. "I'm sorry. I shouldn't have woken you up."

"Nothing to be sorry for, kiddo." He squatted, so they were eye level. "That's what I'm here for. Better safe than sorry."

Unconvinced, Lexi sat down hard in one of the rickety chairs next to the table and continued to clutch her pillow. She stared off into the distance like her mind was a million miles away.

Pulling cans from the cabinets, he sorted through his choices. "Beanie weenies or peaches? We will save the MREs for a fancy dinner."

"I will survive without coffee. I'm not eating cold beanie weenies." Ava shuffled over and pilfered through the cabinet. "Hey, a radio. It's stashed behind a bunch of tuna." She pulled a dusty emergency crank-powered flashlight and radio from the small cupboard. Her voice sounded nasally, sinuses still clogged from crying the night before. "Maybe we will hear something about everybody else. I hate not knowing. How many peaches do you have? Ugh. Only two."

"I want peaches, too, but then you have to eat cold beans and hot dogs." Lexi scrunched her nose at him and gagged. "That isn't fair."

"You guys take the peaches." He dug through the cabinets until he found a can opener and three spoons. He was hungry, but his stomach was upset so he wasn't likely to eat much or keep it down anyway. They could have the good stuff. While he opened the cans, Ava cranked on the radio and found a public station strong enough to understand, and they all sat silently at the small card table eating their cold meal, listening to news of two horrific magic surges that left over fifty people dead. One was in Colorado, the other in Tennessee. The monotonous voice delivered the news with a melodic rhythm that belied the gravity of the situation.

Two gunmen, yet to be apprehended, attacked the Tennessee hospital treating victims of the reported surge, injuring an FBI agent. Three patients were missing, and several staff members were in comas.

"Could that be our parents?" Lexi sounded hopeful. "Three people? The bad guys would have sent more than that. Not put them in comas. But Uncle Finn and that lady, they would try not to hurt people? Maybe?"

He had to admit, the numbers couldn't be a coincidence. He tilted his head in semi-affirmation because Lexi needed something to hope for.

"Of course, it is our parents. Has to be." Ava set the radio aside and dug into her peaches with gusto, a small, hopeful smile playing across her lips. "What's our plan, Mr. Rhodes?"

Both girls looked at him, waiting patiently. "Look, I know it isn't what either of you wants to hear. But we wait. Your parents are still all over the news. It's like they can't stay out of the spotlight."

"Says the platinum-selling country music star." Ava snorted.

Rhodes ignored her. "The Sovereign will focus on them. Bad for them. Good for us. Let's hang tight and stay off the radar. If they aren't okay"—he winced because he hated to plant seeds of doubt already—"our plan doesn't change."

"That's not very heroic." Ava sighed in disappointment. "Nobody writes epic novels about some super-badass dude sitting in a cabin with two kids eating canned peaches and just waiting it out while the world burns. And if they ever did, nobody read it."

"I'm not a hero or writing an epic novel." Rhodes lifted the can of Beanie weenies to his nose and sniffed. He placed it back down on the table without taking a bite, unable to stomach the smell. He wasn't eating today. "I'm just a guy doing his best to keep you two alive and away from the bad guys."

Lexi tapped her spoon on the table thoughtfully. "Maybe you are focusing on the wrong part of the story, Ava. I don't read a lot. I'm not very good at it. But Mom and Tia Blue read to me all the time." Her cheeks turned pink, and she carefully considered her words. "If we can keep you away from the bad guys, we might be the ones saving the world. Maybe nobody ever knows we did it. That's still heroic, right? This might be the most important part of the story."

Rhodes and Ava stared at her in astonishment. She still clutched her pillow nervously and seemed tiny in even this confined space, yet she kept surprising him with little chunks of wisdom far beyond her years. "How old are you again?"

"Why do people keep asking me that? You aren't supposed to ask a lady her age. Mom says so."

Ava chortled, the heavy moment broken and changed the subject. "This new look is so dark. Is this the real you? It's intense. Sinister even. You should be on the cover of vampire books."

Rhodes frowned and leaned away from the table, taking a moment to truly observe both girls' body language. He wanted them to feel safe. They were as relaxed as possible, given the circumstances.

But now he worried he had read them wrong. "Do I creep you out? I was just trying to recharge my magic. I can try to shift to someone else if it makes you more comfortable."

"No. That's not what I meant." Ava waved her hand and slung peach juice everywhere. "You be you. It was just an observation. You aren't actually creepy. I mean, have you seen my dad?" She waved a hand in front of her eye, simulating flames.

"You don't creep me out." Lexi smiled at him. "Tia Blue says we should love people just the way they are and not try to change them to what we want them to be. So I don't care how you look. I'm just glad you are here." She poked at her peaches.

Rhodes hid a flinch. He would not survive this kid.

"Ouch." Ava looked away uncomfortably.

"So, we wait?" Lexi pushed her spoon through her own peaches but did not eat them. "I bet my mom is worried out of her mind."

"Your mom is worried. But she also wants you safe. So, yes, we wait. This place isn't glamorous, but it is sturdy and off the grid. Think of it like summer camp."

Ava's face twisted ruefully. "Yeah, if your parents got conned or were trying to punish you."

Lexi chewed her lip, and Rhodes could see the gears turning in her brain. "They just keep coming. Like when they were after you and Tia Blue. Sometimes you can't fight them all. You run and hide. That's what you said. This is Camp Run and Hide." Resignation stole over her face. "Will I get to go home again?"

"I don't know."

"Did you?"

Rhodes let out a long exhale. "No."

Ava huffed in disbelief and shook her head. "You are great at saving our asses. You are terrible at boosting morale. Just suck it up and lie to make us feel better. Parents do it all the time. Don't you know how to deal with kids?"

"I have no idea what to do with the two of you." The truth was out of his mouth before he realized his brain had sent it.

"My God!" Ava threw her hands in the air and sent Lexi a flabbergasted look that made the girl giggle at his expense. "I saw a deck of cards on the bookshelf. Rummy or Go Fish?"

"Can we play poker?"

Ava cupped her hand over her mouth so Lexi couldn't see but didn't lower her voice. "That's called a distraction. Take notes."

Rhodes shooed Ava away and eyed Lexi as she nibbled on a slimy canned peach. Who taught this child to play poker? "You know how to play poker?"

"Texas hold 'em, five-card draw, seven-card stud." Lexi shrugged. "Mom taught me. She used to play it with her dad when she was a kid. Tio Finn won't play her anymore. He says she cheats. But she doesn't."

Ava bit her lip. "I have never played poker before."

Rhodes set his uneaten breakfast to the side. "Let's fix that. What do you want to teach her first, Lexi Lou?"

Lexi took a bite of her peaches. "Texas hold 'em. I'm going to show you how to take all of their pretzels, Ava."

Monday 2:00 AM

***

Impetuous bravado rush to parry
Find the path you dare not tarry
The popcorn castle kept in secret
Listen close or else they'll keep it

***

22

ZELLA

Zella sat on the floor of Sam's dreary office in the Cahlad Prime administrative office building with her back to the door, trying to relax into a modified lotus pose. Since her hands were bound behind her back, her attempt was lackluster, and her shoulders ached. The space was not conducive to relaxation. Sam volunteered to take the smallest office in the building, despite holding the position of Regent and never cared to make the space comfortable, much preferring fieldwork to the grind of paperwork and administrative duties. They were in the Regent's office for a reason. Making them uncomfortable was a bonus. Larson was making some kind of statement.

Her visions overwhelmed her now, more active than they had ever been. Nebulous and shifting images skated across her vision so often, she needed to keep her eyes closed to prevent vertigo. Anxiety and the overwhelming need to capture her visions on paper clawed at her. Unable to do so, she struggled. The future stubbornly refused to take shape or give her peace. It writhed in wrongness.

Hale leaned against the wall in front of her, hands also bound behind his back and ankles secured with shackles. In the small space, his feet rested mere inches from her folded legs, although he sat with them bent to his chin. A nasty gash ripped through his lip, and his nose was broken. Yet he remained stoically silent.

They had been here for several hours. His hands had to be numb. He studied her with shrewd eyes that were not under-estimating her the way their captors had. She rather liked the young man and hoped no more harm came to him, but his future offered multiple possibilities at the moment. Not all of them pleasant.

Something had shattered the neatly formed paths leading to the future, scattering the shards and tossing them into the sea. They ebbed and flowed together, some dissolving, others warping, all trying to find their way back to one another, twisted and changed. Everything was influx.

The click of a lock allowed her to prepare herself before the door burst open and someone entered the room. Hale's intense expression transformed as a well-practiced mask of Zen-like boredom fell into place. His face gave nothing away, although he gazed at the newcomer. She remained seated, staring straight ahead. Two denim-covered legs appeared in her vision and crossed at boot-covered ankles as the person they belonged to sat on the edge of Sam's desk.

"It's been a long time." Larson Battle's voice grated on her eardrums. "So this is what the once respected title of Regent affords you these days? You've all gone soft."

She struggled to school her features and subdue her physical reaction. Her daughter disappeared, and she lost her ability to communicate with the world the last time she heard his voice. A foot stomped on her shoulder, tipping her forward almost into Hale's lap. As it was, her cheek clipped his raised knee. The man didn't react at all. She raised herself back up, tossing her long, white hair out of her face with a grimace. Larson kicked her right where the darts hit earlier, and she could feel her eye swelling already.

"I see your medical records are accurate." Larson strolled forward, leaning over Hale to rest his forearm on the wall and cross one foot over the other. God, he was a cocky son of a bitch. Even with his arms and legs tied, Hale could do serious damage at that distance, and Larson wasn't the least bit concerned. "No words. No noise." He tsked as she refused to look up at his face. "That's such a shame. I remember Mitch told me once how much he loved your beautiful voice."

She focused on Hale, his blank expression helping to center her emotions. Larson let his words hang in the air for maximum impact. "Where is Mitch? Still putting the position before the people?" She wanted to know where Mitch was, too, but not because she needed a rescue. She hoped he had enough sense to keep his eye on the big picture and stay away.

"Oh, Z." Larson sighed dramatically and stepped away. "Won't even look at me." He kicked Hale's ribs, toppling him over and causing the man to wheeze in a pained and choking breath. He sat back up, his mask returning though his breath was now labored. Zella stared straight ahead, remembering her training. Once a Stalker, always a Stalker. She trained to protect the Cahlad's secrets under the worst of circumstances. Larson knew it, too, because they were in the same unit. That is why he attacked Hale and not her. This was going to get very ugly.

"I'm surprised you didn't see this coming." The man's words emerged with a snarl. "Or did you? But you couldn't tell him?" He snorted. "All that training. But you couldn't protect him or your daughter. Look at you. Useless."

He knelt, putting his face next to Hale's, and she had to look at him. "Who is this?"

The man was speaking to hear himself talk now. He knew she couldn't answer him. Did he think Hale would?

Loud voices in the hallway sliced through the tense silence in the room. Larson leered at Hale despite the noise and didn't react as two quick knocks preceded the door bursting open. "What are you doing here?" Senator Nolan Miller's wing-tip shoes shuffled into her vision, and his angry voice filled the room. "You could ruin everything if the wrong person sees you."

He stood in front of her, hand reaching down and tipping her chin up. His eyes grew wide and panicked as they skated over her face. "My God. What have you done? She was supposed to be at the press conference. If he sees this, he will raze this place to the ground."

"It will be fine." Larson observed Hale for another moment before rising and stepping out of her field of vision.

"Maybe for you," the senator sputtered. "You are the only one who stands a shot at beating him in a fair fight. Hell, any fight. He will slaughter the rest of us. You saw what he did in that field."

A flash of interest crossed Hale's face at Miller's words. She forced herself not to smile. Mitch made it out of Lilac, and Larson couldn't beat Mitch, period. He tried once, a friendly sparring match where Larson stopped sparring, and Mitch barely broke a sweat. That is why they were all here, surrounded by government agents Larson viewed as expendable, instead of tucked away in the Cahlad's secure holding facility. He wanted to force Mitch into surrendering or doing something so egregious, he would blemish the office if he remained. "Get me some ice and an anti-inflammatory right now." Miller spoke to someone in the hallway as he brushed his thumb over her swollen cheek.

"Just get her some makeup."

"This has gone too far." Miller turned angry eyes toward Larson. "I can end this as easily as you started it. Get out."

"What would your family think about that?" The sickening sound of Larson's laughter floated down the hallway as he strolled away. She sucked in a deep breath through her nose and willed herself to remain still. Miller wasn't a raving psychopath, but he was still the enemy.

Miller blanched. "I extend my most sincere apologies for your treatment, Ms. Tyne. Can I make you more comfortable?" He sounded sincere. She suspected it had more to do with what Mitch might do than anything else.

"You can start by getting her some water." Hale finally spoke, drawing Miller's attention his way. "And untie her hands."

"I can't untie her." Miller took an ice pack and a bottle of pills from his aide. "Bring me some water, too."

"At least tie them in the front." Hale motioned with his chin toward her lap. "She's harmless and injured. She needs to draw to manage her anxiety. Get her paper and a pen."

Miller placed the ice pack on her cheek, but she couldn't hold it there herself with her hands bound as they were. He sat the pack on the desk and knelt behind her. "Don't try anything, Ms. Tyne. Larson's men will be here in seconds." He freed her hands briefly and retied them in front of her.

He placed the ice pack back on her cheek, and she lifted her hands to hold it in place. It lessened the throb that had taken up residence in her face. Standing, he rifled through Sam's desk, emerging with a spiral-bound notebook and a pen. "Will this work?"

She nodded as he held the items out to her. "Can I help you into the chair?"

She shook her head and took the notebook and pen, setting them in her lap, immediately sketching the images in her head. Stress drained out of her shoulders. Hale was very observant. She needed to draw and write to deal with her anxiety. Harmless, however, she was not. She just needed to wait for the right opportunity.

Another aide brought three bottles of water. Miller took them and stood looking at her swollen cheek. His expression radiated fury. Loosening the lids on each bottle and lifting the cap on the child-safe pill container just enough to make it easy to get into, he sat everything on Sam's desk. "I'm going to leave these here."

When she didn't respond, he turned to Hale. "I'll have some food sent up." Then he was gone, shutting the door behind him.

She stopped drawing and began unwinding the thin piece of wire that held the notebook together. When she looked up at Hale, he was once again scrutinizing her.

"You know how to use that wire to get these loose." He tilted his head toward the shackles on his feet. It wasn't a question. He figured out a great deal from watching her and listening to Larson. She kept unwinding the wire.

"Get me loose so I can get us out of here, Ms. Z."

She shook her head, pocketing the wire and dragging the ice pack off the desk. She knee-walked over and placed it across his broken nose. If she freed him now, he died. Horribly. That path was written in stone. The other opportunities hadn't coalesced yet. She had to wait.

His body tensed in uncharacteristic anger and pinned her with an intense glare. He hid behind an easygoing façade so people would underestimate him, but he was smart and dangerous. She had his number the minute he walked into the break room at Lilac Avenue. Like recognized like. He sighed in frustration and clenched his jaw.

"Not long ago, I was trapped in this burning building in a place called Kinshasa. Pinned down by snipers. Place was on fire. I had internal injuries and half the third floor laying on top of me."

She moved the ice pack to his cheek. "My team had to fall back, complete the mission. I was glad they did because I didn't want them to die with me. See, I knew." He stopped and took a deep breath. "I knew in my heart I was going to die in that building. Everything was hot. I couldn't breathe from the smoke. The motherfuckers were still setting off explosives. Then an angel appeared, walking through the fire. I shit you not. It was an angel."

He stopped and cut his eyes sideways to look at her over the ice pack. "Her name was Blue. I think you know her."

Zella nodded, a wave of guilt washing over her. She knew Blue very well and often asked for impossible things from the child.

"She had to dig out a piece of me she could touch. She needs to touch skin to do her thing. I couldn't feel the fire, but I could tell she could. Her burns." His eyes closed, and he swallowed hard. "I begged her to leave me. But she told me..." He stopped again, and his eyes squeezed shut even more. "She said that it wasn't her time, so it wasn't mine, either, because she was staying until she got me home. She told me she would die saving her soul mate when dragons descended from the skies. That Ms. Z told her, and Ms. Z was never wrong."

He stared at her in silence for several seconds. "You've seen something. You can't unlock the shackles yet?"

She lowered the ice pack and set it in her lap, meeting his gaze. She never understood why people found comfort in prayer. But she rarely experienced exponential uncertainty. Today, she understood and prayed that she was doing the right thing and not sentencing this man to death.

He nodded and leaned his head back against the wall. "Okay, then. Can you get me some water?"

23

BLUE

A SITUATION

A slow, steady beep sounded somewhere above her head. It was cozy and nice here, but the blankets were scratchy. She wriggled deeper and groaned. Why did she hurt? She rarely woke up, still hurting. What was on her hand? The last thing she remembered was standing in a field in Colorado with a demon and a ghost while the portal to her friends snapped shut. Had she passed out again? She needed to open her eyes and look around. But that was hard. Her eyes wanted to stay closed. Was she hearing the theme song to the *Golden Girls*?

Finding the will to open one eye, she found her surroundings dark. A soft light shone behind her bed, giving off just enough illumination to let her see she was in a hospital room. The beep was a heart monitor, and the thing taped to her hand was an IV drip. *Golden Girls* was on the television. She did a double take. What hospital she was in? She hadn't seen a tube television in years.

Letting her head fall to the side, she frowned. Sam Sotach sat sprawled in an ugly yellow recliner next to her bed. His arms hung so far over the sides they touched the floor. The chair looked like a kid's chair under his frame. He wore rumpled clothes, and his hair stood up in all directions. His head was back, and he slept, mouth ajar. Why was she in a hospital? And why was he, of all people, sitting next to her bed?

"Sotach?" she croaked out, her throat dry and painful. He jerked in the chair, eyes flying open.

"About damned time." He stood, leaning over the bed. "Don't panic."

"I wasn't going to until you told me not to. Did you think that would work?" she croaked out, disturbed by her inability to latch on to the panic she wanted to feel but couldn't. She shrank back, remembering the way he looked in the field. His gaze was intense, and he was really tall. He wasn't trying to loom, but he was looming, at least without demonic solar system eyes right now. She would never scrub that image from her mind.

"You need water." He handed her a small cup of water with a straw. She did the best she could to swallow the liquid, but it was like swallowing around sandpaper. "We have a situation. Follow my lead."

"Sure?" She inspected her surroundings. The room and equipment were outdated, but this was a hospital room. It had a window, so they weren't in some underground experimental torture facility. They weren't playing charades, so Ava wasn't nearby.

Sam started to elaborate but a cheerful, "Knock. Knock," and the click of a door stopped him. His nose flared in frustration.

"Oh! Good! Ms. Keys, you are awake." A short, matronly nurse shuffled in with a smile. She looked through the glasses perched on the end of her nose. "Your husband has been sleeping in that chair for a week. Wouldn't leave your side."

"I gave her some water. I hope that's all right." Sam wore a warm smile on his face. Who was this person who looked like Sam Sotach but acted like a person with people skills? And who was Ms. Keys?

Blue's head whipped around, catching up to his words. "Husband?" she mouthed silently.

"Just go with it," he instructed, just as silently, when the nurse turned her back on him. They had graduated from charades to lip-reading now. How fun!

"What good timing, sweetheart. Let me take a look." The nurse set about taking vitals and changing her IV bag. Blue glared at Sam, who stood to the side silently, hands in his pockets, frowning. A week? What situation were they in? Where were Devon and Greenlee, or even Rhodes? Shouldn't they be here instead of Sotach? And what in the hell happened to Amber?

"Well, Ivy, you look great, considering the shape you were in when you got here. I'm Nancy. I just came back on shift. Your husband met me last night. Real charmer you have here. Lucky girl." The woman's wink couldn't hide her sarcasm, and Blue fought hard not to roll her eyes. Ivy? The woman wrote her name and the date on a chalkboard "I'll get out of your hair, and let the doctor know you have rejoined the land of the living."

The nurse kept talking, saying something to Sam. He answered, but Blue heard nothing else, busy staring at the date Nancy wrote on the board. It was the right day. But the year was off by over three decades. It must be a joke.

Nancy left, taking her cheerful nonsense with her. Prying her eyes from the board, she found Sam standing with his hands still shoved in his pockets, observing her like a person would a bomb about to explode. He was about to tell her this was an elaborate joke, even though he didn't have a sense of humor.

He raised his eyebrows and shrugged his shoulders, glancing at the date on the board. "Like I said, a situation."

24

SAM

APRIL 29. THIRTY-FIVE YEARS AGO

He handled this badly, as usual. Nisha would roll her eyes if she were here. Blue woke a little over two hours ago. Her Zenith training showed as she shifted into observation mode and rolled flawlessly into the scenario she found herself in. Right away, she demanded pants and coffee. Nancy denied both requests, but he convinced her to bring a set of scrubs and help Blue change into them. He agreed coffee was a terrible idea for a week's empty stomach and refused to compel anyone to bring her a cup, which was the first thing he did to piss her off. Telling Nancy he needed a few uninterrupted minutes to talk to his "wife" caused Blue to throw a glare that should have stopped his heart cold.

Brain-dumping everything about the Project Zenith file, Amber revealing her bracelet was the Son Sovaj, and plowing through everything that happened here while he waited for her body to recover

197

from channeling enough power to hurl three people through space and time put the nail in the coffin.

The tiny town's sheriff visited after they arrived in this room. He oversaw the cleanup of their "wreck" and brought a briefcase containing important documents from the site. During his visit, he volunteered himself and a few friends to go haul the belongings that survived the crash into their home, so all Sam needed to worry about taking care of was "his family." This place had strong Mayberry vibes, and it made him nervous. How would they ever blend in?

In retrospect, he should have eased Blue into all the information or waited until she could stomach some coffee, but deep down he was so relieved to confide in someone about this impossible situation that he vomited words in her direction while she sat in stunned silence, face rolling through a hundred different emotions. Eventually, it settled on incredulous outrage.

Now she held out a hand much like she had in the field, signaling him to stop. She scowled in his direction, held tilted slightly. "Let me make sure I'm understanding you. It's thirty years in the past. We are stuck here not knowing if our friends are alive or dead because you told the spontaneous apparition of Amber Collins to "fix it"; of all the words to choose while her spinning bracelet of death tried to murder us." Blue used finger quotes when the words fix it left her lips.

Sam sat in the chair next to her bed and remained silent, feeling he said enough already.

"Spinny death bracelet is the same artifact the Sovereign, as in the psychopaths who hounded us for a week and murdered Ivan, used in some sadistic plot that you are just now mentioning, to grow super Sovaj babies." She waved a hand between them. "Us. Rhodes, Amber, Ivan. In a lab. The bad guys made us?" Voice breaking each time Ivan's name came up, she squeezed her hands together so tight, her knuckles turned white.

"Those same Sovereign assholes started as a shadow organization within the Cahlad, and that bastard Mitch Collins knew and has been monitoring and manipulating our lives since we were infants?" She sent him a disgusted look and snorted. "Unbelievable. And you called me the traitorous bitch?"

Sam suspected she didn't expect an answer, and she didn't give him enough time to offer one, anyway. "Some nonsense about sevens and a powerful conduit if you want to get home?"

"I think you are the conduit."

"I know that." Her tone dripped disdain and impatience as she sat with her legs crossed in the center of the uncomfortable hospital bed, rocking back and forth to spend her pent-up emotions. An uneaten tray of food containing tomato soup and Jell-O with pineapples in it sat to the side of the bed. He now knew the smell of tomato soup made her gag, and she didn't eat "Jell-O with shit in it." Her stomach rumbled, yet she refused to eat anything on the tray. He should ask Nancy to bring her something else. She was skin and bones, and he did not trust Amber or believe there were no other people traipsing through time to cause trouble. They might not be safe here, and it would be easier to keep them both alive if she got back to full health.

She placed her hands on her lap and met his eyes.

"According to that box of impressive forgeries"—she pointed at the box the sheriff left behind—"you are Samuel Keys, the new director of arcana research at a local university specializing in magic artifacts. I'm Ivy Lynn Keys, a high school teacher. We have to stay in this general area so Amber can find us, or I build up enough magic to conduit our asses back to the future somehow." The pitch of her voice dropped menacingly with each word she spoke. "Our cover is a couple moving here for your job, and we will live at 149 Kay Street?"

"I think Amber planted the papers, and she was behind the van and the house, too. I'm guessing time travel."

"Wow, Sherlock. You think?" Throwing her head back, she looked at the ceiling. "How did I not know? Time magic. That's..."

"Rare? Forbidden? Dangerous?"

"Yes. To all of those. Damn it. We were best friends. I thought..." Her eyes closed, and she stopped mid-sentence, taking a moment to collect herself, a sad smile twisting her lip. "Well, I've never been the best judge of character." She looked up. "Have you seen this Kay Street?"

"I went while they were running tests. Took a shower. It's too short." It was the only time he left her side since they refused to let him go with her when they ran the tests, insisting it would take a few hours. Otherwise, he had been in this room doing what Amber instructed and making sure Blue stayed alive.

"Let me guess, it has one bedroom?"

The cottage had only one bedroom and one bathroom, but it was in a cute part of town with a large garage out back. The neighbors descended with casseroles and offers to help clean and mow the lawn when he got there. Considering everything he just shared, why would she care? "Yes?"

"How small is this town?"

"It has one stoplight." The area around the university was dense and the population migratory. The small, quaint community to the east housed most of the permanent residents.

"That heifer." Blue jumped off the bed and paced. "Are you a secret billionaire, by any chance?"

She was having a breakdown. Why did she care about his finances when they were stuck in a time before he had his own money? Regent pay wasn't shabby, and he lived for free in an apartment on the Cahlad campus and invested virtually everything. Financially, he was set in the future, but he would never be a billionaire. "Not a billionaire. No."

She snorted. "You are loaded, aren't you?"

Now, he was irritated. This didn't matter. "What are you talking about?"

"One bed. Forced proximity. Small town. Fake relationship. Not quite a billionaire. We aren't friends. It's all the damned tropes. She did it on purpose. This is so Amber. She's obsessed with those damned books. This is a colossal joke to her."

"I have no idea what you are talking about."

"That's for the best." She stopped in front of the window and stared out, crossing her arms over her chest. "Forget my promise to Ms. Z. Trying to kill me is one thing. But I'm sick of people manipulating my life. I'm going to kill Amber." Once again, feeling like she didn't want him to say anything, he filed his questions about this promise to Zella away and kept his mouth shut.

"This is FUBAR." She spun to face him. "I've dealt with some BS in my life." Her finger hit his chest, and she poked him with each of her next words. "This is epic levels of BS. I've got to pee."

Stomping past him, she slammed the door to the bathroom. He stared after her, agreeing this whole thing was BS.

A loud thump in the bathroom had him eyeing the closed door with concern. A muffled noise that sounded suspiciously like a sob carried through the door, and he ran his hands through his hair. He could not deal with tears today, not from this woman. She was not the crying type, making this situation a literal landmine. Would she prefer help or no witnesses? He sucked at dealing with people. He knocked on the door. "Blue?"

The room had gone silent, and she didn't respond. Worried that she fell because she barely looked strong enough to stand, he opened the door, praying she was no longer on the toilet. The scene in front of him reinforced his uncertainty, and he would have preferred to find her on the toilet. She stood in front of the mirror, mouth agape, and trembling hands hovering over her dazed face. She stared at her reflection in disbelief. "It's me."

It never occurred to him to warn her she looked like Indigo Vale and not Blue West before she encountered a mirror. He never imagined a reaction this intense.

"I thought you fell." Unsure of what to do, he scooted into the room. Her entire body convulsed. She looked frail, adrift, and on the verge of a mental and physical breakdown.

Hazel's eyes, brimming with tears, met his in the mirror. "It's me."

"It is. How can I help?" He wet a washcloth in the sink and wiped at her blotchy face like his mom used to do when he was a kid, mildly surprised Blue let him. "What do you need?"

"Can you get me out of here?" She glanced back at herself in the mirror, tears never spilling over, but shoulders heaving with sobs as she leaned on the sink. Tears or not, Nisha would still call this ugly-crying.

"Of course." His assurance did nothing to stem the intensity of the sobs. "No. No. No. Don't cry. Stop crying."

The sobbing stopped on a garbled intake of breath, and she glared at him with genuine betrayal filling her eyes. "You were being so nice." Her whisper held disappointment and accusation.

"Shit." Frustrated with himself, he kept wiping her face. Her eyes grew large with horror as his magic took hold.

"Oh, my dear God." She shoved him hard with one hand while the other flew to her stomach. "Get out. Get out now." She twisted toward the toilet and slammed the door in his face.

He laid his head against the door in dejection. This is why he lived alone and only socialized with Nisha, who didn't require words to communicate with him. He hadn't slipped up like that in years, because he only dealt with people in brief bursts at work. "I'm really sorry."

"We will never speak of this again, Sotach." The toilet flushed. "Never."

25

BLUE

APRIL 30. THIRTY-FIVE YEARS AGO

B lue shifted in her seat trying to mitigate the pain a bump in the road caused her aching ribs. Troubled by the reminder that her body remained injured five days after they encountered Amber in a Colorado field, Blue took in the details of the quaint neighborhood that surrounded them as Sam navigated their car through the suburban streets of Lakemond. Filled with small one- and two-bedroom cottages on tiny well-kept plots of grass, the cozy town sat east of the city of Whittsburro, which hosted Everdale University, an exclusive private institution known for world-class programs in both music and magic studies. Everything was too perfect, too serene, almost like a 1950s'-era sitcom. Not that she could discuss her observations with anyone.

Since uttering an apology through the door after the mortifying shit incident, Sam had helped her with everything she needed, but refused to say a word to her. Her head ached, and her muscles were already fatigued from the simple task of walking to the car and remaining upright long enough to drive here. She didn't have the emotional or physical bandwidth to handle the silent treatment or an advanced game of charades right now.

A little less than forty-eight hours remained until the seven-day mark when he theorized, before he quit speaking to her, Amber might reappear. Even if Amber showed up, Blue couldn't handle a magic surge of anything close to the one that brought them here. Hell, she couldn't channel enough magic to move herself two feet across the room even if she took all her clothes off to save weight. Meaning they were stuck with each other for at least six more weeks.

"I'm a mess. You are a smart guy. You know we aren't going home this week, right?" He sent a quick, troubled glance in her direction before once again focusing on the road like it held the secrets to the universe. "Come on, Sotach. Talk to me. After everything we have dealt with this week, a little embarrassment has you clamming up?"

An exasperated sigh filled the car like he expected this conversation would happen. She stayed quiet, letting him process the words she could see forming, dying, and reforming on his lips. "I have my reasons."

"Care to share them with the class?"

"I was careless. When I slip up, people leave. The ones who aren't paid to stay or trying to leverage me for some political gain. Every time." He glanced over and read her argumentative expression. "Every time. If you leave, I can't keep you alive. And I don't go home."

"Steaming bullshit."

"I live alone. I rarely speak to anyone except Nisha and Ivan at work. Even my mom only talks to me by video call with the closed-captioning turned on unless it's Christmas."

"That has to suck. I'm sorry."

"I don't want you to be sorry!" Disgruntled exasperation punctuated his words. "I'm sorry." He pointed at his own chest, emphasizing the apology. "Being quiet is how I deal with this."

"This, as in avoiding sudden onset explosive diarrhea? They make a pill for that."

"Oh, for God's sake, are you ever reasonable?"

"As reasonable as the people around me." She looked pointedly around the car.

The conversation appeared to cause him physical pain, and his eyes narrowed. "I lost control in that field and murdered two dozen people with a breath. I almost killed you. You just experienced what happens when I'm careless. And I'm being unreasonable?"

"A little. Yeah. Give yourself a break. The fact that you care so much counts for something."

"I promise you, it won't for long. Experience is the best teacher." He braked a little too hard at a stop sign, slinging them both forward. "Please, just drop it."

The small cottage that would be home for the next few weeks came into view. She pointed a warning finger in his direction. "You will talk to me, eventually. A little diarrhea doesn't scare me. I'm not going anywhere." Other things about him scared her, like the fact he could make her lungs stop working or override her free will, but she would not admit that to him out loud. He would probably go live in a cave if she did.

Sam snorted, a knowing look on his face, and shook his head. Putting his fingers to his lips, he turned an invisible key.

"Fine. Charades, it is." Disappointment laced her words as she turned away, once again wincing at the movement. "I'll deal with it. But for the record, what you are doing is toxic and patronizing."

He mimicked throwing the invisible key over his shoulder and pulled the car to a stop under the attached carport and turned off the engine. He eyed the house like it was a prison where he was about to spend a life sentence.

Giving him a taste of his own medicine, she shot him a bird, then opened the door and climbed out. He understood her charades and returned the gesture.

Trying not to groan in pain, she looked at the tiny old house in front of her. It had green clapboard siding edged in white trim and dark wood shutters and only two doors: front and side. The windows sported thick, wavy glass panels surrounded by layers of scraped-away paint. No doubt the electrical panel held screw-in fuses. Two large trees shaded a backyard that held a workshop larger than the house itself. She hoped it had electricity so she could set up a cot in there.

"Hello, there!" a cheerful voice sang from the driveway next door. She winced and tried to brace herself for social interaction with someone who did not know she was from the future. A woman who didn't look like she had slept in days approached from the neighboring lot with a baby on her hip. She wore green scrubs, her dark brown hair knotted in a frayed ponytail. A teenage boy, with gangly arms and legs that made his stride awkward, followed her at a distance. "I'm Sherry, Sherry Graves, your neighbor. This is my son Ricky. And this little pumpkin is Tiffany." Sherry waved the little girl's hand in Blue's direction, looking at her daughter with absolute adoration.

"Hi, Sherry. Hi, Ricky. I'm..." Blue barely stopped herself from providing the wrong name, "Ivy. I'm Ivy Keys. It's nice to meet you. I just got here."

"The whole town heard about your accident, and I'm glad you are on the mend. You look like you are ready to fall over. So am I, girl. Just got off a double, so I won't keep you. If you need anything at all, just give me a shout." Sherry smiled genuinely, even as her son, already as tall as his mother, hid behind her, looking away nervously.

Blue smiled politely. Sotach wasn't kidding about this place being Mayberry. "That is so kind of you. Please do the same. You know, if you need sugar or any of those things a neighbor might need from another neighbor."

"I will. We are having lasagna tonight. It's leftovers, but the recipe makes enough to feed us for a week, and it gets better if you let it sit overnight. I'll have Ricky bring some over, so you don't have to worry about dinner."

Blue stood, confused. Never had a neighbor offered to bring her dinner, except Mister at the boat dock. But he was Mister. Feeding people was his thing. This was weird. "Oh, you guys don't have to do that."

Ricky rolled his eyes. Sherry graced her son with a look that could kill, and he ran to the house.

"Nonsense. We will be sick of lasagna if we don't get someone else to eat it."

"Well. That's supersweet. I look forward to the lasagna. We are very grateful for your generosity."

"You are very welcome, Ivy." Sherry waved and followed her son to their back door, still smiling, steps heavy with exhaustion.

"See you soon." Blue waved. At least her neighbor would talk to her.

She glared back at the door Sam left open. How did she communicate *Hey asshole, the neighbor is sending over lasagna,* in charades?

26

FINN

The place was swarming with activity, although it was midnight and the FBI arrested most of the Cahlad's staff. The government officials stood out, making the others wandering through the campus even more suspicious.

"White room, Torrin." Nisha huddled in the back seat under a moving blanket, listening to the mental activity around them. "Help me out here."

"Sorry." Forcing himself to stop searching the campus for signs of Agent Richard Mann or Larson Battle, both of whom were on his permanent shit list, he visualized a quiet white room, in his head. Except Larson Battle was in the room with him, and Finn was jamming a knife through the man's skull.

"Oh my God." Nisha sat up, wearing the blanket like a hood, and leaned forward. "You have a very violent brain."

"Can you hear anything over my very violent brain?"

She studied him for a moment before answering. "Zella and Hale are here."

"Where?"

Ravi watched the bustle through the closed gates for a moment. "Larson's there, and it is a trap. He has them in Sam's office. That building, right there." She pointed at the large white marble building that stood behind the ornate cast-iron gates.

Finn mulled over that information. "Battle is holding them near all the federal agents. He's using those agents as a human shield." Knowing Mitch wouldn't abandon his wife or partner or whatever Zella was to him, Larson was a coward to hide behind others like this.

"Not shields. Human sacrifices to make the world see Mitch as a dangerous monster," Nisha corrected him. "Senator Miller was going to put her in a press conference to draw Mitch out. But Larson blackened her eye. Now he's angry at Larson and terrified of Mitch. Dude really hates guys who hit women. But she's fine. We have time."

Finn understood the implications. "Mitch is going to level this place. How do you know she is fine? You said couldn't read Zella."

"I can't. But Hale is loud."

Finn gave her his attention. "How is he?"

Nisha pursed her lips, twitched her nose, and remained silent, which was answer enough. "Hold up, Rambo. They are alive, and Zella is up to something. Let me see if I can establish a rotation or pattern in the guards. Maybe I can find a way in that doesn't involve mass casualties or draw attention to us."

"Fine." He begrudgingly sat back in the seat, hating that her logic was sound. He hated waiting.

She settled back into the floorboard. "White room."

An hour of tense silence passed, with occasional reports of interesting activity or conversations from the back seat. None of it painted a pleasant picture of their odds for getting Zella and Hale out unharmed with the resources they had. His phone dinged from his pocket. Fishing it out, he read the text message illuminating the screen. "Found your sleeping pills."

"Where?" he texted back. That had to mean Trix found Devon.

"Please hold."

"Damn it, Trix." He flipped around in the seat to relay the news before he remembered her magic. She sat in the back seat, upright, uncovered, and alert, looking around them with wild, searching eyes. "What is it?"

She scrambled across the seat and opened the door. "Stay here." Slipping out of the car before he could do a damned thing to stop her, she skulked away and disappeared into the shadows somehow, although she tripped twice before he lost sight of her.

"Ravi. What the hell?" Just when he found five of his people, he lost one. He looked for what drew her away, but the street remained quiet. He slithered out the passenger door and crouched on the sidewalk next to the car to remain out of sight. He listened for a moment. A loud footstep crunched to his right, followed by a muffled curse. Found her.

Staying low, he followed the noise down the street. The woman had many gifts. Stealth was not one of them. Somehow, he still couldn't see her, so he stepped forward carefully, listening for any movement. His knee slammed painfully into... He looked down... nothing. Nothing was there, and nothing hurt like hell. Confused, he put his hands out to inspect the area where his knee had been, feeling the chilly edge of something curved and metal. He shifted farther into the shadows, not letting go of the object he still couldn't see. Between one step and the next, the world in front of his face changed completely. Where there had been an empty street and sidewalk, now sat a black-and-white food truck, bold letters scrawled down the side declaring it Perry's Popcorn Palace. The truck sat half on the street and half on the sidewalk, the rear end facing away from him. A green metal street bench appeared below his hands. Nisha crouched at the other end of the bench, head down and eyes squeezed shut. He stepped to the left. Silent, empty street. He stepped back to the right. Nisha, park bench, and a popcorn food truck. Some kind of cloak or projection surrounded the popcorn truck, making it invisible from a distance of over five feet.

Nisha rose and crept toward the truck, so distracted by whatever or whoever was inside that she didn't hear him sneak up behind her. "What are you doing, Ravi?" He dodged backward as an elbow flew at his face.

"Finn?" Nisha looked furious. "You snuck up on me. I told you to stay in the car."

"Yeah, you did." Finn stood next to her and looked at the van. "Who is in there?"

"I think it's Mitch."

"And you were, what? Just going to sneak up on the most dangerous and emotionally unstable magic user in the world?"

"I wasn't sneaking."

"No, you weren't. But you thought you were."

She glared, looking embarrassed. "We have to get in there. Mitch is losing it." Suddenly alert, her attention returned to the truck. "Damn. Somebody knows I'm here." Her head tilted as if listening to a quiet conversation. "But they don't know about you. Hide."

Finn pulled his weapon and dropped behind the bench. "Where?"

"In the van. I don't recognize them. They are coming. Hide, Finn."

Slinking back into the shadows on the sidewalk, he stood behind a large tree, standing at the edge of a stone fence that rimmed the property behind them. Nisha raised her hands in the air, standing in the open between the bench and the truck as a quiet click reached his ears. The truck rocked slightly, the back door opened, and the barrel of a gun rounded the rear corner and pointed directly at Nisha.

"Kendra?"

A harried and ferocious-looking Kendra stepped slowly around the truck. She appeared unharmed, much to Finn's relief. Stepping closer, she sniffed the air, and a smile broke across her face. "Ravi?" Kendra searched the surrounding darkness, nose twitching. "Where is everyone else?"

"Just Finn and I." Nisha turned toward him, having no trouble picking him out of the darkness, although he stood concealed well enough Kendra still had not seen him and motioned for him to come out. "That's a neat trick. I didn't catch it before. You were drunk or hungover the whole time."

Finn approached slowly as a scowl crossed Kendra's face that turned to guilt when she shifted her eyes to look at him. "What trick?" Was Kendra the person creating this little bubble of altered reality?

Understanding dawned on Nisha's face, and she squirmed. "I'm so sorry, Kendra. I should have put that together."

Kendra remained silent, pinning Nisha with a hard stare.

"Ladies?"

"Hey, boss." Kendra acknowledged him. "Let's get off the street." She stepped back and climbed into the popcorn truck without waiting for them. Nisha climbed in next, and he followed her in. The interior of the truck was dark, and quiet voices reached his ears as he shut the door. Light from a small lantern blinked on and filled the space, revealing a lethal-looking Mitch, leaning against one counter wearing gear Finn recognized from his warehouse, complete with several weapons and a ballistic vest. A duffel bag sat at his feet, contents straining against the zippers.

Harper rested on the floor behind the truck's driver seat, brow furrowed in concentration, body revealing physical strain. Rhodes' dog lay sleeping across her lap. "Look who Kay Kay dragged in. It's wild man and grumpy pants."

"Grumpy pants?" Nisha sent Harper a displeased frown and walked straight at Mitch. "You can't go in there. Larson has set a trap."

"I assumed as much, my dear. I'm not worried." Mitch's face softened slightly, and he squeezed Nisha's arm. "I am very glad to see you safe. Where are Sam and Ivan?" Nisha didn't reply, but Mitch's expression darkened even more as he studied her face.

Finn spoke quietly to Kendra, trying not to interrupt Nisha and Mitch's conversation. "What happened? And why does Mitch have guns instead of artifacts?"

Kendra slid over to stand next to him. "Harper is creating the illusion. She threw something around the Paragon and I at Lilac so the bastards couldn't see us. Zella took two of the darts, but Mitch still took one. He was unconscious. They were inches from us and didn't know it. But they already had Zella and Hale. I confiscated all of his little trinkets before he woke up. He thinks they fell out while I dragged him away. I left the pocket watch."

In front of them, Nisha continued to fill Mitch in on what she learned in the past few hours. Finn studied his employee closely. He hired Kendra as a favor to Blue, although he had no openings at the time and her résumé only listed private security work. One afternoon, running practice drills with Hale's team made it clear that she was more than qualified. Blue and Devon vouched for her, and that was good enough for him. He never suspected she had magic. Herne had a strict policy against hiring magic users because of the company's real purpose: artifact hunting. The artifacts they retrieved would be too tempting for a magic user. They couldn't risk it. "What is your trick, Reyes?"

Kendra looked away. "I detect magic. I smell it."

"Here I figured you just had allergies. The Hounds?" Her documents were fake, devoid of any reference to the military, and fooled Trix. Devon was good at what she did. The military strictly prohibited magic use by forbidding people with magic to even join, and the punishment for breaking the rule was severe. Lifetime imprisonment and death, severe. Did she get caught and needed help?

She nodded. "That's why I didn't complain about the Rhodes' gig. I owed Blue a huge favor. So did Harper, though I didn't know about that or this till today." Kendra waved at Harper on the floor.

"Which branch?"

"It's classified."

"Did Rhodes know?"

"He had no clue."

Wondering who else in his inner circle had secret identities and past lives, he crossed his arms and watched Nisha and Mitch engage in a heated but quiet argument. Lies and manipulation were the reason the Paragon stood here right now, whether he liked it or not. Blue placed two sleeper agents with her ex-boyfriend and accidentally saved the Paragon's life and possibly the magic world as they knew it.

Kendra pinched her nose. "Look at him. He looks like a kid playing with Daddy's toys. He isn't thinking clearly. We don't even know if they are in there. We couldn't track the vans. I've spent the past three hours trying to stall him. This smells bad."

"Ravi has information that might change his mind. You did good. Thank you."

Kendra sighed and looked down at Harper, who remained quiet. "We still clear?"

"Nobody around but us chickens." The dog growled as Harper shifted to a more comfortable position.

"Enough." Mitch spoke loud enough to draw everyone's attention, raising to his full height. He and Nisha stood almost nose to nose, crowding each other's space, the Paragon only taller than his captain by a few inches.

"She did her job, and she would not want you to jeopardize yourself. Respect that." Nisha's voice had gone up.

"I don't care if she thinks she is the Sentinel. Battle has my partner." Mitch leaned down into Nisha's face. The woman didn't even flinch. She stood her ground and leaned closer, eyes narrowing.

"We protect the magic users of this world, and we do that by protecting the reputation and autonomy of the Cahlad. Going in there and slaughtering a few dozen government agents will destroy both things, not just here, but across the world. You won't be allowed to continue as Paragon, which is what Larson wants, so he can step right in. Miller thinks the government will take over. We both know better. Every magic user on the planet has something on the line right now. What do you think the governments of this world will do to us without the Cahlad's protection and governance? How will they exploit us? What will Larson do? This is bigger than you and bigger than Ms. Z." Nisha stepped even closer to the furious man in front of her. "Bottom line, Mitch, you are compromised and unfit to make this decision. As the only remaining member of your cabinet, that means this is my call, and we aren't going in there tonight. Stand down." Nisha's firm words rang out in the small metal box they stood in.

Mitch glowered at Nisha, and a tingle of violent magic energy rippled through the air. Everyone stood in tense silence, watching the two closely. Finn cut his eyes to Kendra, who placed her palm on her weapon, nose wrinkled. She sneezed. He reached for his own weapon, unwilling to stand by and let this man harm anyone in this truck or ruin his chances of getting Hale off that campus alive.

"Get him, Grumpy." Harper cheered and clapped her hands from her spot on the floor. Stunned by the inappropriate outburst, the tension shattered, and they all turned to look at her. An innocent smile decorated her face, an intelligent gleam in her eye.

Nisha stepped away from Mitch and clasped her hands behind her back, where they shivered. Hell, Finn was shaking, and he hadn't been the target of Mitch's ire.

Kendra sniffled. "That took guts." He wasn't sure if she referred to Nisha or Harper.

Finn stepped forward so that he stood next to Nisha. Kendra followed him, standing on the other side. "My team is regrouping. We will have more intel, equipment, and men soon. Zella will be fine at least until Miller's next press conference. I agree with Ravi, and Herne will follow her lead on this."

"Give it up, sugar. You know they are right." Harper stood from the floor cradling the dog in her arms and moving to lean on the counter next to Mitch. She placed a sleeping Lady Lucille in his arms. Surprised, the man almost fumbled the animal, causing another growl. "I love your big loud heart, Fuzzy Bear, but I need you to let your brain talk for a minute." Harper tapped Mitch's temple gently. "Why is this one on Stalker Prime? She is young. They all are." Harper nodded at Nisha, a knowing look on her face. "I know why you haven't killed us yet. You aren't the complete piece of shit we all thought you were. But why are you surrounded by babies instead of a bunch of politically connected gray-hairs?"

Gears turned in Mitch's head as he took a deep breath. "Zella. She picked them. All of them. Put three files on my desk and walked away."

"The lady who sees the future and knows you best wanted this one to have your ear." Harper tapped her chin and cut her eyes in an over-the-top, curious expression. "I wonder why?"

As Mitch pondered Harper's words, Finn leaned closer to Nisha and Kendra. "What is the Sentinel?"

Nisha hesitated, glancing back and forth between him and Mitch. "Paragon's personal bodyguard. Everyone thinks Mitch refused to fill the position. And he did. So Zella kind of took it."

"His wife, that little lady, is his personal bodyguard?" Kendra's tone reflected this new information impressed her. "Sneaky."

"She isn't his wife." Nisha corrected him on this subject for the second time since he met her. Why were they so insistent that Zella was not Mitch's wife? Was it this Sentinel thing?

The Paragon remained silent for a moment, stroking the dog behind the ears. The hum of magic in the room faded, and Kendra stopped sneezing. He glared down at Harper. "How did I get stuck with you?"

"That would be my girl, Blue. Otherwise, I would waste away in one of your two-star holding facilities and would not be here to salvage your image or save your ass." Harper winked. "You should thank her the next time you see her."

Mitch made a face like something tasted bad and focused his attention on Nisha. "Z is okay? You are sure?"

Nisha nodded. "Sleeping right now. Miller sent food. Hale is watching her. She knows something, but she is calm. Mitch, they trained her for this."

Frustration marring his face, the Paragon nodded. He looked at Finn. "Let's go meet your people. I want Z out of there."

27

DEVON

Devon arranged the disorganized paperwork decorating Mr. Robert's desk into a neat pile, then thought better of it and scattered them again. A neat stack would look out of place in this office. She sat down on the laminated top corner of his gray metal desk, taking in her surroundings. Seven Points Memorial Chapel was a dump. Wallpaper peeled off the walls. Everything held a yellowed, aged hue. The furniture looked like the rejects you found next to the dumpsters behind a Goodwill. The sign out front said "Buy One, Get One Free." That should tell anyone passing by everything they needed to know about this place.

The building had no security. It took her less than thirty seconds to get through the lock on the back door. The computer took her less than a minute to crack and held nothing of interest, unless a lonely man's porn habit floated your boat. According to the papers stacked haphazardly on the desk, Mr. Robert had not had a client in over two weeks. He had no regular full-time or part-time employees. From her quick perusal of his effects, he had no family, either, and called a temp service to staff the chapel in the event someone was desperate enough to use his services. He lived in a small, sad apartment over the business's four-bay garage that contained a hearse and an old Mustang convertible. She almost felt sorry for the guy. There was probably a reason he wanted someone to shoot him.

Satisfied she found everything useful, she stepped away silently, making her way out of the office, down the dismal hallway to the back door, which she shut and locked behind her.

Across the small parking lot, Ben stood in the garage's doorway, arms crossed, brows drawn together, watching her as she walked toward him. He was still trying to decide if he trusted her. She could tell by the look on his face. It did not appear his inner monologue argued in her favor. She had a feeling she wasn't what he expected.

He wasn't what she expected, either. The guy was an average size and didn't look like a gym rat. But he just dead-lifted Greenlee, a man most people described as a Viking for obvious reasons and hauled him up a flight of steps without breaking a sweat. And, oh yeah, he fed on people's souls. "Get inside. We don't want to push our luck."

He stepped back into the dark garage quickly. "You didn't have much trouble with that lock."

Devon stepped inside and shut the door, stopping to let her eyes adjust to the dark. "Dad taught me. We can hole up here for a while without being bothered. Nobody will miss this guy. Even dead people don't want to come here." Finally able to see in the dim light, she found the stairs and started climbing to the apartment.

Ben made a noise that she couldn't interpret but followed her. "Ava told me you were a college professor."

Devon smiled as she reached the door at the top of the stairs. "She also told you I am a member of the Hounds of Dawn? And who my dad was?" She opened the door and stepped inside, glancing around. Ben brought the supplies they bought at a local pharmacy up the stairs while she checked the business. The bags sat on the small, green Formica table in the middle of the kitchen. Through a door to the right, Greenlee lay sprawled on a small double bed with scratchy blue blankets. His face looked peaceful, but he was disturbingly pale and still.

"She did." Ben followed her into the room and shut the door. He moved to the table and started opening bags. "But you don't look like a criminal."

"Ouch. I prefer vigilante. Or champion of the oppressed. Either way, the good criminals never look like criminals. No reason to make our lives harder than they have to be." She walked over to the small desk next to the bathroom door and picked up the ancient laptop sitting on top. She flipped it open and typed in the date she found on Mr. Robert's phone. He was a Pisces and took himself out to dinner for his birthday at a place called Calloway's every year. The computer came to life, and she moved toward the table. Ben's eyebrows rose to his hairline again. Her father's voice whispered in the back of her mind. *There are more important things than right and wrong. Do what you have to do to stay alive, Esdevona. Worry about being a good person tomorrow."* She smiled at Ben and settled into a chair. "Does that bother you?"

"Just trying to get a handle on who and what I'm dealing with. I feel like we have established a solid, judgment-free zone in the past few hours." Ben plopped a plastic cup of purple liquid decorated with a bendy straw on the table in front of her. She squinted at her purloined computer and ignored the drink. A medicine cup of clear liquid and a handful of vitamins and supplements hit the desk next to her. "Drink that. Take those. Then go take a nap."

"I need to find Lexi." Devon ignored him and focused on her task. "I'll be fine."

"Devon. You are falling over. I can't do much with what we have." Ben sat across from her at the small dining table and pulled the laptop through the scattered bags to his side. The window air conditioner hummed above the kitchen sink. Since this was Tennessee, it swapped from heat to cool and blasted them with air. "You need to hydrate. And you need to rest."

"Don't you have another patient to bother? I can't sleep when my kid is missing." Devon snatched the glass up and sucked down the grape-flavored electrolyte drink as fast as she could so he would leave her alone. There was no way she could sleep. Her mind dwelled on the fact her daughter was missing, again, and Greenlee suffered from extreme magic poisoning. She couldn't think about Blue. Every time she did, she choked on the frog in her throat.

"He listens much better than you do." Ben hit her with that intense observing gaze again, then glanced at the laptop as she glared at him. Seeming to come to a decision, he didn't argue with her. He must be used to difficult patients. "Thirty minutes. Then rest." He shoved the laptop back her way and poured more purple fluid into her cup. "And drink this while you work."

Disgruntled by the last statement, she set about conducting her searches without leaving a trail. Ben stayed quiet, but he glanced at the clock every few minutes. He was actually timing her.

Finally, the silence got to her. She was making progress in her search, but she couldn't think in the quiet. Her house was loud. Her life was loud. Her people were loud. She wasn't used to quiet. "Ben? How do you know?"

Glancing at the clock again, he looked her way. "Know what?"

Devon stopped typing and looked at his chest instead of his eyes, uncomfortable with the topic she was about to bring up. "The people you fed on. How do you know they will be all right?" His body language didn't change, so she assumed the question didn't offend him.

Sounding philosophical, Ben sat back in the chair, almost slumping, and extended a leg, putting one hand over the other on his chest. "I've found human souls are like human livers. Astoundingly resilient until they are completely poisoned."

Devon considered his answer. "How did you eat before all of this, when you aren't running for your life?"

"I work in a hospital. Nobody thinks twice about a person having a bad day or two when they are already sick."

"Makes sense." Devon nodded and went back to typing on her computer. "Thanks for explaining."

"No problem. Nobody has ever asked before." He seemed flattered. "Find anything?"

"I think I have. Dick Mann's official report states he saw both Finn and Nisha in the hospital prior to the code silver but after the code gray." Devon pushed the laptop away and scrubbed at her straining eyes. She missed her glasses. "Larson didn't flambé them when your shield closed like I feared. Now I wait and see where they pop up."

"The girls?"

"Nothing. I saw them leave Ben. You knocked the last fireball out of the sky, and Rhodes flew them away. They made it. But he has gone full silent. There isn't a trace of them anywhere. I even searched for gigantic-bird sightings. Nothing."

Ben mulled over the information as he sipped on a can of energy drink. "Dick man?"

"It's what Blue calls this FBI agent that gave us some trouble. His name is Richard Mann. Raving case of LDS. Nolan Miller's lackey."

She resumed her search. She had a few more tricks up her sleeve to find the digital bread crumbs people left behind, but she had to be careful not to leave any of her own. Clicking on the link to open a new browser window, she furrowed her brow when a text editor application popped up. She closed it. Maybe Ben was right, and she needed more rest. She tried again, clicking the browser icon only to have the text editor open. "What in the blazes?"

Letters slowly blinked onto the screen inside the editor. "Hello, darling.,"

She sat in shocked silence for a moment. She was routing this connection through so many endpoints, nobody should be able to get to this machine. This person had skills, which meant they already knew where she was. And they wanted her to know they were watching. Pursing her lips, she typed back. "Who dis?"

"Silly Rabbit."

"Ben?" She turned the screen so that he could see the words. "What do you make of this? Does it mean anything to you?"

Ben leaned forward and studied the messages. "Trix are for kids?"

"What?"

"It's Finn's guy. The one named Trix that wouldn't come out of his computer sanctum when the Paragon was there."

"Are you sure?" Devon chewed her lip, hands hovering over the keyboard.

"No." Ben leaned over, watching the screen and her response. "Do you want to run?"

"Not really."

He shrugged and nodded toward the screen.

Lowering her fingers to the keys, she prayed she wasn't leading the Sovereign right to them. In the text editor, she typed "walk round about an oak" and waited. Ben closed one eye and lifted an eyebrow.

"*The Merry Wives of Windsor*? Herne's oak? No Shakespeare in med school?" He just shook his head as letters appeared on the next line: "Hold please."

"That's him." Ben smiled for the first time since she met him.

"What do we do?" She looked through the cracked door into the apartment's bedroom where Greenlee slept peacefully, face still pale and cheeks gaunt.

"We hold." He took the laptop out of her hands and pointed at the bedroom. "Sleep."

She was 90 percent certain that she could trust Ben. She looked at the laptop, then back at the door to the apartment, feeling uncomfortable sleeping with so many unknowns hanging over their heads.

"Greenlee and Lexi need you to be one hundred percent. Nobody is getting in here."

Devon's eyes narrowed. How dare he guilt her into taking care of herself? Even Blue knew better than that, and the woman had a death wish. But he was right. If everything went sideways again, she needed to have her full magic arsenal at her disposal. "Dirty."

"The truth often is. Did it work?"

"Yes." She stalked to the bedroom. "Keep him safe while I'm asleep."

Ben nodded and turned his chair toward the apartment door so his back was facing her. Devon wrinkled her nose and let out a breath. Where did Greenlee find this guy? She closed the door and climbed into the sliver of space left in the small bed and cuddled up next to Greenlee, knowing she couldn't sleep. But she could close her eyes and recuperate. The bed wasn't terrible, and Greenlee was warm. Sleep took her in less than five minutes.

28

FINN

Kendra lounged on the couch peacefully gazing at the ceiling, nose twitching constantly. She didn't suffer from debilitating allergies. The magic in the room overwhelmed her, which explained why she excelled at locating artifacts once their investigations led them to the general area. Kendra held Lady Lucille stretched down her chest, the dog's graying face nuzzled under her chin, relaxing after several hours of keeping the Paragon from getting himself killed or killing a few dozen federal agents. They needed to discuss her secret identity and magic, but he wasn't sure what to say. It was all immaterial. Her job was safe, and she proved her loyalty and competence over the past twenty-four hours.

The remains of a large bag of chicken biscuits decorated the center of the ancient metal desk Mitch sat behind, leaning over the notebook Zella gave Nisha before she left for Denver. The man was barely holding it together and needed something to keep his mind busy. Zella's journal would have him running in mental circles for days.

Harper sat atop the desk, legs crossed, gazing down at the book. Nisha sat backward on a rolling stool, leaning over the seat back, also studying the book intently. Their heads almost touched as they mulled over each passage in the journal.

Finding Mitch, Kendra, and Harper in a food truck called Perry's Popcorn Palace, after reading a passage about a secret popcorn castle, cemented the fact the journal held more than gibberish. It still held the predictions of the most accurate oracle in the Cahlad's recent history, but it held them in a code that only she understood. Deciphering the messages before the predicted events was the challenge.

"One more time, what did Zella write while Mitch was making the video?" Finn picked at the flaky crust of his biscuit.

"The hounds of dawn in blues of bell. Wild children war upon the dell. Roar of brothers. Seven and seven. Vortex cross a violet heaven. Splintered time. Forged love. Staunch Friend. Together stand or all will end." Kendra recited the words for the third time in ten minutes and ran a soothing hand down Lady Lucille's back when the dog growled at the disturbance. "Then she drew some mountains and a Colorado flag. "

"The Hounds of Dawn were on the scene, and there were blue flowers everywhere." Nisha rubbed at her eyes. "The portal was violet around the edges. That one is us, yesterday. What does the rest of it mean?"

"I don't know, but it sounds ominous," Kendra mused.

"What about this one?" Harper tapped the journal. "Dark the harbor to soar round noon. Alight the Zenith by feral tune. Defy the dark and teach them, child. Everlasting hearts and sevens wild."

"Makes as much sense as the rest of it." Mitch placed his head in his hands and leaned on the desk, obviously frustrated and struggling to sit still in the office of the tiny car repair shop Finn commandeered as his new temporary headquarters last night.

"But it says 'Zenith' right there. Must be Rhodes or Blue or Ivan? You said they were all lethal little child soldiers the Cahlad made. They were all also on the scene yesterday."

"They were not child soldiers." Mitch leaned over and read the passage Harper pointed to again.

"Really?" Kendra turned her head just enough to glare at the Paragon. "How old were they during training? Were they old enough to vote? Could they even drive before you sent them on their first missions?"

Mitch lifted his head and met her gaze. "Really? Major? You want to discuss ethics? You think I don't know who you are? We have been looking for you since the government lost you."

"I know." Kendra looked back up at the ceiling. "I could smell you coming. Good thing the Hounds hid me where you would never think to look for me."

"We didn't want to arrest you." Nisha glanced up quickly. "We could use your talents."

"I don't hunt my own kind. And I don't weaponize children. No thanks."

Harper tapped the journal. "Anyway. The can of peaches she drew next to this one about the Zenith is nice. The shading is phenomenal" She ran her hand over the paper again. "I have a feeling about this one."

"I think we should focus on the 'all will end' part of the other one." Kendra continued to stare at the ceiling.

Nisha sent a quick, concerned glance his way. Finn sighed and rubbed his eyes. They weren't getting anywhere except aggravated. Information trickled in from Trix slowly. The order to regroup went out to his men an hour ago. They would gather whom they could and attempt an extraction later tonight.

T: *So sad about Uncle Windsor*

Me: *?*

T: *Overdosed on sleeping pills.*

Me: *Sorry to hear that.*

T: *Service at Seven Points Memorial Chapel.*

"I have something. Let's go." Finn stood and moved toward the door.

"He found them?" Nisha slammed the journal closed and snatched the bag of biscuits off the desk, no doubt ready to get out of the uncomfortable conversation between Mitch and Kendra. She whipped around and pointed at Kendra. "No. We all go. We stay together."

"Bossy." Kendra sat up, cradling the spoiled dog like a baby. "Where are we going, boss?"

"To introduce Mitch to the remaining members of the Hounds of Dawn and hope they like him more than you do."

29

DEVON

"Tomato soup or chicken noodle?" Ben sat at the tiny dining table holding a steaming bowl of soup wrapped in potholders, in each hand.

"Oh, tomato soup, I haven't had that in years." Still groggy from her second forced nap, Devon eyed the bowl he slid in front of her with apprehension and closed the lid of the laptop. The clock read noon, yet she had no desire to eat lunch or much of anything else but tried it since Ben was nice enough to keep offering her food. Stirring the creamy substance and inhaling the aroma, she listened for any noise from the bedroom that remained troublingly quiet.

"Thank you."

"Don't thank me. You haven't been able to eat anything I've made." Ben stirred his own soup and poked at floating chunks of chicken with his spoon.

"It's not a reflection on your microwaving skills, my stomach is just unhappy." Mulling her current situation, she took small, careful sips of the soup. Ben, the soul eater, now held a starring role in her nightmares. Ben, the doctor, and dad reminded her slightly of Blue, hurting and worried, yet still putting the people around him first and making sure they were cared for. His dedication to monitoring Greenlee's condition sealed the deal. He was genuinely concerned, and not just because Greenlee would help him find his daughter. She no longer feared him and considered him an almost friend instead of an ally of necessity. "You aren't bad, Ben. My friend Blue told me that the end of the world was the best time to make a new friend. I think she was right."

"That woman is a little strange." Ben swirled his spoon in his food. "Was strange. I talked to her for five minutes. She was nice. I'm sorry about what happened."

"Maybe they got out. She's lived through crazier things." Forcing a smile, she continued eating, unable to say more, yet still determined to hold it together. Other than her scary new friend, she was alone in this, and falling apart didn't keep her alive or find Lexi. Her insides shook with a persistent urge to steal a car from downstairs and try to find her daughter. Having no plan and no guarantee that either Greenlee or Lexi were going to be okay drove her insane.

A firm knock on the door to their hidden apartment echoed through the space, pausing Devon's spoon midway to her mouth. Neither of them heard anyone come up the stairs. Ben's eyes erupted in flames as he set his spoon down, sloshing soup onto the table and stood, shifting into the frightening predator mode she witnessed in the hospital and moving toward the door. Grabbing his arm before he could get there, she nodded toward the bedroom where Greenlee slept, completely vulnerable and relying on them to keep him alive. "I'll get it. Greenlee needs a doctor. If they get through me, you know, avenge me by eating their souls with a side of nice chianti."

Ben frowned, a puzzled expression on his face that morphed into surprised amusement. "I'm kind of full."

"Oh, aren't you a funny one?" Devon moved toward the knocking as Ben stepped into the bedroom, leaving the door open slightly so that he could hear anything that transpired with their unannounced guest. The entry door lacked a peephole since it led to an interior stairway only accessible from the chapel's garage.

Pulling enough magic to handle a few immediate threats while still heeding Ben's advice, she placed her hand on the knob, opening the door a fraction of an inch. Peering through the gap, a familiar face gazed back. "Dev?"

"Finn?"

Not waiting for her answer, her brother-in-law shoved the door open and wrapped her in a bear hug that crushed her ribs and stole her breath. "Are you okay?"

"I am." Devon squeezed his neck as tight as she could, relieved to see him with her own eyes and relaxing just slightly for the first time since the Sovereign sideswiped their camper on the secluded road in Colorado. "Thanks for the assist."

"Anytime. Lexi?"

"She made it. We don't know where she is." Devon's voice broke as she looked over Finn's shoulder. Four people stood regarding her uncertainly on the small platform at the top of the stairs. Two she knew personally; the other, everyone on the planet would recognize. "Get in here and shut the door, you crazy people. He can't be in the open."

At Devon's invitation, Kendra walked in first, inspecting the space, nose twitching. She peeked out of the window. "Still no unexpected magic. Ravi?"

Nisha Ravi remained on the stoop, waiting for Mitch Collins, decked out in some kind of SWAT gear and Harper cradling the elderly dog from Rhodes' house to file inside before she joined them. "We are clear for the moment."

"Ben, it's Finn and Nisha!" Devon leaned into Finn and let him take her weight. Relief that he was alive, and she had help, swept through her, taking the nervous energy with it, leaving her suddenly drained. This reminded her of the hug they shared at the tiny apartment in front of her strange new roommates and a three-month-old Lexi when he finally tracked her down following his brother's death.

Ben opened the door and stepped out, wearing a genuine smile, her own relief mirrored on his face. "Man, I'm glad to see you guys."

"Hey, Dr. Chuthulu." Nisha took a seat next to Harper on the small couch and scratched the dog's ears.

"Greenlee?" Finn looked past Ben at the still body lying on the small bed. "Did he level that clearing? It looked like a large bomb went off."

Ben closed the door and stepped into the room with them, crossing his arms over his chest and taking on his doctor personae. "He did. He shouldn't be alive. I'm doing what I can with what I have, which isn't much. Luckily, he's just tough as hell."

Finn took a deep breath and tugged her toward the table. Once they sat down, she got a closer look at his face. Dark bags rimmed eyes that were full of grief and worry. The same shroud of dejection loomed over the others, even the perpetually upbeat Harper. "What else has happened?"

"The Sovereign raided Lilac, shot one of my men, took Zella and Hale. They are alive for now. But..." Finn trailed off, leaning over in the chair, placing his elbows on his knees, and allowing his head to hang.

Her stomach sank. "What about everyone else? Tell me they turned up."

Nisha shook her head and answered before Finn could reply, her tone lost and angry. "Nothing. I tried to hear them when I got to the scene. It was loud, but I know Sam's voice. Ivan's, too. I didn't hear them." Devon's heart ached with shared sorrow. Sam spoke highly and often of Nisha during their brief time together, making it obvious they were close.

As a hush fell over the room, the relief of finding one another vanished. Devon's chest grew tight, knowing none of them were out of the woods yet. Nisha cradled her head like she was in pain, prompting Mitch to sit on the arm of the couch and squeeze her shoulder reassuringly.

Finn raised his head. "Were you listening to our conversation with Sam before all hell broke loose?"

"Yes. We all were." Devon glared at Mitch, remembering the look on Blue's face when he implied she should just assassinate a US senator. Just like he sent her to kill Devon's dad. The man loved sending other people to do his dirty work, and she hated his guts. But she loathed Larson more, and Mitch Collins could defeat the bastard.

"Good. The objectives haven't changed. Publicly reestablishing Mitch's control of the Cahlad to prevent challenges and keep Ava out of Larson's hands. How do we do that?"

"The objective has changed. We will still keep Ava safe and hopefully find your daughter." Mitch addressed Ben and Devon as he stood and began pacing. "But we must get Zella out. If I make a stand publicly, he will use her as a bargaining chip immediately. I will not trade her life or well-being for any job or perceived power. I won't do it."

Devon watched the man pace, frustration building. What a selfish bastard. "If Larson or anyone aligned with him gains control of the Cahlad, you are trading the life and well-being of every magic user on this planet, including Zella's."

"Listen to the ladies, Fuzzy Bear. They both speak the truth." Harper's voice was subdued as she scratched Lady Lucille's exposed belly.

"You don't understand." Mitch stopped and faced her, voice raw, looking as on edge as she was. How dare he say she didn't understand?

Emotions boiling over, Devon jumped up and flung the door to the bedroom open and pointed at the motionless body of the man she loved more than anyone except Lexi. "Don't I?" she sneered at the Paragon, voice low with hatred and fury. "He's mine, and Larson might take him from me yet. My daughter is missing. So is Ben's. Missing. My best friend is dead. I haven't seen my dad in twenty years because you tried to have him killed. Larson murdered my husband and experimented on my son until he died on your watch. I understand losing people, Paragon. I understand the stakes. You, however, are just now realizing what reality is like for the rest of us." The tickling sensation of her hair floating above her head alerted her to magic she didn't even realize she had drawn. Her eyes narrowed on Mitch Collins, who still commanded the room, even whining and crying while the world fell apart around him. She wanted badly to put him to sleep forever. Nisha lifted her head and sent an icy stare in Devon's direction, reaching to her hip where Devon knew she had a firearm. Itching for a fight, Devon's lip twisted. "Try me."

Her words caught Finn's attention, and his hand drifted toward his own weapon.

"Devon," Ben warned, even though his reaction communicated he agreed with every word. "You aren't well yet. Don't make yourself sick because of him."

The emotions that played across Mitch's face almost broke through her anger. Quietly, he uttered words that threw cold water on her fury and doused her magic. "I'm so sorry, child. I truly am. He took my daughter that day, too."

30

NISHA

The raw sensations rolling off Finn's sister-in-law scorched ravines across Nisha's mind. Tidal waves of fierce love, crushing grief, paralyzing guilt, and genuine empathy crashed into her. The woman was a roller coaster of violent emotion. She didn't want to shoot her, but if she tried to kill Mitch, Nisha would have to.

Devon's face crumpled when Mitch mentioned his own daughter, but her resentment remained. "I'm sorry for your loss. But at least you didn't have to hide yourself or your grief to keep your freedom."

Mitch's jaw tensed and the man she believed could handle anything broke in front of her eyes. Genuine sorrow and regret twisted his face as he clutched his ever-present pocket watch that pulsed each time she tried to reach into his mind and came away with nothing of sustenance. "You have no idea what I hide."

Mitch's words swept across every person in the room, resulting in a dizzying volley of sensations that translated into spikes of pressure radiating through her skull. Finn and Devon were the only people who trusted each other. Everyone weighed their choices. The already small room grew more crowded as troubling thoughts poured from its occupants. Everything was falling apart.

"Please." Her voice was weak and desperate, but they had to stop. "Let's get this out there. Very few people in this room like Mitch."

She looked up at her unknowing attackers through watery eyes. No one tried to contradict her statement. "I get it." She pointed at Devon. "He tried to have your father killed." She turned to face Kendra, Harper, and Ben. "He leads an organization that forced you to live in hiding your whole life. He didn't fix it when he could have."

Looking each one of them in the eye, she did something she made a point to never do. She reminded them they couldn't hide from her. "But don't forget, I see all of you. All of you. Everything." She tapped her head. "None of us are innocent."

Nisha looked at Ben and held his gaze without flinching. "Everyone here is hiding something. Let's clear the air."

"You first." A *Hell no* rang through his head, unwilling to trust Mitch with their theory about Amber.

She could start if it corralled the roiling emotions in the room. "At the bird attack, a woman appeared out of nowhere and dropped a USB drive. Sam looked at the contents. The Cahlad ran an experimental, top-secret breeding program to create superpowerful Sovaj by exposing the mothers to a dangerous artifact called the Son Sovaj. They called it Project Zenith. Only seven of the babies lived: Ivan,

Rhodes, Sam, Blue, and Mitch's adopted daughter Amber are five of the seven. His signature is at the bottom of all the paper files."

"Whoa," Ben huffed. Harper and Kendra stared with their mouths hanging open. Finn's face remained impassive, but he had questions.

"Excuse me?" Devon deflated visibly with a gasp. "I don't understand. I don't like you, but I never took you for Mengele evil."

Mitch held his ground, a haunted look on his face. "Why do you think I challenged Paragon Johansen for control of the Cahlad?"

Devon shrugged. "I don't know. But it usually revolves around ego, power, and money."

"Professor O'Neal." Mitch used Devon's professional title, causing her to start and narrow her eyes. "Your specialty is magical studies, so I am sure you know that powerful artifact users and eventually Sovaj struggled well before your father went rogue and drew the general populace into it. They had to stay hidden to some extent for centuries even before the Sovaj Registration Act, especially under the previous Paragon, because he conscripted so many into Cahlad service if he deemed their talents either dangerous or beneficial to his needs."

"I read some journals, but they are nothing more than academic speculation. The Cahlad is a secretive organization, and its inner workings remain a mystery to those on the outside."

"Well, I was fortunate. My parents advised me not to share the full extent of my magical abilities. Zella was not as fortunate, and Johansen conscripted her into the Stalker units as a teenager and assigned her to the North American Conclave with express instructions to report back to him anything deemed a threat to his authority. I was a clerk in the North American artifact registry, identifying and documenting discovered artifacts. They did not know I could use them all as well. That's where I met Z. We started dating, and she told me about her terrible visions of Project Zenith. By the time we found it, many had died."

Mitch paused and turned from the others to look at her, letting graphic images of the scene he encountered when he toured the Zenith laboratories flood his brain. She flinched, unable to stop the onslaught of Mitch's motives and actions even as he continued to speak. His signatures in the red files were to shut the project down. "Johansen did and sanctioned terrible things, including imprisoning and killing anyone who showed the inclination or ability to pose a viable challenge for Paragon. He had to go. That left me. No one else was willing or able. I never wanted to kill anyone or carry the responsibility of this office."

Finn sat back in his chair abruptly, mind racing.

Pieces of Mitch's long-buried truth fell together in her mind, and the results stunned her.

Ben rubbed his chin in contemplation. "That is messed up. But let's back up. You can identify artifacts?"

"Any artifact." Mitch nodded. "And use them. Fireballs are not always the solution."

Ben hesitated for a moment, then breezed past Devon into the bedroom, emerging moments later with a clear hospital bag filled with random items. "Tell us what these do." He emptied the bag of items Greenlee had in his pockets onto the small table at the center of the room.

The sudden change in topic surprised Mitch, but he approached the table and picked up a blue-and-white marble. His eyes grew wide as he picked up piece after piece, then looked at Ben with suspicious wonder. "These are masterpieces. Did they come from the same place? Such a wide range." When no one answered, Mitch drew his own conclusion. "This level of quality would require a craftsman to specialize in one type of magic for a lifetime. There must be two dozen types of magic here. This is extraordinary. Where did you get them?"

Ben glanced at Nisha with a questioning gaze. She nodded, only to have him decide her loyalties remained with Mitch and turned to Devon for reassurance. Devon also nodded reluctantly. "That guy did." Ben motioned toward the bedroom.

Mitch wandered toward the room only to have a militant Devon block his path with her body. He stood mere feet from her. "Magic poisoning, dear?"

"Don't call me dear." She glared, squaring her stance, hesitant to let Mitch near a man who was an unregistered Sovaj, just like her father. There was no malice in her action. Only trepidation. Ben and Finn shared a look and approached the standoff cautiously, not having the insight Nisha did into Devon's motivations.

"Devon." Nisha waited for the woman to look at her. "I know you don't know me, but Finn trusts me, and I hope that counts for something. Mitch won't hurt him. I promise."

"You were fine with shooting me earlier." Squinting in discontent, Devon pushed on her nose as if adjusting an invisible pair of glasses. "What do you think, Finn?"

"The enemy of my enemy."

Devon mulled over his words, then stepped to the side.

Mitch walked in first, followed by everyone but Harper and Kendra, who remained on the couch in the living room. Lady Lucille stretched between them. Nisha took her first close look at Greenlee since he dashed past her, carrying Devon into the safety of Ben's soul-fueled shield. His condition was concerning, and she couldn't hear anything happening in his head. He irritated her, but she hated to see him like this.

Mitch held his hands over Greenlee's head, then hovered above his arms. "These piercings. Even the tattoos are magical. They are amazing. There must be fifteen different magics here. He's not tough, Dr. Hughes. He channeled the magic through all these artifacts."

Mitch looked at Devon in wonder. "He can use multiple artifacts at once?"

Devon shifted from side to side before nodding slowly.

"Any artifact?"

"Yes." The admission pained her, and she leaned into Finn's side.

"That's"—Mitch gazed down at the unconscious man, his mind racing through possibilities—"unheard of. It's amazing."

"Mitch also has natural healing magic," Nisha said. "He might be able to help."

Mitch's brow furrowed, less than eager to use his magic reserves for this purpose when he wanted to go find Zella, but he didn't outright refuse. His hesitation was clear as his hands hovered over Greenlee's arm.

Devon looked up at Finn, seeking support and confirmation, unable to trust someone once affiliated with Larson Battle, a man who caused so much destruction in her life.

Finn wrapped his arm around his sister-in-law, a hard professional mask falling over his face to address the Paragon. "You do whatever you have to and bring Greenlee back to us, and I will get your not-wife back home. Deal?"

"That is acceptable, Mr. Torrin." A request from Mitch to bring him a chair from the kitchen crossed her brain.

Nisha brought Mitch a chair so he could settle comfortably next to his patient, pocket watch glowing as Devon crawled into the bed next to Greenlee and laid her head on his chest.

Nisha heard the steady beating of his heart through Devon's thoughts. Her head spun, although the emotional turmoil in the room decreased. The revelations of the past fifteen minutes would be hard to process from a single point of view, much less seven. Finn stopped her when she did not notice he was waiting at the door, by grabbing her arm. "I am going to call in my men and take Kendra to gather equipment from Lilac. Can you keep this location secure? Text me if you detect anything?"

"I've got this. Mitch and Ben are here, too." She blew out a harsh breath, looking up into sharp eyes shielding a brain that doubted her abilities. She missed Sam's unwavering faith. A sharp pang of pain, regret, and resentment sliced through her chest. "She is safe. Get out of here."

31

BLUE

MAY 2. THIRTY-FIVE YEARS AGO

The house was perfectly silent except for the low hum of the refrigerator in the kitchen filtering through the wall. But something woke her up, causing the hair on the back of her neck and her arms to stand up. Sitting up, she stifled a curse because everything still hurt. She would never take being able to do something as simple as sitting up without pain for granted ever again. Her eyes adjusted to the light as she crept down the hall and slipped through the living room, where Sam slept on the couch, and into the kitchen. She half expected to find Amber lurking somewhere with a knife, ready to finish the job. But the house was empty. She grabbed herself a glass of water and ambled back into the living room, where she found Sam sitting up, looking cranky. It was impossible to spend any time on that couch and not be cranky. He stared at her in accusation.

"Thought I heard something. Go back to sleep."

Frowning, he perked up, listening for anything out of the ordinary. He stood and pointed into the kitchen with a question. The asshole still wasn't speaking to her. "Yeah. In there."

He wandered into the kitchen, looking around. She rolled her eyes and waited for him to agree with her. He turned and shrugged, shuffling back to the couch. "Great talk, Lurch. Good night again."

"You made it." A weak voice in the dark caused them both to start. Blue hurled the glass of water at the voice, and it bounced off the window above the sink, shattering and falling to the counter and floor.

A second later, a form materialized in front of the sink and yipped when their hand landed on a sharp shard of glass. Just as quickly, the person faded out of existence.

Blue shook her head to clear it. Maybe she wasn't awake yet. She glanced back at Sam. "You see that?" He nodded but didn't look like he trusted his eyes, either.

Amber blipped into existence again. "Amber?"

The figure peered around with caution, holding a bleeding hand close to her chest. She nodded, and she finally looked up. "Wait here. Sevens."

"Are Devon and Greenlee safe?" Blue took a step but remembered the broken shards of glass on the floor and stopped. "Lexi?"

Amber blipped again and shook her head. "Too many jumps out."

"It's a yes-or-no question." Blue wrinkled her nose in disgust.

"Sorry." Amber blipped out of existence. They waited in silence for a few moments, but it was clear Amber wasn't returning.

"We are so screwed." She didn't yet have enough magic to pull them through another jump like the one that brought them here. But Amber should have more control of her own jumps than she just displayed.

The light flipped on, and Sam stood at the edge of the kitchen, shoving shoes on his feet, eyeing the glass. Walking to the utility closet, he fished out a broom.

She looked around for her own shoes. "It's my mess. I'll get it." He just shook his head and shooed her away.

"Fine." She shuffled to the couch and flopped down on the hideous, lumpy torture device. She could take the couch if he cleaned up the glass. She didn't hang over the edges and wasn't getting more sleep tonight, anyway.

MONDAY 9:00 AM

***

Songs of monsters scrape the toes
Craft new hope with former foes
Truth of matters
Peanut butter taste good on crackers

***

32

DEVON

A frustrated huff drew Devon's attention to a scowling Paragon, who cradled his pocket watch between Greenlee's hand and his own. A soft golden glow pulsed between their joined palms. He had grown uneasy and gruff over the past hour, rejecting all of Devon's attempts at conversation in favor of brooding. Standing, he leaned over Greenlee and lifted an eyelid, unhappy about something. His hands roamed, hovering over each piercing and tattoo before settling over his left ear. He removed one stud from the ear and placed his artifact against Greenlee's skin again. His face shifted to alarm. "The damage has set in. We have to move faster."

Devon shifted upright from where she was laying with her head on Greenlee's chest, slightly alarmed by the Paragon's sudden announcement. "Don't say that. You've only been at it for an hour. Ben said he was stable."

With a look that said she didn't know what she was talking about, Mitch stomped into the combo living and dining area where Harper and Nisha sifted through social media and news sites for any mention of another magic surge or a giant-bird spotting.

"Diva." She searched Greenlee's face for what sent Mitch storming out. He lay perfectly still, but his cheeks now appeared rosy as opposed to the ashen pallor of the past few hours. Something was working.

Moments later, Mitch stomped back in, carrying the reassembled bag of artifacts they left on the dining table earlier. Fishing through the bag, he produced the small white-and-blue marble he was so enthralled with. "Let's see if this helps." Mitch's features smoothed, and his eyes glazed over as he settled back into his seat, grasping Greenlee's hand once again, trapping the marble between them. "Much better. There it is."

Devon relaxed, placing her head back on Greenlee's chest only to have his body seize so violently, she almost fell to the floor, shuddering in a rattling breath. Eyes rolling behind his eyelids, his hands and arms swung with ferocious momentum. Mitch tightened his grip on Greenlee's hand, using both of his to keep the arm steady while Devon dodged a fist. "What's happening?"

Mitch met her gaze, unphased. "This is good. It looks bad. But don't worry." His voice was gentle even as he struggled to maintain control of his patient's hand. "Step away so you don't get hit, dear. He is quite strong."

She reached forward to use her own magic to calm Greenlee, but he was still unconscious, and it would do no good. Instead, she dove off the bed and backed toward the wall, staring at the thrashing body on the bed. "Ben!"

Ben appeared in the door so quickly, he bounced off of the doorframe, eyes flaming, and stance defensive. Taking in the scene in front of him, the flames disappeared, and he rushed in, snatching a flashlight from the bedside table. "Arcana seizure?" He pulled Greenlee's eyelids open and shined the light in his face. Tossing the flashlight aside, he grabbed Greenlee's flailing wrist and started taking a pulse.

Beads of sweat rolled down Mitch's face as he used his body weight to keep the artifact in contact with both of them. He nodded with a grunt.

"I didn't realize he was this bad." Ben shifted from taking a pulse to holding the flailing arm down. "His pulse is still strong."

"The artifacts hid it." Mitch closed his eyes, straining. "They kept him alive, but he couldn't heal. One of them was blocking my magic."

Nisha burst into the room, face etched with concern. "Mitch?"

"I'm fine, dear."

Devon had never heard of an arcana seizure. This looked like a bad thing. She didn't care what Mitch said. "Ben?" Stepping closer to the bed, she peered around Ben's back to where Greenlee lay, both flushed and pale, still jerking violently.

"Hang tight. His body is purging the toxins." Ben kept looking down. "This is good. Most people don't survive long enough to have one." He looked across the bed at Mitch. "Can you hold him?"

Mitch nodded, lips now twisting into a grimace. "I've got him."

"This does not look good!" Devon jabbed her finger at the bed, panic ripping through her body and causing her hands to shake. "What happens if you don't have him?" Everyone remained silent, but Devon didn't miss the concerned glance that Nisha sent in Ben's direction. Devon tried to shoulder her way into an unoccupied space next to the bed, but Ben moved his body to block her path.

Her hair floated above her head, and a fresh wave of nausea came with it. She didn't want to kill these people, but if whatever Mitch had done to Greenlee ended up killing him, she would end him and anyone who got in her way. "So help me God."

An agonized wail erupted from Greenlee's twisted face, ripping through the room with an eerie and menacing echo. His body went rigid, and his eyes flew open as the sound still rushed from his lips.

Nisha screamed in fright, jumping backward, clutching her hands over her heart.

"Holy hell!" Ben ducked, gray mist erupting from his feet.

Even Mitch looked disturbed by the outburst. Devon was too furious to feel frightened.

Mitch's shoulders slumped, and the man fell back in the chair behind him as Greenlee's body relaxed, eyes focusing on Ben's face. "Ben?" He looked around with anxious eyes, taking in Mitch slumped in the chair and Nisha with a hand still over her heart, trying to calm her breath. "Where is Dev?"

"She's good, man." Ben mirrored Nisha's pose, trying to catch his breath, the hairs on the back of his neck still standing.

"Right here." Devon knocked Ben aside and sat on the edge of the bed. Greenlee tried to reach for her face, but his hand faltered and collapsed, so Devon grabbed his hand and placed it next to her cheek. "I never thought I'd see you again." His eyes closed in relief. "Lexi?"

"She flew away, *cariño*. We don't know where she is, but she escaped."

"Blue?"

"Nothing yet."

A long silence followed. The menacing aura of his scream left the room as everyone caught their breaths, and Greenlee opened his eyes again. "I love you, Dev."

Blinking, Devon patted his hand. "I love you, too. Don't scare me like that again."

"You are telling me not to scare you?" Lifting an eyebrow, his face held a touch of humor. His voice did not. "After that stunt you pulled? I thought they shot you full of holes and you were dying, and I couldn't get to you."

"And you just took a decade off my life with that seizure, and I had to stand and pray that rotten turd hole would save you." She pointed at Mitch. "I think we are even."

"Not even close." His expression turned mulish as he stared her down, and she understood where Lexi got it from. "Did you say turd hole?"

"Awww." Harper stuck her head in the door, looking around as everyone loitered. "That is going to be spectacular make-up sex."

"There is something wrong with that woman." Mitch slumped in the chair, now with his eyes closed.

"If you ever get around to having any." Harper cackled on her way to the kitchen.

33

DEVON

Devon set another hot bowl of tomato soup on the table in front of Greenlee. "Thanks. I haven't had this in a while. A decade?"

She watched as he carried on an animated conversation about the intricacies of artifact craftsmanship with the Paragon. He sat at the table littered with trinkets and toys, freshly showered and ready to polish off his fourth bowl of soup, which meant he felt much better than she did, because she hadn't managed more than a bite or two since they left the hospital. Ben observed them both closely, having banned Devon and Greenlee from using magic for the foreseeable future and strongly implying that Mitch should take it easy as well.

The shock and terror of witnessing her first and hopefully last arcana seizure, and having Ben explain the clinical details of how close Greenlee came to the point of no return, left her emotions raw, and she wiped at her eyes as tears leaked out for no reason at all. She apologized to Greenlee for getting irritated when he almost died. She also needed to thank the Paragon, but she couldn't bring herself to do it. The scales still didn't seem balanced after his actions ran her father, the crazy, flawed man that he was, out of her life and drove everyone she loved into hiding.

Currently, Greenlee and Mitch discussed using hair and nail tissue from magic users he collected over the years as the base for some artifacts. Picturing his workshop, the idea of stumbling across boxes of hair and nail clippings made her shudder. Her life was strange. Moments like this reminded her of that fact.

Mitch, though fatigued, enthusiastically peppered Greenlee with questions about each item he inspected, the two of them nerding out between bowls of soup while everyone else tuned out the technical conversation. Not wanting to intrude, she stepped away, intending to join Nisha and Harper on the sofa, where they played a game of Jenga on the coffee table, only to have Greenlee catch her by the wrist and pull her down to sit across his lap. Beaming at her, he wrapped both arms around her waist and settled in. "My timing is terrible. But I meant what I said in that field. I was going to ask you to marry me the day everything went to hell." He beamed up at her. "Lexi liked the ring."

Kissing the top of his head, she laid her cheek against his hair, still wet from the shower, and threw her own arm across his shoulders, happy he finally figured it out even if he skipped a few steps. That was his way. She also wasn't surprised that her daughter was in on it and did not say a word. Those two were as thick as thieves. "I'm not saying no. But should we go on a date first?"

"That's what Blue said." His smile faded when he mentioned their friend, and he studied her face. "Now, fill me in. What happened? The last thing I remember is eating dirt."

They looked around the room at their strange allies. It wasn't the first time she and Greenlee teamed up with strangers to deal with the machinations of Larson Battle. That man needed to die. "Well, that purple portal landed us just outside of Nashville. Rhodes flew away with the girls. You and Ben bought him the time. We don't know where he went after the portal closed."

Greenlee chewed on his bottom lip, head bobbing in a way that meant he was puzzling out a problem, and a brilliant or insane solution would emerge shortly. Knowing he could process multiple trains of thought at a time, she continued. "Ben and I busted you out of the hospital. Where on earth did you find him? He's terrifying." She shook her head to clear it. "Larson's goons captured Zella and Hale. Now he has leverage over Mitch. Finn took Kendra to see what gear they could salvage from his warehouse so they can raid the Cahlad."

"Raid the Cahlad?" Greenlee snorted, then looked around the table. He sobered quickly.

"It was the deal. He gets Zella; Mitch heals you. Then we go get the girls." Devon sent a pointed look in Mitch's direction, even though she suspected he would have healed Greenlee, eventually. Mitch had the decency to look embarrassed.

"Larson is there?" Greenlee turned to Ben for confirmation. Ben gave a grim nod of his head, more familiar than the rest of them with the sheer amount of power Battle could throw around. "He doesn't stand a chance."

"He has a pretty good plan." Nisha stood, abandoning the Jenga contest and coming to lean on the counter behind Mitch. "Small team. Covert in and out. This is one of his team's specialties. The mysterious Trix already has complete schematics on the building."

Mitch's head snapped up, and he craned his neck to look at Nisha. "That isn't possible."

"They are accurate."

Mitch turned around and shook his head.

Greenlee's head still bobbed. "Finns got it, then. If Dr. Chuthulu will lift my restrictions, I might be able to locate Lexi. I could use some solid food. I'm still starving." Sifting through the items on the table with his free hand, he pulled out a wireless earbud, cracking it open to reveal a tiny silver bead. "Lexi has the top half of this bead." He tilted his head. "If she kept my shield necklace."

Everyone turned to Ben, who was torn between finding his daughter and keeping his healed patient healthy. "Explain it. How much magic does it take?"

"Does it matter?" The question stunned and irritated Greenlee.

"Yes." Ben and Devon answered emphatically together.

"Can anyone else use it?" Harper joined them in the kitchen, taking a place against the counter next to Nisha.

Greenlee's head bobbed again as he considered Harper's words. "I think so. Anybody with magic can use it. You need someone with a lot of power. It is also delicate and requires intense concentration.

This one is advanced. Mitch could manage it if he had anything left after taking care of me. Maybe Ben. I don't think the rest of you can control it. No offense."

"None taken." Nisha shrugged, unconcerned.

"If you can describe the mechanics, I will be more than happy to help." Mitch extended his hand, taking the bead that Greenlee placed in it and holding it up to his face for closer inspection. "We need to get you back to your kids."

The many faces of Mitch Collins were giving her whiplash. She wanted to hate him, but all she could manage now, sitting in Greenlee's lap, listening to a voice she wasn't sure she would ever hear again while he offered to help find her daughter, was general annoyance.

"It will show you the immediate area around the bead. You might get audio, maybe not."

"A basic scry?" Mitch rubbed the bead between the palms of his hands and focused on a spot on the wall behind Devon's head, eyes going glassy, rimmed in a faint golden glow. "It feels like more."

"It is." Greenlee leaned forward and stilled the Paragon's hands, directing him to open them so that the bead lay in his upright palm. "Hold it so that you can see it. What makes this special is it will pulse coordinates for the other half of the bead. It's Morse code, so it takes a while. I tried to make it talk, but never got that part right."

A swell of pride surged through her chest as Nisha and Mitch appeared gobsmacked by the capabilities of his craftsmanship. Take that, elitist Cahlad snobs.

"What?" Greenlee looked between them with concern, misinterpreting their silence. "It works. I promise."

"When we are done, I want to know everything." Mitch held the bead up again. "You have an amazing gift."

"When we are done." Ben leaned forward, out of patience. "Can we get on with it? Do you have enough magic left to use that thing?"

"Just try to keep the noise down." Mitch's eyes glazed over again as he stared vacantly at the wall. Everyone fell silent, watching as his eyes moved but never focused, muscles twitching in his forehead. "I see a table?"

Greenlee rubbed a distracted hand up and down her arm as Ben leaned forward practically laying on the table, eyes glued to the Paragon. "It has cans. Beanie weenies? And peaches?"

The bead on Mitch's hand flashed quickly. "Somebody write this down. That's a dot." Greenlee pointed at Nisha and Harper. "Hurry."

Nisha ignored Greenlee's request, closing her eyes, and clutching the edge of the counter. "I see it. It is peaches."

Harper scrambled into the living area and rifled through the drawer of the small writing desk next to the bathroom door. "Got it." She lifted a pen and a cube of Post-it notes from the desk and raced back in time to catch another longer flash of the bead.

"Thats a dash. They should come faster now if he locked on."

"Good." Mitch paused, eyes jerking. "There is a person in a flannel shirt, but I cannot see their face. They are sitting at the table. Are those cards?" The bead continued to pulse, and Harper scribbled the dots and dashes.

"Almost a royal flush. Hearts. That seven was bad luck." Nisha and Mitch sat for another moment, silent and watching. She placed a calming hand on Greenlee's bouncing knee. She didn't care about cards, either. This made little sense.

"I can't hear anything." Mitch frowned. "Nisha?"

"No. I can't hear, either. Whoa!" Nisha started and leaned back, almost losing her footing. "Who is that?"

Devon bit her lip, dying to demand details but afraid to break Mitch's concentration. Ben's hand wrapped around her forearm, his face conveying he experienced the same conflict.

"That is Rhodes Westridge, the way God made him. A striking young man, but he always wanted to make himself look different." Ben squeezed her arm, and she couldn't help but smile at him as they waited for more details. Lexi was with Rhodes and not the Sovereign.

"I wouldn't say striking. He is creepy. No wonder he changes things up." Nisha shuddered. Mitch jerked his head, and Nisha flinched. "I think he saw us?"

"The other bead will pulse, too." Greenlee nodded, excitement lacing his tone.

"Not very stealthy, Thor." Harper hyper-focused on the pulsing of the bead in Mitch's hand, pencil scribbling.

"If you can do better, go for it."

Mitch scowled off into space. "Quiet!"

Nisha frowned. "He is holding the necklace."

Pencil poised over her stack of Post-its, Harper cocked her head to the side. "It stopped flashing, Fuzzy Bear. Is something wrong?"

Mitch shook his head. "No. It feels the same. I'm just..." Mitch's eyes focused, and he dropped the bead like a hot potato. He lunged from the chair and crashed backward, barely stopping before flattening Nisha, whose eyes flew wide open on a gasp and landed on the Paragon warily. He rounded on her once he regained his balance. "Did you see that?"

Ben jumped from his seat. "What is happening?"

Terror ripping through her chest, Devon crawled out of Greenlee's lap and clutched Mitch's arm to get his attention. Harper backed into the living room to avoid the flailing bodies. "What did you see?"

Nisha held out her hands in a calming gesture. "Mitch. I can explain."

Greenlee also stood. "Somebody talk to us."

Mitch's nostrils flared, and his hands clenched into fists like he struggled to control himself. "Was that Amber? Am I seeing things? Who did I just see?"

Nisha stepped forward and took Mitch's other arm, pulling it away from the pocket that housed his pocket watch. "That is Ben's daughter Ava." She sent Devon a pleading look.

But Devon did not know what to do. Blue gave her the basics of her time at the Cahlad. She suspected he just saw his dead daughter. No wonder he was upset. "Come on. Sit down." Devon used her best mom voice, recognizing Nisha did not want Mitch to access his artifact, no doubt seeing some scary intent in his head, so she tugged on the man and pushed him down into the chair as he huffed air in and out of his nostrils like an angry bull. She filled a glass of water and placed it in his free hand. "There you go."

Ben looked hopefully from Nisha to Mitch, not caring in the slightest that the Paragon was one second away from losing it. "You found Ava? Did she look hurt?" He circled the table, crowding their space.

Nisha's focus remained on Mitch. "She looked good, Ben. But we need to tell Mitch what we suspect."

"Your daughter?" Mitch looked at Ben in disbelief, then back to Nisha with a hint of betrayal lacing his words. "You knew about this?"

Nisha took a seat next to Mitch at the table, still holding his arm. "I have a theory. Ben? Tell him your story, and I'll fill in what I know."

Greenlee tugged Devon toward the couch where Harper hovered, clutching the stack of Post-it notes as Nisha and Ben spoke to the shell-shocked Paragon. "That's going to take a while. Trust me." He took the papers from Harper's hands. "What did we get?"

Devon grabbed the laptop Mr. Robert loaned her and entered a search for Morse code charts. "Do you know Morse code?"

Greenlee sent her a crooked smile. "Nope. But you got it."

She converted the dots and dashes to numbers and started to type the coordinates into the search bar but stopped herself. Only three people had seen them so far. "We need a map or an atlas. I don't want it to be in digital format."

They all looked around the small space, finding more board games, a few mystery novels scattered among a library of westerns, and a coloring book, but no atlas.

Harper winked at them with a devilish smile. "You guys take a minute. I'll go look in the cars downstairs. My daddy always kept an atlas in the car." She hurried from the room, leaving them standing in the middle of the living room with coordinates but no safe way to get to them, even if they figured out where they were since they still didn't know how the Sovereign were tracking them.

"I need a Greenlee hug."

He opened his arms.

Devon stepped into Greenlee's outstretched arms and put her forehead to his chest, letting loose everything that had bounced around her mind since he woke up. "If Blue were here, she could go right to them. Everything would be fine." Devon stopped and shook her head. "That sounded horrible. I mean, it would be fine because she was alive. And Ivan. He was so nice and good with Lexi. Sam was even growing on me that last day. I have to tell you about the deal Lexi conned him into."

"Did Blue ever tell you about the dragons?"

Devon frowned at the strange comment. "No. What dragons?"

"Were there dragons at that portal I missed?"

"No."

He squeezed and rested his chin on the top of her head. "Just have faith. She was gone for days the last time, remember? Then, poof, she found us, and we weren't even friends yet. She will find us again."

How did he know about the dragons when she didn't? What else were they keeping from her? "How can you be so sure?"

"Dragons."

Devon groaned in frustration, still staring at the blue cotton of his shirt. "Later with the dragons. How do we get to Lexi? I want her with me."

"I know. But she might be safer where she is. She's eating peaches and playing cards with a Zenith as her personal bodyguard. People in imminent danger don't play cards around a dinner table."

They couldn't teleport unless Greenlee had a stash of Blue's hair or nails somewhere. But a portal could work. "Larson said he only needed pieces of us. If I brought you a piece of the person who opened that portal for him, what could you do with it?"

"Ew." His chin bobbed as he processed her question. "You want me to make a portal to Lexi and Ava? Maybe. Yeah. I'll try. Depends on how the magic naturally works."

"I have an idea, then." Devon stood on her tiptoes and gave him a quick kiss. She had body parts to locate and steal. "I'll be right back. I love you. Eat your soup."

"Nope. Someone else can do it." Greenlee's arms didn't budge. He pulled her chin up so he could look at her face again. "Have you slept? Did Ben feed you anything? You look awful, baby."

"You are so lucky I love you."

34

BLUE

MAY 30. THIRTY-FIVE YEARS AGO

True to his word, Sam had yet to speak a single word to her and avoided any situation that required conversation. He stayed at work well into the evening and rarely made it home before she was sound asleep. They both tried sleeping on the horrible, lumpy couch the first few days in the house and agreed to have mercy on each other and just share the bed. Occasionally, he woke her when he climbed into bed but said nothing. When she woke up at a ridiculously early hour to get to school before the first buses arrived, he still slept peacefully laying diagonally since it was a full six inches too short for him. Otherwise, she wouldn't know he even lived here.

Contemplating whether she had enough energy to bother with dinner, she stared at the color-coded Tupperware containers filled with takeout from her favorite restaurants from all over the world. Her containers had blue lids. The ones she left for Sam were red. Only one of his remained. Her stack contained three. They were out of milk. She rarely went to the grocery store. When she did, she often suffered anxiety or a full-fledged panic attack. Tilting her head, it reminded her how much she had relied on Devon to provide milk for her weird cereal habit. She missed her friend. Standing in the open door of the fridge, she turned her head to the cabinet, thinking maybe she could eat some cereal dry. Opening that door, she found it virtually empty, only holding a large tin of coffee and a stack of filters. Coffee sounded good. Starting a pot, she sat on the counter while she waited and went over tomorrow's schedule. Three periods had tests, and a pep rally would interrupt afternoon classes. Even if she was experiencing high school for the first time as an adult, it was still interesting. But she was thinking she hadn't missed much. Coffee brewed, she filled a mug and settled on the living room rug in front of the insufferable sofa for another night of watching first-run eighties' television classics by herself.

Midway through an episode of *Dynasty*, a strong rap on the door startled her, causing her to spill some of her second cup of coffee. Frowning at the darkness outside, she wracked her brain for any reason someone would knock on her door at ten o'clock on a Thursday night. Another rap jarred her into action, standing from the table and moving to the door to push aside the curtain covering the window. Ricky, the neighbor's son, stood on the stoop, shoulders hunched, clutching his little sister to his chest, eyeing the street in front of the house with apprehension. "Ricky?" She yanked the door open and motioned for the boy to come inside. "What's wrong, buddy?"

"Ms. Keys?" Ricky shifted from side to side, adjusting his semi-sleeping sister in his grip. The little girl who looked to be around one year old was cranky and disheveled, as if she had just woke from a deep sleep. "Um. Can we come inside for a minute?" He looked back over his shoulder toward his house, where the lights were still on, and a strange truck sat in the driveway. Blue's hackles went up.

"Of course." Blue reached for Tiffany and slipped the diaper bag off Ricky's shoulder. The little girl peered at her with suspicion, looking to her brother for confirmation that this new person passed muster. Blue rocked instinctively, years of practiced movements from Lexi's early years taking over.

"Th-thanks." Ricky looked around the house and twisted his hands together. Blue recognized a person on edge and scared. Ricky was both. "Um. Yeah. Thanks."

"What's going on, Ricky?" Blue moved into the living room, knowing he would follow her. "Where's your mom?" Motioning for him to sit on the couch, she sat in the recliner and rocked to calm a fussing Tiffany.

"Well, her ex-boyfriend is here. That's Tiffany's dad. She's trying to get him to leave. He, um, doesn't live with us, but he comes around sometimes. At least this time he didn't bring his friends." Ricky sat on the couch but didn't lean back, perching on the edge and eyeing the door like the boogeyman stood on the other side.

A belligerent voice, loud enough to pierce the walls and closed doors of her house, reached their ears, causing Ricky to flinch and turn wide eyes toward his house. "Your mom is there by herself? Did she call the police before she sent you over here?"

"No. It makes him worse. She told me to go out the window. I think he's drunk." Ricky nodded his head, eyes growing wide when another shout rang out outside. "He's not nice."

Patting Tiffany's back, she listened to the growing ruckus outside and weighed her options. "You did good, Ricky. You are safe here." She needed to figure out a way to get over there if the guy was as "nice" as Ricky said he was, but she couldn't leave the kids. Walking to the phone on the wall, she picked it up and dialed the police first. Convincing the dispatcher that she was not in immediate danger, but her neighbor was, they allowed her to disconnect. The yowling outside continued, seeming to grow closer. Ricky sat on the couch, stiff as a board.

He flinched again as the yelling outside turned into a roar, and glass shattering filled the air.

"Hang tight, kiddo." Tiffany snored on her shoulder, oblivious to the drama happening around her.

"You in there? You got my kid?" The man's voice now came from the other side of her kitchen door.

The loud bang of metal against metal thundered through the house. Tiffany stirred, and Blue bounced to keep her calm. "Son of a bitch." The man hit her door again.

"Ms. Keys?" Ricky turned wide, frightened eyes her way. Sherry's lack of involvement in the situation set off alarm bells. She needed to check on her.

"Come out here and talk to me." Another bang echoed through the kitchen, causing her to seethe. This man did not know what kind of person stood on the other side of the door. But she would be happy to show him.

Walking over, she pulled aside the curtain to the door's half window and peered out at the glazed eyes of a large man wearing a threadbare T-shirt and a trucker hat. A tire iron dangled from his right hand. How had Sherry ended up with this goon? "Leave. Now."

"That's my kid, bitch. What are you doing with my kid?" The angry man slammed his free hand into the glass, all semblance of reason leaving his face. This man was drunk and stoned out of his mind.

"I'm babysitting. Please leave." Blue dropped the curtain and stepped back, familiar with the problem that stood on the other side of the door. A few of the people the Hounds helped over the years were involved in domestics, usually being blackmailed by a partner who lorded their unregistered Sovaj status over them to keep them in line. Cracking her neck, she bounced Tiffany one more time.

"Ricky? Take Tiffany into the bathroom and lock it." The boy flew to his feet and took his little sister, hands shaking as he sent terrified glances at the door. "Go now, and don't come out until I get you." Ricky nodded and ran through the tiny house, clutching the baby to his chest. As the crowbar shattered the window, the bathroom door slammed. Blue stepped back to avoid the glass and waited for the fool on her doorstep to dig himself further into the hole. His second strike obliterated most of the glass, leaving only jagged shards jutting from the edges and tore down the curtain. "Please leave." She watched the man's face turn red when his insane behavior failed to scare her.

"Bitch. Give me my daughter." His words slurred as he reached in through the window to unlock the door, and she pounced. Grabbing his wrist, she yanked to one side and down, slicing his inner arm on a wicked-looking piece of glass. Sirens wailed in the distance, almost drowned out by the man's anguished screams. Blood poured down the bottom half of the door from his wounds as she raked his arm across the bottom and back up the other side, dragging another horrified scream from her visitor. Yanking him forward, she pulled down once again as he lost his balance, dropping his chest across the jagged glass on the bottom of the window frame, a piece breaking off and remaining wedged in his body. Blood spurted from the arm wound, splattering the side of the cabinet and the kitchen sink. Satisfied the injury would incapacitate him until the police got there, she shoved him back through the window and watched as he fell backward off the stoop into a heap in the middle of the carport. Writhing on the ground, he clutched his arm. Blue lights reflected off the windows of the other houses on the street as porch lights flicked on, and neighbors peeked through blinds. If the man got lucky, the cops could call for an ambulance before he bled out. She would not help him.

Careful to avoid the river of blood now covering her kitchen floor, she backed into the hallway and knocked on the bathroom door.

"Ricky? It's Ms. Keys. The bad man won't bother you anymore. I'm going to check on your mom. Stay put." Walking out, she gave the writhing Billy Bob a wide berth and moved toward Sherry's house as the first police cruiser arrived. A tall man with sandy-brown hair and fierce brown eyes got out. A muffled cry from inside the house had them both running. "Stay there." He drew his weapon, slowing to a fast walk, and entered the house. Deciding not to provoke a guy with a gun today, she stood in the front yard where she had a fantastic view of Sherry's busted front window and could monitor the man bleeding all over her driveway. Another cruiser pulled up, this one with two officers. One went into Sherry's house, and the other checked on Billy Bob and called in a medical emergency. Moments later, Sherry, eye black and lip busted, dashed out, followed by the first officer. "Ivy? Where are the kids? He locked me in the laundry room. He said he was going to take Tiffany." Sherry's voice bordered between a scream and a sob as she sprinted toward Blue's house and stopped dead in her tracks to avoid Billy Bob, arm now in a tourniquet, who still cursed up a storm in the driveway. "Oh my God! What happened?"

"The kids are fine. Ricky is a rock star. But that guy is clumsy." Blue pointed at Billy Bob. The officer standing behind her neighbor and wearing a name tag that read R. Miller 5693, raised an incredulous eyebrow her way, but he said nothing, surprising her. Her experience with law enforcement of any sort never left the warm fuzzies or the impression they were useful for anything more than paperwork. "Let's get the kids. I think I have some plywood in the workshop. We can get your window fixed. The sheriff's department was nice enough to salvage our belongings from the wreck. I'm sure they will help a single mother and her neighbor board up a window." She pegged R. Miller 5693 with a meaningful look and put her arm around Sherry.

He narrowed his eyes but nodded. "We will be happy to help." Freaking Mayberry.

35

SAM

MAY 30. THIRTY-FIVE YEARS AGO

Pulling into his quiet and dark neighborhood, Sam wondered what goodness he would find in the red-lidded Tupperware that Blue left for him when he got home. It only took him a few days to figure out her color-coding system, and every night a new dish waited for him. Over the past few weeks, those little containers of deliciousness had become the highlight of his otherwise isolated and boring day. He needed to thank her for leaving them, but they had not crossed paths awake since the day Amber made her brief appearance.

Choosing to eat his lunch and dinner in his office to avoid potentially disastrous social interactions, coupled with working well into the night meant he rarely spoke to anyone. No one questioned his hours. As the director and de facto principal researcher of an underfunded research center, he had more work to do than one person could accomplish in a lifetime. He spent most of his days and nights focusing on the extensive and disorganized mountain of information about obscure magic lore and artifacts his new position gave him access to. The university housed records from rich and ancient sources even the Cahlad's extensive collections did not contain. He suspected most of them were illegally obtained. So many tomes and crates filled the storage rooms of the research wing, he could never read them all in the short time they were here, but he tried.

On the rare occasions he emerged from his office, everyone in the department sent him odd glances. But his interpretation of a few carefully chosen untranslated ancient texts and glyphs in just the short time he had been here took care of any objection they had to his lack of social skills. His secondary magic ability to read any written word gave him an unfair advantage over the faculty in other sections and gave them yet another reason not to like him.

Perhaps the measures he took were extreme, but he couldn't risk saying the wrong thing to someone and drawing attention to his magic. He and Blue landed in the thick of a post-Mullet Roane world, complete with heavy-handed enforcement of the Sovaj Registration Act and a nationwide ten-year anniversary celebration of the thing getting underway in just two months. The Sovaj scare and the beginnings of the Magical Resistance were happening right now. If he slipped up, he could wind up incarcerated or worse, making it very difficult to get back home.

Only three weeks remained until the seven-week mark, when Amber should show up to help them get back to where they belonged.

A small calendar on his desk counted the days. As solitary as his life was before he landed here, the past four weeks had driven him almost insane. He missed one-sided conversations and movie nights even if Nisha and Ivan made him watch those terrible rom-coms. He would never complain about their movie selection again. The reminder of Ivan turned his mood dark, and it grew even darker wondering what was happening with Nisha and Mitch while he was stuck here hiding. What would he be returning home to? So many things could happen in a month. Frustration and guilt for leaving them to deal with the Sovereign and government permeated every minute of his day.

Noticing the light on under the carport, he frowned. Blue rarely left the outdoor lights on. He slammed on the brakes at the end of his driveway because he couldn't go any farther. Reflective police tape circled the entire covered parking area. Jumping out of the car, he rushed forward, trying to identify the large, dark spot in the middle of the drive with trails of droplets leading up to the dented side door. Realizing it was blood, and the door now held a square of plywood instead of glass, he ducked under the tape and raced up the stoop, fumbling with the key.

Things had been so quiet here. He grew complacent, thinking the worst thing that could happen was alienating Blue so much she refused to take him home or slipping up and violating the SRA. Now a million scenarios raced through his mind, none of them good, and every single one could have been avoided if he were here.

Ramming the key into the lock, he shoved the door open and flipped on the lights. "Blue!"

Blood splattered the kitchen cabinets, and some spots still stained the grout between the tile. The scent of cleaner hit his nose. "Please be here." Sam shut the door and locked it. Racing into the living room, he looked for any reason a spray of blood decorated his door and cabinets. He didn't find anything. The house remained silent, and nothing else looked disturbed. The blood could be the aftermath of a Cahlad raid. Stalker arrests in this time frame were notoriously violent. He needed to get some gear and get out of here. They might watch the house, and standard protocol required interviewing immediate family members of the unregistered. They might have a sniffer. Those were also common among the Stalker units of this time period. If they did, they would know before they knocked on the door what he was, and if they took him into custody, there was no way he could find Blue and break her loose and get them home.

"What?" The person he wanted to see climbed out of the recliner in the corner of the living room and stumbled his way, wrapped in a quilt, eyes still closed. "I asked you to leave, Billy Bob. Don't test me again. I need my sleep, you redneck asshole."

Rushing forward with a wave of tangible relief, he grabbed her shoulders and opened his mouth to ask what happened when he caught a left hook to his nose. Slamming his hand over his face with a groan, he stepped away and sputtered, "What was that for?"

Completely opening one eye and shaking her hand, Blue clutched the quilt tighter and squinted in confusion. "Sam? What are you doing here?"

"I live here."

She peered at him, one eye still closed. "Shush. You are going to wake the kids."

He pointed at the blood splatters and stains. "What the hell happened? Are you all right? What kids?"

"Oh. Sorry." She shrugged sheepishly. "I'll clean that up in the morning. By the time we got the windows boarded up and the cops left, it was so late, I just wanted to go to sleep. Don't worry about it. I got all the glass up. Your feet are safe."

Wiping the blood, now dripping down his nose and into his beard, away with his wrist, he pointed toward the mess next to the door. "That's blood."

"Noses bleed. I'll get you some ice for that. But seriously, keep it down. It took us forever to get Tiffany back to sleep." Not fully awake or present, her eyes drifted closed, and she shuffled to the freezer, dragging her quilt behind her like a cape. Opening the door, she squinted with one eye again. "Peas?" She offered him a bag of frozen food, which he took begrudgingly. Confused by his reaction, she shook her head to clear it. "What am I doing?" Shuffling across the floor, she held the quilt together with one hand and reached up with the other, pinching the bridge of his nose gently between her fingers.

Despite the immediate relief from the wave of warm healing magic spreading through his face, his voice was still nasally. "Tell me what happened here."

"So bossy." Blue scrunched her nose and huffed. "The neighbor's drunk ex-boyfriend showed up and caused some trouble." Turning her back, she hit the light switch, throwing them into shadows and shuffled back into the living room. "Ricky grabbed the baby and brought her over. Billy Bob wasn't far behind, so I had the kids hide in the bathroom and asked him politely to leave. Twice." She held up a hand with two fingers raised, still walking away from him. Reaching the couch, she flopped onto the lumpy cushions and somehow rolled farther into the quilt, covering her head. Voice muffled, she continued. "He took a crowbar to our window and reached inside to unlock the door. Asshole almost cut his arm off on the broken glass. Sherry and the kids are in our room. You take the recliner."

"Is he going to live? That is a ton of blood." He eyed the recliner. Could he sleep in it? It had to be better than the couch.

"So talkative tonight. Go away."

Standing in the doorway, staring at the lump under the blankets, he prayed for patience. "Why didn't you call me?"

"Why would I call you? I handled it." She rolled and snuggled farther into the blanket burrito, feet covered in fuzzy socks now sticking out and hanging over the arm of the couch.

He peeled the blanket away from her face. "I thought something happened to you. The front stoop is covered in blood."

"I see how that would pose a problem for you. Don't worry, Sotach. I'm hard to kill." Tone frosty and face unreadable, her hand shot out, yanking the quilt from his hand, tucking it back over her face. "Your conduit home is just fine."

"That's not what I meant. And you know it."

"Whatever." Her hand extended from a crease in the quilt, and the middle finger rose slowly. "Let's go back to charades."

"You are mad."

"I'm tired."

"And mad." He sat on the edge of the couch and watched the hand disappear into the lump of blankets, wondering if he should risk saying anything else.

The lump adjusted, trying to find a comfortable spot facing away from him. "Fuck off, Lurch."

36

NISHA

"This one doesn't have toes, sugar." Harper peered into a plastic bag containing a dismembered leg collected from the scene of what the media had dubbed "Nova-nado." "No toe. No toenails."

Nisha looked away from her own bag, which contained a torso. "That thing is hairy. Grab the leg hair. Maybe that will work."

They stood inside the cold-storage room of the regional forensics lab where the non-magic authorities sent the bodies and random body parts collected from the decimated field. They each carried an unconventional tool kit of nail clippers, tweezers, scissors, a marker, and two boxes of quart-sized freezer bags. Opting for stealth, when Greenlee asked her to run this unorthodox errand to keep Devon from doing it, she chose not to involve anyone else. Only she and Harper had the privilege of standing in the institutional room, surrounded by dismembered bodies, freezing their asses off. Harper generated an illusion around them to prevent anyone, including the cameras, from seeing them. Nisha kept a mental ear out for anyone approaching the room. The tactic worked well, allowing them over an hour to collect enough samples to fill a small backpack and not leave a swath of bodies and destruction in their wake.

"Leg hair, it is." Harper leaned over the leg, wielding her tweezers like a weapon, humming a tune as she plucked several hairs from the leg and placed them inside a bag.

Nisha had to suppress a giggle when she recognized the song. "Is that 'Puttin' on the Ritz'?"

Still humming, Harper sealed her bag so no one would know they had been there. Nisha jumped sky-high when Harper howled out a garbled and high-pitched "Puttin' on the Ritz," just like the monster from the movie.

Nisha shook with laughter, wiping her eyes as Harper did a little tap dance to the side. "Oh, my God. I needed that."

"I adore *Young Frankenstein*." Harper dropped her bag of leg hair into the backpack and looked around, placing a hand on her hip, and blowing a blonde lock of hair out of her face. "Did anybody hear us?"

Nisha listened for a moment to the general low-key musings of the office staff. "No. We are good. They all have on headphones." She listened for a moment more. "Frank slurps his water. They can't stand it."

Harper laughed. "It's pronounced Fronk-en-steen." Sobering, she studied Nisha, her question pouring from her mouth milliseconds after it crossed her mind. "Everyone is all wound up in finding the girls, saving Zella and Sexy, wondering if Blue is alive, but nobody has checked on you. You lost your boys. You doin' okay, sugar?"

Harper was the only person she had encountered who had literally no filter. Some people claimed they didn't have a filter. Most people had at least a small one. This woman did not. If it popped into her head, she said it. It was refreshing. Nisha still waited a moment out of habit for the final message to form after motivation or internal calculations changed the context of the words, but nothing came. Harper truly wanted to know how she was doing.

"I'm fine." She suspected Sam had not died in the explosion. The sheer quantity of dead bodies with no visible injuries recovered from the Colorado site convinced her he had been there. Her gut told her it was Sam's work. He often considered forcing people to stop sharing his air. What bothered her now was wondering where the hell he was and if the Sovereign captured him as well, and instead of helping him, she was standing here harvesting body parts with Sweet Home Alabama.

"I work in the music industry, so I know what a lie looks like." Harper pointed at Nisha and wrinkled her nose, shrugging the backpack full of nail clippings and hair samples onto her back. "That was a lie."

Feeling defensive and avoiding a raw and painful subject because she didn't have the bandwidth to deal with it right now, Nisha couldn't keep the uncharacteristic sarcasm from her response. "You a mind reader now?"

"Honey," Harper admonished softly.

"Let's get out of here." Nisha moved toward the exit, trying to focus on avoiding people moving about the building, but unable to do so as Harper's next words echoed in her mind and ears, rending a chasm through her emotional resolve.

"I'm here when you need me. I see you, sugar."

37

RHODES

Ava covered the bottom of her face with one hand, unable to fully hide the fact her mouth was moving, holding two playing cards in the other, frowning at the line of cards and pile of toothpicks on the table. A few games in, Lexi told her as she chewed her lip when she had a good hand. Now Ava covered her mouth constantly. She pushed four toothpicks from her own pile into the center and hesitated. Rolling her eyes, an irritated huff pushed a strand of hair out of her face. Lexi sat across from her, a security pillow sitting in her lap and her chin cradled in both hands, watching her student try to remember the rules. Currently, a queen, a jack, and ten of hearts lay on the table between them. "Which is a flush?"

"I'm out." Rhodes laid his own cards on the table with a chuckle. Hours had passed since they started playing cards, and he had yet to win a single hand. Lexi was a shark, and Ava had beginner's luck, but it was keeping them entertained and distracted, so losing was fine with him. Both girls turned down the MREs he offered for lunch, opting for more canned goods. They were two of the best-natured kids he had ever met.

"What?" Ava looked at him and Lexi in confusion. "I just asked a question. Why did you fold?"

"If you're asking, you have one." Lexi pointed at Rhodes. "And he obviously doesn't." She studied her own cards and pushed four of her own toothpicks into the pile. "I'll call." Ava's cheeks flushed, and she once again covered the lower portion of her face, chewing on her lip the whole time.

"Ready for the turn?" Rhodes tossed a card into the burn pile and waited on both girls to nod. Flipping over the new card, he raised an eyebrow. "Nine of hearts."

"Um. I'll raise. Right?" Ava looked at Lexi for confirmation, pushing four more toothpicks into the pile.

"Big spender. I'm still in." Lexi pushed in four of her own toothpicks. "Show us the river, Mr. Rhodes."

He tossed the top card into the burn pile once more and flipped the next card over next to the queen of spades. "Ace of clubs."

Ava's face twitched so much from chewing her lip, it shook her eyebrows. Rhodes sent a sidelong glance at Lexi, who sent him a smirk. Lexi believed she had a good hand. The community cards were a solid hand by themselves. This should be interesting. Ava began sorting toothpicks from her pile, eventually pushing twenty into the pot, leaving an anemic pile of wood behind. "Is that a twenty?" For the first time, doubts crossed Lexi's features.

"Yep."

Lexi pushed her twenty in. "Show me what you have."

Ava hated showing her hand first, still not confident in her poker playing abilities. "You first."

Humoring her friend, Lexi laid a seven of clubs and a two of spades down on the table. "Sevens wild. Gives me a straight flush. Give me those toothpicks."

"Wait." Ava frowned at Lexi and laid her own cards on the table, revealing a king of hearts and a seven of hearts.

"Whoa!" Rhodes cheered in disbelief. "Royal flush! That's my girl!"

But Ava didn't share his enthusiasm, looking at Lexi with concern and confusion before turning to him. "Is her necklace glowing?"

Rhodes looked down at Lexi's necklace. The small bead Greenlee wove onto the necklace at the last minute, pulsed a light pink. It pulsed again.

"Take it off and let me see it, Lexi."

She yanked the necklace over her head and shoved it in his direction. Clutching her pillow to her chest, she watched him with apprehension. "Are you better?"

She was petrified and wondered if he could protect them. "I'm better, Lexi Lou. Nothing bad is happening right now." Ninety percent certain he wasn't lying to her, he held the necklace up to his face, unsure of what he was looking for. Ava joined him, forcing her way under his arm, replacing his view of the bead with the back of her head.

Ava jerked back, almost slamming her head into his face. "It stopped glowing. What was that? Is that bad? Is it how they were tracking us? We don't know how they found us. Are they tracking us? Oh my God. We have to go." She clamped her mouth shut, on the verge of hyperventilating, and collapsed into her chair.

"Ava. Calm down."

Lexi stood in her chair and leaned slightly to get a better view of the necklace he still held. "Tio G gave that to me. He wouldn't give me something that would help the bad guys." She looked up, brow furrowed, still frightened. "But why did it glow?"

Rhodes considered his words for a moment, unsure of how much he should share. He glanced at Ava, whose breath still came in pants. "Ava. Breathe."

Ava's eyes narrowed. "You breathe."

Rhodes handed the now dormant necklace back to the girl, who cradled it in her hands reverently. Her eyes grew wide as she slipped the necklace back over her neck. "I think this means Tio G is still alive and is looking for you."

Ava lurched up and marched to the counter where they had a stack of water bottles waiting. "Are you just saying that to keep us calm?"

Lexi clutched the pillow to her chest now. "Should we leave in case it isn't Tio G?"

Rhodes motioned for her to stop standing in the chair. A serious injury to a child in his care from a dining table instead of a small army of madmen would be his luck. "But what if it was? If we move, he might not find us again."

No longer on the verge of hyperventilating, Ava was still on edge, and her words were laced with guilt and regret. "But what if it wasn't? Nobody figured out how those guys kept finding us. I flared when I got here. Is that how they are doing it? Following my surges? And I waved a big red flag, saying *here we are bad guys; come kill us*!"

Rhodes crossed his arms over his chest. "Sweetheart. We need to set something straight. You haven't done a single damned thing to cause any of this. Not. A. Damned. Thing." Ava only rolled her eyes and snorted, mirroring his posture.

Lexi nodded. "You didn't make those people crazy, evil assholes." She looked guilty as she climbed out of the chair. "Sorry, Mr. Rhodes. Ava, there was a busload of people aware of what you could do. They didn't use you as an excuse to hurt innocent people. You can't control how you were born or what other people do, and you can't hold yourself responsible for their poor decisions."

Ava sent an astounded glance his way. Was Lexi as young as Blue and Devon said she was? Ava shrugged her shoulders in semi-defeat. "Oh, great, wise one, please share more of your bountiful knowledge."

Lexi pursed her lips as she inspected the bead on her necklace. "When you have a royal flush, you go all in." She waved a hand at the forgotten cards on the table.

Ava huffed in embarrassment. "Is this what having a little sister is like? Because I'm glad I'm an only child."

Memories of Ivan and all the many ways he delighted in annoying Rhodes when they were younger filled his mind. A pang of grief hit him in the chest, but he still managed to chuckle. "A little."

Lexi ignored them for a moment, then held the bead up. "Do you think he could see us?"

Ava's brow furrowed, and she stepped closer, also inspecting the bead once more. "Do you want to leave him a message in case he looks again?"

"Yeah!" Lexi ran through the kitchen, looking through the drawers. "There is a pen and paper around here somewhere."

As Lexi rummaged, Ava walked across the kitchen to stand next to him, leaning in conspiratorially. "If we are going to wait here while our parents save the world, we need an exit strategy just in case the evil assholes find us."

"An exit strategy, you say?" He wanted to laugh at her choice of words, but he also didn't want to do anything to set her off. "I've actually been thinking about that."

38

FINN

"We really aren't going to talk about the fact I'm a So-vaj?" Kendra sat in the passenger seat of their stolen SUV as they drove back to the funeral home, which appeared to be their de facto base of operations for the foreseeable future or until Greenlee was well enough to move. He and Kendra just spent several hours working with Trix to distribute orders to his men for tonight's raid on the Cahlad, then combing through what remained of the Lilac Avenue warehouse for anything they could salvage. At her suggestion, five teams, a mix of magic users and his men, instead of the single team he planned to take, would be on-site tonight. He chose not to mention the fact she was a Sovaj because they had more important things to discuss.

He navigated the car down a busy thoroughfare congested with commuters heading home or stopping to grab a quick order of takeout. The scent of pizza permeated the air in this car, originating from the enormous pile of greasy boxes nestled among stacks of hard-sided cases and lumpy duffel bags that filled the rear of the vehicle, representing every salvageable piece of equipment they found. The Sovereign destroyed everything else, including his personal vehicle, which was parked in the basement. Repairing his warehouse and restocking his equipment would take several months and cost a small fortune he intended to bill back to the Cahlad. That was tomorrow's problem. Right now, he needed to focus on the potential problem in the seat next to him. "We can if you want to. Are you performing the duties expected of you to the best of your abilities?"

"You know I am, sir." Kendra, though cautious and suspicious, showed not a shred of remorse, most likely expecting to be summarily fired as soon as the immediate danger passed.

"Were you ever tempted to steal one of our artifacts or sabotage a mission?" The temptation to use Herne to gain rare and dangerous artifacts was the main reason he didn't hire magic users.

"No, sir."

"Is there anything else to discuss?" Finn checked the road in front of him, then glanced back at the woman who had remained rock solid and loyal despite everything that happened in the past few days, including his alliance with a man she despised. Actions always spoke louder than words, and while he did not like the fact she and Blue and Devon lied to him, he understood there was no malice involved. Kendra was here because they all trusted him a great deal. A hint of flattery mingled with the betrayal and anger he processed even now. Ever since Devon walked into Alexander's life, Finn understood the risk unregistered Sovaj took daily. He would never fault them for doing what they had to do to protect themselves, especially when it harmed no one.

"You must be angry. I'm prepared to offer my resignation." Kendra looked out the window as they drove past a colorful taco truck in a hardware store parking lot. "But I am going to see this thing through."

"I am angry, Reyes. I'm pissed as hell at all of you." Finn turned onto the last street, the large, ornate columns of the funeral home coming into view. "But if I didn't trust you to have my back, you wouldn't be sitting here right now. I have nothing else to say about it. You do what you feel you need to do."

She nodded, still looking away. "Understood."

Finn parked in the reserved employee parking spaces next to the four-bay garage behind the funeral home, making a mental note to ask Devon or Ben how they came to be here. The place was completely empty and dark.

Kendra sniffled, eyes watering as her nose twitched. Then a sneeze erupted, sounding far more like a goose honking than any sound that should emerge from a human. "Bless you."

Regaining her composure, she looked toward the well-hidden apartment above the garage and scowled. "So much magic." Her nose twitched, and the lines of her face grew hard and focused. "It is foul. So many smells. Something isn't right."

Instantly on alert, Finn moved quickly to the rear door leading into the garage, finding it locked. While the Sovereign hadn't specialized in subtlety so far, and it was unlikely they locked the door behind themselves if they were here, he couldn't rule out the possibility they might change tactics the longer their quarry evaded them. He stepped aside, using his body, which took up more space than Kendra's, to block the door from view, discreetly pulling his weapon and searching the area for any signs of what set her nose off. "Get us in there. Quietly."

The old brass doorknob was more of an annoyance than a real security measure. She quickly pulled a small knife from a pocket on her thigh and jammed it between the flimsy lock and the door, forcing the latch and plate apart with a muted ping. Lacking a dead bolt or secondary security mechanism, the door swung inward. In one fluid movement, Kendra's knife disappeared, replaced by her gun as she nodded and stepped into the dimly lit garage, moving to the side, covering his entrance. Finn followed, concerned that Nisha did not hear them coming. Scanning the quiet shadow-filled room, careful to keep his footsteps silent, he moved up the stairs, knowing Kendra followed even though she made no noise. Reaching the landing in front of the apartment's door, he stopped and waited for Kendra to catch up, feeling her back bump into his own. "On two." He reached for the doorknob, testing it. It turned free, and he wrapped his hand around it. "One." He twisted the doorknob so that only his grip held it closed. "Two."

When he burst through the door, Kendra entered in the opposite direction. "Oh Lordy, Kay Kay, you scared the tar out of me." Finn stopped, lowering his weapon as the insane scene in front of him registered. Small plastic bags filled with what looked like hair and nail clippings littered every flat space of the apartment. Greenlee stood over the kitchen table covered in the contents of every drawer in both the kitchen and bathroom, tongue sticking out of his mouth as he gave a plain spoon his undivided attention. Mitch stood next to him, enraptured by whatever was happening. A storage basket filled with other random objects sat at their feet. Devon sat at the table holding a roll of tape and a marker labeling a few objects arranged in front of her. She gave one to Ben, who scribbled something into a notebook and placed the object into the basket. Harper huddled over a sun-bleached atlas at the coffee table while Nisha lay across the couch, sleeping peacefully.

Kendra sent him an odd look and lowered her weapon. "Are those from dead people?" Her entire face twisted in disgust as she gagged. "I can't." She shook her head and walked out. "I'll be..." A pained retch finished her sentence as she closed the door behind her.

Finn lowered his own weapon, waiting for anyone other than Harper to acknowledge their entrance. None of them looked up. "Anybody?"

"Hey, there, Foxy." Harper closed the atlas and stood, walking over to stand next to him to view the room from his perspective. "Mitch got Thor all patched up, and he scried on your niece. We have coordinates now, but no way to get to them quickly. Sis had an idea to get our Dr. Fronkensteen on from all those folks Larson sent to attack you at the Nova-nado. You know that's what they were calling it, right? She thinks her man over there can make a gadget to portal them to the baby girls and my grumpy-ass boss who is no doubt lost without me. Me and sleeping beauty used our ninja skills to bring back the goods."

"Huh. You've all been very busy." Finn observed the bags full of dead people parts, feeling sorry for Kendra. "Is that all?"

"No, Foxy." Harper bumped his shoulder. "S.S. Dev-lee has set sail. Your boy finally made his move."

Finn's eyes locked on Devon, remembering the first time Alexander brought her home. They were perfect for each other. But so were Devon and Greenlee, and Alex wasn't here anymore. He would want her to be happy. Harper watched him like a hawk, giving him the feeling she didn't miss much. "About damned time." He approached the table to make sense of the chaos. "Anything in there I can use?"

With a goofy smile, Greenlee responded first, holding up the spoon he held for Finn's inspection. "You are going to love this." He motioned around the room at the plethora of bags labeled with dark black ink. "I've hit the lottery. This is amazing."

"You look better."

"I am."

An arm slipped around his waist as Devon gave him a quick hug. "Did you get everything you need?"

"I leave you alone for two seconds, and you go grave robbing."

She remained next to him, staring at the basket of items at Mitch's feet. "Greenlee wouldn't let me rob any graves. Harper and Nisha got to have all the fun." Tell me you won't get killed tonight."

None of the items in the basket screamed portal. They looked like the quarter bin at a yard sale. "Not if everything goes as planned. Can he make a portal?"

"Just in case?" Devon understood his meaning. "Yes. It was the first thing. We didn't want to leave before you got back, since we know they are safe."

"Thanks."

"Finn?"

He squeezed her shoulders, mentally going over his plan to extract Hale and Zella, hoping they were both well enough to move under their own power. He hoped Hale was well enough to don a vest and shoot on the way out. He was counting on it. "Yeah?"

"You had better come back to me."

He couldn't promise that, but he could do the next best thing to soothe her checklist and procedure-driven mind. "Let's get everyone together and go over the plan."

"That sounds perfect." She relaxed at the mere mention of a plan. That was too easy. Greenlee, hearing every word, glanced up with a smirk as he finished the item he was working on.

"Harper, get over here and take these," Kendra's voice bit out as a hand scooted four boxes of pizza through the door. "I'm keeping the Hawaiian. Freaks."

"Ooh," Devon cooed, lunging for the boxes. "Pizza. My favorite."

39

BLUE

EARLY JUNE. THIRTY-FIVE YEARS AGO

Blue glided her bike into the driveway, surprised to see the carport empty. Sam hadn't put in a single late night since the Billy Bob incident two weeks ago, beating her home from work every day to spend his time making a bunch of racket in the workshop and being in her way. Other than the brief interrogation over the broken window, and a stilted thank-you for dinner yesterday, he remained stubbornly silent. Silly as it was, the silent-treatment nonsense hurt her feelings, and it did not incline her to go out of her way to talk to him, so the whole thing was just awkward and tense. She promised she wouldn't leave, not that she would follow him around like a puppy, begging for scraps of conversation. The empty driveway was a gift.

She needed a moment, anyway. The kids were off the rails this afternoon, bouncing off the hallway walls as they collected items from their lockers and dashed out the door in a race to see who could be the biggest menace on the road. Then Mathlete practice ran over when the little fiends wouldn't miss a question.

Since the Billy Bob incident, Ricky and Tiffany stayed here on nights their mom worked. Sherry didn't work tonight, so Blue was free to pursue her own interest. She planned to run inside, change clothes, and skedaddle to the movie theater for a double feature. Hollywood delivered some classics this year, and the novelty of seeing their first run had yet to wear off. Tonight, she wanted to see *Beetlejuice* and eat a giant tub of popcorn with extra butter. Hopping up the steps and unlocking the brand-new door, she flung her backpack to the side and grimaced as the phone rang. Only their employers and Sherry next door had the number. It was probably somebody at school wanting her to cover an after-school event at the last minute.

"Hello?"

"Ms. Keys? This is Mildred, with the Everdale College Department of Magical Studies. I need to discuss a matter of some importance with you. I take it this is a good time?"

Blue made a face at the hard piece of plastic the offensive noise had just came out of. Who talked like that? "Um." Blue stopped when the woman sniffed at the filler word, then stuck her tongue out at the phone. "I suppose it is."

"Oh wonderful." The voice on the other end of the line turned jovial and excited. "I just wanted to know what entrée you preferred tonight. Mr. Keys forgot to send in an RSVP card."

"Oh. W-well," Blue stuttered, unsure of what to say. "I..."

"Of course, you know how important tonight's event is for the Department of Magical Studies and the College."

Blue raised an eyebrow at the strange course of this conversation. "Um?"

"Oh yes, dear. Many important alumni and generous patrons will be present."

Blue pinched her nose, squeezing her eyes tight, and remained silent for a few moments. "Ms. Mildred?"

"Yes, dear?"

"It's been a long week. Can we cut to the chase?" She picked up her house keys and twirled them around her finger.

"If you insist."

Blue smiled at the miffed tone in Mildred's voice. "You know, I didn't know about this very important dinner. That's at what time, by the way? And you know Sam didn't 'forget' to tell me anything. So, tell me why you are sticking your nose in it."

The woman made a noise that sounded both pleased and offended, and Blue hopped onto the counter and swung her legs like a kid waiting for her response. "Simply speaking, Mr. Keys is rather odd, and as director, there is an expectation that he, well, speaks. He's not a bad boy, dear; I'm just concerned that he doesn't always put his best foot forward."

"You hit the nail on the head with that one, Mildred. But what is so important about tonight, and what does it have to do with me?"

"There have been rumors among the ladies on the staff that the dean of the Department of Magic, whom I work for, is lobbying

Dr. Higgins. That's the college president, mind you, to replace Mr. Keys with someone more politically palatable. He has wanted the research institute brought under the umbrella of our department for some time now, but all the other directors have resisted. And Mr. Keys refuses to meet with him. The center operates on a generous endowment that would greatly improve the dean's budget. And he wants access to items from the collection."

"Mm. Juicy."

"I fear if Mr. Keys is less than impressive tonight, that awful twat Ms. Patricks may well replace him in the directorship because she kowtows to the dean. She will be bloody insufferable."

Blue snickered and hummed in understanding. "That awful?"

"Yes, dear. She already makes us take her husband's clothing to the dry cleaners and other rather personal errands, and she is only an adjunct researcher."

"Well, that's..."

"She dry-cleans his underwear."

"Weird."

"There are always stains, miss."

"How rude." It sounded far worse for the dry cleaner than the delivery person, but she would keep that to herself.

"Dr. Higgins is a bit of a traditionalist. They typically expect spouses at these events. Ms. Patricks will bring her husband."

"Mr. Skid Mark himself?"

Mildred sniffed. "Can you imagine what the horrid cow will do if she gains any additional prestige within the department?"

"I shudder to think." Blue leaned back against the upper cabinets, unable to suppress a smile. She had to meet Mildred in person. This entire interaction was delightful.

"I implore you, dear. On behalf of the entire administrative staff, please at least try to make that odd husband of yours look like a better option than the skid-mark twat."

"Your cause sounds dire, Mildred." Blue struggled to contain her laughter, still kicking her feet, loving the familiar tingle of impending shenanigans. It would be nice to talk about something other than school to someone other than Sherry or a bunch of hormonal teenagers. "What are my entrée options?"

"Excellent, Ms. Keys. Prime Rib or Salmon."

"Salmon."

"I've made a note of it. Do you have any formal attire, dear?"

40

SAM

EARLY JUNE. THIRTY-FIVE YEARS AGO

S am hated suits, despised tuxedos, and loathed compulsory social events, yet here he stood, propping up a wall in a small
ballroom on the top floor of the alumni center, staring up at a gaudy
chandelier that needed a good dusting, hoping by some miracle
everyone would overlook him. He wasn't sure what the purpose of
the event was. The whole scenario reeked of an old person's prom.
Considering he didn't go to his own prom, he certainly didn't want
to attend this one. It reminded him a bit too much of his duties as
Regent, at least there he had enough pull to send Nisha in his place.
He owed her an apology.

Hands hidden in his pockets and longing for an excuse to escape,
he watched as every employee of the Everdale College Magic Studies Department and their spouses mingled, sipped champagne, and
chatted like they didn't spend the entire workweek stabbing each
other in the back. The people assembled before him represented

the cattiest bunch of humans he had ever encountered. As the only current employee of the Everdale College Independent Arcana Research Foundation, he worked next to these people, but not with them. Which was just fine by him.

A small army of obviously wealthy alumni and donors laughed and tittered, doing their best not to mingle with the peasants. A flurry of movement from Mildred, a persistent dragon lady, posing as the dean's executive assistant, drew his attention. The regal woman stood next to a man who looked about as happy to be here as Sam was, a warm smile breaking across her face as she waved to someone at the hall's entrance. Startled by the fact she had an expression that wasn't purse-lipped disappointment, it took him a moment to realize the entire room now stared toward the doors, particularly the members of the administrative staff, who looked strangely relieved.

Following their gaze, he tried to place the person standing in front of the doors from the many faces he encountered during his first day of introductions with the department staff and endless alumni introductions. Maybe this was a spouse. His mouth went dry, and his stomach dropped. It was indeed a "spouse" he intentionally did not tell about this event. That explained Mildred's reaction.

He had never seen Blue in makeup or wearing anything other than practical pants and basic shirts. Now she sported flawless makeup and wore a flowing green dress, looking like a complete stranger and waving a greeting to Mildred, of all people. She swept across the room, hugging Mildred like they were long-lost sisters, introducing herself to Mildred's husband, and to Sam's horror, drawing the entire room's attention.

Mildred's face morphed into a smug smirk of victory. Her eyes moved his way. The dragon woman set him up and aligned herself with chaos incarnate to do it. He peeled himself off the wall and made a beeline across the room to head off the inevitable calamity. They could not risk exposing themselves when they were this close to going home. Only God knew what Blue would do, but it would probably end with dead bodies or explosions.

He reached her side as a few of the snobbier members of the party joined the circle. "There you are." He forced the words through clenched teeth, taking a spot next to her right elbow and raising an eyebrow, trying to hide his displeasure.

Blue smiled up and back, mischief written all over her face. "I'm so sorry I'm late. I got stuck at school for Mathlete practice."

Mildred wore an expression so snakelike, he swore her eyelids blinked sideways. "It's no problem, dear. I am so glad you could join us." She plucked two glasses of champagne from a passing waiter and shoved one into each of their hands. Narrowing his eyes, he met the woman's gaze, only to have her wink at him, unconcerned. What had he done to get her attention? She barely spoke to him. This was a nightmare.

Blue's eyebrows raised just slightly, watching his reaction. "Thank you so much, Mildred." She handed her champagne glass back gracefully. "A water would be just lovely right now. It's been a long day. I might just fall asleep on my feet."

A waiter nodded and scurried away.

"Mathlete practice?" A tall, elegant woman with stark-white hair perked up and stepped away from her husband, tilting her nose up and peering at Blue through the glasses on the end of her nose. "I'm Sandy Andreas. It's lovely to meet you. My grandson is involved in Mathlete competitions. Do you teach?"

"Yes! I teach at Lakemond High." Blue nodded with enthusiasm. "Nice to meet you as well."

"That is where Tommy goes. He is a sophomore." Ms. Andreas beamed.

"Tommy Andreas?" Blue quirked a head to the side.

"Yes. Are you the incredible new teacher he has gone on and on about for the past month? Those young people adore you." She bumped Mildred out of the way, taking the spot on Blue's other side as the waiter appeared and slipped a glass of ice water into her hand. Mildred, to his surprise, was unphased and perhaps even pleased, sending a triumphant look to the administrative assistant who handled student paperwork. Intrigue was afoot. But how on earth did they rope Blue in?

"That makes my heart so happy. Tommy is such a wonderful young man."

Digging deep, he braced himself for a night of obsessing over every interaction and word he had hoped to avoid. Mildred moseyed in his direction, dragging her miserable husband in her orbit, and leaned in conspiratorially. "Just smile and nod, dear. And consider shaving. You look like a mountain man." Leaning away again she let out a jovial laugh for no reason at all, tittered about what a wonderful young lad he was, and set her sights on a disgruntled dean. Mr. Mildred sent him a sympathetic look of solidarity before following his wife across the room.

With no good alternatives, Sam stayed where he was. Without missing a beat in her conversation or even looking at him, Blue swapped her water for his champagne and spent the next hour and a half gracefully redirecting every piece of conversation that came his way without seeming obvious or pushy. She excelled at this, almost like she trained in a top-secret program to do it. The waiter arrived with a third glass of champagne paired with an ice water. Blue stepped closer, resting her arm against his, speaking low. "Do you mind if I keep this water? I know you don't drink in public. But I haven't eaten today."

"Of course." He leaned down to get within earshot and to keep his own voice from carrying. "How do you know I don't drink in public?"

"Just a hunch." She sipped her water. "Smart, cautious guy."

He nodded in appreciation. "Why are you here?"

"To foil the nefarious plans of the skid-mark twat." She waved at a couple walking past. "A noble cause."

Sam didn't know what to make of her response. "Not to make my life miserable?"

"That's just a bonus." Her stomach growled, and she looked embarrassed.

"You took the blue container this morning? The manicotti?"

"Didn't have time to eat it." Shaking her head, she waved to someone else. "Helped the theater teacher set up the stage for the summer production. They were running behind."

The waitstaff only circulated drinks. Appetizers were on tables at the front of the room. He jerked his head toward the tables. "Food? No tomato soup or Jell-O, with shit in it, right?"

She stuck her tongue out, crossing her eyes. "That would be great. Thank you." Taking a small sip of water, she turned to yet another wealthy patron and greeted them enthusiastically. They were far more interested in her than him, and he didn't blame them.

Meandering through the crowd, he came to a sudden stop. He didn't want to crawl out of his own skin and run until he couldn't run anymore. At events like this, he ended up being a ball of angry nerves and giving off what Nisha called "big, scary, angry-man vibes." But tonight, he was almost relaxed. Almost. Grabbing a few finger foods, he turned, searching for Blue's present location in the circulating crowd, and frowned. She stood next to a tall, bulky member of the waitstaff. But there was something off about him. He held her arm pulled to the side as if he was trying to lead her away, leaning down and saying something in her ear, a plastic smile on his face as he scanned the room. Blue swayed on her feet, sending Sam's mind back to a few moments ago when she was fine. She wasn't drunk. There was no reason for her to sway. Her glower told him she wasn't afraid of the newcomer. She was furious. That scared him far more than whatever this semi-military brute represented. They were completely screwed if she let loose in here with a fraction of what she was capable of.

Plowing through the crowd and discarding the plate of finger food, he approached, fighting the urge to deliver a stern directive to let her go, not caring if he sounded like a caveman or not. She wobbled again, eyes squinting, trying to focus, hand pressing into her chest, over her heart. The only thing holding her upright now was the punishing grip the man had on her arm, which left white rims on her skin where his fingers squeezed. Tamping down his temper and instinct to fight, from years of Stalker training, he forced himself to deconstruct the details of what was happening in front of him. The man had dark hair and a deep scar across one eyebrow. A tattoo ran up his neck, peeking over the collar of his ill-fitting shirt and into his hairline. The man's hands were rough and cracked. His whole countenance screamed "hired thug shoved in a tux," sending Sam on high alert. "Who is this?"

Relief washed over Blue's deathly pale face as she reached out with a shaky hand, silently asking for help. Astonished, he took it and tugged, forcing the other man to let her go or cause a scene, and she stumbled forward, catching his shirt in her free hand to steady herself, the other still clutched to her chest. "Watch your back. The water. Oh, shit." Her words slurred, and he almost couldn't understand. Her forehead hit his chest as he wrapped an arm around her lower back to keep her on her feet. "Think. Kill you?"

He leveled a stare at the man, weighing his options. Did he tip his hand and make this guy jump out a window, or did he play it smart and see what he could find out? This guy didn't look like Cahlad. "You are?"

The man's eyes narrowed. "Just leaving, Director Keys."

"Not good." Blue's head shook against his chest. She leaned heavily against him as he looked around, making sure no one else in the crowd stood within earshot. Her hand lost its grip, and she went limp, breathing shallow. A whimper muffled by his shirt met his ears. Sam's eyes snapped back to the amused expression of the man in front of him as he struggled to keep a grip on his magic and his temper. The man stepped backward with a satisfied sneer and a small salute.

When Blue survived, this man would learn she had magic. Sam gritted his teeth to maintain control of his own and covered Blue's ears. "Stay there. Don't make a sound." The man's backward progression stopped, freezing in place in alarm. "Keep your hands at your sides."

Sam dropped his head, concerned by the sudden stillness of the woman in his arms. What was in that drink? If they dosed it for someone his size, double hers, intending to kill this quickly, would she be able to handle it even with her enhanced healing? If they dosed the water, it meant whomever they were, they had watched him all night and predicted she would hand it off.

He needed to get out of here without making a scene. If medics or regular human medical authorities got involved, the rate Blue healed would blow their cover. He smiled and tucked his face into Blue's hair like they were having a private conversation, alarmed that he could no longer feel her chest moving. "Keep breathing." He scanned the area for anyone else that looked out of place while monitoring the man trapped next to him. They were in the middle of a crowded room, and he had no discreet exit. Using the arm wrapped around her back, he hitched her higher. "Talk to me."

A deep breath preceded a weak flex of the hand holding his shirt. "Don't." Her body tilted and weaved even though her feet were no longer on the floor. "Let go."

"I won't."

She nodded and rattled in a breath, face still buried against his chest. "Bad. Hurts." Another muffled hiss of pain. "God."

Even with shattered bones and bullet holes, she barely complained. Whatever this was must be bad. Wincing, he placed his face against her ear. "I'm sorry. Stay with me."

"Worst. Go. Twat."

"What?" Her words slurred less but still didn't make complete sense, and he couldn't carry her out of here without drawing attention. "Can you walk?"

"Cold."

"Can. You. Walk?" Sam glared at the would-be assassin, watching the exchange with dark, dangerous eyes. They needed to hurry before the guy got clever.

"With help." Her eyes were still unfocused, lips tinged blue, and grimacing in pain.

Sam stepped closer to the man and covered Blue's exposed ear with his hand. "Follow me. Clasp your hands in front of you. Stay quiet. Walk to those doors and smile. Open them for me and wait. Do anything to make a scene and you are going to chew your own tongue off."

Blue whispered something about "my side." Steering them both in the would-be assassins' stilted wake, through the maze of tables and people, they made it to the double doors leading to the hallway. The man opened the doors with his clasped hands and stood waiting with a large, toothy smile on his face. "Stay quiet. Hands just like that. Follow me."

He led them around the corner to a short, dark hallway, housing administrative offices, and propped Blue against the wall. The shuffling footsteps of his captive whispered behind him.

Sam resisted the urge to say something terrible. "Put your nose and hands on the wall. Don't make a sound. Stay that way until you have counted to ten million." The mercenary dragged his feet to the wall, body tense as his hands fought to reach for something in his pants but couldn't overcome the compulsion. His nose smashed into the wall, followed by his fist, lips moving to count out silent numbers. Sam needed to check for weapons.

Blue attempted to turn toward the wall as well, trying to follow his instructions. She was ghostly pale, face twisted in a determined grimace, eyes looking at him but not seeing him, hand still pressed to her chest. Her feet tangled, and she slid down the wall face-first. Sam cursed himself for forgetting to cover her ears. "Not you." He grabbed her shoulders and turned her around to lean against the wall again. "How do you feel?"

Breathing in pained gulps of air, her free hand gripped his wrist and squeezed. "Better. Thanks." Eyes focusing, pupils so blown out that he could barely see the gray rimming them, she gazed back at him. "They tried to poison you." Taking a deep breath of air that obviously hurt, she only managed a whisper. "They wanted to know where you were. What have you been up to?"

Careful to keep a lid on his words because his blood was boiling, he glared at the counting man next to him who didn't know she would live when he tried to walk away. He had smiled even though she wasn't the intended target. He hated people like this.

A sudden shiver wracked Blue's body and her teeth chattered. She must have used a ton of magic to keep herself alive. He was under the impression only her teleportation magic had this side effect. "Here." He tugged out of his jacket and fed her shaking arms through when her hands shook so badly, she couldn't do it herself.

"Thank you." Wrapping herself in the garment that fell well past her knees, she let her head fall forward again. "Go. Deal with him."

"He's fine for the moment." Sam leaned forward, putting his elbow on the wall and his forehead on his arm, coming to grips with the fact tonight ended with an assassination attempt instead of an annoying conversation. They were supposed to be lying low.

"That keep-breathing trick is handy." She shook her head, sounding stronger and more coherent.

Knowing it meant she came closer than he realized to dying, his nose flared. "Christ. I didn't know you would be this hard to keep alive."

"A recent phenomenon." Her tone held a touch of accusation. "Why is someone trying to kill you?"

"No idea."

Teeth chattering, she nodded her head at the man pressed against the wall. "Well, ask him."

Turning his head to observe the man, he sent a little extra magic into his words. "Tell me what you put in the drink?"

"I don't know. They just gave it to me."

"Tell me what it is supposed to do?"

"Make it look like you had a heart attack."

Blue nodded her head, still rubbing a hand over her chest. "That tracks."

"Tell me who gave it to you."

"Some guy."

"Give me his name."

"I don't know."

"Ask him who he works for." Blue shivered again, though less noticeably.

"Tell me who you work for."

The man gritted his teeth to keep his words in. "Some outfit called the Sovereign. Christ, they are going to kill me now."

Sam's head whipped around just as Blue's did. They both gaped at the man. Thirty years in the past, and they were still dealing with those bastards.

"No, they won't." Blue's voice rang with menace as she clutched his jacket closed with one hand and leaning on the wall with the other. "Why do they want Sam dead?"

"Fuck you." The man sneered and strained to pull his hands off the wall.

"Answer her question." Sam approached the man and searched him for weapons.

"Aww. Thanks, Diablo." Blue gave him a weak but playful smile.

"No problem, angel."

She rolled her eyes. "Not you, too." Yes, him, too. He had lost count of how many times she saved his life.

"They want something in the center's inventory. They need someone in charge who can identify it and sell it to them."

Sam's eyes met Blue's. He told Amber to fix it. For the past month, he tried to figure out why they were here. She dropped him here with an elite magical operative where he stood in the way of something the Sovereign wanted. It was making sense.

"Tell me what they want."

The man gritted his teeth and strained again. "A book."

"Tell me which book."

"I don't know."

Sam finished his search and stepped back. Blue straightened and walked closer, observing their prisoner with a slight tilt of her head and a dangerous glint in her eye. She still shook but appeared alert and ready to rip someone's head off.

"Give me the address where you got the poison and the name of your contact."

"I don't know his name." The man shook with anger now. He let out a long groan that sounded like several curse words jumbled together, straining to resist the magic. "It's 4578 West Nickles Boulevard."

Sam looked back at Blue. "Anything else?"

"What are they going to do with the book?"

"Tell her."

"I don't know, man."

Blue jerked her chin at the man. "Deal with him. I'll handle the body."

"What?" Panic tinged the man's voice. "I told you what you wanted to know."

"And I told you the Sovereign weren't going to kill you." Blue watched the man panic with emotionless eyes, tilting her head with a small smile that made her look downright creepy. "I didn't say we wouldn't."

He hesitated, unsure if she should use her magic to move a body, given the fact she still shivered, even if it was the cleanest solution. But if she couldn't handle it, she wouldn't offer. Nodding in agreement, he motioned for Blue to cover her ears and waited until she took three large steps back and followed instructions. He stalked forward as the man jerked violently, realizing they had no intention of letting him walk away. Leaning in so there was no chance Blue could hear his next words, he fought to rein his magic in. Focusing on concentrating the area of effect to his immediate vicinity, he looked the man right in the eye that strained sideways to see them. "You shouldn't have laughed when you tried to kill my friend. Take your last breath."

The man's eyes bulged, a deep, desperate gulp of air entering his body. Sam stepped away, turning his back on the man, and watched Blue's reaction to what happened behind him. She gazed at the scene with a cold calculation in stark contrast to her typical lighthearted personality, the hand that held his jacket together still pressing the area over her chest like she was still in pain. The body thumped to the ground behind him, and she stepped forward. All business. "I'll meet you back here. Be somewhere without witnesses." Kneeling, she wrapped a hand around the body's wrists and disappeared in a gust of cold air, taking his jacket with her.

41

ZELLA

Zella leaned against the wall and the shoulder of the young man, determined to keep her spirits up with humorous stories and antics, willing the visions to slow down so she could regain her equilibrium. Their intensity and frequency increased exponentially over the past six or seven hours, leaving her exhausted and forcing her to take breaks from sketching and writing. A dark-haired child clutching a pillow while playing cards repeated, followed by a volley of faces and locations passing so fast, she barely had time to process them. Even Hale's horrific attempt to Rick Roll her by burping the song couldn't distract her, though she appreciated the effort.

Two soft knocks on the door gave them a warning a second before it swung open. Peeling one eye open, she left her head resting on Hale's shoulder and found Nolan Miller entering the room. He closed the door behind him and approached cautiously, pulling something from his pockets. Two protein bars filled his hands, both of which he unwrapped and handed to Zella before shoving the wrappers back into his pockets. "There is no sign of the Paragon."

Zella did her best not to respond to the man's words as she broke off a small bit of the bar and fed it to Hale, whose hands remained bound behind him. "Also, no sign of the Regent. Although, Larson seems confident that his men killed Sotach and Lacroix earlier today, but they made a mess of things and can't produce the bodies."

Zella's hand stalled at Miller's words. That couldn't be right, even in the shifting soup of futures that pummeled her mind now. Not one of them showed Sam or Ivan's death. Did she miss something in the brief flashes of random moments? What was happening out there?

"This complicates things. It seems the Cahlad has never endured the loss of both Paragon and Regent. The rules of the challenge are very specific, and this leaves your little magic cult with no way to establish new leadership."

Zella resumed feeding Hale the rest of the protein bar, wondering how Nolan Miller thought unseating the highest ranking official of the world's magical government would play out?

Zella stopped and turned her head, making sure he could see the bruise on her cheek that Hale described as a beautiful violet fading gracefully through every shade of the baby doody rainbow. As she expected, the senator looked away, distracting himself with a few loose sheets holding her most recent drawings and words. "Larson is incensed. It seems he needs the Paragon alive for some reason. A reason he isn't sharing."

Miller flipped through the stack and pulled out a sketch of a three-story house with floor-to-ceiling windows, surrounded by mature trees. "This works." The man flicked the page and stood, moving toward the door slowly. "I'll tell him to look here. Eat the other bar, Ms. Tyne. I don't know if I can get you another."

The door clicked shut quietly behind him, and Hale's gaze turned thoughtful. "What was that?" He turned his head away when Zella tried to give him the last bite of his bar. "You eat it. You look way worse than I do."

At his playful wink, she popped the bite in her own mouth and settled back against the wall to finish the other bar. "Me thinks the honeymoon is over, and Mommy and Daddy are fighting. Stop eating that tasty protein bar if you think I'm wrong."

Zella made a show of nibbling on her snack, closing her eyes against a fresh wave of visions. Whatever was happening remained volatile but shifted in their favor. As the *1812 Overture* delivered via burps, echoed through the room, she leaned her head back just before the door burst open hard enough to shatter the wall behind it.

Two men who looked like the ones who threw them in the van at Herne's warehouse, and broke Hale's nose, lunged in. Stopping mid-burp, Hale smiled. "Hey, guys. Long time, no see."

The taller of the two stayed by the door, while the other locked his eyes on Zella's arms and stalked forward. "Larson was right." Leaning down, he jerked her up by her bound wrist and ripped the ties away, leaving raw scrapes in her skin before hauling her around and binding her arms behind her back so tightly, the slightest movement cut into her skin. Hale watched with narrow eyes as the man shoved her back to the ground with a satisfied smile. Mere seconds of a vision flitted before her eyes as she turned to keep from face-planting into the wall. Her face twisted in a vengeful smile as she watched the man leave. There was nothing fuzzy about the vision. No matter what happened, that man ended up choking on his own blood.

She shifted and tried to get comfortable.

"He's going to die, isn't he?"

She nodded again.

Hale glared at the door, tone dark. "Good."

42

BLUE

EARLY JUNE. THIRTY-FIVE YEARS AGO

The steady drizzle of rain from earlier in the evening turned into a torrential downpour that now hammered the metal roof of the carport so loud, she couldn't hear herself think. The weather was as crazy as their night. Once she disposed of the body, she and Sam left the reception before dinner under the pretense that she wasn't feeling well. She wasn't. Then they drove to the address he provided. The man's contact had even less useful information. Disposing of yet another body after the amount of energy she discharged to survive the poisoning left her frozen. Shivering, although Sam ran the heat in the car on the drive home and now stood drenched in sweat, she waited for him to unlock the door. She wanted to get inside and find the blankets.

"You locked this?" His question drew her attention to the door that was no longer latched and stood ajar. Not waiting for an answer, he stalked inside. "Stay here."

"Are you kidding me?" She threw her arms out in frustration and stood cemented to the stoop, listening to the roar of rain on metal, hoping nobody came out she needed to run from. She also hoped Sam didn't need help in there because she would just have to listen while he died. "Zenith out here. Magic healing. Harder to kill than you are. You stand behind me. You are an idiot."

Sam appeared at the door, looking out into the wall of water instead of meeting her eyes. "I forget. It irritates Ivan, too. You can come in."

"Thanks so much." Shouldering past him, the hairs on the back of her neck stood up. Something was off. "What did you find?"

He walked over and tapped a small, folded piece of paper on the counter next to the coffee machine, decorated in a familiar scrawl. Blue's shoulders sagged. That wasn't good. The last time a mysterious note showed up, the person who left it meant for her to die. "We still had a few days. You said seven weeks."

"That's what she told me." A smothering feeling of foreboding settled over the room. "Is that Amber's handwriting?"

"Yes."

Sam leaned over, bracing on the counter, glowering at the note. "What does it say?"

Flipping the paper open, she read the words twice. Her legs gave out, and she sank to the floor with a thump. "It says I don't know what you are doing. Whatever it is, keep it up. Boom kitty. See you in a few months." She laid her head on her knees and dropped the note to the floor. Sam's hands slammed into the counter, rattling everything in the drawers, and his footsteps stomped away into the house without a word.

Eventually, though she didn't know how long it took, he came back, draping two heavy quilts over her shoulders and handing her a pair of wool socks. She shoved the socks over her hands and rubbed them together to warm them. If they could believe what Amber told Sam, this meant five more months while Devon and Greenlee dealt with whatever nightmare Larson Battle had brewing, and Lexi and Ava lived with neon targets on their backs. She needed to know that Dev, Green, Lexi, and Finn were safe. Hell, she even wanted to know if Rhodes made it to safety. Her family needed her, but she was stuck here.

Sam sat down next to her and leaned against the cabinets, staring into space. "What do you want to do?"

"I want to go home."

"Me, too."

She didn't know what else to do except wait for Amber and keep a low profile. She couldn't time travel. The two men who were sent to kill Sam didn't have time to contact anyone before they died. But the people who hired them were still around and would notice that he wasn't dead, and their men were missing. A low profile might not be an option anymore. "I don't know. Give me thirty seconds to wallow." She laid her face back down on her knees, wrapping her arms around her legs. "Maybe I'll find a bubble and stay in it. The last time she left me a note like that, there were lots of explosions, gunshot wounds, broken bones, and magic poisoning. Not to mention, I ended up three decades in the past, taking a poison bullet for a guy that hates me and tried to leave me for dead in the desert."

"He doesn't hate you. But he sounds like a real asshole."

She tried to smile but didn't have the energy. Seeing the look on his face, she could finally put a word on the emotion currently smothering her. Defeat. "Most days."

Sam snickered, a dry look of mirth on his face. "Tell me how you really feel."

Before she could stop herself, words spilled out. "I think you are entirely too hard on yourself and were surrounded by truly awful people. They should have taught you how to function with your magic, not to stop living because of it. You are different, not broken. It's like Lexi's dyslexia. We can't tell her not to read just because she doesn't do it like everyone else. We have to find a way that works for her." She put her hands over her mouth, but the words kept coming. "It freaks me out every time you sneeze or sigh because it is obvious your magic doesn't rely one hundred percent on your voice. So, the silent treatment is just bullshit icing on the cake."

Sam winced, realizing why she was speaking a mile a minute. His face morphed into an *I told you so* expression, and he raised a hand and opened his mouth to say something else. But she couldn't stop her words and talked through her hands.

"I want to kill Amber. I hate it here. I'm so lonely. I miss my family, and I'm a complete garbage person for leaving the only people who never let me down when they needed me. I love the kids, but teaching sucks. I hate your beard, and I think you are shorter now than when I met you." Jamming her fist in her mouth, she stared at him, wide-eyed and horrified.

His jaw locked in a familiar expression that preceded days of silence, looking as mortified as she was. He struggled for a moment, hands clenching and unclenching at his sides before his shoulders slumped. "Is that all?"

"Yeah."

"I like my beard, and I'm keeping it."

Laughing at the obvious deflection but recognizing the effort, she pointed at the thick layer of hair on his jaw that he hadn't shaved since they got here. "It makes you look mean. But not as mean and scary as the cosmic demon eyes."

Brow furrowed, he tilted his head in confusion. "Cosmic demon eyes?"

"In the field, your eyes went all black and looked like they had little galaxies. You changed. I really thought you were a demon." She wiggled her fingers in the air. "Real nightmare fuel. You didn't know?"

"Is that why you called me Diablo?" He shook his head, a troubled look on his face. "I usually have to use my voice. Especially on that scale. I'm sorry if I scare you."

"Don't do that. We aren't going backward when you are finally talking. You don't really scare me." Most days. She changed the subject to keep him from clamming up or telling her not to lie. "Are you shorter?"

"Yeah. Two inches."

"Huh." Puzzling on that, she wrapped the quilts more tightly around her so they covered her feet, too. The magic Rhodes used on her burned off during whatever brought them here. She was shorter now, too, and her hair turned back to its original auburn, though slightly darker than before. The magic-infused tattoos Greenlee gave her disappeared as well. "Was your height a magic effect?"

"Yes."

"How?"

Sam looked embarrassed. "When I was thirteen, I got upset about not being allowed to share a room in the Cahlad dorms because of my classification and risk level. I didn't want to live alone."

"Okay?"

"I lost my temper and told myself to grow up."

Blue grimaced, understanding where he was going with this. "How much did you grow?"

"Seven inches." He grimaced. "In thirty seconds. I passed out from the pain. They found me the next morning. It hurt so bad; I was afraid to reverse it. I was on crutches for months."

"That's really messed up."

They sat in silence for a few more minutes and she considered just going to sleep where she sat. Sam stood up and started pulling things from the cabinets and refrigerator. "The Sovereign are going to come back when they realize I'm not dead."

"But now we know they are coming." From her spot on the floor, she couldn't see what he was doing, except it involved a knife, and she smelled onions. He cracked three eggs into a pan and dumped something else in. "We need to find that book. It cannot be good if the Sovereign wants it." Gnawing her lip, her stomach growled, reminding her she still hadn't eaten today. She should probably make herself some coffee.

Sam stirred the eggs and pulled a plate out of the cabinets. "I'll start looking Monday. There are thousands of books in storage, donated to the institute and purchased by the previous directors. It could take a while."

"What happened to the previous directors?"

"Good question. I'll ask Mildred."

They sat in silence for a few moments, each in their own worlds, before he tipped the contents of a pan onto the plate. Sitting on the floor again, he passed it over. "I hope you like omelets. It's all I know how to make."

"Oh." She stared at the plate in surprise because she didn't realize he was cooking for her. She hated eggs. Her stomach rumbled again, and she decided she would get over it. "This is great. But you didn't eat anything, either."

"I had lunch."

She moved to stand without spilling the food, not the easiest task wrapped in an oversized jacket and two quilts. "I'll split it with you."

Sam put a hand on her arm. "Blue, I'm going to try. Conversation is exhausting." He paused, looking at his hand. "And terrifying. Especially with people who matter." He waved at the plate and tugged on the edge of the quilt laying on the floor between them. "This is what I can do."

She sat back down. "I knew you weren't a complete asshole."

"Eat the omelet."

"Most days."

Monday 4:00 PM

***

Stalk the singing infant sure
Regret the lyric glow azure
Darling run, your deeds untrue
The wolf opposes what you do

***

43

BLUE

LATE JULY. THIRTY-FIVE YEARS AGO

B lue sat at the small table in the kitchen, watching Sherry try in vain to wipe the chocolate icing out of Tiffany's hair. The sugary brown substance covered both the toddler and the highchair. Ricky stood at the counter, grazing the containers of food on display before reaching into the overhead cabinet and pulling out a plate. Since the Billy Bob incident, Blue babysat often, thus the permanent highchair and Ricky's comfort digging through the cabinets.

"This stuff is fantastic, Ms. Keys." Ricky heaped a pile of fancy filled croissants onto his plate and shoved one in his mouth. "Thanks for inviting us over." Today marked the last day of summer school and almost every single student in her classes brought some kind of food goody. By the end of the day, although she sent something home with almost every teacher in the building, she still had so many she had to ask the science teacher to give her a lift in his pickup truck so that she could get all of it and her bike home.

"Please, son," Sherry said, her own arm now covered in chocolate cupcake. "Don't talk with your mouth full."

"Shorry," Ricky said around a mouthful of food. Sherry just met Blue's eyes with a purse of her lips and a shake of her head.

"Thanks for coming guys. We couldn't finish this before it went bad."

"I'm going to get out of your hair and get this one cleaned up. Sure you don't mind watching the kids tomorrow night?" Sherry plucked Tiffany out of the highchair, still wiping at the child's face and curls. Tomorrow marked the third date with the very handsome Deputy Reginald Miller, the first officer on the scene of the Billy Bob incident, and the man that helped them board up the window. "I feel like I'm taking advantage."

"You go get your date on. I love having them." Blue was glad something good came from that terrible night. She stood as well, offering Sherry a hug and getting covered in chocolate icing when Tiffany squeed and joined in. Sherry was the closest thing she had to a friend in this time, other than Sam. And Sherry's kids were awesome. Having them over all the time made her slightly less homesick, even if it annoyed the piss out of Sam. "They can even stay overnight if they need to." Blue winked at her friend, watching her cheeks grow red as she looked at her teenage son, who was busy filling his plate and ignoring the conversation.

"I think I'll take things slowly after the last guy. I'll be home."

"Offer is on the table." The phone rang as Sherry's crew filed out the door. Ricky took one of her plates with him. "See you guys tomorrow." Shutting the door, she answered the phone. "Hello?"

"Blue?" Sam's voice was scratchy, and he cleared his throat.

"Who else would it be?"

"Change of plans. Can you meet me here? I want to show you something."

"No *Die Hard*?" Disappointment flared, and she sighed dramatically. She really wanted to see that in the theater.

"Not tonight. I'll make it up to you."

Blue frowned and looked outside. The sky was clear, but the college was a thirty-minute car ride away. It would take her forever on her bike. At Sam's insistence, she cut back on jumping to places to minimize their risk of ending up on the Cahlad radar. The Sovereign's radar was bad enough. Except for food. She would not compromise on food. "Sure? It will take a while, but I can do that."

"No. Can you meet me here? Right where I am?" He cleared his throat again. "Right now. "

"Something wrong?" She wanted to ask if she needed to bring weapons, but didn't want to say that over the phone in case anyone was listening. The threat of the Sovereign coming after them again lived at the back of her mind.

"Everything is fine." He coughed again. "But can you get here?"

"I'm on my way."

"Thanks." Sam sounded relieved. "Hey. Can you do me a favor? Bring me some allergy medicine if we have some in the house."

"On it." Blue looked at the food on the counter. "Be right there."

44

SAM

LATE JULY. THIRTY-FIVE YEARS AGO

Door shut and locked, Sam bent over a medium-sized crate he pulled into the center of the room stuffed full of ancient, dust-coated newspapers looking for the actual contents. This crate didn't contain what he was looking for.

Two hours ago, while inventorying the fourth long-forgotten room storing decades worth of magic text and artifacts in search of the book the Sovereign tried to kill him over, a faint electric sensation hovered over his skin. Nothing was out of place, but the hair on his arms stood straight up and a constant hum of magic settled in his spine. Moving to the side, the sensations subsided. Stepping back to the center of the room, they came back. There was no way he was leaving this room until he found what was causing it.

He wiped the sweat out of his face again. The stuffy room had only one tiny air vent, but he dared not unlock the door and risk someone walking in. A cold rush of air told him Blue had arrived, and he turned to find her standing mere feet away, hand hovering over a hidden knife, several dark smears running down her cheek. The magic running across his skin spiked and increased in intensity. Interesting.

She took one look at him, drenched in sweat, and covered in dirt, and wrinkled her nose, which held a dollop of the same substance on her cheek, then sneezed. "We didn't have any allergy meds." Sneezing again, she stepped forward and stopped with a gasp and a hiss. Her shoulders rolled as if fighting off a bad feeling or a chill. "Sam?"

"What is on your face?"

Ignoring his question, she moved past him toward the crates on the back wall. Brushing her fingers over each one, she rubbed her arms. "It tingles." She looked around with trepidation. "What is it?"

He shook his head, relieved that he wasn't out of his mind, and she could feel the charge of magic in the room too, because it seemed no one else could. "I don't know. I wasn't sure if it was real or just me." Stepping forward to join her in front of the pile of mysteriously magical storage crates, he got a better look at the mess on her face. Sherry's daughter Tiffany was always at their house, and she still struggled with potty training. He learned all about blow outs last week. Stuff had been everywhere, including all over Blue. "Please tell me that isn't from a diaper." Reaching to wipe the streak of dark substance from her jaw, a flare of light washed over them as his fingers brushed her skin. Blinded by the flash, he felt but couldn't see Blue being jerked backward by a force so strong her feet left the ground and slammed into his knees. Staggering, the same force enveloped him, and he flew forward toward the sound of splintering wood and large objects smashing to the ground against a concrete floor. Turning just before he hit the wall himself, his shoulder took the brunt of the impact and he slid to his knees, vision returning, heart hammering in his ears. Opening his eyes to the disaster in front of him, he shook his head and searched through the explosion of yellowed newspaper and wooden boards spiked with nails. Huddled under two crushed crates, Blue shifted as she struggled to free herself. A puddle of blood crept across the floor, gushing from a cut just behind her hairline.

Crawling over, trying to make sense of what happened, magic still pulsed through his body, scrambling his brain. Slowly his brain cleared, the pain in his shoulder taking hold as he slung the crates away, careful not to touch her in case it caused another explosive reaction. Freed of the heaviest of the debris, she rolled to her back and looked at the ceiling with glazed eyes. "What hit me?" Lifting a shaking hand to the gash on her head, it jerked backward as she flinched. "Ow."

The gash was deep, gushing a concerning amount of blood. Searching the area for anything to stem the flow, he only found a bunch of ancient newspapers. Yanking his shirt over his head, he extended it to her. Nothing in this room was sanitary, and he doubted his shirt was, but it was all he had. "Put pressure on your cut."

A shaking hand snatched his shirt, wadding it up and pressing it to her head as a fit of giggles rolled through her body. She shook as a peel of laughter echoed through the room. "This is ridiculous."

Concerned, Sam knelt next to her, but not close enough to risk touching. "How hard did you hit your head?"

Eyes still glassy, she smirked at him. "Pretty damned hard." Another round of giggles shook her.

"Why are you laughing?" He found no humor in this situation. There was still something in this mess that had the potential to hurt them, and he couldn't touch her to help.

"We have a gimmick." Blue snorted and winced as her hand shifted, moving the ruined shirt, and letting a trail of blood slide into her ear. "I get the shit knocked out of me and you lose a piece of clothing." She shook her head and closed her eyes, a wry smile forming on her lips. "I'm not complaining about the view. But can we change roles? My part hurts."

Sam gaped, stunned, and irritated by her inability to take anything seriously. "This isn't a joke."

"Not at all." She sobered and lay still for a minute. "That really hurt." Her eyes popped open, and she looked at him warily. "You are bad for my health."

Sinking to a sitting position, he waited while her pained breathing slowed, and his shoulder grew stiff. He had seen this reaction before and knew what came next. He would give her credit for making it longer than anyone else who wasn't on a payroll or able to read his mind.

Sitting up, she surveyed the destruction. "It was cupcake."

Stuck in his own head and expecting different words, Sam couldn't process what she said. "What?"

"The stuff on my face. Icing." She reached up to wipe the smear away and licked it off her finger, then dabbed at the cut on her head with his ruined shirt. "But thanks for being willing to wipe baby poo off my face. And giving me the shirt off your back." Trying to smile and falling short, she winked.

Sam couldn't tell if she was sincere or just trying to walk back her earlier words. She wasn't wrong. Disaster, not just bad luck, followed them. They sat in silence for a few moments, taking in the wreckage. Something red caught his eye laying under a large piece of broken wood, peeking through the cloud of wadded newspaper covering every inch of the floor. "Do you see that?"

Still pressing the shirt to her head, she glanced in the direction he pointed. "I do now." Climbing to her hands and knees, she dropped the shirt and crawled toward the object. "Let's see what it is."

Was she trying to get herself killed? She had no sense of self preservation. He stood to see the object better. He could see more from this angle. The red was the velvet of a bag sealed with a gold rope. "Stay there. I'll get it. You can't take another hit like that."

Her head whipped around, eyes narrowing even as her forward movement ceased. "Of course, I can. But you can't because you don't have enhanced healing. This isn't a debate."

Sam waded through the newspapers and squatted next to the bag, shifting debris away. "You are right. It isn't."

"Let me go, Sam." Blue's voice held a touch of anger.

"You were right earlier, too. I am bad for your health." He looked over his shoulder where she sat exactly where she was when he instructed her to stop. "Go home. Now."

"Mother..." Face twisting in rage and something else, she disappeared, a cold rush of air hitting the bare skin of his back. Taking a deep breath, relieved he didn't have to worry about anyone else getting hurt, he studied the bag for a moment, testing the strength of the magic as he moved his hands closer and farther away. He wouldn't have called her here if he even suspected something would explode. He just wanted to see if she could sense the magic. Finally reaching for the bag, fingers almost brushing the velvet, a large ice-cold object appeared in a flash of red hair and sneakered feet and hit him square in the chest, knocking the air from his lungs and catapulting him backward. His head bounced off the concrete as he slid across the floor, slamming to a stop in front of the door as a weight pinned his body to the ground. Clearing his head, he looked up to find Blue hovering over him, hair flying in all directions, and eyes wild with fury. Straddling his chest, she pulled her hand back and punched him in the throat before he could raise his arms or try to dislodge her. His windpipe spasmed. Choking, he bucked and threw her sideways harder than he intended, but it didn't matter. Rolling gracefully, she surged to her feet, murder in her eyes.

Lunging upright, clutching his swelling windpipe and unable to breathe correctly, much less form words, he prepared for the inevitable attack.

Instead of pushing her advantage, she disappeared, reappearing across the room over the red bag. Bending to pick it up, she winced and hissed, peering inside, then dumped all the contents on the floor in front of her. Sam dared not get any closer while she stood so close to the artifacts. The look she sent him let him know that was her intent.

A heavy red leather-bound tome thumped to the floor, followed by the clatter of red metal boxes. The magic in the room surged but didn't explode. Reaching down, she flicked open several of the boxes, grinding out a pained curse as a flood of magic filled the room before shutting them again. Glaring at him and shaking her hands, she used a foot to push the items farther apart, thinning the density of magic in the air as she did so. "Clear." She threw the red bag to the side and stalked his direction, stopping just shy of his reach, fist clenched. "I promised I wouldn't leave. I didn't promise I wouldn't kick your ass." Projecting an aura of lethal intent and reminding him with only body language that she had once been the Cahlad's best assassin, she stepped forward. "Don't ever send me away again." The anger on her face faltered for a moment, replaced with hurt, then snapped back into place. "Do you understand me?"

Nodding and still gasping for air, he held his free hand in front of him to slow her approach, not wanting to fight. This had not been his intent. Usually, she was easygoing and forgiving to a fault. He had never seen her this mad.

Knocking his hand to the side, she kept moving forward and pulled the hand clutching his bruised windpipe away gently, in stark contrast to the dark look clouding her features. Her hand covered where she punched him earlier and a wave of warmth filled the tissue, relieving the pain and paralysis. "Thank you." He cleared his throat.

"The kitchen is a shit show now." Reaching into her waistband, she ripped a cotton shirt tucked there loose and slung it at his face. Hands clenching at her sides once more, she stepped back, almost snarling at him. "You are cleaning it up."

"I messed up."

"You think?"

"I just wanted to keep you from getting hurt."

"You knew better." Shooting him a bird, she stalked to the door. She waved at the items on the floor as she leaned against the wall. "You're up, Diablo. Avoid the boxes. They hurt."

Recognizing an excellent opportunity to keep his mouth shut, he focused on the brittle and cracked leather of the book, picking it up and absorbing the powerful surge of magic it emitted. He didn't know how old the book was, but it looked ancient. Turning it over in his hands, he found the cover so worn that the ink and embossing were no longer visible. On the first page, he read the printed words in the center and struggled not to drop the book. He looked again. "Can't be."

"What's it say?"

To his knowledge, the term Sovaj and the rare abilities they exhibited did not exist in the magic world until the late 1920s to early

1930s. The book he held in his hands predated that time frame by a century. "Se't Sovaj."

"Sovaj? Like Sovaj, Sovaj?" Blue hopped off the floor and stalked over, body still vibrating with anger. Stopping before the sting of magic became unbearable, she leaned over, squinting. "Se't? That's seven? Wild seven? French?"

Resting the book on a crate that somehow survived the past ten minutes intact, they read the first few pages together. It appeared to be a combination of personal journal and instruction manual. A dialect of Creole comprised most of the prose on the two hundred pages of the ancient tome. "Looks like a Creole dialect." In between the pages of text were sections of what he could only describe as spelled blueprints, the glyphs and shapes undulating on the page as their meaning whispered through his brain like icy wind. He marveled at the magic in the pages and contemplated the significance of the title. Two words jumped off the page. Written in the margin, third in a numbered list of seven items were the words, Son Sovaj.

He ran his fingers over the writing. In this language, Son Sovaj meant wild sound. The other list items all included the word sovaj or wild and translated to wild light, wild force, wild shape, wild sound, wild heart, wildlife.

"I can read some of it." She tilted her head and looked up; forehead furrowed. "But I don't know what language this is." She pointed to the rounded glyphs and schematics below the paragraphs.

"Does it move when you look at it?"

Sending him a look that said he might be the one with a head injury, she studied the page again. "No. It's just funny symbols."

"I don't know what language it is, either, but I can tell you what it says. Those are magic blueprints."

Her attention left the book, and she stared at him. "Is that your secondary?" He nodded.

"Can you speak them, too? "

"If it's a spoken language."

"That's super handy."

"Look at this." He pointed to the list on the margins then huffed in frustration and sent her a cautious look. "Sorry. Ignore that."

"Sam." Blue's voice was resigned. "Look. Just." Putting her hands on her hips, she hung her head so that her hair fell down and obscured her face. "You can't walk on eggshells. I don't expect you to be perfect. You know where the line is. If you cross it, I'm going to punch you in the throat again."

"That's fair." He nodded. "Forgiven?"

"It's fucked up is what it is. We both need therapy. I'm still pissed. But I'll get over it." Leaning closer, she finally read the list and gaped at the page. "Son Sovaj. Wild sound. That thing stuck us here? It made us?"

"Looks that way."

Chewing her lip, she almost tapped the words, but drew her fingers back at the last moment and stood. Picking up the box she opened earlier, she turned it over in her hands. "Fos Sovaj." Flipping the item so that he could see the tiny words engraved on the bottom of the box, she set it down and searched the other boxes. Standing with a different box in her hand, she tossed it. "This one feels light."

"Which one is it?" He didn't need her to show him the words etched on the bottom.

"Son Sovaj." Taking a step away from him, she peeked inside the box. "Yep. Empty."

"Bet I know who has it." Sam reread the moving glyphs of the page in front of him. It gave him the first shred of hope in months. "And I bet this is what they are looking for."

"They are a set? A collection?"

"I'll have to read more. But it seems likely." He slammed the book shut. "They aren't looking for the artifacts. They are looking for the book. Does that mean they don't know about them or that the Son Sovaj isn't like the others?"

"Don't care. You saw what they did with just one. Those are blueprints, right? They could build more."

Sam flipped the book closed. "Agreed. But that means we can, too. We might not have to wait for Amber to go back to our time."

Blue stared at the book dubiously. "Have you ever made an artifact before?"

"No. But maybe I can learn?"

45

NISHA

Nisha sat at the small dining table with Harper listening to Finn and Kendra lay out their plan for getting Zella out of the Cahlad compound without engaging Larson Battle or the small army of goons and clueless FBI agents swarming the place. Kendra stood in the center of the room pointing at its occupants assigning each a task and explaining how to use various pieces of equipment. Finn walked around the room and passed out earpieces to everyone. When he reached Devon, he stood in front of her, hiding his actions with his body, and discreetly handed her a small nine-millimeter. Devon took it, checked it, and tucked it in her waistband out of habit all without drawing attention to herself. There was more to that woman than met the eye. Finn squeezed Devon's shoulder, said something Nisha couldn't hear and continued his path, handing out the rest of the equipment.

She toyed with the idea of removing the necklace Greenlee provided when she woke from her nap earlier, to help her from being overwhelmed by the sheer mental volume of the apartment. It functioned much like the one he made for Ben. He made one for Kendra, too, who could not even be in the building without it because of the magic smell of the body parts they gathered. A sweet gesture, it dampened the voices in her head giving her a level of silence she only experienced when she went hiking or rock climbing in remote areas with Ivan who insisted on tagging along, so she didn't end up like the guy that had to cut his own arm off after a hiking accident. But she had yet to adjust to the stifling sensation of having a magic cotton ball stuffed into her mental ear canal. As much as she complained about the mental chatter, she didn't know what to do without it.

Nobody in this room trusted Mitch yet. She didn't need her magic to see that. Even Greenlee. Devon and Kendra, least of all. Lifting the necklace away from her skin, Harper's mental excitement and wild daydreams over the recent developments in Greenlee and Devon's relationship overwhelmed her and made her blush. Dropping the necklace against her skin to shut off the X-rated images, she rubbed her eyes and focused on Kendra's words.

Finn and Kendra would enter the campus from the South. Nisha, Greenlee, and Harper would find a safe place in an adjacent building close enough for Nisha to listen to the inhabitants and report on anything useful. Harper would provide camouflage. Greenlee would provide firepower and enough chaos to get them out if things went south. A team of Finn's men led by a man named Tanner would cover the rear entrance of the campus to make sure no one slipped out and were prepared to enter if Finn needed an assist. That left Ben,

Devon, and Mitch to cover the front entrance of the Cahlad and make sure nobody left until Finn reported a successful extraction.

Greenlee stood, a deck of cards in his hand. Dealing each of them two cards as he walked around the room, he sat back down on the couch next to Mitch and waited for Kendra to finish telling them how to use the headsets and providing instructions to keep chatter to a minimum. When she finished, he pointed at the cards they held. "They all came from the same deck and work just like the bead that I gave Lexi. For most of you, they're single use. That is why I gave you two. Keep them safe."

Finn leaned against the wall and stared at them. "Our mission is to retrieve our people. That is our only mission tonight. This should go smooth. Kendra and I, with Nisha's help, will be in and out in less than twenty minutes. If anything does not go to plan, do not improvise. Get yourself to safety and use the cards to locate each other." Finn's face held a dark and authoritative look. "We will get ourselves out if we aren't worrying about you. If we need help, my men are on standby. This is what we do." Looking directly at Mitch, Finn continued. "We can't afford to give Larson another valuable hostage. Does everyone understand?" Nobody, not even Mitch, questioned his orders. The room's occupants responded with a chorus of yeses. Nisha watched Mitch. He agreed, but she didn't believe him. If Zella was in trouble, he wouldn't stand down.

Finn nodded in acknowledgment. "Good. Rest up. Grab some food. We leave at twenty-three hundred hours." Kendra joined him in the kitchen and the two of them spoke quietly, no doubt discussing the finer points of their plan.

Ben approached Mitch, likely eager to continue discussing their shared family member. Mitch, though shell-shocked, remained receptive and genuinely glad to still have a piece of his daughter in the world, though none of them were sure how it was possible yet.

Greenlee stood and walked over to Devon, looking less than pleased to be going a different direction than the woman he spent the past week trying to find. Placing something in her hand, the look on his face was grim, but even from this distance, without reading his mind, she could see the words on his lips. "I love you. I'll find you."

Devon nodded and said something Nisha couldn't decipher because Greenlee's head blocked her view. "Aren't they sweet?" Harper leaned over conspiratorially.

"Disgustingly so." Nisha eyed the pair. "They don't seem very upset about their friend."

Harper shrugged. "In fairness, neither do you." Drawing a circle with her finger over the woodgrain of the table, she kept her head down. "But see, sugar, the difference is, Thor doesn't believe his friend is dead. Something about dragons I might have overheard. Sound familiar?"

Tilting her head, Nisha wanted to dismiss the bubbly woman as a brainless ditz, but just like everyone else in this room, she was far more than met the eye. Nisha had not shared her feeling that Sam and possibly Ivan were still alive. But the comment about dragons intrigued her. She took the bait. "Ms. Z?"

"Know anybody else who talks about crazy nonsense like it's gospel?"

Nisha shrugged now. Pretty much every major human institution was based on or morphed into people who talked about crazy nonsense like it was gospel. "Lots of people. But dragons are in Ms. Z's wheelhouse."

"So are peaches." Harper watched Devon and Greenlee, who remained in their own little world. "Didn't you see peaches when you were spying on the baby girls?"

Nisha stared at Harper, dumbfounded for a moment, before scanning the room for Zella's journal. The journal had a sketch of peaches.

She tapped the table twice and stood. "Something to think about, anyway." She walked to the couch, sat next to Ben, and slung her legs across the laps of a soul eater and the Cahlad Paragon, oblivious to their stunned and irritated faces. "I need my beauty sleep. Don't mind me, boys."

46

ZELLA

The door swinging open with a bang had both Zella and Hale raising their heads in alarm. Hale snorted away sleep. She struggled to move her head around stiff muscles. She couldn't feel her hands and her shoulders ached almost unbearably.

The same man who tied her arms stood in the doorway, leering at them with disdain. "Do either of you need to take a piss? Larson doesn't want you to ruin the carpet in his new offices."

A flash of a urinal and a knife skittered across her vision. The images rendered so close she could not tell who was involved, but she saw dirty-blond hair and a gaping stab wound in a broad masculine back. Hale sat up, and she put her leg across his ankle.

He sent her a pleading gaze. "My eyeballs are swimming, Ms. Z. Have mercy." She pressed harder on his leg. Something bad happened in the bathroom.

Slumping backward, Hale gave the man a strained smile. "All's well here, bud. Carpet is safe."

The man knew Hale lied and laughed as he closed the door. Before it latched all the way, a roar echoed down the hallway. "Get her!"

Bedlam broke out outside the office, and the door stood half open. Footsteps raced by and a rapid staccato of gunfire pierced the walls.

Hale bumped into her hard with his shoulder, knocking her sideways, landing on his side next to her. Above them, pieces of the wall exploded out in little chunks. Sam's desk splintered and shards of wood flew through the air. "Did they give guns to the toddlers?" Hale wiggled forward, putting himself between her and the wall. She rolled her eyes, but he didn't see it. "These guys are clowns."

The gunfire stopped. More footsteps thundered by, punctuated by confused shouts and barked orders. Finally, the world outside the office fell silent except for a powerful spray of water they could hear even from here. "This is torture. Evil sons of bitches." Hale scowled. "Somebody shut the damned door!"

They both flopped about until they could sit upright again. The door slammed shut, knocking the framed picture off the wall and shattering it into a million pieces.

"Thank god." Hale sighed in relief and leaned against the wall. "The water was killing me."

47

RHODES

"No." Rhodes repeated himself for the third time. He was understanding why parents were always so worn down and haggard. Children said no all the time. But if they heard it, they sure pretended not to.

The discussion about coming up with an escape plan began well. The girls convinced him that running and hiding should be their first option, since he was the only one trained for any kind of combat.

Both girls were terrified if he fought the Sovereign he would die and then they would be all alone. When Lexi insisted squirrels were the ideal disguise, the conversation devolved. "No squirrels. There are too many owls. I heard them outside last night."

"Well, you won't teach us how to fly." Ava sat on the counter, arms crossed, still sulking about that fact. "We could be owls if you would."

Lexi sat at the kitchen table shuffling cards with the expertise of a Vegas dealer, her security pillow tucked in her lap. The quiet flutter of cards whispered into the room, and she looked back and forth between Ava and Rhodes.

"I told you why." Rhodes leaned against the back door and did his best to look stern and wise, hoping something would get through to the girls, since words weren't working. "Flying isn't intuitive for humans. The learning curve is steep. You will break something, and we don't have access to medical care."

Lexi shuffled the cards with a flourish. "How did you learn if you kept breaking things?"

"I lived with a healer."

Lexi's mouth formed an oh. "Tia Blue?"

"Yeah, honey." Rhodes decided a on different approach. Maybe guilt would work. "She will kick my ass if I let you get eaten by owls. Let's choose something that can defend itself."

"Have you ever seen a pissed-off squirrel?" Ava scowled when Rhodes laughed at her question. "One got trapped in a trash can at summer camp. A counselor tried to help, and it almost ripped her face off." Ava sent him a glare when he snorted. "It launched out of that thing, making this horrible noise, clawing, and biting. Trust me, buddy. They can defend themselves."

"Squirrels can climb. Wolves and dogs can't climb. They are stuck on the ground." Lexi pointed a card at him and flicked it, sending it fluttering across the room. He caught it. It was the same seven of hearts that kept popping up in every hand they played. Someone won with it every time. Ava even inventoried the deck to make sure it wasn't a trick deck. There was only one seven of hearts.

"Bears can climb." Rhodes wasn't willing to compromise. Disguising yourself as a squirrel was ridiculous.

"What will we do when we reach a populated area?" Ava threw out her hands as unwilling to budge on the topic as he was. "They shoot bears that wind up in neighborhoods. Wolves, too."

"Squirrels do this cool superhero landing thing. Even when they fall from super high." Lexi made a fist and posed.

"Nobody is afraid of a squirrel. They are cute. People won't even notice we are around." Ava made eye contact with Lexi and nodded. Rhodes hated to admit it, but they were making sense.

"No superhero landings." Rhodes scrubbed his hand down his face in frustration. "I've never been a squirrel before. I don't know if we'll be able to do that."

Ava's face lit up, smelling defeat. "We can be squirrels?"

When Lexi first appeared and told him Blue had sent her, he was honored by the fact she trusted him. He now suspected the gesture held a touch of revenge and she groomed the child for maximum pain from birth. He could feel his hair turning gray with each passing second. If they wanted to be a squirrel, they would be a squirrel. But he hated it. He blamed Disney. "Fine."

Lexi jumped up from the chair and did a victory dance. "Squirrels!"

Ava winked at Lexi and jumped off the counter. Soon, the two were prancing in a circle with their hands in front of them, twitching their noses, then squatting to the ground in a superhero pose. "Squirrel victory dance."

Rhodes couldn't help the laugh that erupted at the sheer ridiculousness happening in front of him. They needed to discuss where their squirrels would run and a few other important details. He stayed silent. The girls needed this moment of levity, Ava in particular. Her mental state impacted her ability to control her magic. If things went sideways again, he needed her to stay in control. A dire squirrel was just as likely to draw attention as a wolf or a bear. He rubbed his eyes and looked down at the playing card in his hand as he waited for the squirrel dance to wind down and the girls to stop giggling.

"We need to work on your control if this is going to work." He walked over and took a seat at the table, leaning forward and gesturing to the two chairs across from him. A teacher he was not, but he could at least share what his own teachers told him when he started training with the Cahlad. It wasn't ideal. But he was what they had right now. "Welcome to the first class of how to control my magic 101."

Both girls sobered quickly, standing uncertainly. Lexi's face twisted in confusion. "Me, too?"

"You, too, Lexi Lou."

Ava remained quiet, an immense weight falling onto her shoulders again. Both girls sat in the chair and waited for his next instructions.

"Show me where you feel your magic."

Without hesitation, both girls moved, understanding exactly what he asked. Lexi pointed to her palms and Ava pointed at her heart. His own magic was a nagging pressure behind his eyes.

"This is all about building mental muscles. I want you to close your eyes." He waited for the girls to follow his instructions. "Great. Now Ava, imagine you are a super strong superhero. You are wearing a cape and have a super strong super dog."

"I want an assassin outfit. Black. Knives everywhere. I bet that is what Ms. Blue wears."

It was what Blue used to wear. "Fine. Wear what you want. You still have a super powerful dog, and you need to keep a firm grip on his leash, so he doesn't get away."

"She. Her name is Bubbles."

Rhodes laid his forehead on the table in exasperation. Why him? "Just keep Bubbles on her leash."

"I've got her." Ava beamed. "She is a good girl."

Rhodes had to laugh. If it worked, he would take it. But Lexi had different magic. She had at will magic, so he needed a different tactic. "Lexi, imagine you are reaching into your magic and pulling out a whip, like Indiana Jones."

Lexi's eyes peeked open. "Who is Indiana Jones?"

Rhodes rolled his eyes. "Lord help me."

48

BLUE

NOVEMBER. THIRTY-FIVE YEARS AGO

S am stood next to the Christmas tree, feet flat on the floor, begrudgingly placing ornaments at the very top of the tree so that she wouldn't have to dig out the ladder. "I don't understand why we are doing this."

"Because it's the day after Thanksgiving, and this is what you do." Blue swept the glitter and pine needles from the Christmas tree into a dustpan. "Well. It's what Devon does, and I will never take it for granted again. This is work." A wave of homesickness washed over her as Sam secured the gaudy silver star to the top. This tree was pretty, but it lacked the handmade ornaments and mementos from Lexi's early years and copious amounts of hideous metallic garland Greenlee always insisted on. It wasn't the same.

He stepped back and surveyed his work, then adjusted the star again. "Happy now?"

"Yes, dear." Tone dripping with sarcasm, Blue dragged the tree box out of the living room. Chucking the box out the side door into the carport, to deal with later, she snatched a few overdone cookies off a plate. Their Thanksgiving consisted of eating turkey sandwiches and watching television. They tried their hand at home-made cookies with semi-edible results. Sam wasn't kidding about only knowing how to cook an omelet and Blue didn't know how to cook anything. Amber should be here any day now. He didn't want to go far from the house.

She wished Amber would hurry and show up or leave one of her notes. She was tired and irritable. For the past week, she woke with nightmares every night, screaming and drenched in sweat. That meant Sam was tired and irritable as well. He was also anxious and antsy and putting up the tree was more of a distraction to keep her from killing him than anything else. It also helped take her mind off the fact she had been gone for seven months after leaving her best friend and her niece in the care of her ex-fiancé running from madmen who were shooting at them with rocket-propelled grenades. Plopping down on the floor because she still refused to sit on the world's most uncomfortable couch, she handed a cookie up to Sam, flipping the channel to a B-rate science fiction movie, and eyed the Christmas tree one more time. "It needs more garland."

"Well, isn't this domestic?" a pained but familiar voice asked from the kitchen. Still caught off gaurd, although they had expected Amber for days, Blue choked on the bite of cookie in her mouth at Amber's sudden appearance and jumped to her feet. Amber stood leaning against the kitchen counter clutching a bleeding wound in her side. The small bracelet on her wrist glowed pink, beads spinning menacingly slow.

Rushing forward, the instinct to help took over. She jerked to a halt when both of Sam's hands grabbed her shoulders and pulled her back. "The Son Sovaj. You shouldn't touch her yet." A flash of irritation washed over her as she stopped in her tracks. But then her brain caught up with her instincts and she lowered her hands. He was right. They didn't know what would happen if she touched Amber now. They needed to be careful and deliberate.

Amber winced and groaned, focusing on the glowing bracelet. "Got it." Taking it off and setting in on the counter, she leaned farther over in obvious pain. "A little help."

Blue approached, studying her once best friend. Frowning, Blue placed a hand on Amber's wound and let some magic flow between them. Something wasn't adding up. "You don't have any knives on you, do you? Did you come to play more mind games?"

Amber glanced up with tired blue eyes. "I'm sorry about that. I didn't have all the facts." As Blue healed her, Amber's stance shifted upright, no longer hunched in pain. From the side, Sam offered her a glass of water and Amber took it. "Thank you."

Blue tilted her head, still considering this person she thought she knew, but didn't know at all. "Do you have all the facts now?" Amber's wound stable, she stepped away only to bump into Sam, who stood directly behind her. Glancing over her shoulder, it surprised her to find his expression more angry than relieved, piercing Amber with a calculating gaze.

"I know we need to get you back." Amber sipped her water. "I've never moved people with me. I couldn't. I don't think I was ever supposed to."

"How does this fix anything?" Blue asked, making quotation marks with her hands. "Some instructions would have been nice."

Amber shook her head and shrugged. "I don't know. I didn't pick this time. I had no control over that."

"But you left everything at the wreck."

Blue's statement confused Amber. "I don't know what you are talking about."

"Why didn't you come back five months ago?" The sensation of magic washed over her skin even though Sam only asked a question.

"Things were swinging in our favor." Amber ran a hand through her hair. "But everything is a mess. It's a war." She looked up with pleading eyes. "Ava can't help who she is. She is just a kid. But I can't seem to keep her out of it. They all want to use her as a tool in their own plans."

Blue crossed her arms over her chest. "I know a bit about that." A snort of agreement came from behind her. "How long do we have? I have questions. How did I not know you were a time traveler? Fifteen years, Amber." She couldn't keep the hurt out of her voice. In her time at the Cahlad, Amber had been her only friend. They saw each other every day. She was the only bright spot in otherwise grueling and lonely days' training to be a Zenith while other children went to class and made friends and had lives.

"I was scared." Amber sat her water down. "I saw what they did to you. All of you, really. I didn't want that life." She looked over Blue's shoulder at Sam. "I only have a few minutes. I'm four jumps out of my primary timeline."

"I wouldn't have told them. You know that." Blue waved a hand at the glowing string of beads on the counter. "Where did you get that thing?"

Amber's emotional manipulation didn't affect Sam. "What are we going back to?"

Amber answered Sam's question and ignored Blue's. "A war. There's no way around it. I've tried everything. Now I'm just trying to keep Ava alive." She motioned to the blood ringed hole in her shirt. "I've tried to kill Larson. I can't take him." She held Blue's gaze. "I'm not you."

"There it is." Sam stepped forward, radiating menace. "Does she die where you plan to drop us off so you can save Ava? Are you even planning to take us home?"

Blue froze, catching up with his logic, remembering Amber's statement in the field that one of them always died. Apprehension washed over her. But Amber's motivations changed nothing. "It doesn't matter. One problem at a time. If we want to leave here, we have to trust her."

"We have to use her." Sam loomed over them both in the small kitchen. "I don't trust her."

Amber's eyes flashed with the same look they held when she sliced Blue's gut open ten years ago. They were hard and angry and reflected a lifetime of pain. "I'll do anything to save my daughter."

Sam crossed his arms over his chest. "That's the first honest thing you have said since I met you." Blue studied them both, trying to understand what was happening. Amber's behavior hurt but didn't surprise her. The woman had literally stabbed her in the back. But she expected Sam to be overjoyed at the prospect of going back home. He had been on edge for weeks, waiting for this exact moment. This sudden reluctance came out of left field.

"Both of you. Shut up." Shoving her fist into her eyes so that she could think, she took a deep breath. "Look, you both want me to fight your war with Larson for you." She stepped back so that she could see both of them. "There is your common ground."

The comment genuinely offended Sam.

Amber's eyes narrowed.

"I need you to get me home. And I'm not leaving Sam here. So. Here is what is going to happen. Amber, you are going to do the time travel thing right back to where you found us. Sam is going to tell you to do that just to make sure it happens. And only that." She turned to him with a stern expression to make sure he understood she meant he shouldn't give any half-assed archaic orders to fix things. He scowled in response.

"And I'm going to be the best damned conduit I can be. That's what you called me, right? A conduit. A thing to use to get what you want. This is the only way you get it, Amber. Take us both home safe. No hijinks." Blue's eyebrows raised in open challenge as she glared at Amber.

Amber shook her head. "It doesn't work that way. I told him. Sevens. It's sevens there, too. That's thirty-five hours at a minimum."

"Better than seven months." Sam took a step back. "I'll take it. Even if she is lying."

"Everyone agrees?"

Sam and Amber stood staring each other down for a long moment before Amber nodded and picked up the bracelet, which flared to life as she wrapped it around her wrist. "One point two one gigawatts. Let's do it. Same order as last time?"

"Seems prudent." Dreading what came next, Blue found the same reluctance on Amber's face. "Ready?" Not waiting for a reply, she grabbed Amber's arm, the force of the magic surge making her muscles spasm as her feet dragged across the floor in the familiar magnetic pull. Amber screamed, and Blue gritted her teeth. "Sam?"

He wrapped his arm around her waist and put a hand on Amber's shoulder. The second the jolt of magic hit him; he almost snapped her in half. "Take us back to our time." He ground the words out as the world tilted. Blood dripped out of her nose and her vision blotched at the edges. Swirls of light surrounded them, a multicolored rainbow, bright white and a black shadow dusted with flashes of brilliant light. She remembered a little past this part last time. She remembered it hurt far worse than this.

Amber screamed in pain and frustration, laying her head on Blue's shoulder. "I can't lock on. You are too..." She hesitated, a strangled cry escaping. "Heavy?"

Blue was very familiar with that problem. She spent years maxing out her capacity to overcome it. "Pull more magic! Both of you." She already pulled everything she could, quaking with the effort. Without help from someone like Ava, she couldn't offer more just from the environment, and she couldn't sustain this.

"I can't." Amber strained. A surge of black light made her glance over her shoulder. Sam's eyes were gone, replaced with black orbs swirling with fractals of light, and his veins were black tracing under his skin. A crawl of fear rippled down her spine. She figured that was an Ava side effect. But it was an at will ability. What the fuck?

It still wasn't enough. She could channel more power if she could find another source. Deciding and acting before she could talk herself out of it, she slammed her hand down over the furiously spinning beads on Amber's bracelet. The beads tore through the tissue in her hand, spraying blood in all directions as a high-pitched whine rang out. The blinding agony that ripped through her mind made her scream. This is what she remembered from before. They were getting somewhere. As her eyes fell shut and her breathing faltered, an explosive surge of rainbow light burst from her body and collided with the white and violet swirls around them. The piercing ring of the beads echoed in her head with a vague awareness of falling forward, no longer supporting her own weight as the lights flickered around her, along with pulses in her failing vision. Everything hurt.

Someone was saying something. There were words, but she couldn't understand over the ringing. The magic she channeled dwindled. She was tapped out. But a different wash of magic surged over her, forcing her to draw in a breath. "Breathe and let go!" Sam's voice echoed in her mind, but not her ears. Her eyes snapped open, and she yanked her bleeding hand away from Amber's wrist. Amber gasped for air and jerked away, disappearing, hands outstretched as the vortex of magic around them shattered.

Flying backward, she landed hard on something uneven that buckled and crashed beneath her, knocking the air from her lungs. Clutching her throbbing hand to her chest, she blinked, trying to reorient herself as the pain in her head subsided, unsure where or when she was. A silver star appeared in her vision against a field of white. She was still in the tiny house on Kay Street. Turning her head, a wave of nausea washed over her. Sam stopped them. "Why?"

"It was killing you." She couldn't see him, but he was close. Amber was gone and not coming back soon.

She closed her eyes, exhausted all the way to her soul. She was so close to getting at least one of them home. Even if she didn't make it, he would have held up his end of the bargain. Devon, Greenlee, and Lexi would be free to live their lives. "So?"

No words answered, only an angry grunt as he lifted himself off the floor and looked down, eyes not entirely back to normal, glowing an eerie black. He wiped an alarming stream of blood away from his nose with his sleeve. Then he leaned over and used her shirt to deal with her bleeding nose. Lifting her hand to look at her palm, he grimaced and stalked into the kitchen, reappearing with a hand towel which he tied on with more force than necessary. He moved to lift her off the wreckage of their ruined sofa. At least one good thing came of this mess. That sofa deserved to die. "Don't you dare. I'll be fine in a minute."

"It took you five days last time, and you didn't touch the bracelet." Ignoring her, he lifted, causing a wave of vertigo and sickness that made her gag. "What in the hell were you thinking?"

Resigned to the humiliation of being carted around like luggage, she let her head fall to the side, understanding the ramifications of what had just happened. "What if that was our only shot?" She tried to look up, only seeing his angry chin. "What if she doesn't come back?"

Sam sat her down on the bed and stepped back. "You can punch me in the throat later. When you can lift your arms."

"I'm serious. We can't even try again for six years." A ball of grief formed in her throat, making it hard to swallow and tears filled her eyes as the reality of not seeing her family again for years if ever finally sank in. Her eyes leaked and she couldn't even lift her hand far enough to wipe the drops away, voice now a whisper. "Damn it. You said you wanted to go home."

His teeth ground as his jaw worked, expression otherwise unreadable before turning on his heel and stalking out of the room without saying another word.

If she could move any of her body parts, she would have thrown a kicking hissy fit. Blue screamed then closed her eyes for lack of anything else to do.

Two days later, she finally made it out of the bedroom under her own power in search of food that was not an omelet. She found Sam sitting on a brand-new sofa, sound asleep with the Se't Sovaj in his lap. The Christmas tree was smothered in garland. It still wasn't the same. But she appreciated the effort.

MONDAY 11:00 PM

***

The Se't Sovaj. A tome and tale.
A dulcet cure to break the spell.
Beware last child of Zenith, the sentinel guard and carry.
Douse the flames of war's inferno lest hope's bloody corpse they ferry.
The stars know not if she portend rebirth or ruin?
When release the arrow aim be true, but for reign or revolution?

***

49

SAM

DECEMBER. THIRTY-FIVE YEARS AGO

A bottle of single barrel hundred-proof whiskey thumped onto the coffee table in front of him, followed by two glasses full of ice and another of water. He stopped reading his book. Night had fallen outside, and the clock told him it was almost midnight. Blue sat down on the floor on the other side of the table and poured three fingers into each ice filled glass. They hadn't spoken much since the day after Thanksgiving. Things were tense, to say the least.

Picking up her glass, she took a sip and stared at the wall behind his head. "I'm gonna fuck some shit up."

He weighed his choices. Even though he never drank around other people, choosing water would not change anything when a conversation started with a declaration like that from Blue West. Reaching for the glass of whiskey, he took a sip and leaned back, stretching an arm across the couch. He hadn't had a taste of alcohol in months.

When he looked back up, Blue watched him with a calculating gaze, eyes darting between his face and the glass like she hadn't expected him to pick it up. "You want in?"

He sipped his drink knowing whatever she was up to was dangerous and ill-advised. He also knew he would not say no. "Sure."

"Are you going to get in my way when things get hairy?" Swirling her whiskey with an innocent look on her face, she raised an eyebrow.

Noting that she said when and not if things get hairy, he shrugged. "If I think your death is imminent, yes. Every time."

Judging by the way her eyebrows furrowed, that was the wrong answer. "I don't understand. Our whole arrangement is predicated on me doing things for you and your interest that have a high probability of imminent death." Frustration laced her words.

He wasn't sure how to pass this test. "You want me to be honest?"

"That's why I brought the whiskey."

Afraid she was going to say that he tossed back the rest of his glass and sat it back on the table. She refilled it. He waved at the whiskey. "I don't do this around other people. This is dangerous."

"Yep."

"You don't know what I'll say."

"Nope." Topping off her own glass, she settled in. "You have to tell me what's in your head. We probably should have done this before everything went to hell with Amber. Let's practice."

"Christ." Sam put his head in his hands. He was about to make a huge mistake. "Please understand. I've lived alone since I was thirteen, except for a week or two here and there to go home and visit my parents. That stopped before I graduated. There are reasons for that."

"Reasons." She nodded seriously. "Got it."

"My social interactions are thinking things around a mind reader, interpreting Ivan's grunts because he is resistant to my magic and a dating profile that says I'm mute."

"I've seen your profile now that you mention it. Smart move not using your actual picture. I can see the headlines now." She waved her hand across the sky. "Cahlad Regent's Preference for Kinky Silent One-night Stands Revealed." Frowning, she knocked on the coffee table. "Otherwise, it reads Cahlad Regent uses magic to coerce women into sex. No way to defend yourself from that one unless you recorded it. And that's a whole different headline. I see your pickle."

"See. This." He pointed at her, then at the whiskey between them and swirled his finger around the house. "I've never had this before. Never dreamed I could. Whatever it is? Without mind reading. Normal?"

Holding up a finger, she took another sip of whiskey. "Are you telling me you blew what might have been our only shot to go back to our own time so that we could stay here and playhouse?"

"No." Sam shook his head. "Not even close."

"Good. I'm glad I don't have to punch you in the throat. Drink some whiskey and try again." When he didn't respond, she continued. "I've got a few years."

He looked down at his hands, struggling to form words and hoping she would give up. They both sipped their drinks in silence for a long time. Eventually, the whiskey kicked in and his judgment flew out the window. "You know what staying this close looks like. And look at where you are. That's why."

"Because I am hard to kill?" She made a face. "Then you should have just let me get us home."

"You are hard to kill. Not immortal. But that isn't what I meant."

"I'm a pretty good listener?"

"You are. If I talk. Still not what I meant."

"It's the little containers of lasagne verdi al forno from Bologna, isn't it?"

"That stuff is amazing, but it is going to get us caught one day. I know you are getting it in Italy."

"Not the food." She scratched her chin and hummed. "So emotional support Zenith?"

He pinched his nose in frustration and almost laughed. "Fuck me, Blue. Are you being dense on purpose?" Blue shifted to stand, and he jerked his hand away from his face to find her watching him with a raised eyebrow, waiting to see what he did next. "Disregard that."

Erupting with laughter, she tossed her head back, plopped back on her butt and pointed. "I've been waiting for that one since we got here. You should have seen your face." A fit of giggles followed until she sobered but still smiled. "This is good. We have the big two behind us. Shit and fuck me. Lo-and-behold, we survived."

Finishing her drink, she slammed it on the table. "No more eggshells. Once more with feeling."

"What if I hadn't told you to disregard that?"

"I knew what I was doing." She looked him up and down playfully. "You aren't hideous. Even with the beard. And you aren't that guy. So, talk."

Jerking his head back, an indignant snort erupted before he could stop himself. "Not hideous?"

"I said what I said."

Clearly, he feared what he would say more than she did. So why not? "You asked for it."

An amused smirk settled over her face, and she made a give me motion with her free hand. "I did."

"I haven't had a place to call home since my magic manifested. Where people who couldn't read my mind weren't terrified of me. Somewhere safe? I forgot what that was like. It's priceless." He waved a hand again, just like he did before, encompassing the room and everything happening in it. "But I have that here. I've spoken more in the last six months than I have in twenty years."

Leaning forward to make sure she understood they were no longer joking around, he looked straight into her eyes. "I care about you. A great deal. I want you to see your Greenlee and Roane's daughter, and her little evil genius again. So, you can stop with the self-sacrificial B.S. Even if we never stop Larson, and I have to live through six years of big hair and grunge music again. Even if it pisses you off and you punch me in the throat. Even if it means I don't see the time I started in until I'm old and gray."

Her expression grew more stunned with every word he said.

He took a deep breath. This was a disaster, and he couldn't seem to stop himself. Damned whiskey. "I don't know what tomorrow looks like without you anymore."

She turned her head away and blew out her cheeks, no longer smirking.

"Did I get it right that time?"

Still looking away, she whispered her next words. "That's a lot to unpack."

"Much easier than charades." Scooting his glass away, he sat back, hoping he hadn't gone too far. This is why he didn't drink around people.

She sat stock still and stared at the wall so long he began to think he had gone too far. Finally, she sucked in a deep breath and squared her shoulders. Facing him again, she eyed the whiskey with equal parts appreciation and concern. "Can we fuck shit up now?"

"Isn't that what we just did?"

She laughed and extended a hand. "Nah. Not yet."

Relieved, he took it. "What are we waiting for?"

"I kinda like whiskey-Sam." The living room disappeared, replaced with a poorly lit concrete hallway filled with the squeals of happy babies.

50

SAM

DECEMBER. THIRTY-FIVE YEARS AGO

Blue crept forward toward the sounds and peeked around a door. She motioned for him to look as well. Taking a moment to orient himself because he just learned that mixing whiskey and teleportation was ill-advised, he followed. The world stopped spinning, but his head still ached like spikes of metal pierced his skull. He looked into the room, a large rectangular space with doors every six to eight feet lining the walls. Between the doors, cribs took up the space. Two baby girls crawled across a carpeted floor. In the corner, a gaunt, frail woman with bright red hair cut in a bob wearing a green pair of coveralls sat in a rocking chair watching them play with affection. Sam pieced together who he was looking at. The woman in the chair bore a striking resemblance to the one standing behind him. A man in white scrubs stood in the corner and looked at the clock on the wall. "That's it. Lights out."

A sad expression crossed the woman's face as she stood and knelt next to the babies. Picking one squirming infant up, she held her close to her chest and kissed the girl's cheek before setting her into a crib against the far wall. "Good night, my sweet girl."

The man picked up the other child and plopped her down into another crib, wheeling it into one of the many rooms. Despite the instant wailing of both babies, the woman shuffled without emotion to stand in front of one door and waited. A tug on his hand turned his attention back to Blue, who motioned for them to move back down the hall. "He will lock her in soon. Then go back to doing rounds. The one baby will cry all night."

There were a lot of things he wanted to say now, but he would wait until they reached wherever she was leading them. Two things were obvious. This was not her first visit. And one of those babies was baby Blue. Coming to a stop in front of a door with a gold tag proclaiming it "Administration", she took his hand again and a flash of rainbow and cold enveloped him. Then he stood on the other side of the door, looking through a window into the dark hallway they just stood in. It wasn't him. Her jumps were much rougher than before. Maybe the whiskey was getting to her, too. "Security?"

"Even less than the last Sovereign house of horrors I visited." She waved at the walls of filing cabinets and rows of desk filling the room. "Maybe because this one is Cahlad sanctioned. I need a lookout. It will take forever to dig through all of this."

Glancing out of the tiny square window in the door at the still empty hallway, he turned to find Blue digging through the files in one of the desk. "One of those girls was baby Blue?"

"Never say those words together again." Cutting him a sharp warning look, she moved to the next desk. "And Amber. That's how I found the place."

Content to stand and make sure neither of them wound up in jail or worse, he crossed his arms over his chest and watched. "Isn't there some rule about never meeting yourself?"

"The space-time continuum seems fine so far. Besides, a bunch of writers wrote those rules looking for plot devices to drive their stories and explain why the characters make stupid choices." She moved to the next desk. The efficiency with which she moved through the office impressed him. It was like she'd done it before. He supposed she had.

"This is Project Zenith?" He already knew where he was. "Should we be messing around here? I don't want to end up being my own grandpa."

Stopping and placing both hands flat on the desk, she struggled to suppress a laugh, face twisting ridiculously with the effort. "What exactly do you think we are doing here?"

"You were the one that said it involved fu..."

Her choking laugh cut him off mid-sentence. "Oh, my God. You are a lightweight." She shook her head still smiling and dug through the desk drawer. "And fourteen. Good to know."

"What exactly is your plan?"

"I'm going to find their records. Shred them, doctor them, maybe just steal them." Flipping through, she shrugged. "General shenanigans. I'll figure it out as I go."

"What about the Son Sovaj?" A movement in the hallway drew his attention. "Down." Kneeling, he watched as her head dropped below the desk, but the sound of papers continued to rustle.

"I've looked everywhere but in here. The only room with a damned window in the door." Crawling across the floor, she pulled another drawer out. "I don't feel it, either. Not like the others. I don't think it is in this building anymore."

Thirty minutes passed before the guard came back. Sam knelt on the floor, waiting for the man to move. "What about that woman, your mom?"

Blue peeked around the side of the desk, hiding from the door and chewing on her lip. "If I get her out, they will know I've been here. I need to at least throw a monkey wrench into this thing first. Ooh. What is this?" Plunking a folder onto the floor she flipped through. "Study 5. Red paper."

"That's familiar." Resisting the urge to walk over, he watched the window as the lights went out in the hallway. "Do they turn the lights out overnight?"

"Not that I've seen." She pulled folders from the drawer. "Why?"

Shadows moved in the hallway, and he ducked. "We have a problem."

Emptying the contents of a trash can into the floor, she stuffed the folders into it and pulled the bag out. Tying it off, she peeked around the desk, watching the window intently.

The doorknob turned, and Sam flattened himself to the wall behind the door. Two figures in black entered, guns raised. The familiar voice of Larson Battle sent chills down his spine. "Find the records. I don't know which child it is."

"The white witch isn't far behind us," the other shadow said. "She probably knows exactly what we are doing."

"I kept her on the other transport for a reason. She needs to be close to be accurate." Larson stalked forward, beginning his search just like Blue had earlier. "Shut up and get to work." The second shadow moved forward to the second desk. Just one desk over from where Blue was crouching. He could no longer see her.

The last time he saw Larson Battle, the man blew an entire floor off an office building, killing over a dozen people. If not for Ms. Z, known in some circles as the white witch, he would be dead as well. It changed the course of his life. His muscles tensed as he waited for his opportunity.

The second man moved to the third desk. A smaller shadow stood silently, wrapped its arms around the man's neck, pulling him to the ground but not without some noise. Larson shifted to identify the sound and Sam slid forward, doing his best to target his magic but choosing a useful yet benign command in case things went wrong. "Sleep."

Battle tried to turn, and Sam worried in his attempt to keep the effect from reaching an ally, it had not been effective. But Larson's body crumpled to the ground, the gun falling to the side. A soft struggle continued from the floor behind the third desk and Sam moved closer to find Blue crushing the man's windpipe in a brutal choke hold. Finally, he fell silent, and she kicked away, standing and picking up the trash bag. She ambled over to the prone Larson and looked down at him, the room too dark for Sam to see her face. Her foot reared back, and she kicked the man in the ribs, causing him to startle awake and cough in agony.

"Larson. Sleep." Sam hurried to reissue the command. He lunged forward and grabbed Blue's arm as Larson fell unconscious again.

She kicked again, this time catching him in the face. The man jerked awake, groaning in pain, and rolled, extending a glowing hand on the verge of letting loose one of his infamous fire balls. "Larson. Sleep." He jerked hard on Blue's arm, pulling her backward and out of Larson's line of fire so hard she bounced off his chest. "You aren't that drunk. Stop it."

Chest heaving, she looked around searching for a weapon. She reached down for Larson's weapon, and he pulled back again. She stood in front of him, glaring at the unconscious man. "Tell him to stop breathing. Kill the monster."

A door banging shut echoed through the hallway. Whoever was coming wasn't bothering to be silent, probably someone on Larson's team warning him by making noise that Zella had entered the building. Thoroughly irritated, he jerked her toward the door. "Do you want to get your mom?"

"Yes." She shook with rage. "Why didn't you kill him?"

"You were too close." And he had no idea what that would do to the future. But he was certain it would put the Cahlad on their trail in their present. "Put your fingers in your ears." He led them into the hallway, away from the sound of the opening door. The guard from earlier rushed toward it, almost plowing into them, lifting some kind of weapon. Sam knocked his raised hand away. "Sleep." This man crumbled to the ground as well. "Don't wake until someone shakes you."

Stalking down the hall as footsteps and shouts rang out behind them, they darted into the carpeted room from earlier.

"I would have been fine. You should have taken the opportunity." Blue pulled her fingers from her ears and looked at the six doors leading out of the nursery. "I also could have jumped us here." In the pale light of a wall sconce, he read the look on her face. She was going to go back and finish Larson.

"Stay with me. Leave him."

Her fists clenched, and she exhaled a literal growl in frustration.

"He will kill you and everyone in this building."

"I'll be fine."

"They might not be." He pointed to the door Blue's mother had entered earlier in the night. "I don't need you fading out of existence in front of my eyes."

Anticipating a promised throat punch as she stalked forward, a barely contained ball of fury, he was shocked when she snatched his arm instead. Instantly he was standing in the dark and quiet room where the haggard woman with red hair slept curled in a ball on a basic metal bunk. His head spun. That jump was quick and brutal, the rainbow almost black.

"Get the baby." She knelt next to the bed and grasped the woman's hand. Bowing her head, she sat as Sam moved to the crib and picked up the baby, trying not to wake her and failing.

A cry erupted from the little girl as Sam held her. He had never held a baby before in his life and the kid knew it. He bounced like Blue did with Sherry's daughter Tiffany. "Don't cry, sweetheart." The little girl fell silent but watched him nervously, her tiny lip jutting out and quivering.

He looked down at the young mother's gaunt, sleeping face. It reminded him of what his mother looked like during chemo. The ravages of the cancer caused by the Son Sovaj were clear and he suspected untreated. Blue studied the sleeping woman with a grave expression. "I look like her. I don't remember her. She died when I was four. That's what the nice lady told me, anyway."

"The nice lady?"

"The lady who kept me after Mom died. Until Larson came for me and killed her." Placing a hand gently on her mom's arm, Blue stood silently frowning while Sam processed the statement she just made so casually.

"Larson killed your guardian?"

"Yep. I was standing next to her, picking green beans from the community garden. He said it was my first lesson in Zenith training and if I told anyone, he would kill everyone else there, too." Shaking her head in frustration, she gripped her mother's arm tighter. "I can't heal it all. It's? I don't know, I just can't."

A wave of rage at Larson and cancer hit him and he had to take a moment to collect himself before he risked saying anything. "What about the other baby?"

As if on cue, a familiar female voice rang out in the hallway. Zella was on the scene and not happy. "No time now. We have to get them out of here." She extended the hand holding the bag of folders.

He took it, and an icy wave washed over them. Blue's mother woke, screaming in terror as they all shifted through the strange rainbow space between Blue's jumps. They landed in a clearing surrounded by giant trees, quaint cabins, and a few large yurts. Blue's mother landed on her side and backed away, pushing with her feet, face etched with terror. The alarmed voices of the cabin's inhabitants reached his ears as he stepped slowly forward, sitting the baby down on the grass as close as he dared to the hysterical woman. Blue's hand slide back into his when he stood.

"It was really nice to meet you," Blue said to her mother, barely loud enough for him to hear. Then they were back in their kitchen, and he was leaning into the sink, trying not to lose his dinner before she finished the sentence.

Blue stood shivering in the door between the kitchen and living room, clutching the bag of red folders looking lost.

"You okay?" Still leaning over the sink, he tried to remember if he told Blue that her mother escaped to a commune. He hadn't. She did that all on her own.

"No. You could have killed him. A clean shot. Negligible collateral." She looked through him instead of at him. "All the pain and suffering he causes. All the lives lost. Is my life worth all of that?"

Did she just ask him that after the conversation they had earlier? "We've been over this already." Forget the consequences killing Larson could have on the futures. The man was formidable could cause serious damage or possible kill her if she went at him without a plan or backup. "Don't try to take him alone. I'll help. You are not negligible collateral."

Nose flaring, she took a stunned step back. The color drained from her face, and she clenched her fists when his magic hit. "It's better if I go alone."

"Why?" Crossing his arms over his chest, he turned to face her.

"You don't know what he's capable of. The only person I would consider for a moment taking with me would be Ivan."

"Oh, I know what Larson is capable of. I've already survived Battle up close and personal. I was in the room when he blew the top floor off the Cahlad administration building trying to kill Mitch." His back still hurt occasionally, though Mitch did an amazing job patching him up. No need to tell her he wouldn't be standing here if not for the Paragon and Ms. Z.

Though stunned by that revelation, she didn't back down. "It's not the same."

"How is it not the same? I led Stalker Prime for ten years when the Zenith program shut down. Who do you think took over the high-risk assignments? I'm still here. I'm the one that put Larson on the floor tonight. Not you. Do you think I can't hold my own? Or do you think you are negligible collateral and I'm not? Because you are wrong, either way."

Magic flared in the room, but nothing happened. She was trying to go back for Larson despite what he said. Her mouth opened but formed no words, just a sound that communicated absolute fury and a touch of betrayal. She chucked the bag of folders onto the dining room table and stalked away.

He leaned back on the counter and rubbed his already aching head. That went well.

51

BLUE

FEBRUARY. THIRTY-FIVE YEARS AGO

N ibbling a pretzel, Blue listened carefully as Ricky repeated the phrase he practiced for the millionth time.

"Te gustaria ir al baile de invierno conmigo?" He waited for the inevitable correction that didn't come and looked at her with hope and dread.

"Perfect." Blue clapped enthusiastically. Ricky now attended the high school where she taught. At the beginning of the year, the French teacher asked her to pop in and let the kids see an actual conversation in the language they studied. That day, Ricky caught up with her as she walked home and asked if she would help him with French homework. Now he found a reason to walk home with her most days. Recently, he expressed an interest in Spanish because he wanted to ask the foreign exchange student from Chile to be his date to the winter formal. Fortunately, that was one of the five languages she was fluent in, so she was helping with that now.

"Really?" His face brightened. "I got it?"

"Yep." A car door slammed outside, letting her know Sam made it home from work. She somehow quelled the urge to punch him in the throat after he told her not to go after Larson alone and accused her of having double standards. But she needed time to cool down. The past few weeks, they operated on an uneasy truce.

The files she stole that night were written in Bengali, a language she could not read or speak. So, she had to rely on Sam to unravel the documented horrors.

Helping Ricky get a date was a pleasant reprieve from the files and the tense atmosphere of their house. "Say it again to make sure you remember."

Sam opened the door as Ricky began his statement, unsurprised to see one of Sherry's kids in their house. It was a daily occurrence at this point. He shut the door and unpacked a grocery bag containing two brightly colored boxes of cereal. Setting them on the counter, he put a gallon of milk in the fridge and listened.

"Te gustaria ir al baile de invierno conmigo?"

"Me encantaria." Sam smiled. "Especialmente si le recuerda a mi hermosa esposa que no soy un idiota malvado."

Ricky frowned and looked at her for a translation. "He said he would love to. Looks like you have a date for the formal." She left off the part about convincing his wife he wasn't an evil jerk and waved a dismissive hand in Sam's direction. He wasn't evil or a jerk. Just overprotective and prone to taking responsibility for things outside of his control. "Se que no eres malo. Simplemente sobreprotector."

Tossing his keys on the counter, he put his hands on his hips, giving her his undivided attention. His mood shifted from playful to serious, making Ricky squirm in his seat, even though he obviously couldn't understand what they were saying. "Estamos bien?"

Were they good? She stewed for a moment, crossing her arms and staring at him, not answering. No apology. But, so far, the only directives he purposefully sent her way were meant to protect her. But it felt uncomfortably like what Rhodes had done. He meant to protect her, too. She kept replaying the Larson incident over in her brain. Sam had not told her not to go at all. Just not to go alone. Which really translated to don't go without me because who else could she take? That detail made his words strangely forgivable and fundamentally opposite from what happened with Rhodes, who summarily and brutally sent her on her unhappy way. She still didn't like it.

Sam warned her something like this would happen. And she told him she wouldn't leave. But they couldn't keep living like this. It was time to let it go. "Sí."

"Bueno." With a nod, Sam turned back to Ricky. "Aren't you learning French?"

When Ricky only sat and gaped at Sam, Blue answered for him. "Cute girl speaks Spanish."

Sam snagged a cup from the cabinet with a knowing smile. "There it is."

Ricky's face flushed with embarrassment. "I didn't know you spoke Spanish, too." He scrambled from the table.

Sam slapped Ricky's back as he ran out of the kitchen. "Good luck, man."

The screen door slammed behind the teenager as he called out, "Um. Thank you. I guess."

Blue eyed the cereal boxes on the counter. She could see the words Bill and Ted's Excellent Cereal on one box. The other appeared to be Fruity Yummy Mummy with Monster Marshmallows. That one looked good. "Are those a peace offering?"

"No. I just thought you would like them."

"Thanks."

52

BLUE

APRIL. THIRTY-FOUR YEARS AGO

Dragging her exhausted body into the kitchen, Blue wanted nothing more than to collapse onto the first soft object she could find and go to sleep. Even the floor would do. The clock over the kitchen table read eleven forty-eight. Her day started at five o'clock this morning. She worked all day, then helped set up the gym for the spring formal dance. She chaperoned the dance, changed clothes, and helped break everything down. Shutting the door, she kicked off her shoes and dropped everything she carried in a pile at her feet.

She shuffled into the living room and found Sam sitting on the couch watching a twenty-four-hour news channel currently reporting on Mitch's impending challenge for Paragon. The headline read "Records clerk issues Paragon formal challenge."

He held one of the study folders from Project Zenith in his lap and looked up and raised an eyebrow when she walked in. "Have you had dinner?" Not waiting for her to respond, he nodded toward a glass of water and two plain turkey sandwiches sitting at the far end of the coffee table. An empty plate and half-full glass of whiskey sat on the table in front of him.

"I don't think so." She continued her zombie shuffle to the couch and picked up a sandwich. Collapsing onto the couch, she sighed in relief and ate half of the sandwich in one bite. "You are my hero."

He just grunted and rubbed his eyes, propping his head up on the arm of the sofa. He looked as exhausted as she was. Over the past few months, he had translated five of the Project Zenith folders, figuring out the convoluted data structure and reporting methodology. Folder one, with details about Rhodes, read like a horror movie. Reasonable humans would have shut the program down and cut their losses. But the assholes forged ahead. Folders two and three were the worst, nothing but death and evil. None of the mothers or children survived those studies. According to Sam, all the information he translated tracked with the documents Amber left in the future, only with more gruesome detail. The folder from study five contained details about the woman who donated the eggs his mother eventually received, as well as a tracking sheet predicting when cancer for the surrogate might manifest. He hadn't seen that before. He didn't say anything, but she could see it took a toll. The details disturbed her, and he didn't tell her everything.

"Had to break out the whiskey?" She ate the other half of her sandwich.

Sam reached for his glass and finished it. Then he gestured to the plate in front of her. "Both of those are for you."

Nice deflection. Blue picked up the other sandwich, growing concerned. "Maybe you should take a break."

"I just want to get this done." He sounded resigned and opened the folder for study six.

"Want another drink?"

He didn't even look over. Just kept reading the horrid details of how the Cahlad systemically killed mothers and babies for almost a decade. "I've already had three."

"Oh." This wasn't happy Whiskey-Sam. This was drink-ing-to-numb-the-horror Sam. It explained the terse answers. Prob-ably best to let him be. Blue settled back into the couch, grabbed a blanket, and got comfortable. The least she could do was to be present for moral support. She finished the second sandwich at a slower pace, chewing this time.

Knowing Sam would likely read all night without stopping, she turned her attention to the television, where pundits predicted Mitch's defeat in the upcoming dual. Nobody was taking his chal-lenge seriously.

Just as she was nodding off, he grew agitated, flipping back and forth in the folder, searching for something. Raising her eyebrow, she stayed quiet, wondering what he had found. Finally, he sat the folder in his lap and sighed. "The participant information is missing for study six." He referred to the running numbered list of partic-ipants, mothers and fathers that grew larger with each consecutive study. Details for the children, both living and dead, only listed participant numbers, so he had to use the list as a reference to figure out who the humans were. "But I think I found the two participants they lost track of. There are adoption records. Two boys, both adopted by wealthy Cahlad benefactors." Placing the folder between them, he pointed at a paragraph toward the bottom of the page that she couldn't read. "Baby boy one, adopted by Gregory and Marie Hughes. Given name Benjamin."

Blue's head reared back as she pieced the first and last names together. "Ben Hughes. Ring any bells?"

At first, he didn't seem to recognize the name, then she watched his jaw drop as the puzzle pieces fell into place. "Ava's dad? Did he have magic?"

"Not that I know of. But I met him for all of five minutes." She glanced down at the folder. Did Amber know about Ben? She had to.

"This explains why the Sovereign were after him." He pointed to another paragraph she couldn't read after flipping to another page. "Adopted by Clay and Lydia Greenfield. They paid for the park and the statue. Real pieces of work. Given name Andersen. Andersen Greenfield doesn't ring a bell, though."

A memory from the stairwell of the Sovereign facility where she met Devon and Greenlee bubbled to the surface. She ran her finger over the section he pointed out. "I'm Andersen Greenfield. If I don't make it out of here, can you tell my parents they were terrible and they can go fuck themselves?" She repeated the words Greenlee said to her in the stairwell. Every moment of that day played on repeat in her nightmares. She fought back a sudden wave of shock and acute homesickness.

"What does that mean?" Sam glanced up and did a double take. "What's wrong?"

"It's Greenlee. He said that to me the day I met him."

"Your Greenlee?"

"Yes. My Greenlee. Do you know anybody else with that name?" Rubbing a hand against the sudden ache in her chest, she closed her eyes. "I can't believe this."

The folder snapped shut. "Want to talk about him? It always made Nisha feel better when she missed her nani." He shifted on the couch to face her. "I could use less doom and gloom right now, too."

Greenlee's goofball face flashed in her mind, and she smiled even with her eyes closed. "He's a complete slob and makes the best hot chocolate. Even if he isn't Lexi's father, he's a great dad. He was going to propose to Devon before all of this happened. Before he even asked her on a date, the goober. Completely backward. But the ring was beautiful."

"He lived with her the whole time? It took him ten years?"

Blue glanced over, wondering how to explain the dynamic of her family. His head rested on the back of the couch, and he stared up at the ceiling. "Devon's husband, Alex, died horribly. She feels responsible. She always felt guilty if she even looked at someone else. When she did finally, try to date... we think she picked assholes she wouldn't get attached to on purpose. And when he dated, he felt guilty because it wasn't Devon. Drove me and Finn crazy. In short, Green had to wait for Alex's ghost to move out of our house."

"Did the ghost finally move out?"

"I hope so. I paid for an exorcism. Two, actually. Religious and magical. Just to make sure it took."

Sam guffawed and raised his head. His smile twisted when he realized she wasn't joking. "You didn't."

"I did." She took in the astounded look on his face and shrugged. "What? He's in love with her. I had to help my boy out."

He stared at her for a moment, like he didn't know what to make of her. "He's really lucky to have you."

"No. I'm lucky to have him." Her mind went back to the first few weeks after she escaped Larson, Amber stabbed her, the Cahlad drove her underground, then Rhodes sent her packing with a new face and nowhere to go. No job, no home, no friends, a broken heart and no identity in less than a week. Those were the darkest, loneliest moments of her life. If not for Devon and Greenlee, two people she barely knew at the time, she might not have made it. "When we met, we both tried to be strong for Devon. She was going through so much. She is the strongest person I know. But she was pregnant. Grieving her husband and son and stuck hiding in a tiny, awful apartment with two traumatized and depressed strangers. I don't know how she did it. So, I couldn't dump my shit on her. You know?" She leaned back in her own corner of the couch and stared up at the ceiling, too. "But Greenlee. God, I dumped my shit on him.

I told him everything. Some days, he held me together. Literally. With his arms. He kept me from breaking into a million pieces. I never would have put myself back together if he hadn't." She looked up to find a somber Sam watching her carefully. "You needed less doom and gloom. I'm so sorry. I'm just tired." Smiling sadly, she shrugged. "I miss his hugs. And Lexi's wiggles. I miss Devon, always telling me to breathe."

"I tell you to breathe all the time. But I'm usually trying to keep you alive." Setting the folder aside, Sam extended his arm. "Come here. I'm not Greenlee. But I give hugs, too."

Scooting over, she leaned into his side, accepting a hug that actually made her feel better. "Do you miss anyone?"

"Nisha." A deep breath expanded his chest, but neither of them moved.

"What is she like?"

"She's my Greenlee. She's been my best friend since I was thirteen. Only kid at the Academy brave enough to talk to me. People were scared to even be in the same room as either of us. Didn't want to lose their free will or have anyone know who they really were in here." He tapped his head. "I was just relieved to talk to someone, even if it was with my thoughts. She's a klutz. Completely ruined one of my office chairs. She spills coffee on it every time she sits in it. Next time I buy leather. Huge fan of rom coms."

"Eew."

"I know." A chuckle rumbled under her ear. "Eats constantly. Fearless. A peacemaker. She was leaving Stalker Prime. I don't know what I'm going to do without her. She kept me sane."

He looked down at her, face shifting from reflective to horror in a flash, and his body tensed suddenly. He threw his arms out to the sides like touching her burned him. "Jesus."

She jerked upright, looking for whatever set him off. "What?"

"I just made you hug me."

She relaxed. She didn't notice the command. "Oh. You scared me. It's fine."

"Still. I'm sorry." Running a hand through his hair, he sighed deeply and swapped the study six files for the study seven files.

She scooted back across the couch. "It's fine."

He didn't respond and remained quiet for a long time as he went back to reading, and she dozed off. The sound of papers furiously flipping back and forth woke her. Sitting up, she rubbed her eyes as he looked between two different folders and then flipped to the familiar participant matrix in the back of study seven. "Something good?"

His jaw set in a familiar expression that meant he didn't want to say anything, and his finger moved down the list and stopped. He swallowed hard and sent her a sideways glance. "I assumed you and Amber would have the same father, since your mothers were identical twins."

"No?" He shared that theory in the hospital when he dumped the whole Project Zenith saga on her. "Or Yes?"

"No." Covering his mouth with his hand, he stared straight ahead, lost in thought. The slight tilt of his head and the hesitant intake of breath made her nervous. The fact she and Amber didn't share a father didn't seem like this big of a deal. "Indigo Vale and Andersen Greenfield." He opened the two folders side by side and pointed at lines in the same place on two forms. The lines had the same number: eighty-six. "This is the paternal participant."

Frowning, she folded her arms over her stomach and leaned forward as she processed what he was trying to tell her. She rocked backward when she finally put it together. "Oh, my God. He's my brother?" Her hand flew to her heart and her eyes grew wide. Then she smiled. She and Amber, being sisters, never resonated. But this did. "I have a big brother?"

Sam just nodded, his finger now pointing to a line on the participant list. "A half-brother."

"Well, Maury Povich, spill it. Who is the daddy?" The look on his face made her heart hammer. Delivering this news, whatever it was, pained him. Immediately, a horrific possibility popped into her head. "Is it Larson?"

"No."

"Thank God." She waited, and he said nothing else. "Damn it, Sam."

"Mitch Collins."

Her hand flew out to point at him in accusation without her realizing it. "No." Shooting up from the couch, she paced, trying to calm her rapid breathing while Sam watched her like she might explode. "Read it again. It's another guy named Mitch Collins."

"The age is right. Hair color. Eye color. Type of magic. It's him."

"Your Bengali is rusty." That was the only explanation. She might be completely broken, but Greenlee wasn't.

"No. It isn't."

She pointed at him again, this time in warning. "You should be quiet."

Sam dipped his head and showed her his palms, signaling he was bowing out of the conversation. He watched her pace.

Finally, she stopped and put her hands on her hips, still unable to accept it. Her voice was quiet when she finally said the words on repeat in her brain. "Greenlee has a bigger heart than anyone I've ever met. He is a genuinely good person. There is no way half of Greenlee came from Mitch Collins. Me? Maybe. Greenlee? No."

Sam sat the folders aside and leaned forward, elbows on his knees. "What's his magic?"

She jammed her palms into her eye sockets and stopped in the middle of the living room. She didn't like where he was going with this. "He makes artifacts."

"Can he use them, too?"

She sank to the floor, pressing her eyes so hard white spots flashed across her vision. "Yes."

"And you can heal?"

"Stop." Finally, she looked up in defeat, unable to argue with his logic. "Stop making sense."

"You didn't have a Luke and Leia moment, did you? Is that why you are so upset?"

Sniffing in disgust, she glared. "No. He's Greenlee. He's like my brother!"

Sam looked mildly amused by her statement. "He is your brother. Thus, the question."

"Smart ass. You know how Mitch let Larson treat me. Greenlee ended up in Larson's sick experiment on Mitch's watch. Who does that to their own kids? How would you feel right now?"

"Angry." He stood and walked into the kitchen, then back into the living room. Standing above her, he looked down with something close to sympathy. "Overwhelmed."

"Yep." She looked at his shins. "But it doesn't matter. We are who we are, and we are where we are. What happened, happened." Her voice fell to nothing more than a whisper.

Squatting so he could see her face, he closed one eye and tilted his head to the side, the three whiskeys he drank earlier making themselves known in the uncharacteristic movement. "Seems like it matters."

"Changes nothing." It didn't.

He sat down on the floor across from her and held up the almost empty bottle of whiskey and a clean glass. "Whiskey or hugs?"

"I think I need both."

53

DEVON

Devon held Greenlee's hand as they all moved down the stairs to the various vehicles Finn and Kendra assembled to transport them to their assigned positions. Even when Finn explained he wanted her to go with Mitch and Ben because they were the two most powerful magic users on the team and he calculated she would be safest with them, she still didn't like his plan. She wanted to stay with Greenlee, but he pulled her aside and pressed a red marker into her hands, explaining it would create a portal to Lexi's last known location if she used the activation word 'peaches.' It only had two charges. Showing her a green marker, he explained it would take him anywhere he wanted to go, and his own magic fueled it. "No matter what happens, I'll find you."

Nisha and Harper and Greenlee would leave first, but she struggled to stay calm. Everyone milled around, Kendra and Finn wearing Kevlar vest and several weapons. The sight of their attire made her stomach drop, driving the reality of what they were attempting to do home. Nisha stood to the side, talking with Mitch. She carried a weapon, but Devon couldn't see it from here. Finn refused to give Mitch any weapons and to Devon's surprise, Nisha agreed, reminding the Paragon he had never trained with traditional weapons and might shoot himself or an ally.

Even Harper, sitting behind the wheel of a cheap economy car, was more subdued than usual as the minutes ticked down to their departure. "I don't like this. Do you trust Nisha? She's Cahlad."

"I do." Greenlee looked at her with worry as he put his hands on her shoulders. "Stick close to Ben."

"Don't worry. I'll keep him safe." Greenlee rolled his eyes, then quirked his head in real consideration.

Ben joined them, looking at the other groups. "Can you check on the girls again?"

"Sure, man." Greenlee retrieved the small bead from his pocket and held it in his open hand. His eyes lost focus, as Mitch's had earlier, and he was silent for a few moments. "Oh, man." Swallowing hard, his face melted into a soft smile before his eyes snapped back into focus. "They left a note."

"What did it say?" Devon asked.

"We are safe. Go save the world. We love you. Mr. Rhodes says hi."

Ben rocked back and forth on his feet. "I want this over." All of them itched to get to their girls, but knowing that they were somewhere the Sovereign hadn't tracked them yet made the decision to stay away less painful.

"I know, man. We all do." Greenlee handed them both a pink princess Band-Aid. "For emergencies. They aren't much. Won't reattach an arm, but they are better than nothing. Try not to have to use them."

"You should keep these." Devon shook her head. "We will be with Mitch."

"It's time." Nisha climbed into the back seat of the car Harper sat in. "Let's go."

Greenlee leaned down and gave her a proper kiss this time. "I love you, baby. See you soon."

"I love you, too." She held his hand as long as she could while he nodded to Ben and walked to the car. Handing a large backpack to Nisha in the back, he wedged himself into the passenger seat. Harper opened the garage door and pulled away almost immediately, the door rolling shut behind their car.

Finn walked over, a different stride to his step. This wasn't the Finn she knew. This was someone else. "Can I have a moment with my sister, Ben?"

Ben nodded, shuffling toward the cleaning service van they would ride in with Mitch. Kendra walked over, giving the two men one more round of instructions on how to operate the earpieces and the protocol for communicating. Her voice echoed louder than normal in the cavernous space of the garage.

Standing in front of her so that his back was to the others, Finn crossed his arms instead of reaching out in his usual hug. "Did Greenlee give you the portal?"

Taken aback, Devon nodded. "He did."

"You have the nine-millimeter?"

"Yes."

Finn considered his next words, summing her up with a calculating stare that made her uncomfortable.

"What's going on, Finn?"

"My agreement with Ravi was to keep Mitch safe. He's a wild card with a dangerous temper. He is also the girls' best chance of staying alive. I had to let him in on this to keep him cooperative." He stopped himself from looking over his shoulder. "If anything, and I mean anything, goes wrong, I need him off the playing field. You are the only one who can and will do it. Knock him out and use the portal to get him to the girls. Take Ben with you. He's solid. Mitch will come around when he sees Ava with his own eyes."

Devon snorted in disbelief. "You want me to kidnap the Paragon and blackmail him with his long-lost granddaughter?"

"If it comes to that." Finn's tone left no room for argument. "Greenlee will find you."

She stared him down, but he refused to look away. "You are so full of crap. You told Greenlee you wanted me with the most powerful people here."

"I do, to control them. I need our heavy hitters with the girls if anything happens to the rest of us. You know how to hide. You know how to survive. Keep them all safe until we can stabilize the situation or Greenlee finds you."

"What about you?"

"I have a good team." Finn dropped his arms, looking like her big brother again, and gave her a hug. "Lexi's all I have left of Alex, Dev. She's my priority."

Refusing to cry, she squeezed his ribs with all of her energy, despite the bulky vest. "Finn Torrin, you are all she has left of Alex, too. Don't forget that."

"I won't, sis." Letting her go, his face slipped back into the cool professional mask he needed to wear right now. "You've got this."

"You do, too." Walking together, they stopped between the two remaining vehicles. "Stick to the plan, Collins." Finn climbed behind the wheel of a sporty luxury SUV.

Mitch helped Devon climb into the rear seat of the van before sitting in the passenger seat and scowling at Finn. "Remember the deal, Torrin."

54

SAM

MAY. THIRTY-THREE YEARS AGO

"Seriously, how do you let yourself get killed by a baby doll?" Blue huffed as credits rolled on the screen. "It only had one knife. Shameful."

Sam laughed at her reactions through the entire movie and every other horror movie they had watched in the past two years. She didn't get scared. She either got mad at the bad guy for being a bad guy in the first place or the victim for being too easy to kill. It wasn't normal. But he found it endlessly amusing. "I can't believe you have never seen *Child's Play*."

"I didn't miss much. Eddie Murphy should have popped in and told that horrid little baby doll to give him the knife. Please." She snapped her finger. "Problem solved. That is a decent movie."

Rewinding the cassette, he flipped the input on the television back to cable and turned it to his default CNN while they waited. The minutiae and growing pains of the twenty-four-hour news cycle during this time frame fascinated him. Blue groaned and rolled her eyes, flopping backward on the arm of the couch dramatically. "Not the news again."

"It's worth watching for the hair and fashion alone."

"I would rather suffer the shame of death by baby doll than to have that hair."

"What's the next movie?" Eyeing a stack of VHS on the coffee table next to a box of pizza from some place in Chicago by Wrigley Field, he went through his options for getting rid of the box with no one noticing where it was from.

"Bartender makes bad life choices to a Beach Boys song."

"You haven't seen that one, either?"

"Eat, sleep, train, and kill people." Blue shrugged. "Then eat, sleep, Lexi, hide people. Not much time to watch movies."

"In that case, I will suffer through it again." Ejecting the cassette, he looked up to see the blurred genitalia of a man running down the Las Vegas strip at the end of his nose. "My eyes."

"That prick." Blue sat up and glared at the screen.

"Exactly." Sam backed away from the television as the shot panned out to show large pieces of metal dangling in the air behind none other than Mullet Roane.

"He just robbed the casino." Blue jumped up and started hopping into shoes. "How long ago was this?"

"I don't know." Sam shrugged and looked between the television and the furiously hopping woman in confusion. "It says this afternoon. Why?"

She pointed at the television. "I'm going to go knock some sense into him."

Fighting for patience, he put both hands out, motioning for her to calm down. "Blue?"

Stomping her left shoe into place, she held out her hand. "What?"

"Can you slow down for a minute and tell me why you went from zero to whatever this is in less than a second?"

Blue pointed at the floor in jerking motions to emphasize her words. "Because right now my three-year-old friend is sitting alone in a dark house with nothing but her stuffy waiting for her mom or dad to come home. But they aren't coming. Mom is banging the new boyfriend and writing the handbook on how to ghost your kid and dodge the therapy bills. Dad is streaking down the Vegas strip after snorting God knows what up his nose." She held her hand out, pushing the rolled sleeves of her flannel shirt up past her elbows, and motioned for him to hurry. "She has already been there for a day."

Sam sympathized for Devon, Blue's friend and Mullett Roane's daughter, but this was rash, even by Blue's standards. "We are just going to teleport to Vegas and hunt him down?"

Hand still extended, she shoved some cash in her jeans. "I can get us closer than that. In or out?"

Sliding on his own shoes, he took her hand. "How?"

Blue just smirked and laughed. "Magic." With a whoosh of rainbow light, they stood in the gaudiest hotel suite he had ever laid eyes on in his life. Even the walls had shag carpeting, lit only by the sparkling lights of Las Vegas streaming through the torn curtains because this place had no electricity. Bottles of alcohol and bags of every drug known to man lay strewn on each gold flaked flat surface.

Moans and grunts of pleasure filled the air, followed by a loud slap. A woman screamed something that included the word daddy from somewhere in the suite, and the frantic pounding of a head-board hitting a wall took up a steady rhythm.

The scene surrounding them in full pornographic stereo did not phase Blue. "That asshole."

She moved toward the noise, and he followed equal parts, amused, and horrified by the situation. "Are you sure this is a good idea?"

"No. But it feels right." She stomped into the bedroom and stopped, slamming her hands onto her hips. Mullet Roane knelt on a bed covered in heavy canvas bags of cash, going to town on a blonde, wearing nothing but gold high heels and handprints on her ass. His heavily lined eyes were closed, and neither person heard Blue enter the room. She cleared her throat.

Roane's eyes popped open, but he didn't stop what he was doing. "What in the hell?"

With a disapproving huff, Blue let loose with her fist, catching the man across the jaw in a brutal hit that sent him flying backward off the bed mid thrust.

Sam pinched the bridge of his nose and shook his head in disbelief as the room erupted into hysteria. The blonde flailed on the bed, screaming in shock and terror. Blue stalked toward Roane, who sprawled across the floor with his legs in the air, ass on full display. She yanked him up by the spiked hair on the top of his head as the naked woman lunged from the bed, tripped on her ridiculous heels, and fell right next to Sam.

"Leave now and forget you were ever here." He sincerely wished he could do the same. Of all the things he had seen in his time on Stalker Prime, this took the cake. Crossing his arms over his chest and looking at the ceiling, he did his best to ignore the woman as she snatched up clothes. She fled the room, screams echoing off the walls of the dark, empty hallway.

Blue and Roane brawled in front of him, slamming off every surface in the room. Roane was larger and fighting hard, but still drug and sex addled. Righteous fury fueled Blue's efforts. The carpeted walls of the room muffled the brutal sounds while Sam continued to focus on the yellowed popcorn ceiling, wondering how in the hell he ended up here.

A lamp hurtled itself off the nightstand, slung by an invisible force, and hit Blue in the back. It shattered into several large pieces on impact. Shaking off the blow, she reared a fist back. "Try harder, asshole." The next punch landed with even more force.

A gaudy chandelier jettisoned from the ceiling, narrowly missing Sam's head as it hurtled toward the fighters. She shifted them somehow, pinning herself to the wall, and used Roane as a shield. The man shook off the self-inflicted blow and punched Blue in the ribs, making her double over in a wheeze. Then she laughed.

Should step in? And why on earth did she bring him with her? Remembering his time on the other side of Blue's rage and acknowledging that this might be personal, he stayed put. The guy had it coming, anyway.

"Go." A punch landed, and they shifted off the wall. An ice bucket bounced off of Blue's head with a clang. An electric sizzle of magic washed over the room and the almost deafening sound of hundreds of pieces of metal pinging loose from their homes filled his ears. He looked over his shoulder just in time to see a barrage of loose metal zipping toward him. Sam flattened himself on the floor as the newly liberated chunks of metal whizzed by.

"Home." Another punch, then a groan as several metal chunks of hotel room junk embedded themselves in her back.

Roane punched back with surprising force, snapping her head back. "Who are you?"

The screams of the fleeing woman in the hallway stopped suddenly, drawing Sam's attention away from the fight. Her voice changed to plaintive wails of, "I don't know." A deep voice, speaking quietly but still carrying in the empty, silent building, responded. Sam could only hear a few words, but what he heard made his blood run cold. The words Roane and white witch found his ears.

Cahlad. How did Blue keep doing this? She put them in the path of a Stalker unit every time she did something rash. They were going to discuss this.

Creeping to the door of the suite that stood slightly ajar, he peered down the hallway. Five figures and the blonde. He clicked the door closed and put the lock in place to at least slow them down. Racing back into the bedroom, he found Roane pinned to the wall, both of

Blue's hands in his hair and one of his hands wrapped around her throat, trying to push her away.

She slammed his head into the wall hard enough to bust the sheetrock with each of her words. "To. Your. Daughter." A shower of flying metal objects pummeled her back. Blue finally stepped away. Wiping her busted lip with the back of her wrist, she landed a kick to Roane's groin and watched impassively as he crumpled into a ball on the floor with a groan very different from the ones he made when they first arrived. The rest of the room's flying metal objects fell with him.

"Stop. Both of you. We have company."

Blue turned a furious face his way. Eyes wild, hair disheveled and cheeks red, she looked like a complete psychopath. Roane looked relieved as he clutched his naked privates. "Who?"

"Stalkers. In the hall."

Both she and Roane cursed. Roane crawled to the bed, grabbing two canvas bags in each hand.

"Come on, Roane. Your ass is about to win an all-expense paid trip to a magic gulag, and you are worried about the money?" Blue huffed and looked at Sam is if this was the craziest part of the night. "Devon got her brains from her mother."

The suite's doorknob rattled in the other room. "We need to leave."

Blue stalked to the bed. "Fine. But I can't leave him here. He's a complete piece of shit, but he's all Dev has left."

Roane clutched the bags of money in a way that covered his privates. "How do you know about Esdevona?"

Someone outside issued a command to "Move." A blast flashed in the next room, sending the door flying off the hinge.

Larson. Blue slapped her hand onto Roane's arm, and Sam grabbed her hand. Seconds later, they stood in a dark and quiet room devoid of decorations or furniture. Roane dropped the moneybags, the sound echoing off the bare walls and hardwood floors and vomited on his own feet. Sam jumped back, trying to avoid the splatter, and looked around. They were in a small, quaint home. No curtains covered the large plate-glass window looking out onto a dark suburban street.

"Who's there?" a scared, youthful voice trembled somewhere deeper in the home. Blue's eyes closed, almost in anguish.

"Oh, sweetheart," she whispered. She turned to Roane, who still leaned over, catching his breath. "She deserves better than this you."

Roane looked up, taking in his surroundings. His eyes grew wide, and he stared at them with a mixture of wonder and fear. "Are you Cahlad?"

Small footsteps echoed in the space, and Sam stepped forward to grab Blue's arm. "We need to go before she sees us."

"The Hounds of Dawn." Blue stepped backward as Sam pulled her away. "Don't mess this up. Not everyone gets a second chance."

"Daddy? Is that you? I don't know where Mommy is. I'm scared."

"Daddy is home, sweetheart. Stay there." Roane, still shaking, took in the house's emptiness. His face shifted as he looked between the bags of money in the empty house and the dark hallway where his daughter waited, understanding what had happened. His eyes landed on Blue. "Thank you. Do you want dinner or something?"

Sam huffed in surprise. The man just offered them dinner. He was still bleeding from the beating she gave him.

Blue shook her head. "Hounds pay it forward, Roane."

Roane nodded in understanding as his eyes darted toward the hallway.

"Ready, Diablo?" Not waiting for an answer, she hurtled them through the rainbow, but not to their living room. Hot wind hit his face and honking horns filled his ears as their new location came into focus. They stood atop a tall building at the very end of the Las Vegas strip, staring out at the flashing lights of the city bustling below them.

"We shouldn't be here." He did not know if they were in the same building as before, but if that Stalker unit had a sniffer, her magic burst would bring them running. They shouldn't be anywhere near this town right now.

"There is nothing to worry about." She looked around, seeming to relax as the wind whipped her hair around her head. "Unless they can fly." Climbing onto the edge of the wall rimming the roof, she stood and leaned her head back, closing her eyes. "I need a minute to wind down. I can't take this energy home."

Walking over, he rested his elbows on the wall next to her feet and looked out over the stunning sight. The town was beautiful in its own garish way. Glancing sideways at the black Chuck Taylors she wore, he tried to understand how her brain worked. How could she slide so comfortably in and out of different personae and still be one hundred percent Blue? And why on earth had she brought him along on this little jaunt? Obviously, she didn't need or want his help to handle Roane. "Why did you bring me?"

She threw her arms out like she intended to sky dive off the roof. "So, you could keep me alive if things got out of hand."

Knowing she wouldn't hit the ground if she fell, he still couldn't resist the urge to wrap a hand around her ankle. "Please get down?"

"No." She shook her head and took a deep breath. "I like it here."

"We need to talk about your impulse control."

"What impulse control?"

"Exactly."

Looking down, she smirked in amusement; her face already bruise-free from the brawl earlier. "You have enough for us both."

"I really don't." He stared out at the lights again, spotting a flurry of activity in front of an abandoned hotel. He recognized the stark white hair from here. But nobody was coming their way. "There is no containing your chaos."

"Come on. This was fun. Did you see the look on his face when I punched him the first time?"

"Other things distracted me."

She laughed as a powerful gust of wind hit her, pushing her forward slightly so that her toes hung over the edge. "That's understandable."

His hand tightened on her ankle, and his heart stuttered. "Damn it, Blue."

The tone of his voice drew her attention, and the smile fell from her face. "This really upsets you?"

"I'm not upset." He offered her his hand. "But please come down."

Pouting, she ignored his hand and jumped to the roof. "Better?"

Tilting his head in silent thanks, he went back to leaning against the wall. She leaned next to him, no longer phased by the sudden silences. "There's a great little place right down there. Been there forever." She pointed into the lights below them and squinted. "Spectacular French toast."

"We've already had pizza." He looked at her with fake irritation. "From Chicago."

She feigned a look of playful confusion. "And that has anything to do with French toast in Vegas, how?"

"You are ridiculous."

"You know you love me." Turning back to the view in front of her, she didn't see how hard her words hit him.

He didn't know when it happened, but it was true and she remained oblivious because, except for Devon, Greenlee, Lexi and, to some degree Torrin, she happily kept everyone at a deceptively friendly but firm arm's distance. "Yes, I do." Not trying to keep his tone light, he watched her reaction out of the corner of his eye.

Blue went completely still and. sent him a forlorn look. She quickly covered it with a half-smile that didn't reach her eyes. She started to say something but shook her head instead. Sam could feel her pulling away, even though she didn't move. She gazed back out into the night with a guarded look on her face. "Let's go so we can beat the breakfast rush."

55

RHODES

Rhodes wedged himself into the corner of the kitchen next to the old orange ceramic sink with his hands firmly clasped behind him. He could not get any farther away from the girls unless he went outside or hid in the bathroom. A tiny one-bedroom cabin in the middle of nowhere did not provide the best conditions for what they were attempting, especially given the type and power of Ava's magic.

He watched as Lexi snuck across the floor, slowly creeping up on Ava, who sat on the couch reading a ten-year-old magazine. She gleefully agreed to help Rhodes after he reluctantly agreed to her terms. They intended to surprise Ava to help her practice controlling her magic when she found herself surprised or afraid. He regretted throwing Ava into the deep end with this lesson. But unfortunately, that is exactly where they were. If he couldn't help Ava control her magic, not only could he suffer side effects or lose control of a shift and accidentally hurt one of the girls like he had Blue, but the surge could give Lexi magic poisoning. He still didn't know how she used so much magic in the field with no significant issues.

When Lexi stood directly behind Ava, she leaned down and released a high pitched, ear-splitting scream directly into her friend's ear. Ava lurched forward with her own scream, hurling the magazine into the air and tripping over the coffee table in her effort to face the noise.

Before the magazine hit the floor a wave of Ava's magic flood his system. Claws erupted from his hands and his perspective changed as his body grew several feet taller, causing the extra tufts of hair on his head to brush against the cabin's low ceilings.

Ava screamed and clutched at her chest, on the verge of hyperventilating, as Lexi erupted into a fit of giggles. Ava's eyes landed on Rhodes and grew wide. "Down, Bubbles! Down, Bubbles!"

Immediately, Rhodes shifted back to its normal size and the claws that gouged the hideous sink shrinking back into his hands. He let a smile form on his face and clapped his still slightly misshapen hands. "Very good. Very good. You pulled Bubbles right back."

Ava's face morphed into a mask of fury as she looked back and forth between him and Lexi. Her mouth opened to yell. He could tell by the way she took a deep breath and her face turned beet red, then a flash of realization crossed her features. "I did it?"

"You did it." Rhodes looked at his hands, that now looked completely human. He took two large steps across the room, patting a still giggling accomplice on the back as he went, and extended his other hand to Ava for a high five.

Ava smiled and gave him a high five. A flare of pride crossed her face before it turned dangerous once again. "I'm going to pay you both back. Double." She pointed at Lexi, a promise of retribution in her eyes. It only made Lexi giggle harder.

The younger girl looked up at him and smiled before vaulting over the back of the couch and landing with a bounce. "Pay up, Mr. Rhodes."

He pinched the bridge of his nose. "Stop jumping on the couch, Lexi Lou. Does your mom let you climb on the furniture like this?"

"Tia Blue does." Lexi soared into the air. "Sometimes she does it with me."

Rhodes rolled his eyes. Of course, Blue let the kid do anything she wanted. She could heal her before her mom found out anything happened.

"Are you sure you don't want to hear another song?" He held his breath, hoping the answer would be any song other than the one Lexi requested. He had plenty of other number-one songs, and he already sang *Baby Blue* for them at least twenty times before he put his foot down and refused. But to gain Lexi's help, he agreed to sing it one more time.

"I want *Baby Blue*. I love that song and Tia Blue never lets me hear it."

Rhodes glared at the scheming smile that crossed Ava's face.

The creak of a board on the front porch made them all freeze. "Mr. Rhodes?" Lexi landed hard and stood on the couch, subdued and scared.

"I'm sure it is nothing. Get down. The house is old, and they did not build it to hold a trampoline." Rhodes stood and moved to the window, peering through the narrow gap without moving the curtain. The porch remained empty, but a crawling sensation flitted across the back of his neck. Someone was watching him.

Ava spun, looking around like something might jump out and grab her at any minute. "Should we go with the plan?"

"Hang tight." Rhodes looked out the other window. He didn't want to abandon their safe house without an excellent reason. An empty back porch met his eyes. Regardless of what his eyes told him, he couldn't shake the feeling that someone or something watched him. "I'm going to step outside. Stay on the couch."

Ava looked horrified and on the verge of anger. "Don't leave us here."

Rhodes' claws sprang from his fingers and fur sprouted from his arms and face, but not as much as a few moments ago. That was a good sign, but he still needed to stay human to protect these girls. He didn't want to lose his ability to speak again. He schooled his face, trying not to show his exasperation. "I will stay on the porch. I promise. Can you talk to Bubbles for me?"

Ava grimaced and wrung her hands. "I'm sorry, Mr. Rhodes. I'll try."

At least the clothes in this house were several sizes too large. If he got lucky, he wouldn't rip the seams on these. Sliding out the door and standing in front of the stairs, he took advantage of the unexpected shift and used his enhanced eye site to inspect his surroundings. He didn't see or hear anything out of the ordinary.

Eventually, the feeling of being watched faded away, as did the effects of Ava's magic surge. Taking a deep breath, a faint hint of ozone tickled his nose, making him scan the horizon for any sign of storms. A few dark clouds littered the sky and at this altitude, storms could roll in without warning. Waiting another moment to make sure he wasn't missing anything; he stepped back inside and locked the door.

"Good job keeping that magic in check." Rhodes patted Ava on the back, noting the seams on all his clothes were still intact and his nose remained human shaped. "There is nothing there."

"I don't think I did very good." Ava frowned and put her hands on her hips in disgust. "I'm not getting the hang of it fast enough."

"Magic takes practice. Years. You just started this morning. I'm impressed with your progress. You should be proud."

Lexi sat on the couch, still rattled, and clutching the pillow. He needed a distraction. "It's okay, Lexi Lou. How about another round of poker?"

"How about another round of *Baby Blue*?" Ava crossed her arms, a mischievous twinkle returning to her eye as she looked directly at Rhodes, almost in challenge. Even if her sudden shift in mood was at his expense, he would take it. She sat down next to Lexi on the couch.

Lexi nodded, still glancing at the doors in trepidation, oblivious to the vengeful subtext in Ava's words. "I really like that song." Lexi forgot about the noise from earlier and leaned into Ava, but she held tight to her pillow.

"She likes the song, Mr. Rhodes. It is your best one." Ava smiled sweetly, putting her arms around Lexi protectively.

His eyes narrowed and his lip curled. Ava was doing this on purpose to make him hate his own song. It was working. "I know what you are doing, Ava."

The lift of her eyebrow told him she didn't care. "I just want Lexi to feel better." Ava squeezed Lexi's shoulder and mouthed the word payback in his direction. "Sing for us, Mr. Rhodes."

"I'll sing with you this time." Lexi turned large brown eyes his way. Puppy dog eyes.

How was he supposed to say no to that?

56

BLUE

FEBRUARY. THIRTY-THREE YEARS AGO

R olling over and pulling the covers over her head, trying to block the light that interrupted her sleep, Blue let out a groan of frustration. "Turn the light off, Sam." Obsessed with figuring out a way to engineer another spinny bracelet of death using the Se't Sovaj, he'd developed a bad habit of staying up half the night and turning on all the lights in the house getting ready for bed. First, a drink of water, then a few minutes with CNN, then pulling clothes for the next day out of the closet, followed by brushing his teeth. Since she had to get up at an unholy hour to teach math to disinterested teenagers, it had become a point of contention.

"The light isn't on," came the disgruntled and groggy reply.

Peeling an eye open to see if she had dreamed the light so bright it pierced her eyelids, she found the bathroom light off just as Sam said it was and the man himself sprawled across the bed next to her instead of banging around in the bathroom. Yet flickering shadows bathed the room. Sitting up in confusion, brain slow to process what she was seeing, she turned toward the source of the light to find an orange glow dancing outside the bedroom curtain. Fire.

Lunging out of bed, she raced to the window, jerking the curtain to the side to see flames roaring from a window of Sherry's house, siding melting down the exterior wall. Panic filled her chest at the sight of the flames and the location, Tiffany's room. "Sam!" Racing to the door, where she kept a pair of slip-on shoes, she banged on the wall to wake him. "Call the fire department."

Voice rough and sleepy, he sat up. "I said it wasn't on." He jerked out of bed when he saw the scene next door.

"Fire department. Now!" Dashing from the room before she heard his response, she burst out of the kitchen door, feeling the heat from the flames next door instantly. Searching the visible portions of the yard for any signs of Sherry and the kids, she raced forward, circling as far from the flames as she could. Bounding up the steps to the front porch, she checked the doorknob, only to pull her hand back with a curse when it scorched her palm. Hurtling off the side of the porch and running through the small shrubs to the side door, she launched herself onto the stoop and reached for the doorknob. Hands gripped both of her arms from behind and lifted her off the ground. But the grip wasn't strong enough to be Sam and he would have said something. Why did people keep picking her up? Focused on getting to Sherry and the kids, it took her longer than it should have to process what was happening. This wasn't an accident. This was arson. The person she couldn't see took advantage of her surprise and dragged her away from the house. "You son of a bitch. Put me down." Throwing her head back, she caught the person in the nose and heard a crunch. A man howled and dropped her where she stood. She left him without looking back, racing to the side door to get into the house. As her foot hit the step, her head jerked backward, a brawny hand almost pulling her hair out by the root. She should have teleported him into the middle of the ocean. She did not expect him to recover that fast, and she didn't have time for this.

"Let her go!" A tall black shadow barreled into the man, taking him off his feet where he landed with a harsh thud, letting go of her hair on the way, but not before it spun her around. Sam pinned the man to the ground face first, slamming it into the ground without mercy. He had this.

She needed to get to Sherry and the kids. She entered the house, covering her mouth with her shirt. Dropping to her hands and knees to get below the roiling plumes of acrid smoke, she crawled through the kitchen to the hallway that led to the bedrooms. One leg of the hallway was far longer than the other, and she didn't know which one to choose. "Sherry!" Even the air near the floor was hot and filled with particulate, causing her to cough. "Ricky!" Crawling forward a little farther, she listened for any noise over the roar and pop of the fire consuming the home.

"Ms. Keys!" A strangled cough sounded somewhere to her left.

Eyes watering from dripping sweat and stinging smoke, she couldn't see, but she crawled forward. "Ricky! This way." Blistering heat fanned her.

"I can't find them!"

Blue patted in front of her blindly, losing hope that she could get them before flames fully engulfed the house with each passing second. If she could locate them, she could get them out. Coughing and fumbling in the dark, she bumped into Ricky. Forcing her eyes open, she focused on the boy. Ricky's breathing came in quick gasps, punctuated by racking coughs.

She risked standing in a crouch as a loud bang of the screen door slamming sounded from the side of the house. "Come on, Ricky!"

"Blue!" Sam's voice cut through the hellish nightmare surrounding her.

"I can't see." Ricky clutched at her with his free hand. "Someone wedged the window shut."

"I've got you. Close your eyes, buddy." Jerking him into a similar crouching position and making sure his eyes were closed, she took a step through a cold rainbow and walked straight into a tall, coughing form, crouched to stay below the smoke and not as close to the door as she wanted him to be. "Get him out of here. I have to get Tiffany and Sherry." Shoving Ricky, eyes still closed and body trembling in terror, into Sam's arms, she turned back toward the flames.

"Blue." Sam coughed, grabbing her wrist before she could get away. "It's too far gone! We have to leave!"

"My mom!" Ricky gripped Sam's arm for dear life.

"I have to try!" Blue coughed. "Get him out. Get me an anchor point."

Only a moment passed before Sam nodded his understanding, the smoke so thick she barely caught the movement. "Thirty seconds. Then you have to leave." Pulling Ricky closer, he disappeared into the kitchen.

Knowing Sam was right, she started her countdown. Flames rolled across the ceiling now as burning chunks rained down in her path. Unable to yell anymore and knowing the roar of the fire would swallow the sound anyway, she fumbled in the opposite direction from where she found Ricky. Fifteen seconds. Coughing and lungs burning, she fought for every ounce of speed she had. With five seconds left, drenched in sweat and out of air, her hand bumped into a soft, still lump on the floor. Got her. She patted her way up the body. It was Sherry, but she still needed to find Tiffany. Blinded by the smoke, she patted her way farther up to a small arm flung across her mother's chest. She had them both. Pulling in her magic, surrounding them in a cold bubble, she focused on Sam and released it. Landing hard somewhere cool and dark but still close enough to be surrounded by smoke, her arms gave out and she fell on top of Sherry's limp body in the grass already wet with dew.

Raising to her hands and knees and coughing, she tried to see where she was through stinging, tear-filled eyes. They were behind the house, still close enough to feel the heat, but not visible from the street. Frantic screams and a calm voice met her ears, but she couldn't see the source. Plucking Tiffany's limp body from the ground, Blue pushed as much magic as she could muster into her. "Come on, baby." A vision of Devon's son, his tiny face, pale and terrified, flashed through her mind, and she clutched Tiffany tighter. "Please. Please. Please." She could not watch another child die in her arms. The ominous cracking echo of the collapsing house filled her ears and a billow of fumes and heat surrounded her, but she didn't move. Her hands grew icy and numb, and her stomach rolled from the amount of magic she pushed into the small limp body, but couldn't stop herself. A wail erupted from the tiny girl, and Blue pulled the screaming head of dark curls against her chest with a sob that turned into a cough.

Sam appeared in the smoke above her, coughing and covering his mouth with his arm, eyes black and a wild expression on his face. Letting out a huge breath, he took all of them in, then knelt next to Sherry's prone body. "We need to move. Follow me."

He dragged Sherry through the grass into the fresh air of a cloudless night. Blue scooted across the wet ground, coughing, and drawing deeper and clearer breaths of air the farther she got away from the ruined building. Sirens wailed in the distance, and Tiffany screamed. Ricky rushed forward, choking on his own coughs, and snatched Tiffany from Blue's arms, rocking the sobbing girl as he stared at his mother's lifeless body in horror. Sam stumbled forward and laid Sherry on the ground as gently as he could while coughing and fighting for his own air. He wheezed as he checked her neck for a pulse. Then he leaned forward, tilting back their neighbor's soot-covered face. Sam started CPR, breathing twice, followed by a series of compressions snapping bones and cartilage. Blue crawled faster and sat across from him. She positioned her hands on Sherry's chest and pressed down hard when he finished the second set of breaths. Pushing a tremendous wave of magic into Sherry's heart and lungs, Blue counted out the compression, still coughing and now shivering. Sam sent her an irritated look but said nothing.

Ricky's coughing sobs grew louder behind them. She wished she could stop to comfort him, but if they didn't do something now, even with magic, his mother might not live. The red flashing lights of the fire trucks finally lit the street. Sam leaned over, waiting for her to finish the compressions. "Breathe Sherry." A tingle of magic and two more puffs of air and Blue started compressions supplemented with magic. Halfway through the third set of compressions, a rattled breath leaked from Sherry's lips, followed by another. She wasn't conscious, but she was breathing on her own.

"That's it. Keep breathing." Sam released a wave of magic that made her own chest expand. Ricky and Tiffany took deep, audible breaths. Taking Sherry's pulse, he nodded and fell backward onto his butt, head falling back, to look up at the sky. "Are you hurt?"

She laid down, resting her cheek on the cool, wet grass. "I'm fine. Take care of the kids." She kept a hand draped across Sherry's arm so she could continue healing her with the magic she had left. Ricky rushed to his mother's side and held her other hand, begging her to please be alive.

The fire trucks screeched to a stop somewhere out front. In response to Ricky's distraught cries for help, an army of men in reflective rollout gear and a frantic police officer she recognized as Sherry's boyfriend Reggie swarmed them within seconds, forcing

Blue to roll out of the way. They gave Sherry an oxygen mask, shifted her onto a gurney, and loaded it into an ambulance. It took both Sam and Reggie's help to pull Ricky away from his mother and load the kids into a second ambulance, assuring them their mom would be okay.

Though she was content to stay where she was, two firemen refused to leave her laying in the grass and helped her walk to the front of the house, insisting she wear an oxygen mask of her own when she wouldn't go to the hospital. From this vantage point, she had a front-row seat of Reggie telling the EMTs to stuff their protocol as he climbed into the back of the ambulance with the kids before Sam slammed the doors.

A fireman tried to get an oxygen mask on Sam as the ambulance left, only to be swatted away. Spotting her sitting by herself on the ground draped in a scratchy blanket one fireman brought for her, Sam's long strides ate up the distance between them despite a constant cough.

She stood, a wave of fatigue washing over her and making her sway slightly as her adrenaline rush crashed. But her lungs were clear. She took the oxygen off her own face and extended it to him. He took the mask with an irritated shake of his head and placed it back over her nose, securing the strap in place, then swept her into a bruising hug. "I told you thirty seconds." Violent coughs rattled his chest and shook them both.

"I counted to thirty." She peered up at his soot-smeared face. He was wrecked. "I'm better. Please take the oxygen."

"It was a full fucking minute." He sat down on the ground hard, pulling her with him to sit sideways across his lap. "I didn't know a minute could be so long."

They both reeked of smoke and chemicals, and his body shook with coughs. She put the mask firmly over his face and slid a hand over his ribs, pushing some magic into his lungs to clear them and repair the damage the smoke caused. "I'm healing. Take the damned oxygen."

He closed his eyes and rested his face on the top of her head, breath echoing against the plastic mask. "Ricky tried to run back in, and I had to move him." She kept pushing magic into his lungs and her hands went numb from the cold, but his breathing evened out. "The house collapsed, and you weren't there. I didn't think you were coming." A long breath shuddered out and he pulled her closer.

She scanned the scene. Her old friend Billy Bob sat on the sidewalk in handcuffs, bruised and bleeding, talking a million miles a minute to an officer scribbling in a notebook. In the dancing light of the fire and emergency vehicles, his face contorted in the obvious effort to stop himself, but his lips kept moving. "What did you tell him?"

"To wait for the cops and confess everything."

"That might take a while." Who tried to burn a house down with their own kid inside? A man who had surely committed other horrible crimes. That's who. She laid her head on his shoulder, still exhausted and enjoying no longer sitting on the wet ground. She wedged her hands between their bodies, trying to keep them warm.

Listening to the shouts of firefighters and the indistinct murmurs of gossiping neighbors, she shut her stinging eyes against the whirlwind of activity, thankful for a moment of peace and that everyone got out alive.

"Blue?

Humming in acknowledgment, she reluctantly lifted her head, eyes still closed. She gasped in shock as warm lips sealed over hers. Before her brain caught up and warned her this was just a stress response for them both, she relaxed into his arms, burying her icy hands in his hair and pulling him closer.

The chaotic world around them melted away. This was farm than a stress response. No one had ever kissed her like this before. This kiss was a question. But it was also an unmistakable declaration and a promise. Was she ready to deal with what that meant. Alarm bells rang in her mind, telling her she wasn't and might never be. After the way things ended with Rhodes, there weren't enough pieces left of her heart to live through that again. She needed to protect herself.

His hand cradled the back of her head to deepen the kiss, stopping her train of thought like he knew what she was thinking, demanding she come back to the moment.

Too soon he pulled away, resting his forehead against hers, leaving her more breathless and terrified than when she fought for air in the house. With their faces so close they still exchanged air, his eyes bounced between hers, communicating the same question, and the same promise. A swell of conflicting emotions tightened her chest. He was too close, but not just physically. Letting someone in meant getting hurt. She fought the urge to jump anywhere but here. Witnesses be damned. She needed distance.

His hands tightened where they held her, and he looked at her with a mix of hope and dread. That he remained so carefully silent despite the fact he sensed her struggle was the only thing keeping her in place. She sat perfectly still, catching her breath, hands still in his hair, because she couldn't bring herself to let go and she didn't know why. She squeezed her eyes shut. Her brain shouted fearful warnings that her heart didn't heal the way her body did. But her instincts screamed, hold on and don't let go.

So, she held on. She didn't want to ruin the moment with words. Instead, she pulled his head back down, brushing her lips gently across his before letting her hands slide to his shoulders. Relief flooded his eyes as he softly ran his hand over her hair, staring at her for a heartbeat, before tenderly kissing her forehead. She let him pull her even closer and rested her head in the space between his neck and shoulder, soaking in how right it felt. She prayed she wasn't making a huge mistake.

The clearing of a throat and a deep male voice from above startled them both. A police officer stood silhouetted against the glow of Sherry's burning house.

"Mr. Keys? You live next door?" The man waved toward their side door, which hung wide open, light spilling into the carport. She hadn't stopped to shut the door, and as fast as Sam followed her, she doubted he had, either.

They both nodded.

"I need to take your statement." The officer's words were grave even for the situation, and for a moment Blue feared Sherry hadn't made it despite their efforts.

Her brow furrowed, and she stood, body tense and once again cold, waiting for the news. "Is it Sherry?"

"No." The man gestured toward Billy Bob. "The man who set the fire claims someone paid him to create a distraction. Something about one of those magic artifacts. I sent a deputy over since your door was open."

His meaning clear, they both stepped forward to see through the doorway of their home. She cursed. The contents of all the kitchen drawers and the shattered contents of their cabinets littered the floor. In the living room, stuffing spilled from the couch cushions. The bookshelf's contents lay shredded on top of everything. Someone tossed the place while they were next door.

The deputy gave them a moment to digest the destruction before getting back to business. "You were probably targeted because of your position at Everdale."

"Did he say who hired him?" Blue asked the deputy. Of course, the deputy knew who Sam was and where he worked. Everyone knew everything about everyone else in this town.

"He's saying a lot of things right now, Mrs. Keys. Never seen anything like it." The deputy snorted. "They almost have the fire contained. I'll have someone over here to dust for prints."

"Don't waste your time with us. Let me talk to the man who started the fire." A vein pulsed on the side of Sam's face as he issued the order.

Struggling not to react in front of the officer, Blue sent Sam a warning look. The deputy shifted from foot to foot, looking uneasy. "I guess we can do that. Come with me." Stepping away, he waited for Sam to follow.

Tugging on Sam's hand so that he would lean down, she stood on her tippy toes to get close to his ear. "What are you doing?" Using his magic in front of others, especially law enforcement, invited trouble. This wasn't like him.

He sent a menacing glare in Billy Bob's general direction. "The police don't know what questions to ask. You know it's the Sovereign. When they find out he is talking, they will kill him. I have to get over there."

She studied his eyes for any sign of the shift to black that occurred before he truly lost it. And they were darker than they should be. "Are you in control?"

"Is everyone still breathing?" The way he asked and the brief flash of black in his irises filled her with dread.

She contemplated how she could stop him without making a scene. She couldn't. She could stop him, but it would be a scene. "Did you mean it?"

He frowned in confusion for a moment before understanding crossed his features, and he stepped closer. "Yes."

She looked past him to the deputy, who waited, growing impatient. "Then you can't get us both arrested. Not now."

"They won't arrest us." He rubbed his thumb across the top of her hand. "No one will remember I was there."

"You can make people forget?"

He nodded and glanced at the group of people now surrounding Billy Bob. "But it's tricky."

Eyes narrowing, she rolled her shoulders past a chill of discomfort. "It's too risky."

"They almost killed two innocent children tonight." His eyes flared black again and his jaw tightened. He was furious. An inky string of black crept up a vein in his neck. "Again. They are escalating."

Sighing in resigned displeasure, she tugged his collar over the dark vein on his neck and stepped away. Sending the deputy, a long, concerned look, she pulled the blanket more tightly around her shoulders as her stomach rolled with anxiety. This could go so terribly sideways. "Be careful."

He looked around the bustling scene surrounding the burning nightmare that used to be Sherry's house, still filled with firefighters, police, and nosy neighbors. "Please, stay where I can see you, just in case they are still around." Turning he stopped and glanced back over his shoulder. "But not too close. I really don't want you to forget anything." No magic lined his words, but their sincerity glued her feet to the ground. She was in so much trouble. He waited until she gave him a small nod. "I'll be right back."

57

ZELLA

Knocking pierced the veil of sleep, but it took her a moment to claw her way to consciousness. Pealing a bleary eye open, she found Hale gazing into the distance like he did when someone else was in the room with them. She sat up, body aching from sleeping upright on the hard floor, but she could not bring herself to take advantage of the chair while the young man remained tied up on the floor. Swiping her hair out of her eyes with a shake of her head, she glanced at the clock on the wall next to the door. Unsure of how much time she lost in the closed room, she did not know if it was afternoon or early morning. A delicious smell reached her nose, and her head followed it.

Nolan Miller stood to the side of Sam's desk, holding two bags of takeout food and a carafe of water, looking like he had just stepped off the golf course. His gaze was dark as he ignored Hale and focused on her. Wishing she could ask Hale how long the senator had been standing there staring at her, she shifted into a more comfortable position and returned his gaze.

"Your face is worse." He sat at Sam's desk and continued to study her. "One of the staff said this was your favorite." Zella fought through a moment of vertigo as contradictory visions flashed through her vision. "I have some cream for your bruise, and more pain killer. Please use it once you have eaten." She did not know how he expected her to do that with her arms bound behind her back as they were.

Miller surprised her. No sign of the bombastic political anti-magic evangelist Mitch dealt with in meetings or events sat before her. His contemplative and disturbed demeanor unsettled her more since her most recent visions wavered wildly between her and Hale dying horribly in the hallway and walking out of the building unscathed. Over fifty visions of just the two of them from the next twenty-four hours were etched into her brain and in most of them, at least one of them died. Other visions of Mitch and Nisha accompanied them, some so horrible she almost lost her lunch.

She did not know what was going on, but intense waves of visions hit her every time Miller entered the room. The broken pieces of the future that surrounded him refused to go back together, causing chaotic ripples for everyone near him.

Eventually, the man stood and walked over to Hale, looming above him, looking down. Zella tensed and pulled her legs underneath her body, preparing to lunge if she needed to. Hale shook his head slightly, looking directly at her for a moment.

"Larson is unhinged." Miller squatted and revealed a pair of scissors from Sam's desk. "Every minute the Paragon doesn't show up, it gets worse."

All of them were silent as the moment dragged on. The senator finally leaned over to bring the scissors down and push Hale's upper body away from the wall. The scissors disappeared from her vision, and Hale's arms sprung free. He hissed in relief, shaking his hands and rotating his shoulders.

"He is getting suspicious. The two guards at the south end of the hall have noticed my visits. But the FBI agent that took over Ms. Ravi's office is the one who told Larson about them. I made him angry by delaying the press conference. I will have to schedule it soon." Miller glanced back at Zella. She watched, waiting for any sign that Miller intended immediate harm. He walked to Zella next, cutting her wrist loose and laying the scissors back on the desk. "I don't have keys to those." Miller pointed at the shackles around Hale's ankles. "This is bigger than me and my family. Larson is far more dangerous than I realized. I'm arranging to have Ms. Tyne transported off site. Do you understand?" With that, Senator Miller walked out of the room without looking back.

"God, I've got to take a piss." Hale tucked the scissors into his back pocket and shook his hands out. "Give me the wire, Ms. Z."

Zella shook her head, even more fearful for his future with this strange recent development. Miller knew something and wanted them to act, but she still didn't trust his motives.

"I've watched you draw, Ms. Z. I've seen your reactions. You don't know what happens next anymore." He extended his hand, tone gentle. "Now you are just scared. Give me the wire."

Reaching into her pocket, she prayed for only the second time in her life, but hesitated as the wire cleared the opening. She had no reason to sit here and wait for this young man to defend her and possibly die doing it. If she weren't dealing with constant visions, she could get out of here on her own. Sighing in resignation, she admitted to herself that she needed his help.

"Come on, Ms. Z. He told us where the guards were. We need to move."

He was right; she didn't know what was happening. What if they walked out of this room into something worse?

"Now." The command in his words spooked her, and she pulled the wire backward, a scolding frown forming on her face. If she could speak, right now she would tell him to go fuck himself. "I'll take it if I have to. This is our window."

Throwing the wire in his direction, she climbed to her feet, legs stiff from sitting for so long. Just like the past several times Miller paid them a visit, the visions amped up in quantity and intensity. Hale freed his feet and grabbed a trashcan, moving to the corner of the room and turning his back. A sigh of relief escaped him as the sound of liquid hitting the plastic liner reached her ears. Closing her eyes to give him some privacy, she leaned on Sam's desk and tried to parse the visions into something that made sense. Moments later, the sounds of drawers opening, and the smell of hand sanitizer broke her concentration. A hand grasped her elbow gently, and she sat in Sam's uncomfortable desk chair. "Eat something. Quickly." The sight of Hale shoving an entire cheeseburger into his mouth in one bite greeted her when she opened her eyes. A greasy bag of food plunked into her lap as he ran his hands along Sam's desk.

Zella snatched her own meal out of the bag and watched Hale curiously. He looked up, still chewing, and held up a finger as he continued to search. Swallowing, he disappeared below the desk. "This is Sotach's office?" His head popped up long enough to view her nod of affirmation. "That bastard has a gun in here somewhere." Giving up on the desk, he moved to a cushioned chair covered in coffee stains. Tipping it, he searched the fabric lined bottom carefully. "What do we have here?" A ripping noise followed as he pulled the flimsy black fabric away and produced a small handgun and an extra magazine covered in tape away from the bottom of the chair. Peeling the tape away, he checked the weapon and pocketed both items. Stuffing the fabric back in, he sat the chair back on its feet and repeated the maneuver on the other chair. Two more guns with extra magazines emerged from the second chair. Zella smiled, a gun for each member of Stalker Prime. Bless Sam's paranoid heart.

"I knew he wasn't a suit." Checking one weapon, he flipped it over and extended it to her. She took it and checked it for herself out of habit, impressed that he didn't even ask if she knew how to use it. Eyes hard and jaw set, he took a knee in front of her chair, no longer the jovial, easy-going man who sat in the room with her for so many hours. "If you know I'm going to die, do me a favor and don't tell me. I'm getting you out of here."

58

SAM

JULY. THIRTY-TWO YEARS AGO

A hideous noise met his ears when he approached the back door. For the first time since they arrived, Blue elected not to teach summer school. She never had a summer break as a kid, so he convinced her to try one out as an adult. Instead of shopping or sleeping late and watching bad television, she was teaching herself how to play every instrument known to man. At least no one lived close enough for the noise to bother them. The barren ground where Sherry's house once stood served as a reminder that the Sovereign were still out there and what they would do to achieve their goals.

After the fire, Sherry's ex confessed to many crimes; however, he knew very little about who had hired him. Just like the attempt on Sam's life, the man who committed the crime only knew money was involved and the name of the guy who gave it to him. Sam followed the trail of money and names through a series of low-level criminals and con artist until he hit a literal dead end. The next man he needed to talk to died in a freak boating accident hours before Sam got there. The whole situation left him on edge. So far, the Sovereign were outsourcing henchmen duties, but their core values remained the same.

He wanted to move, but Blue refused to budge, insisting the Sovereign would track them to a new address through their work. He suspected the real reason was the fact she itched for someone to come at them again so she could exact revenge. Ricky had a car now, so he drove Blue home from school most days, but then he had to go to his new job to pay for the car. Sherry and Tiffany still dropped by for dinner at least once a week and Blue babysat all the time, but Sam could tell she missed the constant activity of having them right next door. Staying home by herself for two months straight was a dare, using herself as bait. He alternated between extreme anxiety that someone might take it and feeling sorry for the poor soul that did.

Stepping inside, a whishing noise alerted him to a projectile hurtling at his head. He ducked, and it crashed into the doorframe behind him. A broken violin bow clattered next to his feet. Blue stood in the living room, violin still tucked under her chin and arm outstretched from throwing the bow like a knife. "You could have put my eye out."

Setting the violin on the coffee table next to a small keyboard, she walked into the kitchen and picked up her ruined bow, wincing as it fell apart in her hands. "I would have healed it. What are you doing here?"

"I live here."

She looked around in mock confusion. "Oh yeah. You are the one always leaving the lights on. I guess I should invite you to dinner. Sherry is bringing it over later. We need to work on the seating chart for the reception. Apparently, Reggie's parents can't sit near each other."

"Funny." Taking the bow out of her hands and setting it aside, he pulled her to him, tilting her chin up to give her a kiss. Most days, he still couldn't believe she didn't disappear into thin air or punch him in the throat in Sherry's yard. Pulling away, he watched as a thoughtful smile crossed her face, no longer playful. "What are you thinking?"

She just patted his chest. "Why are you early?"

She didn't want to talk about it. Fine. He pulled the file Mildred, the dragon woman, brought him after lunch out of his bag and walked over to the couch. He spent almost four years looking for the origin of the Se't Sovaj collection and came up empty. Finally breaking down and asking Mildred, who he hired away from the dean about a year ago, for help, the information was in his hands in less than eight days. "Mildred is amazing."

"I already knew that." Blue flopped onto the couch next to him and started reading the papers. "No need to come home early to tell me."

Leaning back and stretching out, he watched as her brow furrowed, then her eyes grew wider with each page. The report Mildred secured, at first glance, read like a simple history of a few family heirlooms labeled as the Mirialas estate lot that eventually found their way to a forgotten room in Everdale University's basement. The crates containing the Se't Sovaj belonged to a woman who lived near Bayou Lafourche in Louisiana in the late 1800s and early 1900s. Rumored by locals to be a voodoo priestess, she married and buried five husbands but bore no living children. Upon her death, her property, including the Se't Sovaj collection, transferred to a distant cousin, a young lady named Ruth Mirialas. The newlywed Ruth helped her husband run a rather infamous boarding house in Houston, Texas.

Uninterested in the belongings of a relative she did not know, Ms. Mirialas placed the items in the attic and preceded to live a long life. She, like her distant relative, endured several pregnancies that ended in miscarriage or stillbirth and left no living heirs. The collection remained hidden away until a lengthy legal battle over the contents of her estate between even more distant cousins and various debtors reached an end, resulting in an auction where the crates wound up in a lot that also contained a set of china with a very rare pattern. The couple who bought the lot kept the china and donated the rest to Everdale because the contents looked "magicky."

Within the context Project Zenith and the results of exposing pregnant women to one artifact, the pedestrian narrative became compelling.

"Sam?" Flipping another page, she scanned and then looked at him, almost fearfully. "Do you realize what you have?"

"I want your take on it. That's why I came home early."

She covered her mouth and looked over the papers again. "I think if we dig, we will find that the earliest Sovaj had an ancestor that spent some time in a seedy boarding house in Houston. That explains why it is a mostly North American phenomenon." Somber and quiet, she handed the papers back to him. "You've solved the great mystery of the Sovaj. You've done what the Cahlad and every nut job conspiracist on the planet have tried to do for over a hundred years."

That was where his mind went, but the concept was too big too big until she said it out loud. "Technically Mildred found it. She just didn't know what she had."

"These weren't pregnant women. They were just people passing through the area for a while. And the women who owned them and were around them for extended periods of time. None of their babies lived just like in Project Zenith." Blue looked up at the ceiling. "If anybody found out about this." Shaking her head in disgust, she crossed her arms. "This stays between us. We need to burn these papers. And maybe that book, too."

"Let's slow down. You can burn the papers, but I need that book to figure out how to get us home without killing you."

Blue's nose wrinkled in agitation. "I don't think it is worth the risk. Neither of us can make artifacts." When he started to argue, she held up a finger. "You've tried. Artifacts are not your thing. The book is worthless to us at this point. But to someone who can make them, it's the holy grail."

"I might have missed something."

"You don't miss things, Diablo."

He folded the papers and swatted her knee. "We don't have to decide now."

Chewing her lip, she shifted to straddle his lap, looking far too serious. She was trying to figure out how to convince him to get rid of the book. She would not change his mind.

He wrapped his hand around the back of her neck and rubbed his thumb over the edge of her jaw, watching her mind work. "I'm not giving up on getting you home safe. We both go or we both stay."

Blue stilled and the same thoughtful expression from earlier crossed her face. She closed her eyes, letting her head fall forward. He kept rubbing the back of her neck. It always grounded her. "There's that look again. What's in your head?"

She placed her hand over his heart, but her eyes remained closed. He stayed silent and wrapped his other hand around hers, waiting. When they first got here, she promised if he slipped up with his magic, she wouldn't go anywhere. And she hadn't. But every time he tried to get through the emotional fortress she surrounded herself with, he knew she was one second from disappearing and never coming back, like right now. The tingle of her magic was in the air, and he needed to let her work through whatever this was in her own time.

"It's not important."

He rubbed the back of her neck. "It is to me."

She made a nose between a huff and a laugh and stared at their hands. Finally, she met his eyes, looking uncertain and uncharacteristically fragile. "I love the way you say I love you."

His grip tightened instinctively in a not-so-subtle attempt to anchor her and keep her here while he made sure he understood what she meant. He hadn't said those words. Her reaction that night on a rooftop in Vegas made him hesitant to try again. As a matter of fact, he avoided it like the plague.

In that uncanny way that she had; she knew exactly what he was thinking. She leaned forward, brushing her lips against his then pulled away just enough to meet his eyes, her own now soft and for the first time since he had met her completely unguarded. "Yes, you do. Your way."

Still stunned but awash with relief and elation, he used the hand on the back of her neck to pull her closer. Her emotional fortress was still there. But he was inside the wall now. A part of him never thought this would happen and he still wasn't sure what had changed to allow it. But he never wanted to leave. "Come here, Angel."

Just as she smiled and placed her forehead against his, the kitchen door flew open with a bang and bounced off the wall. Blue jerked back, eyes completely wild, reaching for something in her belt as a teenager in baggy jeans steamrolled into their kitchen with a tray of food. Groaning in frustration, Sam caught her wrist before she could throw whatever weapon she reached for and pulled her head down to his shoulder with the hand already resting on her nape as her magic flared. Turning his head away from Ricky, he whispered in her ear, "Stay here." Her magic faded, but he still fought to keep her hand in place. Her pulse hammered where he practically crushed her wrist.

"We brought lasagna and stuff for S'mores." Ricky dumped the pan of food on the counter and turned his attention to the living room, taking in the way Blue sat straddling Sam's lap with her face pressed into his shoulder and neck. By this point, they were both breathing heavily from his efforts to keep a clueless teenager alive. She was much stronger than she looked. Fortunately, so was he.

"Oh. Sorry. Sorry." Ricky pushed his now long wavy hair out of his face and turned a shade of red usually reserved for beets. Dashing for the door, he called back, "I'm going to go knock."

"Relax. It's just Ricky." He let go of her hand and released the hold he had on her neck.

Blue slumped as the door slammed behind Ricky's retreat, her hand no longer reaching for what Sam suspected was a knife. He didn't realize she was so on edge. And he forgot to lock the door.

"Knock." Ricky's voice carried through the door, followed by a bang so loud he might have been using a battering ram. "Knock."

Sam let his head fall back onto the back of the couch. "I'm going to kill that kid."

Blue shook her head, her hands still trembling. "Thanks for not letting me do it."

"Yeah. No problem."

Another loud bang echoed through the kitchen. "Knock."

"Jesus, Ricky! We are going to need a minute!" He certainly needed a moment and Blue still hadn't moved from where she sat trying to switch from killer Zenith to friendly neighborhood high school teacher.

"Sure! Sorry!" Ricky's clearly embarrassed reply reached their ears, followed by a muffled admonishment from Reggie about knocking first.

Reggie and Ricky kept arguing on the other side of the door. Blue finally sat up and a contagious smile stretched across her face as Tiffany's tiny voice demanded to know what S.E.X. was. Sherry's muffled, chiding voice joined the fray. He shook his head, trying to keep a straight face and failing.

"Do you and Reggie do the S.E.X., too?" Tiffany howled, Sam could only presume at her mother. Ricky made a horrified noise. Blue snorted and covered her mouth.

Tiffany's little voice rang loud enough for everyone in the neighborhood to hear. "What? Is S.E.X. bad? Why do I have to be quiet?"

Blue collapsed in a fit of giggles, falling sideways onto the couch, and he erupted in laughter. He never imagined his life would ever contain moments like this or that he would feel anything other than fear and discomfort if it did. But he loved it, and he wouldn't trade it for anything in the world.

However, he needed to have a serious conversation with Ricky about knocking first.

59

ZELLA

Holding her weapon at the ready, Zella covered the hallway while Hale dumped the body of a guard he killed soundlessly and with his bare hands into a supply closet. The light in Nisha's office shone underneath the door and the FBI agent Miller warned them about sat behind it. Deep voices floated down the hallway from the break room at the south end of the building. Hale emerged from the closet, tucking an extra gun into his waistband, and motioned for her to follow him to the North stairwell. She walked backward down the dim hallway, occasionally bumping into Hale's solid back. Her stomach fluttered with nervous butterflies. In all the missions she ran during her time as a Stalker, she never ran one completely blind to the future. Worse, she never ran one with a clear view of multiple grisly potential outcomes. They reached the stairwell, and he slipped in quietly, waiting for her to follow him and shutting the door behind them without a sound. They hurried down the stairs. When they reached the third floor, Zella opened the door and exited the stairwell even though Hale kept going, trusting he would figure it out. Hale followed a moment later, eyes raking over the empty hallway, checking for threats before sending an irritated look her way. "What are you doing? Did you see something?"

In every vision that involved them surviving this escape attempt, which was less than half of them, they wound up in the South stairwell, somewhere between the third floor and the basement. That is where they needed to be. She jerked her head to the south and walked that way without waiting for his agreement. He didn't respond, but she knew he had followed. They had only taken a few steps when shouts rang out upstairs so loud they echoed down the concrete stairwell and through the closed door. Metal slammed above, and the sounds of feet thundering downstairs filled her ears. A hand landed on her shoulder and pushed. "Run, Ms. Z."

They were as good as dead if they tried to hide in any office, so she dashed down the hall as fast as she could. The door flew open behind them, and Hale opened fire before their pursuers could even clear the door. Five men struggled to get out of the stairwell as they climbed over the bodies of two men who hadn't expected their quarry had guns.

"Larson wants her alive!" one man screamed behind them. "Don't shoot her."

Bullets pinged off the walls and floors. Only feet from their goal, Hale cried out in pain, and his body careened into the wall. "Keep going!"

Skidding to a stop, she whirled to find the young man leaning heavily against the wall, clutching a gushing wound in his hip with one hand and shooting at the men rushing down the hall with the other. He spared her a glance, lips forming into a thin line when she didn't follow instructions. "Get out of here!"

Forget that. She wasn't leaving him. They were both getting to that stairwell, or neither of them were. Larson wanted her alive and she would use that because she didn't care if anyone left in this building lived other than she and the young man in front of her. Opening fire, she raced back into the fray, startling the men running toward them. No one ever expected the tiny white-haired hippy woman in a broom skirt to know how to use a gun or take the offensive in a life-or-death fight. The dumbfounded looks of the people who underestimated her would never get old. The men stopped shooting when she planted herself in front of Hale and continued firing. "What are you doing, Z?" Hale moved when she pressed backward, although he tried to shove her behind his body despite his wound. She shot one man in the throat, his body twisting and spurting blood onto the wall with the rhythm of his heart. Three of them dove into offices for cover, and one kept coming, landing a brutal punch to her left cheek. He tried to shove her aside and get to Hale, but she shook off the ringing in her ears and held her ground. Hale knocked the man's weapon skyward before it roared in a flash of flame inches from his face. Zella used her shoulder to wedge herself between the men and shoved their attacker away, pushing as hard as she could to force the asshole back down the hall. Before he could level his weapon back at Hale, she put her own under his chin and pulled the trigger. The body fell backward, and Zella sent a thank you to Nisha for being the only person in the entire organization willing to defy Mitch and continue training with her. A hand wrapped into the back of her shirt and pulled. "Let's go!" Hale dragged her toward the stairs, his steps lurching as she peppered gunfire at the occasional head poking out of office doors. The stairway door squeaked open, and she backed through it, pulling it shut hard behind her.

"Reload. Leave me. I'll slow you down." Hale's voice sounded pained and weak, but he remained on his feet, back planted against the wall, and facing the door. He shook his head, no doubt dealing with the aftereffects of having a gun go off so close to his ear. "I'll cover you."

Ejecting her now empty magazine, she pulled the extra out of the waistband of her skirt and slammed it into place. She squared her feet and waited for the next wave. "Ms. Z. Go." Hale shifted against the wall, forcing himself to stand straighter with a pained grunt. "They know you are gone. There will be more than that. Take my other gun and run."

Zella backed up and nudged him toward the stairs leading to the second floor. Neither of them would budge. He stumbled slightly, face growing hard, but resisted her effort. Then the hiss and clank of the automatic door locks echoed in the stairwell and the lights went out, sending them yet again into inky darkness.

60

SAM

APRIL. THIRTY-ONE YEARS AGO

An aura of tension hit Sam as he walked into the building. The usually boisterous group of people who worked here bustled around in hushed silence. A few, realizing he had arrived, sent him worried glances, then disappeared into their respective offices.

A flustered Mildred hustled his way, heels clicking on the marble floors of the entryway, clutching a leather planner to her chest. As she drew closer, he could see that her face was pale. More than the strange behavior of the building's other denizens, Mildred's nervous state put him on red alert. Nothing ruffled the dragon woman's feathers. Behind her, the dean of the College of Magic, and President Higgins approached, looking worried and grim.

"Good morning, Mildred." Sam kept his eyes on the two men approaching. "What is going on?"

"The Paragon is here." Mildred cast a worried glance over her shoulder like the devil himself followed. "He is in your office. He only wants to speak to you."

Dread filled him as he forced himself to take a breath and stay calm. This was not good. "The Paragon? Did he say what he wants to speak about?"

"No." Mildred shook her head, knuckles white from clutching the planner. "But the Regent is with him."

Sam barely contained a curse as he worked through the likely reasons both the Paragon and the Regent would visit and speak only to him. "Mildred. Do me a favor. Call my wife and tell her who is here. She should be home. She is on Easter break. We were planning to have lunch today." He had to get a message to Blue. If he didn't come home, no doubt she would jump to him, eventually. She'd find a way around it, even if he told her not to. Or there was already a Stalker unit at their house waiting for a signal. He needed to make sure she understood the gravity of the situation, either way.

"Right away, Mr. Keys." Mildred turned on her heel and scurried back to her office.

Passing the dean, the man looked furious, face red and body rigid. President Higgins appeared much more diplomatic but still worried. "This could have a great impact on the university's continued autonomy to operate a magical studies program. Please try to..." The man stopped and struggled with his words. "Try to make a better impression than you usually do."

The man was drenched in sweat for a reason. The basement storage rooms were full of unregistered artifacts and text waiting to be cataloged and studied without Cahlad oversight. The university's published research and content was curated to contain only items that would not draw the Cahlad's ire. Not responding, because he rarely responded to most things either man said, he walked around them and approached his office. He passed the room housing the administrative staff where Mildred held a phone between her chin and shoulder, hands flying as she spoke.

Reaching into his bag, he pulled out the reading glasses she had gifted him a few months back because he was struggling to read smaller print. He could still hear her voice in his head when she set the glasses on his desk. "No shame in flaunting our wisdom and experience. It happens to us all after forty." Sliding the glasses over his face to do his best Clark Kent impression and hopefully protect future him, he opened the door to his office with confidence, extended a hand and deployed a classic Mitch technique. He hoped Larson didn't recognize his voice as the person who told him to go to sleep. "To what do I owe the honor of speaking with the Paragon this morning?"

Neither Larson nor Mitch had subtle magic, so they were unlikely to let loose in a public building for several reasons. Sam had more options. He forced himself not to look at the towering figure of Larson Battle leaning against the wall, looking sinister and dangerous. He also burned with curiosity to know why the Paragon came here off the books with his second and no security or pre-screening? It flew in the face of every standard operating protocol that existed, and Ms. Z would have a conniption when she found out.

A young Mitch Collins, the stress of the job already apparent in the lines on his face, and the white hair at his temples, stood from a chair where he lounged and took Sam's hand, shaking it. Mildred bustled in, setting out a full tea service on his desk. He didn't know where she had gotten it or why she thought this meeting called for tea. They all watched in quiet irritation as she bustled around arranging things. "Thank you, Mildred."

"Yes. Thank you kindly." Mitch nodded with thin lips. Larson scowled.

Mildred tittered a response and excused herself.

The door shut, and Mitch snapped his fingers in a familiar motion, and a quiet thump buffeted the room. A magical barrier surrounded them, separating them in every way from the outside world until Mitch dropped it. Its primary purpose usually revolved around interrupting magic or mundane ease dropping. But it also meant he and Larson could throw around magic without collateral damage. Most people wouldn't understand what Mitch had done, but Sam did, and he started sweating.

"Thank you for letting us interrupt your morning in this manner. This is Regent Larson Battle, as I am sure you are aware. I understand you are the subject-matter expert on an item that is of great personal interest to me."

Sam looked for any sign of an interrogation artifact while pretending to smile. If there was one, Mitch had it. Larson, to his knowledge, could not use most artifacts, only blow things up. Still, he should avoid telling a flat-out lie. "How can I help?"

"There is a book containing information about an artifact called the Son Sovaj. It might be in the university's stores." Mitch picked up a teacup and sniffed the contents. "Does that ring any bells?"

Something about Mitch's mannerisms convinced him Mitch would know if he lied. But it was Larson's eyes that bored a hole in his skin. "It does. I believe I read something that referenced that when I first got here. But that was years ago."

"Would you be able to find it for us?" Larson exuded an oily evil, playing his role as a hard-nosed enforcer perfectly.

"Of course." Sam hated that guy. "May I ask who referred you here? Anyone I would know?"

Mitch sent Larson a sideways glance. "No one you would know, just someone very well-connected in the community." A weak blue glow flashed at the Paragon's wrist. Sam leaned back in his chair, projecting a relaxed air. Both of their eyes fell to the revealed artifact, then met in cold challenge. Larson didn't react because he couldn't see the object from his vantage point. The look Mitch gave him dared him to acknowledge the artifact. Interesting.

"I will do everything I can to accommodate a personal request from the Paragon. How should I contact you when I locate the item?"

Mitch reached into his pocket and handed Sam an official business card. "I appreciate expedience."

"I understand." Sam placed the card in the top drawer of his desk and stood. "Can I arrange a private tour of the campus? I'm sure President Higgins is eager to thank you for the honor of your visit." Playing nice made his teeth grate.

"Thank you for the offer, but we have a busy day and must be leaving." Larson stepped forward, no longer leaning on the wall, glaring at Sam with more menace than necessary. Mitch stood. "We will see ourselves out. I look forward to hearing from you."

"Yes, sir." Sam opened the door, and the Paragon wasted no time exiting the office, snapping his fingers on the way out to release the field. "Paragon." Sam nodded. "Regent."

He watched from the door of his office while Mitch stopped and spoke to President Higgins and the dean, shook hands, then slipped out the door with Larson stalking by his side. Mildred's head popped out of the room that housed her desk, eyes wide. Seeing that the Paragon was no longer in the building, she hustled to his door. "I called Mrs. Keys. She said an unexpected guest was knocking on the door as we spoke, so she couldn't make lunch, anyway. You should probably call her. She sounded miffed."

Stifling a curse, Sam stepped back into his office. He needed to get home right now. Unaware of the shift in his mood, Mildred looked back to the exterior doors where Higgins and the sniveling dean still stood in quiet conversation. "What did they want? That man with the Paragon exudes evil from his dark soul."

"The Paragon had a question about an item in the center's possession. I will be busy with a project for him for the foreseeable future.

Please discreetly clear my calendar." He nodded at the two men, still speaking at the end of the hallway.

She still stared down the hallway where Mitch and Larson had disappeared, obviously rattled. "I'll keep the hyenas at bay."

"Thank you, Mildred. I don't know what I'd do without you." Slamming the door in poor Mildred's face and locking it, he turned to find a person standing right behind him.

"Don't move." He said it without thinking and his hand flew out to wrap around their throat, squeezing. Blue choked out a pained exhale, eyes bulging, and she grabbed his wrist with both hands. He jerked his hand away in horror. Blood caked her lip and chin, and her right eye was swollen shut. Both sides of her jaw were black and blue. Her shirt and pants sported various puncture marks rimmed in blood. Deadly wild eyes landed on him after taking in the rest of the room. Concerned by her obvious injuries but still aware of his surroundings, he placed a finger to his lips and pointed at his desk to let her know he suspected a listening artifact. "I'm sorry," he mouthed silently. "Got it. Spider. Feel free to move." He covered for his slipup.

"Are you okay?" She mouthed the words, understanding his signal. He nodded and formed the same words. She shook her head and placed a trembling fist in the center of her chest where she once explained she experienced the pull of magic when she focused on a person. She almost whispered out loud but stopped herself. Her lips moved. "You were gone." Face crumpling, she threw herself into his arms, pushing him a step back, and buried her face in his chest.

Even through her clothes, he could feel that she was ice cold. But that wasn't the reason she was shaking.

The magic barrier Mitch deployed must have blocked her ability to know where he was. She thought he was dead. The intensity of her reaction stunned him, but he was far more worried about what had happened to her than what had happened here.

Wrapping his arms around her, his hand slid over her back in a soothing motion and stopped at a hard object shaped like a knife. Continuing the circle, another knife and a small handgun met his hand on the other side of her back. Inspecting the two hair sticks secured in her uncharacteristic bun, he pulled them out. Her hair tumbled loose, and he ran his thumb across one edge, confirming it was sharper than it should be. He leaned away and held them up in question. She shrugged and stepped back, pushing her loose hair behind an ear. Continuing their silent conversation now that she had regained her composure, he formed the words, "What happened?"

"Five minutes? Home?" she mouthed back and held up a hand with five fingers extended.

Nodding, he jerked his head toward the door. Motioning like he was locking it, he jerked his thumb in a *let's go* motion.

Taking his hand, she hurled them across the nightmare rainbow to their destroyed kitchen. The side door hung open, the lock shattered, and part of the frame littered the floor. Cabinet doors hung on broken hinges, a puddle of water originating from the still spraying broken faucet wet their shoes. The window was cracked. A man-sized dent graced the door of the refrigerator. None of the furniture in the living room remained unscathed. The coffee table he built earlier in the year was nothing more than a pile of kindling. Bloodstains covered the sofa. The television lay shattered on the floor, and several holes graced the Sheetrock of both the walls and ceiling. Blood splattered everything. Seething, he held her at arm's length. He counted five stab wounds. "How many were there?"

Shivering, she rubbed her arms to warm them up. "Eight. Thanks for the heads-up. You saved my ass." She jerked her head toward the hallway. "I left them alive. Can you make them forget?"

She said the number with such nonchalance. "Eight?" She pulled his hand, and he followed her down the hallway, past a pile of guns, knives, and other weapons, into their dim bedroom. Sure enough, eight large bodies lay hog-tied at random intervals around the room. Most were conscious and struggling, and they were all equipped for a raid. Every one of them was twice her size. "Jesus Christ." Checking to make sure they were all secured, he pulled her back into the hallway and shut the door.

Misinterpreting his reaction, her brow furrowed as she looked up at him. "I can kill them. That might wave a red flag to Larson. I think they are his. Sorry." She moved to go back into the room.

"No. I'll handle it." Closing his eyes and shaking his head, he wrapped his arms around her, allowing himself a moment like the one she had earlier. Eight people. Blood covered his hands from touching her soaked clothing. They could have killed her. And she still came to his office, ready to fight two of the most powerful magic users in the world. "Were you seriously going to stab the Paragon with a hair accessory?"

"If I had to. But that was plan Z." Her words were light, but the look on her still bloody face was serious.

"I love the way you say I love you, too."

That earned him a scowl and a push. "Would you please go deal with those assholes before someone misses them?"

"Give me a second, Angel." He stepped back and rubbed at the dried blood on her lip and below her nose, thanking the heavens she was healthy enough to be cranky. "How are you? Really?"

Waving a dismissive hand, she opened the door. "Some of them are beat up. I didn't want to waste magic healing them. I don't know how you want to handle that."

"I'll think of something. I need you out of range." He stopped with his hand on the doorknob.

"Workshop far enough?"

"That works."

Blue disappeared before his eyes in a puff of cold air.

Stepping into the room, he found the smartest-looking guy in the bunch and propped him up against the wall, squatting so they were at eye level. This was a complicated directive since it involved multistep orders to many people. And he couldn't push too far, or the mental gaps would become obvious. He needed all his magic and concentration to make this work. "Tell me why you are here."

Choking and trying not to answer, the man turned red and gave in. "To take the woman who lives here into custody."

475

"Tell me why they want her."

"Her husband knows something. They need leverage."

His give-a-shit slipped away. The last time that happened, a lot of people stopped breathing. "Tell me why you stabbed her."

"They wanted her roughed up."

Stabbing someone five times was a far cry from roughing them up. They intended to kill her. "Tell me why you tried to kill her instead."

The man's eyes filled with embarrassment. "We couldn't catch her."

That made Sam smile. "Tell me what the husband knows."

"Something about the Paragon's kid."

"Tell me who sent you."

"The..." The man strained, turning so red, Sam worried he might have a stroke. "The... Regent."

"There it is." Sam stood. "Tell me if the Paragon knows."

A pissed-off grunt preceded a no.

"Stay there. Be quiet. Don't move unless I tell you to." Sam went about waking up the other men and giving them similar orders. When all the men were untied and glaring at him, some in fury and some in fear, he crossed his arms and leaned against the wall, taking in the lot of them. He wanted to teach them all a lesson that would leave them celibate and frustrated for the rest of their lives. But Nisha's voice was in his head, telling him not to go too far and to remember he was one of the good guys. He didn't want to be a good guy right now. Pulling as much magic as he dared, he watched their eyes grow wide in horror before he spoke, and knew his own eyes were changing. "Tell me what you wanted to be when you grew up."

They all responded at once. He heard firefighter, electrician, chef, and strangely, mortician, but he heard nothing that concerned him like a serial killer or hit man. "Excellent, gentlemen. Here is what is going to happen. Forget that you were ever here today. You never made it. Forget you ever saw this house or anyone in it." He watched as their eyes glassed over.

"Tell me who drove." He searched the men and directed his attention to the one who responded. "Tell me your name and which direction you came from."

"Robert. East."

"Robert. When you get back in your vehicle with all of these guys, drive exactly fifteen miles east and run it into the first tree you see." The man nodded blankly. That should explain their injuries.

"One more time." He addressed everyone in the room again. "Forget you were here. Forget you saw this house. Tell me if you understand."

A chorus of yeses met his ears.

"Never hit a woman again." For a moment, he again considered taking them out of the gene pool but stopped himself. "Stop doing this job. Figure out a way to be what you wanted to be when you grew up."

They stared at him, eyes dilated as their minds worked to follow his commands. "Pick up your weapons on the way out of my house.

Get back in your vehicle and get out of my neighborhood as fast as you can."

One by one, the men stood in confusion and picked their weapons out of the pile on the hallway floor and filed out the side door. Walking down the street, they all climbed into a telephone company truck, and Robert drove it away.

He knocked on the door to the workshop after they left. The door opened, and Blue peeked out. Pushing his way in, he shut the door and took a good look at her. Her swollen eye was open again, and most of the bruises on her face had already faded to nothing. "They are gone. I'll come home."

She shook her head. "I think you are safe at work. They can't play the Paragon visit card again for a while."

"They beat the hell out of you here."

"I heal." She shrugged.

He couldn't suppress the surge of frustration in his voice. "You aren't invincible."

She took his hand, hers still as cold as ice, and spoke softly. "I know. But we need to get you back before Mildred misses you. Act like everything is normal. They might still be watching your building. If you disappear without an explanation from a locked room, someone will notice." Before he could argue, they blinked through the cold electric rainbow to his office. "I'll be fine. See you tonight." Standing on her tiptoes, she pecked him on the bottom of the chin and disappeared.

61

BLUE

APRIL. THIRTY-ONE YEARS AGO

B lue stood under the scalding hot water of the shower and still shivered. She had a plug in the tub so hot water covered her feet, but they remained so cold they ached. Feeling the water temperature shift cooler and knowing that Sam still needed a shower, she turned off the water. Wringing out her hair and pulling the drain, she stepped out just as the door opened slightly and Sam's arm appeared, trying not to let any warm air out. He handed her a towel so warm it almost stung the cold skin of her hand. "Here you go, Angel."

"Thank you." Snatching the towel, she wrapped herself in it. His hand appeared again, holding another towel and a bag full of clothing. Wrapping the second warm towel around her hair, she looked through the bag.

"Warmed up your pajamas and robe, too. There are two hot packs. I think I have all the nails and splinters up but watch your feet." The door clicked shut.

Drying quickly so she could get into the clothes before they cooled, she smiled when she found two sets of wool socks and a pair of fluffy slippers. Pulling the still warm socks over her feet, she sighed in relief. The warm robe felt so good it almost brought tears to her eyes.

She spent the morning and most of the afternoon disposing of their destroyed possessions, living room carpet, and dozens of bags of debris, dumping every piece of furniture they owned except the bed and a dresser directly into a lovely-smelling land-fill. They couldn't risk dragging everything out the front or back door in case anyone was watching. It took several unpleasant trips. Couches were heavy, but what surprised her was the sheer weight of the carpet and what the pain-in-the-ass tack strip could be. Between that and the fact she lost count of the jumps it took her to take those men down this morning while trying not to kill them, she might never be warm again. She shoved the hot packs into the pockets of her robe and wrapped her hands around them.

Sam came home after lunch and took over cleaning and re-pairs. It was well past dinner now, and they still hadn't talked about the reason for Mitch and Larson's visit. As she shuffled into the kitchen, Sam finished installing the new doorknob. He closed the door, making sure it would latch and lock.

"Thanks, again."

Looking over his shoulder, he frowned. "Sure. Still cold?"

"Much better now."

"I'll make another pot of coffee." Setting his tools to the side, he scanned the bare particle-board floor of the living room, the destroyed walls, and the complete lack of furniture with a disgusted shake of his head. "Those guys weren't Cahlad."

"I figured that out." Blue looked at her feet. Eight magic users likely could have taken her out or at least made her run and leave them alive and unaltered to spill all their secrets. "It would have been a very different fight."

Sam took out the coffee tin and slammed the newly repaired cabinet door with an angry grunt. "I should have fucked with those assholes more than I did."

"Then Larson would have had ammo to come at us even harder." Jumping up onto the counter, she watched him start a pot of coffee using one of their pans in place of the shattered coffeepot. "What did you do?"

"Gave them new leases on life." His tone was dark. "I should have taken them out of the gene pool, too."

She was glad he was on her side. Sensing a downward spiral in his mood, she changed the subject. "They left something in your office?"

"Mitch did. A business card. My gut says it's a magical bug."

"So, he suspects you of something?"

"He asked about the Son Sovaj." Sam walked to stand in front of her, leaning in and resting his hand on the counter on either side of her hips.

"By name? Why would Mitch think you have it?"

"Yes, by name. But specifically, about a book that references it. It's like he knew I didn't have the artifact, and he lied about who told him to look at Everdale. We both know it was Larson."

Eyeing the coffee pan as the percolator dripped, she chewed on her lip. "How do you know he lied?"

"His artifact reacted. And he knows I saw it."

"Did Larson?"

"No." Sam lifted an eyebrow to emphasize the gravity of that statement. "It's like Mitch was daring me to say something that would out him."

"Mitch is now looking for the same book as the Sovereign. We know why Larson wants it. What is Mitch up to?"

"No idea. Those men came to use you as leverage against me. Larson sent them personally because he thinks I know something about the Paragon's kid. Mitch didn't know about it."

"How lazy. Take the love interest hostage. Motivate the hero. He can do better than that." Blue hissed in irritation. "I hate that one-dimensional asshole."

"Blue, this isn't a joke. They meant to hurt you."

"I'm aware. And they did." She absentmindedly ran her fingers over her abdomen where two of the worst wounds had been. "But it could have been a bad day if they went after someone else. What if they went after Mildred?"

The look on his face told her he hadn't considered that possibility. He hung his head, his next words emerging pained. "We need to keep their attention on us, don't we?"

"Yes, we do. Why would Larson need leverage if Mitch was asking?" Fiddling with the tie on her robe, she struggled to figure out the motivations of all the players. "I don't think Larson wants Mitch to have that book. And he doesn't want us in official custody, or he would have sent Stalkers by now."

"We still have a problem, then. I had to admit I had heard of the book." He retrieved a mug, filled it, and handed it to her. "At least the dishes survived this time. This is getting expensive. I liked that couch."

"Me, too." The coffee was wonderful, but she was still freezing. "I have an idea."

"I'm listening."

"We have the book, the artifacts, their history, and the real Project Zenith records. The only advantage we have at the moment is information. Doling out misinformation and half-truths is incredibly effective at throwing other people off the trail or pushing them where you want them to go." Her words set gears turning in Sam's head. She could see plans forming.

"Give them enough to make Mitch happy, but not enough to make Larson more volatile than he already is. Take out some pages and make some creative edits?"

"You read my mind."

"It's risky. Mitch is sharp, and Larson knows something is up and will keep coming until he gets his leverage or Mitch gets that book." Sam looked down at her coffee cup, like it held the answers to all of their problems. She usually just went with her gut. Sam didn't do anything without thinking things through at least three times.

"Then we should get to work." She squared his glasses on his face. "I love the glasses, by the way."

"Thank Mildred." He fiddled with the stem of the glasses over his right ear.

"Oh, I will. I'll get her some Black Forest cake from the place in Lucerne. She loves that stuff." Her stomach chose that moment to rumble angrily.

Sam gave her a stern look. "You haven't eaten today, have you?"

She sighed. "I've been busy."

Immediately turning, he pried the dented refrigerator door open and pointed. "There are three blue lids. Why don't you eat?"

She shrugged and sipped on her coffee. "Your glasses distracted me."

Sam's eyes flew to the ceiling, and he put both hands on his hips before shaking his head and pulling two containers out. Grumbling something about fighting eight assholes and not being capable of feeding herself, he popped the lids off and stuck them in the microwave, then used his shoulder to force the warped refrigerator door closed again.

It was probably best not to remind him of the difference between capability and motivation. The hum of the appliance filled the kitchen, and his lips formed a thin line. He started to say something, held a finger up, then shook his head, struggling with his words but not with his magic, for a change.

A mischievous smile formed on her face before she could stop it. "I am not the Lord, and I can't grant you patience."

Sam laughed despite himself and pinched his nose.

"But I will go get the book and files so we can work on our plan."

"Not tonight, you aren't. You are done." The microwave chimed, and he pulled the dishes out, setting them on the counter next to her. Placing a fork in her hand, he pointed at the container of pad Thai. "Please eat."

"Since you asked nicely."

62

NISHA

"This is Silly Rabbit," a deep, smooth voice that continued to catch her off guard, chimed in her ear. She assumed someone named Trix would sound nasal and awkward. "Alpha team, give me a comm check. Over."

"Control, this is Alpha One. Good copy." Finn's voice reached her ears.

"Alpha Two, Good copy," Kendra said.

"Charlie Team, this is Control."

Finn's men, using signs one through four, checked in next. "Delta team, this is Control."

"Control, this is Delta One. Good copy." Nisha stood in front of the car, currently parked on the fourth floor of the parking garage of a medical complex across the street from the Cahlad's administration building. She would have a clear view of Mitch's office and Zella's big comfy chair if she had a pair of field glasses. As it was, she could see almost the entire campus and stood a scant distance from the primary administration building.

Check-in complete, she removed her necklace per Finn's plan and leaned against the low concrete wall of the garage and reached out with her magic. It took a moment to readjust to noise, but it was also a relief. She searched for Hale or Larson's familiar voices.

"Delta Two. Copy." Greenlee sat on the hood of the car, keeping a careful eye on their surroundings.

"Mississippi Delta Three. I hear ya, sugar. What happened to Bravo?" Harper sat relaxed, with her eyes closed in the passenger seat of the compact car, her magic already in place to hide their small group from view.

Trix's voice held a touch of humor. "Nobody wants to be on the B team, Mississippi Delta Three. Echo, team, this is Control."

"Control, this is Echo One. Good cop," Mitch said. Devon was next with Echo Two, followed by Ben's quiet voice declaring a good copy for Echo Three.

"Good copy for all teams."

"Alpha team is moving." Finn waited a moment. "Delta One confirm HVT location."

Nisha frowned, struggling to grasp Hale's voice. Some people were excited, and others panicked in the building. One was furious.

"Repeat. Delta One confirm HVT location."

"Negative." Nisha concentrated harder. Greenlee jumped off the hood of the car and moved to join her by the wall, staring at the dark shadows of the Cahlad campus in concern.

"Say again, Delta One," Kendra's voice crackled in her earpiece.

Finally, Hale's familiar mental voice caught her attention. He focused intently on a task, moving fast through a dark hallway. Someone was with him. A flash of white hair made an impression. Zella.

"Control," Finn said. "Door 4E."

"Copy," Trix's voice clipped back, no trace of the usual joking demeanor present. "Go."

"Entering the building," Kendra said. "Comm check."

"Still good, Alpha Two." Nisha began to sweat as the exchange continued.

Positive she understood Hale's perspective correctly, she relayed the information. "HVT is on the move with Alpha Three."

"Copy that," Finn said.

Harper stretched across the back seat, searching for a comfortable spot. "I'm craving alphabet soup now."

Focusing on the mental noise erupting in the building, it became easier to tell what was happening. And it was a cluster. An angry mind roared in fury and calculation. He was searching for someone, but it wasn't Zella or Hale. Most FBI agents left the building for the day. Almost everyone else was Sovereign goons. The familiar sound of Agent Richard Mann's slimy brain tickled her senses, followed by a few aids and the frightened mind of Senator Nolan Miller. He was fleeing in the opposite direction.

She weighed whether she should mention Miller at all. The plan was already completely off the rails. "HVT moving southeast on the third floor. Five in pursuit."

"This is Charlie One to Alpha One."

"Hold position, Charlie One," Kendra gave the order, surprising Nisha.

"Acknowledged."

Greenlee fiddled with a small object in his hand. "This is not good."

Cutting her eyes at him in irritable agreement, she focused again. He had no idea how bad it was. Larson was going to kill Miller.

"Fi..." Nisha corrected herself. "Alpha One. Battle is in pursuit of Miller. Northwest corner nearing the main entrance. He intends to kill him."

"Acknowledged. HVT Status?" Finn's voice held no emotion. She could feel her heart slamming against her chest. Listening and not being able to do anything was frustrating. She was used to being the person on the ground. Finn wasn't concerned about Miller. She could tell by his tone. Her unit would have made the effort. Sam would have sent Ivan. She ground her teeth.

"Entering the stairwell. Two neutralized; three still in pursuit on the third floor. Alpha Three is injured. Three more incoming at the first-floor stairs. He's pinned in."

"This is Control. What is your position, Alpha One?"

"Southeast corner. Basement stairs," Kendra said calmly.

The building was chaos. The only two minds not swimming in fury or panic were Finn and Kendra. Miller fled for his life, doubling back. He wanted to buy them enough time. The mind of the FBI agent now joined the fray, not hunting Hale and Zella. He, too, pursued Miller but planned a few stops along the way to deal with various aids and clerks who could prove to be witnesses. Miller was about to be murdered at the hands of a magic terrorist organization with inside help from his own government.

Nisha stared at the deceptively quiet campus in growing horror. "Miller changed direction. He's moving east toward the HVT."

"Overriding safeties, sealing off the third floor and above, and cutting power in three."

"Copy that, Control."

"Two."

She heard when Finn and Kendra reached the stairwell seconds before the group on the first floor got there as well.

"Contact." Finn's voice joined rhythmic pops and echoes of gunfire in an enclosed space carried over all of their earpieces.

"One."

63

BLUE

MAY. THIRTY-ONE YEARS AGO

Blue lay perfectly still, flat on her stomach, with her chin resting on her hands, peering through the slats of an air vent in the hospital wing of the Cahlad's health and science complex. Spying on Mitch and Larson occupied her time several hours a day since they ambushed Sam in his office and sent a pack of mercenaries to her home. Both used artifacts to jam listening devices in their offices, so she had to eavesdrop personally.

She and Sam needed to figure out the Paragon and Regent's motivations to determine how to enact their misinformation campaign. Sam was cranky about it, but he couldn't argue with her logic.

Her evening started off peering through the ceiling tile of Larson's office since Mitch currently attended a conference in Singapore. When a staff member delivered news about Zella, who stayed behind for Amber's kindergarten choir program, things got interesting. According to the staff member, Zella's eyes turned white, and she collapsed on the floor and dropped Amber, breaking her arm. Zella suffered a concussion and currently rested in the infirmary. But that wasn't what sent Larson into a tizzy. The report containing the words Zella uttered while under the influence of the vision sent him over the edge. He jumped to his feet, slamming his hands on his desk, burning handprints in the wood. The poor woman who delivered the message literally whimpered and ran away.

When he stomped from the office, Blue knew she needed to find Zella quickly. Fortunately, she could locate Zella with her magic, so she easily beat Larson to the hospital room, settled on an uncomfortable portion of the drop ceiling and waited for the show to start.

Right now, Larson stood leaning casually against the wall by the door of Zella's hospital room. Zella, dark circles under her eyes, sat, reclined in the bed. On a cot under the window, little Amber slept curled around a pink stuffed kitty, clutching it to her chest with an arm wrapped in a purple cast.

Larson read from the note in his hand, tone accusatory. "The Se't Sovaj. A tome and tale. A dulcet cure to break the spell. Beware last child of Zenith, the sentinel guard and carry. Douse the flames of war's inferno lest hope's bloody corpse they ferry. The stars know not if she portend rebirth or ruin? When release the arrow aim be true, but for reign or revolution?"

Zella's face held no emotion. She just stared at Larson, blinking occasionally.

Larson straightened and stepped closer to the bed. "That is the third time you had this exact vision." He waited for Zella to respond, and she remained quiet. "Are you finally going to tell me what it means?" Zella's visions always came in coded words and images. But until her accident, she could translate them into messages other people could understand and find useful.

"No."

"Come on, Z. If you talk to someone about it, maybe they will stop." He folded the note neatly and tucked it into his pocket.

"I see what I need to see when I need to see it. I have no control over when a vision comes or what it contains, whether I speak of it or not." Zella rubbed her forehead, obviously suffering from a headache.

"But you got hurt. Amber is hurt." Larson waved to the sleeping child wearing Rugrats pajamas. "Let me help you."

Blue tilted her head and studied this version of Larson. She had never seen this side of him before. He spoke to Zella like Greenlee would speak to her, with familiarity and friendship. She didn't know he had it in him.

Zella glared up at the harsh light above her bed. "Could you turn that light out?"

Larson reached back and turned off the row of lights directly over Zella's bed, leaving the one over Amber on. "Better?"

"Yes. Thank you." Zella sounded resigned as she leaned back in the bed. "You can't help me with this. I've talked to Mitch. But I appreciate your concern."

Larson sat in the small reclining chair next to Zella's bed and leaned forward, placing his arms on his legs. Right now, he could pass as a human. No trace of the monster that lurked beneath the surface. "You haven't told Mitch about anything other than the book. And it is at Everdale, just like you said it would be."

Zella's posture remained relaxed, but eyes narrowed slightly as they cut to Larson's face. "How did you know I only translated part of the vision for Mitch?"

Blue perked up at Zella's tone and the hard flash in Larson's eyes. She caught him in a lie. He recovered quickly, falling back into concerned-friend mode effortlessly. "I'm his right hand. He told me."

"No, he didn't." The way Zella delivered the words almost made Blue laugh. This was getting good. "He promised me he wouldn't tell a soul anything about the vision."

"How can you be so sure he kept his promise?" Larson cajoled. "He is the Paragon now. He has to consider the bigger picture."

Zella's hands fell to her sides, and she looked up at the ceiling, seeming to consider Larson's words. When she finally spoke, her voice was powerful and filled with certainty. "Because I know Mitch. And because I know you well enough to know you have bugged our home to get the information you have."

Larson remained in a relaxed position, leaning forward, and studying Zella, his face conveying an emotion that Blue couldn't put her finger on. "You wouldn't be the first person in this room to be betrayed by someone they thought they could trust."

Blue stifled an oooh, and her head involuntarily bounced back and forth between Zella and Larson as they stared at each other. The tension in the room grew thick enough to cut with a knife. What was happening right now?

Zella's lips thinned, and she shook her head slightly. "I didn't betray you."

"You didn't? You told me I would challenge the Paragon one day. I was in your vision. But when I had the opportunity, you ratted me out to Johansen, and he put me in jail. I'm lucky he didn't kill me." Larson still spoke softly, but his voice held a touch of anger and hurt. "Why, Z?"

"You were the only person I told about that vision. But I know you don't believe me." Zella sounded exhausted. "I never should have told you about it. It was a grave mistake." She looked at Larson, and she sounded almost apologetic. "And you didn't let me tell you the rest of it. You ran off thinking you would soon be the most powerful man in the world."

Larson's jaw twitched, and his hands turned to fists. Zella hit too close to home with that one. "You've kept nothing from me before. Not just because we were in the same unit. We were friends."

Zella's head turned to the side, and she took a shocked breath. "We aren't friends now?"

Voice cold, Larson asked a question of his own. "What did you see that made you betray me and have me sent to prison?"

Zella's face fell, and her right hand fidgeted with the blanket next to her thigh. "I saw my friend die horribly."

Larson lunged from the chair and stood over Zella's bed, putting his hands on his hips, and leaning down so they were at eye level. "You saw me die?"

Remaining silent, Zella didn't seem concerned that an unstable human fireball loomed over her bed.

Larson rose back to his full height again and began pacing. "This vision is about me, too, isn't it? And Mitch. That's why you won't tell him." He stopped pacing and turned to face Zella. "Do we die?"

"I'm not saying anything else. I've already said too much."

Larson's eyes narrowed, and the menacing look Blue knew so well settled on his face. "I won't stand by and wait for the 'Sentinel' to stab me in the back again." He used his fingers to make quotes as he said the words. "You will tell me everything I want to know." Now his words rumbled low with an unspoken threat that made Blue shiver, remembering the punishments he doled out when he used that voice during training. She would be a walking ball of scar tissue without her enhanced healing. Rhodes had a few nasty burns when he wore his own face. Blue bit her lip. Zella was hurt and alone. Should she get involved?

"You should go now." Zella's face and voice shifted to icy stone in an instant.

"Mitch is still in the air. He won't be here for hours. He can't protect you now." Larson looked smug as he stepped forward.

A creepy smile crossed Zella's face, and faster than Blue could blink, the woman lifted her hand and pointed a small gun directly at Larson's head. "I don't need him to."

Larson barked out a humorless laugh. "Amber is behind me. You won't risk missing and hitting her." Blue's gaze fell to the still sleeping Amber, completely oblivious to the drama unfolding just feet away.

Zella's eyes never left Larson's face. "I don't miss." The certainty of the statement shocked Blue and made her smile. She knew Zella was a Stalker. But she didn't know Zella had flex. This was amazing.

Larson laughed. "I will incinerate the bullets and everything in here." He raised his hands, and Blue's eyes grew wide. She looked to the small body lying on the cot behind him. If this went any further, she was going to grab Amber and go. Old habits died hard.

"Really?" Zella raised an eyebrow.

Larson's own flew up in surprise. He stared at his hands, then clenched them closed with a snarl. His eyes flew around the room searching for something. "You have an anti-magic field?"

"Leave. Now."

Blue held her breath as the Regent and the Paragon's partner stood off in a hospital room. Finally, Larson took a step back. "This isn't over."

Zella followed his movements with her weapon as he moved to the door. "I know." She kept the gun aimed at the door for several moments after it closed behind Larson. Finally, she lowered the gun, flicking the safety and tucking it back under her leg. After a moment, she climbed out of bed, crossed the room, and lifted Amber from the cot. Carrying her back to her own bed, Zella climbed in, and rolled to face the door, tucking Amber and the pink stuffed cat into her side.

Zella stared at the door for a few moments and made no move to call Mitch and tell him about what just happened. Why would she keep that to herself? Something didn't add up. Blue couldn't wait to tell Sam.

Letting the cold rainbow cloud her vision, Blue landed in the kitchen with a whoosh, to find Sam leaning against the counter in front of the sink, scowling at a stack of creamy-white papers he held in his hand. A dark look marred his face, and a black vein on the side of his neck pulsed. She held perfectly still. That only happened right before he completely lost his temper and did questionable things with his magic. What happened while she was gone? "Hey, there, Diablo. What's wrong?"

Finally, he lifted his face and met her eyes with black, inky orbs. She had to resist the urge to take a step back. "Tell..." He stopped himself and tilted his head, his lips thinning in an effort not to use his magic. "Did you know Ricky's middle name?"

Blue wrinkled her nose, confused and struggling to shift from the drama in the hospital to the unknown drama in her kitchen. Whatever it was, Sam was pissed. "Um. His school records were just N."

"Just an N?" He sounded skeptical, and his eyes darkened even more.

She didn't recall ever seeing a full name. "That's all I saw. I don't know the actual name. Why?"

He extended the papers he held, and she took them carefully. It was an envelope with a heavy card laying on top, embossed with beautiful script-like lettering. Instantly, she knew it was the invitation to Ricky's graduation. Sherry called to tell her it was on the way. As a teacher, Blue would be at the graduation ceremony. But Ricky wanted to make sure that Mr. Sam knew he wanted him there, too, so he insisted Sherry send a formal invitation. "I've been waiting for this. It should have his new name. The adoption paperwork with Reggie went through last month. Ricky isn't a Groves anymore."

Sam's fist clenched, and he looked at his feet with a huff. Tilting her head in confusion, she inspected the paper. In the center of the lovely card were three words that narrowed her vision and made her ears ring: Richard Nolan Miller. "You are kidding me?"

"You really didn't know?"

Eyes wide, she looked between the paper and Sam and back again. That stung. "You really think I would sit on something like this?"

They stared at each other for a minute. His face said everything. "No. But..."

The kitchen fell silent again as the words he didn't say sank in. But he knew she kept secrets from everyone, even the people closest to her. "I didn't keep this from you."

He shook his head and looked up, closing his eyes. "I know. I knew. I lost my temper, and I pointed it at you."

She understood where he was coming from. What he must have thought and with good reason. "It's all right."

"It's not."

"You are human, and you are allowed to have emotions. You caught yourself. This is..." Her words trailed off as she stared at the papers again. She didn't believe it.

Slumping against the counter, he shoved his hands in his pockets. "I told her to fix it. All this bullshit is on me."

Blue slung the papers on the counter and scowled at the random pile they formed. "Just hold off on the self-flagellation. We don't know that this is a bad thing yet. Maybe we have fixed it."

"Or we accidentally made the stuff that needed to be fixed happen." His face twisted with a mixture of receding anger and self-loathing. His eyes were black, and she could feel anxiety rolling off him in waves. He might not be mad at her anymore, but he was a long way from calm.

"What did Mitch tell us about Nolan Miller's childhood? Someone burned his home down with his mom and sister inside." She stepped forward into his space and pulled his hands out of his pockets and gripped them firmly, so he understood she wasn't leaving, even when the cosmic demon eyes made an appearance. "They were inside. But Tiffany was just over here last week, grinding Play-Doh into our carpet. Sherry is very much alive and in love with a decent guy."

"They lived."

"Right." She squeezed his hands. "Maybe not all of your slipups are bad. Did you ever think about that? You said fix it. All juiced up on the Son Sovaj and Ava. To all three of us. Not just Amber."

His eyes flared, and for a moment, she feared he would storm out or tell her to leave. Instead, he took her face in his hands. "Thank you." He held her that way, silent for a moment. "You really think we have been following a directive for the past five years?"

"We never had that mandatory conversation about the dire consequences of changing anything in the past because it might change the future."

"Just by being here, we are changing it. There wasn't anything to discuss." Sam's body relaxed, eyes shifting back to normal. "I don't feel guilty about buying the Apple stock, either."

She laughed and stepped away. "Good. Now I have to tell you what I just overheard."

64

FINN

"Miller has issued a press release. Scheduled for the front steps at six hundred hours." Trix talked in his ear. "You have two hours before the press shows up."

They didn't need additional civilians in the area. Crouched and moving low through a well-manicured courtyard, between a building labeled on the schematics as the Paragon's residence and the administration building, Finn followed the glowing, green form projected in his goggles of Kendra's body convinced now she spent the entire time on his team sandbagging. Being in charge was her default mode.

"What's Bravo team's status?" Laying out this plan, he agreed with Kendra's assessment that the horrific deaths of a cadre of FBI agents and government aides would play far worse for the magic community, and thus his sister-in-law and niece, than the assassination of the Paragon's partner. Larson didn't care if he started a war. He would kill whomever they left in the building. Finn needed them off-site in case Larson did what Nisha said he did last time, erupt in a fireball that leveled most of a building. Bravo team began the covert and probably forced evacuation thirty minutes ago, leaving the hallway containing Mitch and Sam's offices alone.

"Seven heavy and clear."

Kendra looked back, waiting for his signal. They needed to move before anyone missed them. "Go for phase two."

Trix began the comm check, looping the rest of the team in on what they thought was the first and only phase of the plan.

Kendra stopped at the brick pillar, capping the end of a cast-iron fence covered in climbing vines, and gave him a signal for two.

Halting behind Kendra and covering their rear, he waited for everyone to finish checking in. "Delta One confirm HVT location."

Pulling a crossbow from its location on her back, Kendra took careful aim to the right, letting a quill loose with barely a whisper, then shifting seamlessly to the other side and firing two more. Nodding, she went right. Finn moved to the body on the left with an arrow sticking out of its eye. Dragging it back into the courtyard, he dumped it into the vines with the body Kendra had dealt with. Hearing no response, he made another call. "Repeat. Delta One confirm HVT location."

Kendra stepped back to the pillar, nose twitching wildly, looking back and forth between the direction of the main entrance and the loading dock. She pointed to the southeast corner where the loading dock waited and motioned for him to follow.

"Negative." Nisha's voice carried through their headsets. Kendra didn't slow down as Finn swept the roof and their surroundings for other patrols or issues.

"Say again, Delta One" Kendra reached the ramp to the loading dock and moved in the shadows cast by a yellow-tinted security light.

They both reached the door, and Finn looked up, reading the small label in the center of the doorjamb, and turned back to the large, empty parking lot. It remained motionless. "Control. Door 4E."

"Copy." A moment later, the door buzzed quietly. "Go."

Kendra moved through, sweeping the entrance. "Entering building." Reappearing at the door, she motioned for him to follow.

Finn closed the door silently behind them and followed her down the hall. Her nose still twitched and wrinkled with every step. This portion of the building was dark and quiet.

Kendra called for a comm check as they moved farther into the building.

"Still good, Alpha Two." Trix's words let them know any devices the Cahlad might have in place did not yet block their signal.

Kendra picked up the pace, looking at the ceiling and rounding the corner, gun raised and alert.

"HVT is on the move with Alpha Three." Finn scanned the building. Pointing up in question, Kendra nodded and moved toward the location of the stairs. Nisha reported a direction that confirmed their general bearing, showing five incoming. Tanner checked in, and Kendra gave instructions to hold position. They were almost to the stairwell. Kendra sniffed and pointed north, waved a hand, pointed up, and nodded. Their magic target was above. He was glad she could tell the difference. Stepping into the stairway, she cleared the door, and he fell in behind her.

Lights flicked on with their movement. His glasses compensated, Greenlee's magic stifling the flare before it could blind him, but he had to flip them up. Ahead of him, Kendra did the same.

A volley of gunfire from above had them moving faster but still cautiously. The basement stairs had three flights as opposed to two, with two 90-degree angles.

"Fi..." Nisha's voice halted in his ear. "Alpha One. Battle is in pursuit of Miller. Northwest corner, nearing the main entrance. He is going to kill him."

"Acknowledged. HTV status?" A door banged above them, echoing through the stairwell. Two more gunshots echoed in the concrete space, followed by the slamming of a door. Finn heard a pained grunt that told him Hale was in the stairwell with him.

Nisha told them about an injury and three remaining enemies above and three incoming on the first floor. Trix called for their position, and Kendra responded before her head jerked, and she sent a worried look to the west. Signaling incoming magic from that direction, she crossed the first-floor landing and dashed up the stairs to the turn, crouching and sighting on the door from the first floor. Stopping just short of the first-floor landing, he crouched and raised his weapon, listening for Hale's and Zella's footsteps.

"Overriding safeties, sealing off the third floor and above. Cutting power to the east in three." Trix clipped.

"Copy that, Control."

"Two."

The door to the first floor opened, and two men barreled through, followed by a third man, who had more sense about him. Finn waited for the door to slam shut behind the last man and fired. "Contact."

"One." The stairway went dark.

65

BLUE

AUGUST. THIRTY YEARS AGO

B lue sat in the grass in the backyard, watching the fireflies glow and glitter in the dimming light. Yoga hadn't helped calm her nerves, so she gave up. A cool breeze tickled her face, so she pulled a thin sweater over her shoulders and just focused on breathing. Today she planted subtly rearranged data from Project Zenith in the guest bedroom of the director's home. Knowing the Cahlad had taps on all the man's phones, even though he remained in custody, she called, posing as the man's mother and left a message asking when he was going to come home and get all the boxes she was storing for him. Since Larson showed an unexplained interest in information about the Paragon's kid, they redacted the paternal information for both her and Amber and forged Greenlee's. Keeping the information from Larson meant keeping Mitch in the dark about his biological children, but it was the safest course of action. They also removed any documents mentioning who adopted Ben or Greenlee.

She might have also spent a great deal of time sneaking around the Cahlad's new main campus. She hid Mitch's favorite coffee mug, replaced his underwear with new ones that were a size too small, arranged for a flea infestation in Larson's personal quarters and taken the firing pins out of two of his favorite guns while she was at it. Now she sat here in the open to make sure it looked like everything was normal in case someone watched.

Her part of their misinformation campaign was simple. Sam, on the other hand, had to sit across from the Paragon and Regent once again and not get caught in a lie while presenting the heavily doctored Se't Sovaj.

An hour and a half ago, she lost any feeling when she focused her magic on him. They expected that, but she still didn't like it. The panic of being unable to get a lock on his location or even a hint that he was on the planet ran on replay through her mind. Since then, she had given serious thought to the repercussions of murdering both the Paragon and the Regent twenty-five years in the past. Her moral compass didn't run true enough to care about them. If Mitch or Larson harmed a hair on Sam's head, she would find them and make their deaths excruciating, even if she died doing it. Future consequences be damned. She'd had enough of both men.

Instead of maintaining a constant pull of magic, she checked in every few minutes on both Sam and Mitch. She couldn't make herself sick. If things went wrong, she had to operate at full capacity. She checked again, and an intense, comforting sensation swept through her torso. Sam was moving in her direction and very much alive. Larson, the bastard, never let her teleport him anywhere, so she couldn't lock on to his location. Mitch she could find, and he currently moved in the opposite direction. That information and the fact a raving pack of Stalkers or fresh criminal henchmen hadn't shown up to take her into custody meant the meeting must have gone well.

Lost in the random pattern of fireflies, she didn't hear Sam's car pulling up until the sound of his door closing let her know he was home. A moment later, he joined her in the backyard and sat down silently next to her, stretching his legs out. The residual stress of the meeting lined his face as he gazed out at the fireflies as well. "They bought it."

"Did they react to the book?" Even though removing the schematics toned the magic of the book down considerably, it still pulsed with it. They both worried that Mitch or Larson would pick up on the magic coming off the book and misinterpret it as an attack or demand additional information.

"No." Sam looked down. "It's just us. Did you get in and out without issue?"

"Of course I did."

"Of course you did." Sam smirked. "Did you cause any issues?" When he looked at her face, he smiled wider, and his shoulders relaxed. "Of course you did."

Glad that he didn't sound mad about her additions to the plan, she scooted across the inches that separated them, closed her eyes, and leaned her head against his arm. The anxiety that formed from the weeks of painstaking preparation and constant dread of the impending meeting finally left her body, and she relaxed for the first time in recent memory. "What now?"

He put his arm over her shoulder, and they sat on the grass quietly for a long time. They never discussed what they would do if they pulled this off, both half convinced that it would blow up in their faces. Sam took her wrist in one hand and placed something cool and small in her hand, wrapping her fingers around it with the other. The air rushed out of her chest as she unfolded her fingers and stared at the object he placed in her palm. It was a dainty silver band rimmed in small sapphires. Quashing her panic response, she looked up to find a question in his expression. His hand gripped her wrist almost too hard. He knew she was a second away from disappearing into thin air, but his jaw remained set in the familiar expression that told her he didn't want to use his voice.

Swallowing around the gigantic lump in her throat, she stopped herself from shaking her head in disbelief. Normal people got teary and said yes. Here she was, trying her best not to run away and pretend this had never happened. He couldn't take it back if it never happened. She never wanted to hurt that way again. Heart twisting, she just stared for a moment, knowing her face clearly communicated all her emotions, and unable to do a thing about it. If this meant what she thought it did, charades weren't going to work. "I need words."

Sighing deeply, as if nothing about her response surprised him, he looked back out into the sea of fireflies and closed her palm over the ring again. "I'm terrified I will forget to say will you and screw this up forever."

He meant what she thought he meant. Her hands were cold, and she was subconsciously drawing magic, a rainbow haze forming at the edges of her vision. "Forever is a long time."

Shifting slightly, he looked back down, more serious than she had ever seen him, and spoke very slowly. "That's why I can't afford to screw this up."

"When?" The question left her lips before she consciously made a decision. She slapped her free hand over her mouth in disbelief and released the magic she summoned into the universe, unused. She was terrified. But it felt right.

Sam's eyes crinkled around the edges, and the tiniest smile touched his lips. "Tonight."

"You are serious?" She leaned away slightly to get a clear view of his face. He meant it. "My God. You are."

Standing, he began pulling her toward the house. "Vegas. Then I will buy you French toast."

"You've thought about this." Her words were a statement, not a question. Of course, he thought about this and worked through every contingency before he risked saying a word or not saying a word as it was.

"This is plan Z, but I'm running with it." He still hadn't let go of her hand, and he squeezed it now.

"We went straight to Z?"

"Plans A through R were all the ways I would find you after you disappeared."

Blue wanted to feel indignant but couldn't. He wasn't wrong. "What were plans S through Y?"

"S was just surviving the throat punch. T through Y involved lots of words I would probably screw up if you stayed, but said no." He opened the door to the house, led them inside, and locked it behind them.

"Can I hear plan T?"

Sam tensed and glanced away. She almost told him not to worry about it, feeling bad for forcing him to do something that caused so much anxiety. But his focus returned to her face, his expression determined. He traced his finger down her jaw. "Well, plan T was where you argued we don't know if we can make it home, and everyone here already thinks we are married."

"Plan T me would have a good point."

"Yes. And plan T me would have told you that marriage is a choice. One you wake up and make every day. I want to make our choice official. Now. In the future. Whenever and wherever we end up. Even if no one else ever knows, we will." Somewhere between marriage and official, her breath caught. He was right, and somewhere along the way, they had already made the choice. She expected him to tell her to breathe. But he didn't. Instead, he took a deep breath himself. "Blue. Angel. I choose all of your tomorrows."

He was too careful with his words to say this if he didn't mean it. She wasn't sure what to say. "All of them?"

His face answered before he could, but he still gave her words. "Every. Last. One."

"Starting today?"

"Starting today." Raising her hand to his lips, he kissed it and held it there, studying her face for a long moment. "Yes?"

"Yes." Twining her fingers in his, she nodded. "Ready?"

"I've been ready."

Blue released her magic, and they landed, surrounded by neon lights and warm, dry air.

66

DEVON

"HVT moving southeast on the third floor. Five in pursuit." Nisha's words jolted Mitch upright to peer around Devon's head, where she sat on the console between the two men in the van.

Placing a steadying hand on his arm, Devon scanned the area. A news van pulled up, parking on the street across from the Cahlad's main gates, a tall antenna extending up. A man in a suit got out, followed by a cameraman munching on a doughnut.

The voices in her ear kept talking, warning each other of Larson's movements and more enemies incoming in the basement.

"Do you see that?" Ben stared at the newsman, seemingly disinterested in the drama unfolding on the Cahlad campus. "Why would a news van be here?"

Temporarily distracted as the newcomers walked across the street to line up their shot, she almost missed Trix counting down to cut off the power. She didn't miss Finn's terse announcement of

"Contact" or the sounds of gunfire before the entire campus fell into darkness. Heart pounding, she held her breath, praying for Finn's voice to fill her ears again.

Mitch jerked for the door, and she clamped down on his hand. Gunfire continued to ring out over the communication devices. "Stop. Finn has got this."

Mitch's face grew dark, and Devon's eyebrows drew together as they stared each other down. "Let go, dear. Before I make you." His eyes flashed gold, and a wave of magic pulsed out, filling the van and making the hair on the back of her neck stand up.

A feral smile twisted her face. She grew up surrounded by criminals and thugs, learning everything they had to teach, all while dodging assassination attempts ordered by this man. He had no idea what she was capable of or the things she had done. He intended to scare her. Cute. "I'd like to see you try, old man."

67

SAM

APRIL. TWENTY-NINE YEARS AGO

S am lay on couch number four staring at the ceiling as the television bathed the room in flickering light. Blue curled half on top of him, wedged against the back of the couch on her side, head tucked under his chin, and one of her legs thrown over his where she fell asleep earlier while watching one of the late-night talk shows.

This was how they ended the day during the week since he was a night owl, and she had to be up early. He would carry her to their room when he finally went to bed. On the weekends, Blue always found some adventure to take them on. Beaches, mountains, jungles, cities. She could go anywhere in the world, and he could speak any language. It made travel easy. But his favorite trips were the simple ones. They spent one Saturday afternoon at a skating rink near a mall in Minnesota just so she could laugh at a man six and a half feet tall trying to master roller skates for the first time in his life. His pride would never recover. His tailbone probably

516

wouldn't, either. They drove go-carts at a tourist trap somewhere in Missouri and were banned for life thanks to Blue's terrible driving skills. Her pride was not involved at all. They attended a rave in a firetrap of a warehouse near Atlanta and a Nine Inch Nails concert at the Hollywood Palace. A year ago, she convinced him to sing karaoke at a bar in Oklahoma. It took them two hours to pick a song safe for him to sing, only to be booed off the stage. The audience demanded an encore when Blue sang. Last month, they sat in an airport at the gate without a ticket, drinking coffee and watching planes land and passengers disembark.

Despite the weekend adventures, they spent most of the past two years monitoring Mitch, Larson, and the children of Project Zenith. Recently, Blue discovered the nice lady she told him about, the night they rescued her mother, planned to sell her to traffickers for a few thousand dollars. Strangely, Larson had saved her from a worse fate than the one he provided. She hadn't smiled for weeks after the revelation.

Amber should return any day now, and he didn't know if he was ready or if he even wanted to go home. The past four years were hands down the best of his life. He still had a plan to do it, but no guarantees that it would work. The red velvet bag containing the schematic pages of the Se't Sovaj and the six remaining artifacts sat on a bookshelf in the room's corner, emitting a low hum of magic. Last time, he and Amber couldn't pull enough power. When Blue touched the Son Sovaj, the power surge was incredible and overloaded her ability to channel it. He hoped the other artifacts would provide the raw power he and Amber were missing and divert some of the energy through them. He prayed, since everything about these artifacts hinted they worked best as a set, that having all seven would allow them to channel the magic safely as well. That is where his plan got dicey, and his mind refused to let go. Blue wasn't worried at all, telling him all about Zella's vision and the dragons. It shed light on her habitual disregard for her personal safety, but it did not make him feel better at all.

If he had to choose between going back and one of their lives, even if he didn't see a single dragon, they stayed here. Scowling at the ceiling, he dragged a blanket over them. He remained torn because this plan would likely fail, but he needed to try.

A noise outside drew his attention to the door, and he readied his magic to deal with whatever it was. A moment later, a familiar face framed by dirty-blonde hair stepped inside. Shoving a key to the house that neither he nor Blue had given her into her pocket, she met his gaze with sad and worried eyes. The familiar beaded bracelet spun to a halt, still glowing. Blowing out a breath as if her presence was an everyday occurrence, she leaned against the counter. "I don't think I can get you home." She flinched the moment she reached the ambient magic in the room, and looked around, trying to find its source. "What is that?"

"How long do you have?"

"A few hours."

"Grab yourself a drink and sit down." He nodded to the recliner in the corner. "I have some questions for you." Perfectly content right where he was, he had no motivation to move or wake up Blue at the moment, especially not on Amber's account. Whatever came next would be hardest on her. She needed the rest.

Amber's eyes narrowed as she did as she was told, settling into the chair and taking a big drink of water. "I don't like you."

"Feeling is mutual." Sam studied her face for a moment. She wore the same clothes that she wore on her last visit. Evidence that her assertion time might not be moving as fast in their original time line, might be true. "Tell me where you got the Son Sovaj."

"My first fiancé, Percy, gave it to me." Touching the bracelet, a sad smile crossed her face. "You don't have to force me to answer."

"Where did he get it?"

"I don't know. I've never been able to figure it out."

Sam considered her answers while he studied her surroundings. "It didn't give you cancer? Ava was born healthy?"

"No cancer. No complications. And she was just perfect."

"How did you meet Ben Hughes?"

Amber's face twisted in confusion, clearly not expecting that question. "I met Ben in group therapy. He was there because his parents died. I needed help to deal with murdering my best friend." A subtle shudder rippled across her shoulders when she looked at Blue again. A strange expression crossed her face. "She warned me about the explosives, even though she was dying."

Shifting to get a better look at Amber's face, because he didn't trust her answer, he asked again, "Did you know he had magic?"

She frowned and shook her head. "Not while we lived together. I can't believe I missed that." Her answer reinforced one of his theories. Seven artifacts and seven children, all drawn to each other like magnets. Amber's eyes darted to the fridge. "Do you have any food? I haven't eaten in, I don't even know." Amber shuffled to the kitchen, not waiting for an answer. She looked tired and walked with a slight limp. Watching them as the food warmed in the microwave, she raised her eyebrows and waved a fork at them. "Want to tell me what's going on with you two?"

"No."

"Doesn't matter, anyway. We are all screwed." Puffing out her cheeks, she dragged the food out of the microwave and began shoveling it into her mouth like she had never eaten before.

Sam ignored her comment. "What are we going back to?"

Finishing her bite, she finally gave an answer. "The Salem witch trials on steroids. Damn social media. Every iteration I have seen. In all of them, something happens with Larson and Dad. A news anchor with millions of followers on some tok thing meets a pretty gruesome demise on air every time. That makes the internet angry. But Senator Miller gets diced and barbecued, too. Usually well-done. That's what gets the government involved."

"No way around it?"

"Different details, same general result every time." Amber moved to the second container. "This is fantastic. Did you make this? Boom Kitty." She flopped into the recliner, cradling the dish. "Look, I even tried bringing Ava back with me to see if we could get you home that way, but I can't shift anyone other than me through time by myself, even with this. It just helps me shift more often. I need you guys." She tapped her fork absentmindedly on the bottom of the container. "And there was a werewolf in the way. That's a new one."

"In any of these futures, do you get us home?"

"No." Amber's head dropped, hanging in defeat. "You know the saying I've lived a thousand lives? Well, I have. No matter what I do, the future finds a way to be what it wants." Raising an eyebrow in their direction, she looked from where Blue slept and back up to him, still shoveling noodles into her mouth. "But this has never happened before. You guys have always disliked each other. So maybe." Amber shrugged. "Because if I can't get you home this time, you will die of old age before I can come back."

He tightened his arm around Blue, already painfully aware that possibility. And while he had come to terms with it, Blue's heart ached to see her family again. "Can I trust you?"

"At the moment, our goals align." Stirring her food with jerky movements, she couldn't meet his eyes. "They are hunting Ava, too. I need all the help I can get."

"I have a plan." He shook Blue's shoulder to wake her up.

"I'm awake," Blue grumbled and sat up, rubbing her eyes. She slid to the middle cushion to let Sam sit up, pinning Amber with a hard glare.

"Hey, there, sleeping beauty." Amber smirked. "You always could sleep anywhere."

Leaning back into his side like she was settling in for a night of watching television, Blue pointed at Amber. "Drop the bullshit, Amber. I don't care what I promised your mother. If anything has happened to my family, or you stab us in the back again, what I do to you will make what I did to Percy look like a walk in the park."

The tone of her voice made Sam's blood run cold. Blue rarely showed this side of herself, but when she did, it was truly terrifying. He wrapped his arm more firmly around her shoulder just in case Amber said the wrong thing and Blue tried to murder their ticket home.

Amber froze in shock with a forkful of food halfway to her mouth. Her face ashen and rattled by the visceral sincerity of the statement, Amber whispered, "Jesus, Blue. What did you promise Mom?"

"That I would protect you. Mitch was Zella's job. You were mine. Only I screwed up and believed we were friends."

"We were friends. I just... you killed him. I watched. I loved him." Chin jutting outward, Amber's face twisted in disbelief. "When did you make that promise?"

"Thirteen-ish."

"But you wanted to leave." Amber looked even more stunned. "That's why you stayed?" Amber leaned forward. "I didn't know."

"Now you do."

"Then I stabbed you and left you for dead."

"You sure did." Blue's posture looked relaxed, but he could feel the tension rolling off her in waves.

No wonder she kept people habitually at a distance. Between her upbringing and double betrayals by Amber and Rhodes in a matter of days, he couldn't blame her. No wonder she took the news that her guardian planned to sell her to traffickers so hard. "Angel?"

Blue waved a hand dismissively. "That hasn't happened yet. Let's focus on the important stuff. How are Greenlee and Devon? Lexi?"

Slow to respond and almost on the verge of tears, Amber put down her food and sighed. "I have screwed up so much." This emotion was real, and he couldn't muster an ounce of sympathy for her. "They were all alive when I left. But things are about to get bad. What is your plan, Regent? My way isn't working."

Both women looked at him expectantly. Sam still hesitated. Blue looped her elbow through his. "Your idea? Does it feel right?"

It did. The artifacts called to him, but that was the only thing he was certain of. "I don't want to kill you."

Leaning in, she was calm, but the intensity of her voice told him otherwise. "Not what I asked."

"Yes."

"What are we waiting for?"

It was so infuriatingly in character, he wanted to grind his teeth. But he didn't. He gave her a quick kiss, then stood and pulled the red velvet bag off the bookcase shelf, moved the coffee table aside, and distributed the artifacts around the room. As he did, the beads on Amber's bracelet moved into an even spacing around her wrist, glowing a subtle, distinct color. It gave him more confidence in his plan. Amber didn't notice, too focused on what he was doing and the shift in the room's magic. "Don't touch each other. That's very important."

"What are these?" Amber scooted out of the recliner and onto the floor, holding her hand out toward the boxes and pulling it back, manipulating the intensity of the magic in the room.

Blue scooted onto the floor as well, and he sat across from them both. "They are the Se't Sovaj. The other artifacts are in the set that one came from." He pointed to Amber's bracelet. "They need each other to work properly."

Noticing that the beads no longer moved, Amber looked suspicious. "Where did you find these?"

Both Blue and Sam ignored Amber's question.

"The Fos Sovaj is a belt. It's long. All three of us can hold it. The others are small." Sam flipped open one box, and an electric surge of magic erupted, causing them all to squirm in discomfort, but nothing else happened. He put the ring on, and the electric buzz went away. "We each wear two. Then all three of us grab the belt and try not to knock out any teeth or break any noses when the magnet effect hits us."

Blue, familiar with his plan and habitually accepting of bad ideas, remained unphased. Amber pursed her lips and glared. "Using one screwed things up this bad, and you think using seven is better?"

"We were driving a car with one wheel before." Blue flipped open a case and extracted a bracelet that looked like cheap elastic play jewelry. A zap of magic hit them and subsided. "That's why it crashed. This time, we make sure it has all of its wheels before we drive it off the lot. It makes sense." Snatching up another box, she winked at him. "Very logical."

"It's a wing and a prayer, is what it is," Amber grumbled as she gingerly picked up a box. A haircomb emerged, and she wrapped her hair into a bun and shoved the comb in.

"I know." Blue dropped a dainty silver necklace over her head. "That's why I like it."

Pinning an ornate lapel pin into his shirt, he looked at the box containing the last item, feeling more confident by the minute. With each item that emerged from its protective case, the magic stabilized and became more harmonious, just like when he tested this a few weeks ago while Blue was at school, just in case he exploded the house. Wrapping the rope of the velvet bag containing the schematics around his wrist, he anchored it. "Let's talk about when and where we are going."

"The closest I can get you is just shy of two days after you left." Amber scooted forward, eyeing the last red box like a snake might jump out and bite her. "They are monitoring the burst now. They are on me so fast." She shook her head in exasperation. "Do you remember that place you took me when Jonas Archer dumped me senior year?"

"Yeah? That's not exactly remote." The suggestion confused Blue.

"But it is where everything goes down."

"Wanna fill me in?" Sam scooted toward the last box and dumped the belt on the floor.

"Parking garage across the street from the campus where the groundskeeper kept his tequila stash in the maintenance closet?" Blue cast a suspicious look in Amber's direction. "That's mighty close to where Larson was holed up while we were running for our lives with your daughter across the American Southwest. Convenient."

Amber nodded in agreement. "Nolan Miller is there, too, spouting his propaganda. He gets caught in the crossfire."

Blue closed her eyes and dropped her head. She would go now, even if Amber admitted to having an execution squad waiting on the other side. Blue looked his way almost apologetically. "I don't trust her. If I'm down, you will be on your own."

"If you get us there, I'll handle it." He looked pointedly in Amber's direction, but she didn't seem phased.

"It's not a setup. Come on, Blue. We've known each other our whole lives."

Blue's outraged reaction would have been humorous if he weren't so pissed off about the statement that caused it. "And how many times have you tried to kill her?"

"He almost killed you in that field this time." Amber pointed at him in accusation. "He has killed you before, by the way. A few times."

"Really?" She didn't sound like she believed Amber's assertion. Her head tilted to the side in curiosity. "Have I killed him?"

"Yeah."

"Cool."

"What? Wait. Cool?" Exasperated, Sam's words got away from him. "Never mind. Answer her question."

Pouting, Amber spat, "Seven."

Blue's jaw dropped. "What the hell, Amber?"

"Well, you didn't die this time. And it was to save Ava." Amber now pointed at Blue, whose eyes narrowed. "And how many tips did I give you for Sovaj that needed help?"

"You should have just asked me to help." Blue's shoulders slumped.

"I did. But I also stabbed you in the back and left you for dead." Amber crossed her arms defensively. "You were more over me than you were Rhodes. That dark-haired woman with the glasses always convinced you to send me packing, even when you were thinking about helping. I really upset you once, and that Viking man chased me down and made me forget three days of my life, among other things. He's scary and disturbingly creative when he gets mad."

"Yeah, he is." A wistful smile crossed Blue's face before she sent him a warning look. "Watch your back. Fuck her up if she gets stabby."

"I get no points for hundreds of assists. Fuck you, too." Amber seemed almost indignant, which irritated him. As if bored with the conversation, she shrugged with attitude. "Only one way to find out, I guess. I'll drive the time. You drive the place. And he handles whatever is on the other side."

"I've got this, Diablo. Don't chicken out." Blue rolled her shoulders and hovered her hand over the belt. Looking straight at him, she nodded, projecting an aura of utter confidence. "Start the countdown."

"Try to get us there in time to fix it, Amber." Sam moved his hand into the same position. "Three."

"Oh yeah. Sure. Simple." Amber's eyes rolled, and her hand hovered over the belt. The area immediately around them fell almost completely silent, both audibly and magically. She whistled. "Here goes."

"Two."

They all shared a troubled glance.

"One."

TUESDAY 6:00 AM

68

FINN

F inn flipped his glasses down to compensate for the sudden darkness. Several more gunshots echoed in the confined concrete space. One man crumpled to the ground from a fatal shot from above. The other grunted and stumbled but didn't fall. Taking careful aim, he fired, and the man's head exploded, body falling against the door.

"Clear." A whistle sounded from above. Surging up the stairs, he found Kendra in the corner of the mid-point landing, sitting on her knees, covering her nose with her elbow, gasping and gagging for air.

"Come on, Ms. Z. Not now." Hale grunted and coughed somewhere upstairs. Heavy footsteps echoed, followed by the sound of something dragging across the floor.

"Miller just fell out of a window." Greenlee was on the verge of panic.

"Alpha One, what is your status?" Trix's voice remained monotone, even in the chaos.

Hale rounded the top of the stairs, leaning on the wall, blood streaming down his leg from a wound Finn couldn't see. One hand held a gun, the other clutched a limp and seizing Zella to his side, trying to keep her on her feet. Finn didn't know how the man kept from falling down the stairs in the dark or where he secured a weapon.

"HVT acquired." Finn knelt to Kendra as he relayed the message. They had Zella, but he was the only person moving under his own power.

He opened his mouth to call in the Charlie team, but Nisha's urgent words cut him off. "Battle is right on top of you. He is charging his magic."

He couldn't stop himself from looking up. How close was right on top of you, in Nisha's mind?

"I have eyes on Battle in the window." Finn didn't know who was talking now. Probably Greenlee. "He's glowing. Harper..." His words cut off suddenly with a whine.

More chatter filled his ears as one by one Trix tried to get a response from the Delta team, with unsuccessful results. What was going on out there? Whatever it was, there was nothing he could do for them. He needed to take care of the people in front of him. "Are you hit?" Holstering his weapon, he checked Kendra for injuries.

"Huge magic surge." Kendra coughed and fumbled with the necklace that dulled her magic. She shoved it into her shirt under her vest, and she leaned back and gulped in air. "I've never... That was... Something big just happened."

His fingers landed on a smashed hunk of metal low on her rib cage. It still hurt like a bitch to get shot, even with the vest. How had she not felt this?

Kendra leaned back into the corner, holding her chest and gasping for air. "Now that you mention it, I think my ribs are broken."

"Stay here." Finn rushed up the stairs, whistling again to let Hale know not to shoot him. "Give her to me." Finn yanked a still jerking Zella out of Hale's grip. Her eyes stared absently into the dark stairway, flaring a bright green in his glasses. "What's wrong with her?"

"Visions. She shot two guys, saved my ass, and then that happened." Standing easier without Zella's added weight, Hale released an involuntary sigh of relief. "Good to see you, boss."

He inspected the source of the blood running down Hale's leg. A grazing bullet wound oozed blood just above his hipbone. "You, too, man. That's it. Desk duty for you."

Hale scowled into the darkness. "I can still shoot."

"I was counting on it." Finn unclipped the extra bag he carried and handed it to Hale. "Brought you some things. Vest, gun, night-vision glasses, mask, in case those bastards try to gas you again."

Hale took the bag like a kid opening a Christmas gift. "I don't know how you are still single, Torrin."

Finn pulled one of the bespelled playing cards Greenlee gave him out of his pocket and extended it. "Take this, too."

Hale took the card and put a ridiculous pair of yellow plastic glasses, shaped like flowers, on his face. "Night vision. Nice. Where did you get these beauties?" He looked down at the card he held, a crumpled seven of hearts. Stuffing it in his pocket, he continued putting on the gear Finn provided. "What's that about?"

"Long story. Don't lose it." While Hale suited up, Finn carried Zella down the stairs to the landing where Kendra waited, breathing pained and shallow. He sat Zella down on the floor next to Kendra and turned to Hale, who labored down the stairs, grunting in pain. "You got this?"

"Yep." Hale forced himself to stand up straighter.

"Alpha One, you have six incoming, west basement. Charlie One won't get there in time."

"Where are they getting these guys?" Kendra shifted to her feet and crossed the landing to look down the stairs toward the basement entrance.

"Incoming from the basement. No help." Finn exchanged a quick look with Hale and moved back down the stairs. Hale lumbered behind him. "Get ready."

Kendra limped across the landing, hunched to the side, eyes and gun still focused on the stairs leading to the basement. Frowning, Finn scanned the floor next to her. "Where is Zella?"

Kendra scanned the area in confusion. Together, they looked to the door to the first floor, which now stood propped slightly opened by the foot of a corpse. "Larson is on that floor."

Hissing a steady stream of curses, Hale limped the rest of the way down the stairs, stronger with each step. He waved his hand in exasperation. "Follow her. She saw something."

Finn rushed through the door, not waiting for Kendra or Hale. He had to stop Zella. They could not engage Larson. They didn't have the firepower, and he didn't plan to end up roasted to perfection tonight. Entering the first-floor hallway, he caught the brief swish of her skirt disappearing into a room, emitting a red glow. Finn ran as fast as he could, wondering what in the hell possessed the woman to run toward a man who threw molten lava balls around like baseballs and flinched when gunfire erupted behind him. Hale and Kendra yelled at each other over the gunfire, but he didn't turn back. He trusted them to handle it and barreled into the room behind Zella to a sight that left him both unsettled and amazed. Larson stood in front of an open window, staring out into the lawn, facing the parking garage and outpatient medical center, where the Delta team were supposed to be. His whole body glowed a sinister red, so deep it rippled with blackness. In horrific slow motion, Zella took three long, graceful, and powerful strides, then launched herself into the air without a sound. She flew so high, it reminded him of the action movies where they attached people to wires to lift them and twist them for impossible stunts.

As she sailed toward Larson, a chorus of trills and hollow sounds reverberated musically in the night air outside, accompanied by what sounded like the frenzied flap of thousands of wings. A voice carried into the room through the open window that did not belong to Nolan Miller, and a tingle of recognition crossed his mind, but he couldn't focus on it, too distracted by the impending Armageddon in front of him. Larson remained oblivious to both of them as he focused, shaking with fury at whomever the voice belonged to.

An explosion flashed outside. But Zella still sailed through the air, hanging for a moment, flexing her muscles so that her body formed a predatory midair crouch. Her skirts and hair flowed behind her like a flag as she sailed straight toward Larson's back. Two things happened at once. She tackled the unsuspecting man as a flash of fire and heat rolled from each of his hands, forcing Finn to throw an arm over his face to protect it from the heat and blinding light. But not before Zella wrapped her arms and legs around his head and torso, sending them both toppling out the window.

Finn tried to rush forward but stumbled when Hale careened into the room, clipping Finn's shoulder before falling to his knees. Kendra, wheezing, followed Hale into the room and slammed the door shut behind her. A hollow bang blasted the door, and she backed away. "That should slow them down."

Hale peered up at him from the floor, taking in the mask covering Finn's face, and fished his own out of the bag Finn had handed him earlier. "Where's Zella?"

"Control, HVT just jumped out the goddamned window." Finn rushed across the room, leaping out the window after her.

"Copy that, Alpha One. We are fucked."

69

NISHA

A flare of alarm from Kendra's mind knocked her backward with a gasp. Greenlee caught her before she fell flat on her ass, eyes wide in alarm. A tsunami of fear, pain, and confusion rolled over her, and she had to put both hands to her head to stop the overwhelming sensations. Her head was going to explode. What was happening?

The lights in the main building and all the landscape lights clicked off in a split second, throwing everything into almost complete darkness except for a blindingly bright light from a news van aimed at the main entrance of the Cahlad.

"Miller just fell out of a window," Greenlee barked, snatching up his backpack to rifle through its contents. Even from here, while she tried to hold her brain in, Nisha could see the flailing form of a man pushing himself out of the bushes and dragging himself to his feet.

A moment later, a flash of sinister intent entered her mind and a deep-red glow formed in the window Miller had just exited, directly above the flare of alarm Kendra had produced just moments before. "Battle is right on top of you. He is charging his magic."

Rushing back to the wall, she watched in horror as the glow of Larson's magic grew brighter, and Miller ran as fast as he could toward the fence surrounding the campus, though he stood no chance of getting over it. If Larson only wanted to kill Miller, he would have done it by now. He intended to do more damage with this charge.

An amplified burst of elation mingled with raw fury caused Nisha's eyes to water. "Damn it." The emotions hitting her were so overwhelming, she could no longer decipher anything coherent, only roiling, supercharged emotions, and she couldn't think. She fumbled with the necklace Greenlee provided earlier, stuffing it down her shirt and holding it against her skin.

Greenlee still dug through the backpack, mumbling and cursing his own lack of organization skills. "Harper!" He stuck his hand back into the bag and a tiny pop sounded. "Shit! I didn't mean to do that." Her earpiece erupted in a shrill shriek.

Tossing the small metal object away before it could do permanent damage, Nisha shook her head to clear the ringing. Greenlee did the same to his own earpiece. Scrambling from the car and swatting at her own ear without success, Harper ran to his side. Lady Lucille sprawled on one arm. "What do you need, Thor?"

Greenlee reached up and snatched the squealing earpiece out of Harper's ear, then pointed at the fleeing figure of Nolan Miller. "Hide him!"

With her eyes on the lawn, Harper nodded and blew a long breath out. "Got it." A little puff of magic swept out around them, and Nolan Miller disappeared from view on the lawn, like he had never existed.

"What are you doing?" Nisha placed her hands on the concrete half wall and looked between where Miller had been and the two people standing next to her. "We aren't supposed to improvise." They both ignored her.

"I told you to hide him." Greenlee sounded desperate, looking over his shoulder at a perfectly still Harper. Nisha frowned, not understanding what he was complaining about. Miller was nowhere to be seen. She followed his eyes and groaned. A very lifelike illusion of Nolan Miller ran for his life toward the front gates of the Cahlad on the other side of the lawn.

"I am hiding him and giving the old battle ax another target." Harper scratched Lady Lucille's belly, eyes still closed, looking serene and unbothered by the unfolding chaos.

"Your target is running right for that news truck." Greenlee found something he was looking for and took it out of his backpack. "And Devon."

"Oh fudge." Harper's eyes popped open.

"No. No. No." Devon was with Mitch. Her eyes flew back to the red glow of Larson's growing charge, illuminating his body in the window. Scanning the yard, searching for his now invisible quarry, his face twisted into a sneer as his gaze skipped past Harper's fake senator and landed on the street in front of the Cahlad. "We have to distract Larson!"

Mitch stood in the middle of the street, steps in front of the cleaning van she remembered from the funeral home's garage. Devon had both hands wrapped firmly around his forearm, wrestling with all her might to pull him back into the van, to no avail. It looked like she was skiing behind the Paragon as he pulled her along behind him. She screamed something Nisha couldn't hear. A gray mist erupted from the van as Ben stepped out of the driver's seat, a long tendril snaking forward. For a moment, Nisha thought Ben would attack Mitch, but the tendrils passed Devon and the Paragon and wrapped around the cameraman and journalist standing just steps from the Cahlad's main gate and directly in front of where the fake Nolan Miller ran.

"Damn it, Devon!" Greenlee shoved something into Nisha's hand. "Throw this as hard as you can."

Nisha didn't even look at what he handed her, entranced by the growing sneer on Larson's glowing face and the potential disaster unraveling at the Cahlad's main gate. "At what?"

"Just throw it!" Greenlee hurled his own object, a saltshaker, into the air in Larson's direction.

She hurled with all her might, and a loud hum filled the air. The items they hurled erupted into an explosion of birds that flocked together, morphing into a massive shadow, following the trajectory of her throw. They both stood watching the feathered nightmare as it swirled above the lawn.

Harper walked up to stand between them. "That's something, Thor. But should we worry about that red dot on your chest?"

Nisha looked at Greenlee's chest at the same time as he did. A small red dot decorated the blue fabric above his sternum. Nisha twisted, grabbing Harper around the waist, throwing them both to the side as a thump and roar sounded, and dove for cover. Greenlee's eyes grew wide. "Pineapple!" He threw his body on top of them. Harper cried out, losing her grip on Lady Lucille as she landed, and the dog rolled away from where they landed hard on the concrete floor of the parking garage, growling and snarling in indignation. The force of an explosion and a hiss pushed Greenlee down on top of them, pressing the air from her lungs. A cloud of green gas enveloped them, causing them all to cough. Feet away, Lady Lucille righted herself, shook her head, and sneezed, then keeled over sideways.

Greenlee's weight was gone in a heartbeat. "This stuff is nasty. Get up." He jerked her up so hard, she was momentarily airborne. "Get the dog!"

"I think it's broken, Thor," Harper whimpered from behind her. Nisha scooped up the limp pug and turned to find Harper clutching an ankle and Greenlee scooping her up off the ground, causing her to let out a startled whoop.

Greenlee raced for the stairwell door. Nisha ran ahead of him, snatching the door open. He ran through just in time for her to shut the door and block the gas. "Keep going. We have to get away from the gas."

Footsteps in the stairwell above them had her jerking her weapon loose with her free hand, her other still holding Lady Lucille like a football. She stepped in front of Greenlee and Harper.

"Hang tight, honey." Harper closed her eyes and released a breath. "Shooting is so messy." Her eyes flew open in horror, and she looked at Greenlee. "I can't use my magic!"

Greenlee's lips drew into a thin line. "I know. The gas neutralizes it."

Two sets of feet appeared on the steps above them, moving fast.

"Can you make that portal without your magic?" Nisha needed to know just how screwed they were.

Greenlee shifted Harper's weight so he could pull a marker out of his pocket. He closed his eyes and strained, but nothing happened. "No. I breathed too much of that stuff."

She leveled her weapon at an emerging set of shins. "Stay behind me."

70

BLUE

Her head bounced off something hard, but she couldn't see what it was or feel the pain that should accompany an impact of that magnitude. Her vision and every sense in her body burned with a buzzing electric mixture of rainbow and white and black glitter, leaving her unable to process her surroundings. She felt like she had spent too much time holding an electric fence. But she was still breathing, not in much pain and conscious. This Son Sovaj experience was better than the last two.

A wave of nausea hit her, and she tried to roll, not knowing if she had managed or not. A smell filled her nose, the terrible mixture of urine and rubber only found near parking garage stairwells. It didn't help her rioting stomach, but at least she got them to the right place. Were they in the right year, and did they all get here? Braving another wave of nausea, because she couldn't see or hear, she focused on Sam and was rewarded with a tug of magic low in her chest. He was close. Relieved, she focused on Amber with the same result. They all made it. She hoped Sam was in better shape than she was, otherwise they were sitting ducks.

Muffled voices reached her ears, which meant they were working, but she couldn't tell what was being said or who was speaking. If her eyes worked, she'd be in good shape. She floated somewhere in between *I feel great* and *I think I drank too much.* Reaching up to the magic necklace she wore, she ripped it off, snapping the chain and yanked the bracelet away as well, dropping them on the ground next to her.

A shadow crossed her dim vision, and she blinked. Her right eye hadn't turned back on yet, but in her left eye, the shape of a person leaning over her came into focus. Sam's face filled her vision as he squatted next to her and shoved the artifacts into the red bag around his wrist. Somehow, he looked a lot better than she felt, and that struck her as unfair. Sam stood, dragging her with him, and wrapped her up in a tight hug that pressed her face into his chest and left her feet dangling somewhere above the ground. Peering through her left eye, she saw Amber resting on her hands and knees, divested of the two artifacts she wore, vomiting next to a late-model work truck. Blue couldn't stop the smile that broke across her face, so big she could feel her skin tighten to make room for it. She was home, and everyone was alive. "You did it."

"You did it." Pulling her away, he looked down with worried eyes. "I would kiss you right now, but I just puked all over a Buick. Can you stand?"

She couldn't feel her feet, just a cold sensation where they should be. "Nope. And my right eye is on the fritz." Still smiling, she closed her left eye and Sam's face disappeared. "Yep, still fritz'd. This is so awesome."

"Are you drunk?"

"I think so." A giggle erupted.

"It hasn't happened yet!" Amber called from where she hauled herself up on the half wall at the edge of the parking garage, a red glow silhouetting her figure. Amber pointed into the night, reaching her feet with a pained grunt. "What is Miller doing out there?"

Sam moved them to the wall to get a view of whatever had Amber so excited, and Blue fought a wave of vertigo. Through her left eye, she saw a man fleeing across the lawn and an imposing figure lurking in a window, glowing red. "Oh no." Amber looked over at Blue and Sam. "Dad is getting out of the van. This is where it goes south."

In the blink of an eye, Miller disappeared, and Blue squinted to make sure she wasn't looking out of the wrong eye. "Where did he go? Did everyone else see that?"

"I did." Sam's head tilted to the side. "Amber?"

"I saw it. But it wasn't me."

"How magic-drunk are you?" Sam's voice rumbled in her ear as Miller appeared just as quickly as he disappeared on the other side of the lawn.

"I've felt worse." Blue took a closer look at Miller and cursed. Devon stood right next to the Paragon in the middle of the street, mere yards from a news crew conducting a live broadcast right in front of Miller. "Is that the guy that dies live on television right next to my crazy friend?"

"Yep."

Blue cut her eyes at Amber and couldn't hide her sarcasm. "Wonderful."

"Can you get us down there?" Sam sat her feet on the ground, and after a moment of uncertainty, her legs held. She couldn't see his face, but he didn't sound happy.

A saltshaker sailed into the air, its origins a floor or two below where she stood, and a voice echoed. "Just throw it." A green plastic toy sailed into the air behind the saltshaker. Both objects arced over the street in the general direction of the window Larson stood in, exploding into a wall of feathers, trills, and utter chaos. Even through the feathers, she could see Larson focus on this building.

Blue's heart thudded. The voice from downstairs belonged to Greenlee, and the crazy man was trying to draw Battle's attention here and away from Devon. "Sam. That's Greenlee." Turning in his arms and looking up into a face that grew grim at her words, a wave of desperation washed over her. If she didn't save Ricky, it started the Salem witch trials part deux and the unwinnable war Amber said followed. If she did, Larson was going to level this place with Greenlee in it. "I can't do both."

"We have to do something!" Amber's eyes darted from Mitch to Larson and back. "Dad! No!"

Sam's jaw clenched and his eyes flashed black. He kissed her forehead and let her go, stepping away. "I'll get him." It looked like he wanted to say more, but he turned and grabbed Amber's arm, racing across the dark space without looking back.

Watching Sam drag Amber into the stairwell, she locked on to Ricky, aka Nolan Miller, and let the cold rainbow blur the vision in her good eye.

Landing unsteadily, head swimming, a body barreled into her before she could find her feet or remember to open her good eye, knocking her flat on her ass. Above her, an army of birds swarmed, the sound of their collective flapping and trilling almost deafening.

Battle loomed in the window, still glowing red with unspent magic, looking at the parking garage. The man who ran into her stumbled to a stop, fear and confusion plastered on his red and sweaty face. "Ms. Keys?"

"Hey, Larson!" Ignoring Ricky, she struggled to her feet and did a few frantic, exaggerated jumping jacks as she backed toward her former student. She needed to pull Larson's attention away from the parking garage and Devon's fool ass standing exposed on the street. She waved cheerfully. "Good to see you again! Still compensating for something, I see!"

Larson's eyes narrowed, and she bumped into Ricky, grabbing his wrist. He tried to pull his arm loose. "What are you doing?"

She pinched her fingers together, demonstrating something tiny, and Larson moved his hand in their direction, taking the bait. She winked at him. "I hear they have a pill for that."

"I think you made him mad." Ricky shifted to stand behind her.

"That was the idea."

An explosion erupted behind her, causing her to flinch and cover her head. Ricky dropped to his knees next to her, also covering his head. She turned toward the noise, horrified to find flame and smoke belching from the center floor of the parking garage she had just left, the parking garage Greenlee and Sam were still in. Worse, the smoke held a green tinge. Her heart stuttered in fear, and she focused on Sam and Greenlee, finding their signatures and letting out a relieved huff of air. They were moving, but they were still in that building.

Whipping her head back to the Cahlad administration building, she scanned for anywhere that the projectile could have come from. Larson still loomed in the first-floor window, glowing brighter by the second, attention back on the garage. He was charging for an epic detonation of molten magic. But he wasn't the only threat. Larson didn't shoot projectiles full of green, magic-neutralizing gas. "Oh yeah! Remember the flea bites on your balls?" She kept scanning the building, and shouted as loud as she could, "I didn't know testicles could swell like that. Did it do permanent damage?"

Larson bared his teeth, and his focus shifted her way again. That distracted him. Movement in a third-floor window drew her eyes to none other than Agent Dick Mann standing in a window reloading a rocket launcher. She should have killed Mann when she had the chance. Ricky spouted a string of curses and backed away from her to resume running for his life. She snatched at his hand, but he moved too fast, fueled by the fear of impending death. What she did not miss was Larson tumbling out of the window, ass over teakettle, with something white clinging to his back. His arms flailed, and molten jets of brimstone erupted from each of them. A blistering gout of flame rolled in her direction. Diving for Ricky, she caught him by the ankles, intending to jump them both to safety, but her skin only touched his clothes. She sent them both slamming into the ground instead as a wave of fire and heat rolled over their heads.

71

SAM

S am raced down the stairway, dragging a grousing Amber along
behind him.

"You can let me go, asshole, I'm not going anywhere." The building rumbled and shook, the muffled sound of an explosion echoing
through the space. She looked up and around in alarm, still yanking
on her arm, trying to get it loose. "What on earth was that? Seriously,
let me go."

Sam shook his head, trying to rein in his magic, furious with
himself for letting Blue jump into this new nightmare alone. But
there was nothing he could do now except what he told her he would
do, which was to get her brother out of his building before Larson
blew it to smithereens. "Which floor did that come from?"

"Right below us," Amber wheezed, struggling to keep up with his
much longer stride.

He needed to get Greenlee out of this building. No way did they
figure out how to survive another thirty-year jump through time

just to have the people they were trying to get back to killed by a meteor-slinging psychopath as soon as they got here. He was not telling Blue her brother had died.

"Stay behind me," a familiar voice, filled with stress and steel, sounded from below.

"That gas is getting around the door." A very Southern feminine voice carried through the stairwell.

Sam took the stairs two at a time, ducking to see who stood at the bottom of the stairs sooner. His chest tightened. His best friend stood with her feet squared in front of Greenlee, who carried an unfamiliar blonde woman. "Nisha?"

She bent forward to get a better look up the stairs, but still pointed a gun at his chest as her eyebrows drew together, and her jaw fell slack. "Sam?" Her eyes watered, and a sob erupted from her chest as she reholstered her gun.

Now they had to get out of this building. He spent seven years missing his friend. Like hell were they dying in a parking garage. "Run. We need to leave." He waited for the group to move before following them down the stairs.

As her body responded to his magic, Nisha's eyes widened. "Wait. Greenlee, give him the portal thing."

Greenlee, also compelled to run, joined her on the next flight of stairs, sending his passenger an irritable look as she kicked her legs.

"I can't help myself, Thor." The woman clung to his neck and winced with each kick.

Struggling not to drop her, Greenlee ground out a frustrated, "What are you talking about, Nisha?"

"Sam still has magic." She raced down the stairs, even though she looked behind her.

"Brilliant." Greenlee turned sideways, still moving down the stairs, and waved an object in the hand that supported the blonde woman's feet, at Sam. "Take it. It takes a ton of magic if you don't have precision."

Without thinking, Sam reached out and took the object, continuing down the stairs so that he led the way out of the building. He frowned at the purple marker now in his hand. "What is this? How much magic?"

"It's a portal. Give it everything you have, and take the lid off." Greenlee still navigated the stairs sideways, causing the blonde woman to wince in pain. At this angle, Sam had a clear view of her swollen ankle. "Sorry, Harper."

Sam wanted to argue. He had never used an artifact before in his life, if you didn't count the Se't Sovaj. But the look on Nisha's face stopped him. A low rumble shook the building, knocking dust and grime loose from the ceiling. "Just do it, Sam."

He clamped his mouth shut and pulled every ounce of energy he could muster, suspecting his eyes would shift, and his veins would turn black. Nisha, Greenlee, and Harper shrank away from him, their eyes growing wide in horror, confirming his suspicions. Amber watched him nervously and flinched. He popped the lid off the marker, and a twirl of purple sparks sprang to life, growing into a ten-foot circle that led to a dark wooded clearing. Never taking her eyes off him, Nisha shoved Greenlee through the portal, then raced through behind him. A rumble thundered, and a flare of orange light filled the stairwell. Amber stepped through but turned and grabbed the front of Sam's shirt, hauling him through the portal into the darkness. Cold air and the smell of pine filled Sam's senses, and a wave of heat and dust hit his back and he stumbled forward, trying to stay on his feet. He slammed the cap back onto the marker with a loud click as Amber fell to the ground and rolled on her back in front of him.

Close to Amber, Nisha stood, eyes wide, shielding her face from the flame and debris that was cut off with a pop.

Harper sat on the ground clutching her ankle in front of Blue's Greenlee, who stood with his hands on his knees, panting. Sam patted at the smoldering portion of his shirt and nodded to Amber in thanks.

"Oh my God." Nisha looked at Sam in confusion and trepidation. "What is wrong with your eyes, Sam?"

His shoulders dropped with a measure of relief, knowing he got both Nisha and Greenlee out of that garage before Larson leveled it. "I'm so glad to see you, Ravi."

Any fear she had of his appearance burned away, and her face pinched in fury. She advanced, punching him in the chest twice before swinging wide and punching him in the arm. "You scared me to death, asshole. What happened? Where have you been?"

Sam rubbed his bruised sternum and backed away. "What in the hell, Nisha? You have to ask?"

Nisha glared at him, fist still balled at her sides. "They gassed us. I don't have any magic."

Frowning, Sam started to reply, but a flash of purple light bathed the clearing.

72

DEVON

Devon stared at Mitch, both threats hanging in the air between them. A low buzz emitted from her earpiece as Finn announced they had eyes on Zella.

Ben's gaze shifted toward them with an eerie slowness, flames slowly licking from his eye sockets. Her hair floated around her head as she drew her own magic into the fray. The buzz grew into an angry hiss as the magic ramped up and covered Nisha's anguished announcement of "Battle is right on top of you," before a metallic screech cut her off. Devon slapped at the small device in her ear to stop the painful noise, finally prying it out and throwing it into the floorboard. Ben worked at his own earpiece, wincing in discomfort.

But Mitch lunged out the door before she could stop him. She scrambled out of the passenger side behind him using her angry-mom voice. "Mitch Collins, get your keister back in that van this instant." He rounded the front of the van, ripping the earbud out and tossing it to the side, and strode into the street toward the main gate where the reporter and cameraman now stood. Grabbing his arm, she dug her feet into the ground and skidded along behind him. "Good god, old man, how often do you work out?"

The terrified screams of a middle-aged man in a rumpled suit drew her attention away from their tug of war long enough for her to notice the glowing red figure in the window behind him. Fear surged down her spine. "I'm not kidding. Get back in that van." In the blink of an eye, the screaming man disappeared and reappeared, running straight for them and the waiting camera crew, drawing Larson's attention in their direction. "Oh boy. Ben! A little help."

"Last warning, dear." Mitch didn't even break his stride, now standing in the middle of the street.

"My brother is in that building, you arrogant hotheaded jerk. You are just going to cave the building in on them."

His steps slowed a bit as two misty gray tendrils streaked by, wrapping around the journalist and cameraman. That was not the help she was hoping for.

A cacophony of trills and screeches erupted over the lawn across the street from the parking garage, where Greenlee was waiting with Nisha and Harper. A flock of birds materialized out of nowhere, diving toward the building, and blocking out the light generated by the news van's antenna and lighting rig.

"What on earth is going on?" Mitch parroted what she was thinking. A thundering explosion reverberated off the surrounding buildings, and Mitch broke into a run. Devon's toe caught, and she almost lost her grip on his arm. A jolt of sleeping magic erupted from her before she could rein it in. Mitch crumbled mid-stride, and they both fell, limbs tangling, face-first, toward the concrete. Stunned by the force of the impact, it took her a few seconds to raise herself up onto her elbows. What she saw caused her arms to give out again. The parking garage was on fire, belching green-tinged smoke. "No."

"You are outside of my range!" Ben's footsteps thundered behind them. The journalist and cameraman screamed in terror as they dangled from Ben's ghost arms in the air and flew toward Mitch and Devon. She couldn't process Ben's warning. She could only stare in horror at the parking garage.

A primal rumble shook the ground and rippled the surrounding air. Dislodging herself from Mitch's dead weight, footsteps and screams filled her ears. The journalist and cameraman rolled to a stop next to her, and a blinding flash of light erupted from the Cahlad building. The two men screamed in horror and scooted backward as the wave of light, fire, and debris rolled toward them, shaking the ground. Throwing her hands over her face, she almost missed a swirling gray wall of magic slam into place mere inches in front of them just as a gigantic wave of fire splashed off Ben's shield, followed by a steady rain of rocks, fence, and trees. He fell next to her, grimacing with the strain of holding the barrier. That blast was ten times more powerful than anything Larson threw at them in the field.

The rumble subsided, and Ben's barrier dropped with a whoosh, leaving them sitting surrounded by a three-foot-tall pile of rubble, dirt, and rock. A cloud of dust and debris filled the space. The buildings all remained standing, though damaged, but the Cahlad's south lawn was nothing more than a fifty-foot-wide smoking crater.

"Get us out of here." Ben fell to his elbows, eyes generating flames almost three feet high.

A loud groan preceded a rending noise, and the parking garage collapsed into a pile of concrete and rebar, jettisoning dust and debris in all directions.

Was Greenlee still in there? Her mind buzzed, floating somewhere not here, unwilling to believe what she was seeing.

"Devon!" Ben grabbed her shoulders and put his own face inches from hers. His dark eyes still flamed slightly, and he shook her shoulders. "Open the portal."

Hands shaking, she pulled the marker from her pocket and popped the lid off. "Peaches." A purple shower of sparks erupted next to them. Cool air and the smell of pine rolled through the tear it created in space. Devon sat on her knees, chest tight and staring at the collapsed building as Ben grabbed Mitch by the ankles, dragging his dead weight backward toward the purple portal.

Looking behind her, she searched for another purple portal in the clearing they were trying to get to, but she didn't. Maybe Greenlee had to go somewhere else. She had to believe he went somewhere else.

The cameraman looked around, stunned, still sitting on his butt. Somehow, he held on to his camera in the chaos, and he lifted it, pointing it at the destruction surrounding them. The reporter stood, taking a gigantic step back, also looking around, dazed and disbelieving. The terrain no longer looked real. "Is that... is that the Paragon?"

"Come on!" Ben barked, still dragging Mitch across the ground.

Devon stood on shaky legs. "It is."

The cameraman turned his tool in their direction, no doubt capturing the portal and everything behind it. "You saved us."

Ben glared daggers at them all, taking in large breaths, eyes back to normal.

"Aaron, get your camera on that." The journalist pointed toward a flurry of activity on the ten feet of withered grass between the Cahlad's main building and the edge of the crater where the lawn used to be. Squinting, she could see two figures brawling on the ground, one much smaller than the other, a bloom of white surrounding her head. The larger of the figures glowed orange. The other was Zella. She mauled Larson like a deranged spider monkey. If Zella was there, where in the blue blazes was Finn Torrin?

Right on cue, Finn flew out the window, landing in a crouch. He stood, lifted his gun, and raced toward the human fireball. She threw her hands out in exasperation. "What is wrong with you?"

"Devon!" Ben stood on the other side of the open portal. Mitch lay unconscious in the grass at his feet, purple light shimmering over his sleeping face.

She looked into the portal for any sign Greenlee had made it out of the collapsed garage. She didn't see him. He would have gone straight to Lexi, and he wasn't there. Her stomach sank as she looked back at her idiot brother-in-law. Something snapped in her chest, releasing a wave of anger and fury that had stewed for a decade and exploded in a blistering burn that swallowed her. She had done what Finn asked her to do. The two most powerful magic users in their group were now with the girls. But they would never be truly safe as long as Larson Battle drew air into his lungs. Devon didn't start this fight. But she could help finish it. It was time for Larson Battle to die. "Take care of Lexi, Ben. Tell her I love her more than anything."

Ben tilted his head in confusion, not understanding what she meant. "What are you doing, Devon?" He lunged for the portal a split second too late. She slammed the cap onto the marker and watched the purple sparks fizz into nothing. Then she was climbing the wall of dirt and rubble and racing across the crater, intent on murder. The fence surrounding the campus did not survive the blast, so she had an unobstructed path to Larson and Finn. She charged her magic as she ran, and her hair whipped around her face. Now she just needed Finn to get clear so she could put Larson asleep forever. Movement in a window on the third floor drew her attention, and she missed a step. Dick Mann, the FBI agent who inquired about the Hounds of Dawn the day before all hell broke loose, stood in the window with a weapon on his shoulder. He tipped the gun downward, aiming for something on the lawn.

"Like hell you will." Throwing her hands up, careful to aim high and well above Finn and Zella's heads, she sent out a wave of magic at the man in the window who heard her words. Running again, she watched the ripples of her magic scorch toward him, grazing his side as he leaned away. He wobbled, eyes growing heavy. He should have toppled out of the window, but he didn't. Instead, he pitched forward, dropping the weapon out of the window and withered out of sight. The gun tumbled to the ground, bounced, and jettisoned a smattering of objects into the air.

Devon skidded to a halt and threw her arms over her face, waiting for the explosion. It didn't come. The objects hit the ground softly and puffed out thirty-foot clouds of green gas that caught the wind spiraling into the air, enveloping everything she could see, including Larson. She couldn't send another burst of magic. "Dang it!"

73

BLUE

The world cooled off, and the scent of burned hair joined the mixture of dust and smoke filling her lungs. Ricky's arms covered his head, and he huddled against the ground like he wanted to crawl into it. His body quaked and his breath came in shuddering gasps. Blue recognized this. Some days she still woke from nightmares having this same reaction. It must have been the fire. She patted the back of a man now in his late forties who she taught in high school. Weird. "Breathe for me, kid."

They sat on the fifteen feet of wilted grass that remained in front of the Cahlad building before the ground dropped off into a crater Larson's fireball created. An otherworldly groan of metal howled through the night and the parking garage across the street caved in on itself, sending a plume of dust shooting out around it. Without thinking, she focused on Sam and Greenlee, and rode the resulting wave of nausea. She could feel her feet and her right eye were working, but she was pushing her limits. Both men brushed against her senses, alive and far away. Now she just needed to get Ricky out of here before Larson exploded again.

Something hit her head, sending a wave of pain down the side of her face. It wasn't a rock, but it was heavy. It bounced into her lap, followed by rhythmic thuds and squelches of other objects hitting the ground. Looking at the thing in her lap, she blinked and swallowed hard. It looked like a miniature dragon. A tiny roasted miniature dragon. Turning her face to the sky, hundreds of smoldering miniature dragons rained down from above. Not all of them were dead. A sizable flock still flew in a disorganized figure eight above them. Too stunned to even cover her head, dread filled her stomach. Dragons were falling from the sky.

"What is happening?" Ricky sat up, facing her, still trembling, gaping at the surrounding carnage. A charred, winged creature bounced off his shoulder. Covering his head, he picked up one of the roasted critters. "Is this a great eared night jar?"

"A jar of what?"

He looked at her with a confused expression. Focusing over her shoulder, he frowned and pointed the dead bird at her. "What is that?"

She smelled it before she saw it. The putrid scent of Larson's nightmare gas filled her nostrils and a green cloud filled her vision, rolling over Ricky with a gust. Ricky's eyes grew heavy, and he listed sideways, landing with a thump on the ground as her magic dwindled away. Now she had to drag Ricky's overweight, middle-aged ass out of here instead of teleporting. "Come on!" She turned her face to the sky once more, looking for whoever was running this circus, only to find a small flock of tiny winged dragons, harbingers of her demise, still swooshing in a pattern that looked suspiciously like a middle finger above her head. She didn't even get fierce, fire-breathing dragons with scales that inspired fear. No. She got teensy, little feathered dragons that were so cute they made you want to cry. Worse, she was going to die wearing rubber ducky pajama bottoms. This was bullshit. She screamed at the sky. "Work with me!"

Standing, she waved away the green gas that clung to the ground in a heavy cloud. Muffled gunfire sounded from inside the building, corresponding with flashes of light strobing from the windows. The unmistakable sound of flesh hitting flesh registered to her right.

"Get out of the way, Ms. Z! I don't have a clean shot!"

Blue recognized that voice. She squinted through the green fog. "Finn?"

"Get off me." Larson's infuriated roar echoed through the night.

The green fog cleared enough to reveal Larson spinning in circles, fighting with a blur of white that harried his back. Blue blinked, realizing it was Zella punching, clawing, and giving Larson hell. How did Finn and Zella end up here?

Finn, wearing a gas mask, circled them, trying to get a clear shot at Larson. A thinner cloud of gas surrounded them than the one she stood in, but Larson no longer glowed. Whoever gassed them neutralized Larson, too. She looked at Ricky's unconscious form. She needed to get him to a vehicle and hope he woke up in time to drive it. The only way to do that was to drag him through the melee or down and back out of a twenty-foot crater. At least if she hauled him through the melee, she might get a swing at Larson. Though it looked like Zella had things well in hand. She grabbed Ricky under the arms and pulled, a strained grunt leaving her mouth as his dead weight refused to cooperate. She kept pulling, a sweat breaking out on her forehead at the effort.

Halfway across the small space, a ball of flailing limbs and firing weapons exploded from a window in the building like cowboys flying out of a saloon in an old western movie brawl. The mass of bodies landed just behind Larson and Zella, still fighting and shooting.

She knelt, trying to shield Ricky from any stray bullets. She should have braved the crater. Five people writhed on the ground, fighting for their lives. She didn't sign up for this.

"Kill them!" Larson pointed in Finn's direction. One of the new arrivals with a nasty-looking gun lunged to his feet, freeing himself from the tangle of fighters and whipped his weapon in Finn's direction.

"Look out!" Blue surged to her feet and ran as fast as she could, tackling the man just as he swung in her direction. They both hit the ground, rolling and fighting for control of the gun. He almost pinned her to the ground, but she twisted and wound up on his back, wrapping her legs around his waist and her arms around his throat. She couldn't get a good grip on the bastard. His neck was huge. Using her heel to dig into his groin, she punched the back of his head with everything she had.

Someone tried to yank her away. Bodies collided next to her and a large man wearing a gas mask and ridiculous daisy shaped yellow sunglasses took the man trying to drag her away to the ground. He bellowed the Flight of the Valkyries at the top of his lungs as he wrestled the man's gun arm up and away. She did a double take. "Hale?"

He lifted his head, tilting it in question, looking completely ridiculous in the crazy glasses. "Angel? Is that you?" The man below him punched his ribs, and Hale turned his attention away before she could answer.

She fished around her opponent's waist and thighs with one hand while hanging on to his neck with the other. These guys always had some gigantic knife strapped to them somewhere. Finding what she was looking for, she pulled it loose as the man's fist swung over his shoulder and connected hard with her jaw. She fell to the side but held on to his knife. He twisted onto his knee and drew another weapon as she hurled the blade, then ducked as he fired. His knife struck him in the side of the neck and he dropped his gun, both hands flying up to cover the wound that sliced his airway and an important blood vessel. He pitched to the side. Blue picked up his gun and shot him in the head, then yanked the knife out of his throat.

Next to her, Hale got the upper hand in his own fight. He pinned his opponent to the ground and shot them point blank at an angle that sent the bullet under the edge of the ballistic vest the man wore and up and under the rib cage. Sitting back on his heels, he sent her a goofy smile. "I would recognize your voice anywhere. You changed your hair." He rose to his feet, revealing his pant leg soaked in blood. He leaned over, obviously in pain, and sent her a weak smile. "I like it."

"Thanks. Love the glasses."

Two loud gunshots cracked next to them. "Would you two quit playing around? We need to kill that asshole." Blue recognized that voice as well. Kendra stood over the dead body of her own opponent, gun still in hand, glaring in their direction.

More gunfire erupted from the window everyone just fell out of. Finn screamed, legs flying out from under him as he landed on the ground. He clutched at his leg and one arm dangled uselessly. Kendra lunged for Finn, backing into position next to him as she returned fire. "Where are you hit, Torrin?" Now the man in the window shot at her and she crouched, shielding Finn with her own body. Blue raised her own weapon and Hale did the same, but neither of them had a clean shot of whoever was shooting. All that Blue could see was part of a shoulder.

A muzzle flashed in the darkness to their right, shedding momentary light on a lone figure standing next to the building just outside of the cloud of gas. The shooter in the window jerked and twisted, a bright red spot forming over his eye. Blue blinked in disbelief as the body of Agent Dick Man fell forward, the top half of his body dangling out of the window. Several small objects toppled from his pockets and rolled across the grass beneath him.

Someone screamed peaches and a purple light flared behind the mystery savior, blindingly bright, and sparks created a perfect circle obscuring the building and the lawn behind it, replacing it with a view of the tops of trees bathed in moonlight.

"Kendra!" To Blue's amazement, Devon stepped forward slightly, holding a small handgun and a dark, distant look that hadn't graced her friend's face in years. Why was she here, and how did she make a portal? "Get him to me." Devon coughed and shook her head in frustration, then waved furiously for Kendra and Finn to move toward her.

Larson turned, zeroing in on the portal even though Zella punched him in the rib cage.

A loud groan behind her told her Ricky was awake. Sparing a quick glance, she rolled her eyes as Ricky stumbled toward the portal, and directly into the cloud of green gas, only making it two steps before he collapsed again. "Come on, kid. You are smarter than this."

"The fucker is glowing again!" Kendra leaned down and grabbed Finn under the arms.

Kendra was right. Larson's hands were sparking with a low, ominous glow. His magic was returning. Her own magic trickled in, but not enough to get anyone else away from here. Even Larson.

"Hale!" Blue pointed at Ricky, then to the purple hole in reality. "Get him through that thing!"

Hale only hesitated for a moment, glancing at Finn, who raised a weapon and pointed it at Larson, even as Kendra dragged him away. He limped to Ricky's side and lifted him over his shoulder, stumbling for a second under the unconscious senator's weight, then lunged across the field toward Devon's escape plan. Overhead, the flock of miniature dragons trilled and changed direction, flying toward the bright violet light.

Blue set off at a dead sprint toward Larson, intent to help Zella, but the woman, still clinging to Larson's back, went stiff as a board as her muscles spasmed. Her head flew back and her spine arched as her eyes glowed white with a vision. Larson roared and seized the opportunity. Reaching back with both hands, he grabbed Zella around her neck and slung her over his head like a rag doll, slamming her body into the ground with a thud. Even from here, Blue heard bones snapping.

She fired her weapon, taking the opportunity to shoot Larson without hitting an ally. More guns barked next to her. Devon raced toward Zella's crumpled and still body, firing as she ran. Finn fired as well with his good arm while Kendra dragged him backward across the lawn. But Larson simply waved his hand, incinerating the bullets before they could reach him, striding with purpose toward the portal and the people trying to retreat through it.

Larson raised his arm, and his palm glowed. Blue reached for her magic but struggled to draw enough. Her gun clicked empty as she raced forward, and she threw it at him. It hit him but didn't phase him. She frowned, still drawing magic and trying to figure out why the gun had hit him, but the bullets hadn't. Because he didn't hear it coming. Still running, she pulled the stolen knife out of her rubber ducky pajama waistband, flipped it into her palm as a last resort, and hurled it. It spun silently toward its target and sunk into his bicep, knocking his arm to the side. The fireball flew high and soared through the portal, barely missing her friends. Hale ducked as it singed his head and fell flat on his face. The flames ignited the back of Ricky's shirt as his body fell off Hale's shoulder and disappeared through the portal. Devon rolled to the side with a scream but stood and resumed her charge toward Zella, even though she batted at her flaming sleeve. Kendra kept dragging Finn with a single-minded focus.

Larson screamed in pain and pulled the knife out of his arm, rounding on Blue, eyes alight with fury. Devon reached Zella and picked the woman up under her arms.

Larson glanced back at Devon, a snarl curling his lips. Devon raised a hand and released a small bolt of magic, swaying as it left her hand. It didn't even reach the target. Devon's magic had not returned completely, either. She was virtually defenseless.

Without thinking, Blue sailed into the rainbow and emerged just in front of and above Larson, using gravity to land a brutal blow to his face that whipped his head around and forced him back several steps. His glowing hand swung her direction, and she zipped back across the rainbow, landing where she stood before, chest heaving and stomach rolling. The fireball he chucked exploded in the crater behind her. Larson's stony gaze zeroed in on her with single-minded focus and he drew himself to his full height, smiling. "I'm going to make you hurt." He spat a stream of blood onto the ground.

Devon glanced at Larson, then her eyes met Blue's for a split second and filled with tears.

"Go." Blue did her best to look confident and uninjured. "I've got this."

Devon's lips thinned, seeing right through Blue's façade. She gave Blue a single lift of the chin before she looked away and began pulling Zella across the ground.

Blue knew what she had to do to buy her family and friends time to get to safety. She knew what it would cost her. And she was ready. She met Larson's infuriated gaze. "Come and get me."

74

RHODES

A purple flash in the window woke Rhodes from a fitful sleep. Blinking, he let his eyes adjust to the darkness, wondering if the flash was real or if it was a carryover from a nightmare. But the glow still rimmed the edge of the window.

"Shit." Rhodes grabbed for his shoes.

Ava threw the covers off and ran for the window, pulling the curtain aside and peeking outside. "It's one of those portals. I count five." She stayed in the window, squinting into the darkness.

"Mr. Rhodes?" Lexi bolted upright in bed and immediately jumped to the floor, running to his side, looking lost and unsure.

Standing, he picked her up even though she was entirely too big to carry around, because it didn't feel right to leave her standing alone in a dark room. But he needed to understand what was happening. Crossing to the window, he pulled back the curtain. The portal vanished as he arrived.

"What do we do?" Ava stood sentry at the window, not looking at him. "Some of them looked hurt."

Lexi buried her face in his shoulder and wrapped her arms around his neck. "I'm scared."

"It's okay, Lexi Lou. We have a plan." Rhodes sat her down on the floor and squeezed her shoulder. He continued to watch the group out the window until the portal blinked out of existence. This wasn't an attack. Yet. But he wasn't willing to chance it.

Another burst of purple illuminated the clearing again, this time from the opposite side, and two figures emerged, one dragging the other. Their entrance gained the attention of the other group, and he could see their figures, illuminated by the sparking outline of the portal, as they raced across the grass. This portal stayed open longer. The upright figure was talking to someone on the other side. Then he lunged forward as it blinked out of existence, stumbling into a grove of trees instead of wherever the portal led. The clearing was several football fields long, so the two groups hadn't made it to one another yet, but he heard them shouting at each other.

"They don't seem like they want to hurt us. Or like they know what they are doing." Ava chewed her lip and sent him an uncertain look. "I think they are running from something."

"That's a problem." Rhodes didn't like it. He didn't want to deal with whatever was chasing them.

"I don't want to run into the dark by myself." Lexi's voice wobbled.

"I'll be with you." Ava squeezed Lexi's shoulder.

A light clicked on, and Rhodes counted seven people moving in the darkness outside. One was prone, and another looked around in agitation, as if expecting someone or something to appear. Rhodes didn't like that one bit. Ava might be right. Jerking the curtain closed, he grabbed both girls and ushered them to the back of the building.

"Stick to the plan." He cracked the window. "Remember the signal?"

Lexi held on to the pillow she had yet to let go of.

"Be careful?" Ava's statement turned into a question at the end. "Don't die."

"I won't. It's a good plan. Keep a leash on Bubbles. You've got this." He took a moment to give them both a quick hug. "Ready?"

Ava nodded, her face taking on a fierce mask of determination. Lexi seemed less sure.

Touching both girls' hands, they morphed into fluffy, brown pine squirrels native to the surrounding area. Swaddled by clothing, the smaller squirrel sat atop a pillow, twitching its nose. The other's tail flicked in agitation.

"Watch out for owls." He still hated their choice of disguise. The voices outside sounded angry and panicked now. Bending down, he extended an arm, and both squirrels climbed up to his elbow, then stepped onto the windowsill. Squirrel Ava scurried outside, hopped to the porch, and waited for Lexi, who sat on her haunches for a moment looking at Rhodes, twitching her nose and jerking her tail in agitation, before following Ava out the window. The girls dashed across the yard in a flurry of brown fur, then disappeared into the trees. They had two hours before the magic wore off.

Sure that they were at least pretending to follow the plan, he grabbed the windowsill and morphed into a squirrel himself, clinging to it until he could boost his body up. He was heavier than he should be and his claws sharper, gouging the windowsill. But so far, Ava was keeping her magic in check. He slid out the window and raced into the forest, scampering up a tree. He jumped from branch to branch until he was close enough to hear and see exactly what was going on. Harper sat on the ground near where the first portal formed, clutching her ankle and performing Lamaze exercises. Amber Collins slunk down the edge of the clearing toward the cabin. Nisha Ravi knelt next to a prone Mitch Collins, who snored and rolled to the side, tucking his hands under his chin. Ava's dad stalked across the clearing toward Harper, a dark look on this face. Lexi's Tio G thundered behind him, fist clenched. Even from here, Rhodes could see a vein throbbing on the side of his face. Sotach stood equidistant from Nisha and Greenlee, with his hands on his hips, grinding his teeth, looking up and around expectantly.

Rhodes crept out onto a branch until he sat directly above Nisha and the Paragon.

"What do you mean she went back?" Greenlee's face was red and twisted with disbelief and anger.

"She didn't go back," Hughes raged. "She never came through. And she kept the artifact."

"What in the hell, Ben?"

Hughes threw his arms out, a mixture of guilt and anger on his face and in his words. "I tried! Just find the girls, then go back for her."

"I can't!" Greenlee threw down his backpack in frustration. "They gassed us!"

"Well, who can!?" Ben turned on his heel and reached Harper's side. Kneeling, he gently took her ankle, swollen and sporting a deep shade of purple in his hands. In a far gentler tone than the one he used with Greenlee, he instructed her to lie back and try to stay still.

Amber Collins burst onto the front porch of the cabin, panicked. "They aren't in here!"

"Sarah?" Ben fell back, staring at the woman in disbelief and causing Harper to cry out when he dropped her ankle. He blinked and shook his head, hand flying to his chest.

Rhodes' nose twitched. As far as Ben was concerned, Amber, aka his dead wife, Sarah, was dead. The man was seeing a ghost. If Harper wasn't in excruciating pain right now, she would love this.

"What do you mean, they aren't in there?" Greenlee raced back across the clearing toward the cabin.

"I mean, they aren't in here." Amber ran down the steps and turned in a circle, scanning the area.

"Everybody calm down." Nisha jumped to her feet and raced to Greenlee's discarded backpack. "Are the artifacts neutralized, too? Maybe Sam or Ben can use them."

Greenlee's shoulders slumped, and he walked to Nisha, taking his backpack from her hands. "It was set to here as default. To go anywhere else will take someone who knows what they are doing." He pointed to Sam. "He has the juice, but not the precision. What was that, by the way? And where the hell is Blue?"

Sotach's chest puffed out, and his voice broke. "She went to get Miller."

Greenlee blinked, then threw his head back in a scream of otherworldly rage that echoed across the night, and all the hair on Rhodes' body stood straight up. The man was losing it. Judging by their faces and movements, Ben and Sotach looked like they were right there with him. Rhodes considered shifting forms and letting him know the girls were safe, but his gut told him to wait it out. This was not a coordinated rescue effort. Something else was going on here. Finally, Greenlee took a breath and ran his hand through his hair. "We need Mitch."

"Yeah, well, Devon knocked him out. I can't wake him up." Ben called over his shoulder as he examined Harper's ankle once more. "Nisha? Can you sit with her while I find something to splint this with?" He stood and wandered in the cabin's direction, stopping when his path would have crossed Amber's. He glared, huffed and changed direction, walking the long way around the clearing, his face a stony mask of anger and barely contained rage. Each step of his foot sent a small puff of gray mist into the air.

"Hey, there, Fronkensteen." Nisha scurried across the clearing, seeming uncertain and uneasy, and knelt next to Harper. "Hang tight."

"I can wake him up." Sotach's words sounded like a threat. He stomped to Mitch's side and stood over the man. Greenlee joined him, leaning against a tree and fishing through the backpack. "Wake up."

Mitch startled awake, and so did the surrounding forest. Birds chirped, critters chuffed, and insects sang. A few worrisome howls echoed throughout the night. The overall effect was eerie. Rhodes tilted his head, keeping an ear out for any problems that might cause Lexi and Ava. Especially owls. He didn't like any of this.

Mitch jerked upright. "What happened?" He clutched his head and groaned in agony. He looked at Sotach, rearing back in confusion, and his eyes narrowed.

A purple light flashed on the far side of the clearing. Another sparkling circle formed and expanded roughly fifteen feet in the air. A ruined urban landscape came into view. From his vantage point, fifty feet up a tree, he had an impressive view of the side of a tall marble, white building, a charred and blackened crater, and a familiar man with glowing hands staring through the opening. Rhodes' tail twitched in agitation, and he backed up.

Ben was the closest to the new portal. He raced toward it, screaming Devon's name. Greenlee sprinted after him, but he was all the way across the clearing. Taking only a moment to help Mitch to his feet, Sotach followed Greenlee, quickly catching up. Mitch, squinting into the portal and still clutching his head, ran behind at a slower pace.

Devon stood on the other side, shooting at someone. People were on the ground and dragging each other. He had been on enough missions to know what one going sideways looked like. Whatever was happening on the other side of that portal was bad. He backed up farther. Larson Battle was going to come through that portal. He needed to get to the girls.

Seconds later, a molten ball of rock flew through the opening and struck the tiny cabin he and the girls had called home for the past day. The roof caved in, and it burst into flames, walls exploding outward. Without waiting to see more, he turned and ran in the direction he had instructed Ava to take Lexi. He had to get them as far from this as he could.

75

SAM

S am raced across the field next to Greenlee, fighting the icy chill that ran down his spine when he finally got a clear view of the carnage on the other side of the portal that hovered fifteen feet in the air at the edge of the clearing. Ben said the blast was bad, but Sam was still stunned by the sheer magnitude of the damage. It remained dark in Nashville, but the purple sparks illuminated the dark outlines of people moving across what little grass remained in front of the Cahlad's administration building. None of them had red hair. Blue would have been on the lawn with Ricky, and she would have used him as an anchor. If not him, then Greenlee. But she hadn't reappeared.

A bright orange glow flared to life, then grew impossibly bright as a dark object radiating heat surged through the purple ring, burning across the sky. The molten chunk of flaming rock that sailed their way made him feel sorry for the dinosaurs.

Sam threw an arm over his head and kept running but missed a step and stumbled when the cabin behind him exploded in a shower of splintered wood. Greenlee stumbled to a halt as well as they both stared slack-jawed at the destruction. He hoped the girls really weren't in that cabin.

A sickening thud drew his attention even as a chorus of trills filled his ears. He turned back to the portal to see a man's body lying twisted on the ground below it, shirt smoking, and a flock of birds flying through the opening. Some, aflame or smoldering, plummeted to the ground. They strafed by Greenlee and turned toward Sam, buzzing only a foot over his head. He had never seen birds like this. They had two ridges on their face, one on each side of their head and a rounded nose where a beak should be. They looked like baby dragons.

The flock zipped over Ben's head as he ran several paces behind Sam and Greenlee, then turned toward Amber, where she now stood next to Nisha and Harper. They circled her head, and she ducked with a startled scream. Then they flew into the trees. The h igh-pitched cry of a small animal rang out in the night.

"Were those baby dragons?" Greenlee turned to Sam with a look of disbelief, and the color drained from his face. "No!" His eyes flew to the portal. "Blue! No, you will not!"

Sam stared at the flock of birds as their dark silhouettes disappeared into the forest, and Greenlee's words sank in. Dragons. Sam suddenly didn't know what to do. Dragons were falling from the sky, and Blue hadn't reappeared. He thought Blue must have misunderstood Zella's prediction, but now a sick feeling settled over him, and his skin grew clammy.

By the time he turned back to the unfolding nightmare, Greenlee was running toward the portal again, screaming for Blue and Devon. Ben passed him, dark puffs of mist and ghostly appendages writhing from his feet. Sam did a double take. Ben was a soul eater. And right now, he didn't care. A barrage of gunfire erupted overhead on the other side of the tear in space.

He looked up to see a flash of red hair appear for a moment as a figure barreled into view and lunged for Larson. Larson raised a knife and swung as the two bodies collided and fell out of Sam's sight. That was Blue, and she was fighting with Larson. It did not look like she had help. Everyone else was running. He had to get up there somehow. But even he couldn't jump that high.

Two more bodies tumbled over the edge, erupting in screams as they plummeted to the ground. Sam recognized one of them as Finn Torrin. The other was a small woman with dark hair that Sam didn't recognize.

Ben planted his feet, and his mist appendages shot out, snatching the people from the air and setting them gently next to the body that fell out earlier. Torrin bled from wounds in his arm and a leg. Immediately, the woman patted out the small flames on the body next to her and ripped off her belt, threading it around Torrin's leg to form a tourniquet.

Greenlee stood next to Ben, looking up. "Ben. Get me up there."

Sam's eyes stayed fixed on Larson and Blue as the two circled each other gracefully underneath an open window with a body hanging out of it. Larson threw out small jets of fire, and Blue disappeared into thin air just before they hit her, reappearing closer to him, only to be driven away by another jet of flame. She wasn't gaining ground, but Larson had to stay focused on her to keep her from getting to him. It was buying people time to escape.

Devon appeared at the edge of the portal, face illuminated by flashes of Larson's flaming projectiles. She held a limp body with stark-white hair and gazed down at the people below with a grim expression, then glanced over her shoulder quickly. "Catch her. I have to help Blue." Hurling Zella's limp body over the edge, she raced back into the dark Nashville night.

With a curse, Ben sent his magic swirling upward, snatching Zella out of the air.

"Devon! Baby! Dammit!" Greenlee screamed in frustration.

"Pick us up, Ben!" Sam demanded. He could at least put everyone on the battlefield to sleep, but he had to get to it first. Right now, Ben was the only way up. Ben's magic snaked out of the cloud below him , wrapped around him and Greenlee, and lifted them.

Blue manifested slightly above Larson's head, careening through the air toward him. He sent a jet of flame her way, and this time it caught her in the chest, sending her flying backward. She slammed into the ground and rolled out of Sam's field of view.

A man wearing a gas mask and yellow-daisy sunglasses limped into the fray from somewhere, carrying a wicked-looking weapon.

Sam blinked at the surreal image outlined in purple sparkles above him. The man picked something up off the ground under the window. He tossed it at Larson. It puffed into a cloud of green gas right at Larson's feet, obscuring him from view and snuffing out his glowing hands. Sam did not know who he was, but right now, he would kiss him if he could. The mystery man stepped forward, disappearing from view for a moment. He reappeared, holding Devon by an arm and the back of her pants, and chucked her through the sparkling vortex like a sack of potatoes, straight at Greenlee.

Floating ten feet in the air, surrounded by Ben's magic, Greenlee reached out and caught her as she screamed in terror, pulling her close in a death grip. "Gotcha!"

Ben's arms still lifted Sam, and he reached out to grab the edge of the portal. He was almost there. The green cloud surrounding Larson shifted, and the man pulled something off the body, hanging from the window next to him, before the gas obscured him from view once again. Muzzle flashes lit up the green cloud. The mysterious man, wearing novelty sunglasses, returned fire immediately, advancing on the area where the flashes were visible. Sam's hand reached the edge, the burnt grass of the Cahlad's lawn brushing his fingers when a puff of the green gas brushed the edge of the portal, and it blinked out of existence.

"No!" His hand floated in midair, and he stared at the dark shapes of tall pine and birch trees where a portal used to be. The world around him slowed down. His body went numb, and his ears started ringing. People shouted and screamed around him, but he couldn't focus on their words or care about what they were saying. He was vaguely aware of Ben's magic lowering him to the ground. He felt the impact when he touched the ground, but his legs gave out, and he ended up on his knees, still staring at a now empty piece of sky. Blue was trapped up there with Larson, and he had no way of getting to her.

Devon's heartrending wail tore his attention away from the empty sky, twisting his own stomach with the intensity of the grief and pain it carried, dwarfing his own. "Lexi! Baby!" She ran across the clearing toward the burning cabin, clutching her blistered and burnt arm to her chest. Her face was pale, and her hands shook violently from shock. Horror etched her features.

Greenlee struggled to stop her without hurting her injured arm more, stepping in front of her and blocking her view. "She wasn't in there, sweetheart! Listen to me. She wasn't in there."

Devon stopped running and stared at him, breathing heavily, face streaked with tears. Her eyes went from wild to confused to relieved in seconds. A garbled sob erupted, and she collapsed into Greenlee's arms.

Ben knelt next to Zella as Mitch and Amber skidded to their knees next to her. Mitch dropped Greenlee's backpack on the ground and dug through the bag frantically. Ben's face was grim as he assessed Zella's injuries.

"Help her, Ben." Amber grabbed her mother's hand, pulling it to her chest. "Please."

Still working, Ben didn't look up. "I'm trying, baby."

"Sam!" Someone was talking to him, but he didn't care. All he could think about was how they finally got back home, only for things to end this way. He hovered somewhere between fury and numbness. His ears rang, and he could only focus on the hollow emptiness in his chest. Someone shook him.

He tried to focus on the voice and found Nisha on her knees in front of him, holding his face in her hands, saying his name. He blinked. "Nish?"

"There you are." Nisha threw her arms around his neck and squeezed. "It's okay."

Sam hugged her back, needing to hold on to something so that he didn't collapse.

Greenlee and Ben yelled at each other about princess bandages. Kendra threatened to shoot a pallid and weak Torrin again if he didn't hold still. Everyone was losing their minds. Maybe this wasn't real.

Nisha leaned back and grabbed his face again, forcing him to look at her. "Look at me. I've got you." Her brow furrowed when he just stared at her. "You are fine. Do you understand?" She nodded and moved his head up and down with her hands. "Finn gave Hale a tracking artifact. As soon as someone can open another portal, we will go get them. She's tough. She isn't fighting eight men at once this time. Just one and Burpmaster Flash is up there with her. Keep it together."

He grabbed Nisha's wrist and focused on her face, replaying her words. Eight men? Had her magic come back?

"Yes. And we are going to find your wife, then kick Larson's ass."

76

BLUE

Rocks dug into Blue's back and side as she skidded to a stop a few feet from the jagged edge of the crater in front of the Cahlad administration building. She blinked up into the darkness and agony flared in her chest from the fireball Larson had hit her with. She had burns and cracked bones. The smell made her gag and flinch at the pain the movement caused. He caught her mid jump, so she at least didn't have a flaming hole all the way through her chest. It could have been worse.

The portal still illuminated the sky, casting a purple glow on everything. Sirens wailed far away. Miniature dragons still circled overhead. She really hurt, and she wanted nothing more than to lay here and try not to while reveling in how amazingly bonkers watching a baby dragon fly around in the sky was. Instead, she rolled onto her hands and knees, hair dragging on the ground, and used all of her energy to lift herself up. She wasn't healing as fast as she should be. But the portal was still open, which meant Devon and everyone on the other side of that thing were still in danger. Job wasn't done.

A fresh cloud of gas exploded at Larson's feet, surrounding him, and he cursed in anger, running toward the window where Dick Mann still dangled lifelessly across the ledge. The gas wafted between her and the portal, making Larson nothing more than a shadow. She couldn't see Devon or anyone else, either. A burst of gunfire and a muzzle flash strobed in the green fog. Larson scavenged Mann's gun. And someone returned fire. Who? Whoever it was, she had to help them. A wave of pain ripped through her as she struggled to her feet. "Over here, asshole! Thought you wanted to make me hurt!" Bullets pinged off the ground in front of her. Chunks of dirt flew into the air and she should try to take cover, but she was afraid she wouldn't be able to stand back up again if she did.

Two figures moved in the cloud of green gas. Bullets kept coming her way despite the hollow click of a gun running out of ammunition. She stumbled back as one figure threw something that generated more green gas and raised something that looked very much like a gun, turned bat into the air and clubbed the other shadow with it. The gunfire stopped, and the gas expanded toward her. Her heel dangled over the edge of the twenty-foot-deep crater behind her, and she couldn't retreat any farther.

The portal sputtered out of existence, leaving only the light of the many fires burning in the surrounding structures to illuminate the decimation. She wheezed a sigh of relief, positive Larson remained in the fog. Devon and Finn were safe for the moment. And maybe she at least slowed down the apocalypse.

But now she had a new problem. She couldn't teleport yet without hurting herself. The gas would surround her before she found enough reserve to make a jump safely, and she couldn't beat Larson in a conventional fight in this condition. She couldn't outrun him, either.

A brief pang of regret washed over her. The lone miniature dragon trilled over her head, rubbing it in. She shot the thing a bird and rolled her shoulders. She needed to find a gun or a knife and at least go down fighting. She took a halting step forward, stifling a cry of pain.

A large man charged out of the green cloud, running right for her, face still covered in ridiculous yellow daisy sunglasses and a gas mask. He ripped the mask from his face without breaking stride as soon as he cleared the rolling plume of gas. "Fuck those dragons, Angel! Get out of here."

"Hale?"

Larson emerged from the green plume behind her friend, holding a gun. His forehead was bleeding, and his eye was swelling shut. He fired and solid hollow thumps echoed.

Hale jerked, grimacing and shouting in pain, but kept his own body between the bullets and her. He slammed the mask over her face, holding it in place with his palm as the gas washed over him. His eyes fluttered closed, and he fell into her, sending them both over the edge of the crater.

She had to get Hale out of here. Larson or the twenty-foot fall would kill him otherwise. She prayed she had enough magic, and energy left to get him to safety and locked on to the closest signature she could feel. It was so weak she wasn't sure who it belonged to.

"You crazy bastard." She grabbed the hand still somehow holding the mask to her face, gripped his belt with the other and wrapped her legs around him so she didn't lose him in the space between here and there. She let the cold rainbow take over her vision as they fell. "Fuck those dragons." She never really liked Zella's ending, anyway. Maybe she could write her own.

Also By

The Hounds of Dawn

Hounds of Dawn
Sevens Wild
Flying Fluke
Zenith's Child

ABOUT THE AUTHOR

H.S. Torben weaves urban fantasy tales filled with humor, heart, and whimsy, inviting readers to explore a realm where magic and reality intertwine.

She lives in Tennessee with her husband, two children, and a snoring dog named Pickle. She spends Friday nights dungeon crawling, summers at the lake, and the rest of the year putting up or taking down Christmas lights.

Website: hstorben.com
Facebook: HSTorben
Instagram: hstorben

Acknowledgements

Thank you again to Caitlin for being the world's best beta reader.

    And to my editor Beth at Magnolia Author Services.

    Thanks to Paula at PaulaProofreader for the extra set of eyes.

    Thank you Chris for the Superman consult.

    Thank you Rachel for helping with Spanish.

Dramatis Personae

Blue West (aka Indigo Vale)
Independent contractor/ Former Cahlad Zenith
Faction: Hounds of Dawn

Devon O'Neal (aka Esdevona Irving)
Associate Professor of Magic Studies and Arcane History/ Mother
of Lexi O'Neal /Step Sister-in-Law of Finn Torrin
Faction: Hounds of Dawn

Greenlee Anders (aka Anderson Greenfield)
Self-Employed Artist
Faction: Hounds of Dawn

Finn Torrin
Owner Herne Tactical/Brother-in-Law of Devon O'Neal/ Uncle of
Lexi O'Neal
Faction: Herne Tactical

Lexi O'Neal
Fourth Grader/Goalkeeper/Daughter of Devon O'Neal
Faction: Unaffiliated

Sam Sotach
Regent of the Cahlad and Team Leader of Stalker Prime
Faction: Cahlad Prime

Nisha Ravi
Stalker Prime Captain
Faction: Cahlad

Ivan Lacroix
Stalker Prime Lieutenant /Former Cahlad Zenith
Faction: Cahlad

Cade Rhodes (aka Rhodes Westridge)
Platinum selling crossover country music artist /Former Cahlad Zenith.
Faction: Unaffiliated

Harper Kilgarden
Professional Diva Wrangler
Faction: Unaffiliated

Kendra Reyes

Security Specialist
Faction: Herne Tactical

Christopher Hale
Director of Operations
Faction: Herne Tactical

Trix Carpenter
Intelligence Specialist
Faction: Herne Tactical

Ben Hughes
Orthopedic Surgeon/Father of Ava Hughes
Faction: Unaffiliated

Ava Hughes
High school Senior/Daughter of Ben Hughes
Faction: Unaffiliated

   Amber Collins (aka Sarah Hughes)
Adopted daughter of Zella Tyne and Mitch Collins/Mother of Ava
Hughes/Former wife to Ben Hughes
Faction: Unaffiliated

Zella Tyne
Stalker Prime Lieutenant, Retired /Partner of Mitch Collins
Faction: Cahlad

Mitch Collins
Paragon of the Cahlad /Partner of Zella Tyne
Faction: Cahlad

Larson Battle
Former Cahlad Regent/ Former Captain Stalker Prime
Faction: Sovereign

Nolan Miller
United States Senator/ Chair, Magic Relations and Regulation
Committee
Faction: United States Government